IN THE SKIN OF A NUNQUA

IN THE SKIN OF A NUNQUA

R. J. POURITT

Cover design by Damonza
Interior design by Damonza

For Joani

TABLE OF CONTENTS

Escape 1

Gray Streak, Flat Face, and the Weevil 8

A Hidden Agenda 15

Scheming Women 25

Turning the Screw 39

The Daughters of Fortunate Birth. 56

Hexed 66

The Thrill of the Race. 74

Infestation 80

An Unholy Baptism 100

Queen of the Bugs 113

Apprentice Monk. 134

The Sword and the Swarm 148

Chameleon 157

Banishment 163

Thief 173

A Ruby Ring 182

Scapegoat. 187

An Interrogation 195

War 205

A Luxurious Cage 214

Blood on Her Hands 223

Newly Ordained Brother Monk 231

Poisoned 240

Women's Work 256

Burning Books 266

Snapping the String 274

Uncle Seiko 284

A Roll in the Hay 294

Quest for a Sword 303

The Arena 314

Catacombs 325

1
ESCAPE

HE WAS CLOSE enough to kill.

She couldn't do it—not even if she ran him through with a sword and shot him with a poisonous dart. Nothing could kill Caravey.

He poured whisky into a cup and gulped it down. "Show me."

Shanti adjusted the strap securing the sword across her back, then tightened the wristlet of attached darts on her forearm. "Show you what?" She would pay for such an insolent remark, but she played the fool anyway, just to deny him complete domination.

Leopard's spots patterned his smooth skin, and his lips were more brown than red. Caravey unsheathed a knife from his belt and scratched the tabletop with the point. The table had been carried off from a local tavern after a night of drunken revelry and brought to his quarters by Shanti and five of her fellow warriors. The battered surface showed the abuse from men who cared more for fighting than for furniture. Two chairs, a bench, and an ample supply of liquor with mismatched cups were also in the room.

"Of all my warriors," he said, "you're the most trouble. Why should I keep you?"

Shanti went to the table and poured herself a drink. "Because I've brought you the most honor by competing in the arenas."

The knife swung at her, and Shanti blocked the weapon from piercing her flesh. A mistake. Defending herself from Caravey's attacks would only prolong her suffering. She braced for the cruelty to come.

He seized her shoulder and pulled close, plunging the blade into her abdomen.

The air left her lungs, and she dropped to her knees. Shanti covered the wound with her hand, blood seeping through her fingers.

Caravey calmly wiped the knife with a cloth before returning it to its sheath. He knelt beside her. *Close enough to kill.*

"Who are you loyal to?" he said.

The steady tone of his voice made her flesh crawl. She envisioned drawing a blade across his gut and plunging a poisonous dart into the vein in his neck. And he still wouldn't die.

"Answer me," he whispered.

Always the same. He would hurt her then heal her, hate her then love her. How she tired of playing the dutiful servant, dependent on him for her very life. Saliva drained into her mouth, and black fog consumed the edges of her vision. The pain made her want to retch, but the shame of having to grovel before him was far worse. What choice did she have?

"You," she said.

She leaned against him, her head resting in the hollow of his neck, skin touching skin. Healing power, like rays of light, coursed from his body into hers, and the nausea subsided. The bleeding from the gash in her abdomen eased as skin sewed itself shut. She inhaled fully and trailed her fingers along the newly formed scar, disheartened that the miraculous recovery should come from the source of her suffering.

Caravey lifted her jacket and shirt to examine the scar. With the same cloth he had used to clean his knife, he wiped away the blood. "All better," he said, acting the part of the kindhearted physician.

Caravey and his crazy moods. She wondered whether power and madness were two sides of the same coin. She was tired of playing his games, tired of *him.* "I can't do this anymore," she said, knowing that his violent outbursts were followed by flashes of benevolence but never by regret.

"Then why disobey me?" He took off her wristlet, revealing more scars along her forearm—parallel scars made by the blade of a sword. "Show me," he said. "Change for me."

Shanti willed the scars to disappear, and it was so. A familiar flush warmed her cheeks, and her lips cooled in response to the change as she altered her appearance from a spotted Nunqua into a clear-skinned Willovian—a feat she had mastered as a child.

"Shanti, my sweet," he said. "My glorious witch."

Power and madness—two sides of the same coin. "I'm not a witch," she said.

"You've been distant." He stroked her cheek, and she moved away from the touch that had once pleased her. "I know how you miss Willovia, so I'm sending you back to the land of your birth. It's time to act on the prophecy concerning the king of Willovia."

More madness? Caravey always put too much faith in the supernatural. "A prophecy by an old hag," she said, "whose teeth were stained gold from chewing beetle wings. You can't trust a woman looking for gold to support her addiction."

"Three summers, and the king of Willovia will be dead," he said. "Three summers left to prepare. We know little of their society, their royalty. The king's daughter, Rega Bayla, is heiress to their throne. Our mystics have been unable to tell us about her. It's time to gather information in a more practical manner.

"I want you to seek out Rega Bayla, get to know her, provide us with information. What sort of queen will she be? Who are her advisers, her military commanders, her lovers? What's the biggest threat to her reign? Determine her weaknesses, her strengths. How do the commoners feel about Rega Bayla as their future queen?"

"You want me to spy?"

"It's the reason I chose you," he said, "the reason I trained you. You can travel as you please in Willovia, without suspicion. Hide the scars and spots on your skin that prove you're Nunqua. Once you've gathered the information we require, you can return home. Your fame will be greater than it is now."

Shanti had grown up in Willovia but spent the last few years with Caravey and the Nunqua. She considered both kingdoms home. Why was it so important for her to return to the land of her birth? The answer hit her like a bolt of lightning. "Are the generals planning war?"

"As soon as their king dies, we will combine our resources with theirs."

"War," Shanti said.

"An acquisition."

"A forced acquisition."

"It may not come to war," he said. "A peaceful alternative can be pursued dependent on the next monarch."

Now Shanti understood the real reason that Caravey took the time and effort to train her. He needed a liaison to communicate with the Willovians, someone they could trust and he could manipulate. She also knew that Willovia would never willingly unite with the Nunqua. No use telling Caravey. He thrived on conflict, chaos, the struggle for supremacy. Caravey wanted the fertile lands of Willovia. He wanted war.

"How am I supposed to access royalty?" she said.

"You'll find a way. You always do."

Shanti stood and arched her back. The muscles of her abdomen where the knife had penetrated were stiff but otherwise intact, and the bloody undershirt clung to her skin. She wiped her hands on her pant legs then retrieved her wristlet. "I'd like to visit my uncle before going to Willovia." Both Caravey and her uncle held the rank of general, but Uncle Seiko was more moderate and thoughtful. If she could consult with him concerning plans to overthrow . . .

"You leave tomorrow for Willovia."

So soon? Three years until the king of Willovia's questionable death, and Caravey wouldn't give her three days to see her uncle.

A knock sounded at the door. "General Delartay."

"Enter," Caravey said.

Gitonk and Tracker came into the room, glancing at Shanti and the blood on the floor. "The men are ready for your review."

Caravey straightened his black uniform. He was the perfect image of confidence and cunning. Men would kill to be welcomed into his unit of warriors, and women would sell their own mothers for the opportunity to bed Caravey. If only they knew the price!

"Shanti," he said, "you're exempt. Get your things ready. We'll discuss this matter in more detail tonight."

Gitonk snickered.

"Find someone to clean this mess, maggot," Caravey said.

Gitonk's demeanor changed under Caravey's scrutiny. "Yes sir."

One more night with Caravey. One more night to pretend she still cared. Caravey offered her the drink she had poured for herself. She took it with a bloody hand, swallowed, and returned the empty glass to the strange table. Scratches and crude carvings marred its surface, and stains from unknown concoctions discolored the wood. The table, which received the occasional waxing, was strangely pleasing to the eye and touch. More than a conversation piece, it was a piece of history, every outer imperfection a test of its inner strength and durability. Perhaps that was why Caravey coveted it.

She was the table.

Shanti brushed past her two fellow warriors on the way out, changing in appearance to a spotted Nunqua.

"You're beautiful," Gitonk boomed. Oval spots stretched wide over his bulk.

She was a pawn, a candle that could be lit, blown out, then lit again until all the wax had burned away and the wick was a black crinkle of ash.

"Remember, Shanti," Caravey said, "some fates are worse than death."

She left the room, wondering whether escape was possible.

*

After washing and putting on a clean uniform, she wrote a letter to her uncle to inform him of her return to Willovia. Nothing in the letter gave any hint of her mission to gather information concerning the princess.

She had no intention of becoming a spy.

Shanti searched the grounds for Tracker and found him in the stables. He scooped oats into the horses' feed buckets. "I need a favor," she said.

Tracker always rolled up the sleeves of his uniform, no matter what the weather. Leather bands circled his biceps. Shorter than most of Caravey's handpicked warriors, he could sniff out a trail better than any hound. "What happened between you and the general today?" he said.

"The usual."

He continued filling the buckets. "Why anta . . . antagin . . . why defy him? You can't fight a healer and win."

"'Antagonize,'" she said, correcting his Willovian—a language that Caravey insisted she use when speaking with the warriors under his command. "I thought the abuse would have ended by now. After all I've accomplished, he still treats me like a dog on a leash."

"You mean a bitch," Tracker said playfully.

"It's good to know you've mastered some of the language's subtleties," she said. "I'll be leaving tomorrow."

"Leaving?" He sank the scoop into the bag of oats and left it there. "Why?"

"General's orders." She removed the wax-sealed envelope from her jacket. "Can you see that this gets to General Seiko?"

"Why not give it to General Delartay? He can give it to Seiko."

"He'll read it first. It's just a personal letter to my uncle."

Tracker took the letter. "Uncle Seiko, huh? I could get into trouble for this."

Always a catch. "What do you want?" she said.

"There's this woman at the inn. I need some funds to treat her to a special night. I'll pay you back."

"You want to treat her to a special night, or to yourself?" She gave him a coin from her money bag.

His hand remained raised. "A very pretty woman."

Shanti dropped another coin into his palm.

"I know one of the warriors under General Seiko's command, who can deliver your letter."

"Thank you."

"Are you going to the inn tonight?"

"No," she said. "I have to pack."

"When are you coming back?"

"In a few summers," she lied. As long as Caravey lived, she wouldn't return. And healers were rumored to live a long, long time. Did they even die?

She would go to Willovia, blend among the people in a way that Caravey, with his spots, never could, and find a job in the military—a way of life she had already mastered. Besides, being surrounded by soldiers would give her a certain degree of protection in case Caravey ever came looking for her.

Tracker wrapped his arms around her legs and lifted her over his shoulder—an overzealous and awkward, yet much appreciated, gesture of good-bye. She put her hands on his back for balance.

"It'll be boring here without you," he said.

A horse in its stall neighed in annoyance, waiting for its oats.

"I'm sure General Delartay will find someone to take my place."

"Nobody can replace you, Shanti." Tracker put her down. "Nobody."

That's what I'm afraid of.

2

GRAY STREAK, FLAT FACE, AND THE WEEVIL

S HANTI LEANED WITH some other women against a split-rail fence and watched the Willovian soldiers attempt to impress their giggling spectators. No spots were visible on her skin, and she dressed in the attire of her youth: long sleeves, skirt, and vest appropriate for the weather. Her sword was secured in a back scabbard.

Soldiers marched with spears in the open field, and horses galloped along the fence line in the distance. Archers shot arrows at gourds. Two men had taken off their shirts and were wrestling, sweat shining on their spotless, sun-pinked backs. In a pit lined with timbers, another pair fought with swords, hacking at each other without any real skill or purpose. Shanti laughed loud enough for them to hear.

"Look at the girlie with the sword," one of them said.

"Who does she think she is? Want to fight, girlie?"

"I doubt she could even lift that steel."

"It's a short sword, jackass," the soldier said. "Made for weaklings."

"You should know."

Their banter made her smile, but these boys didn't have the clout to help her achieve her goal. No women practiced on the field, and Shanti realized that working her way into the Willovian military would be harder than she had thought.

"Bet you a gold coin she could beat you in a sword fight," the soldier said to the other man. They shook hands and climbed out of the pit.

"I'll split the take if you win," the young man said to Shanti. "On my honor."

The other soldier craned his neck. "You're a tall one."

"Afraid?" his friend said.

"She can't beat me. All right, girlie, let's see if you know how to use that scrap of tin on your back."

They were cute, really they were, but she had no time for games. Other soldiers joined in the fun and taunted her. Even some of the women catcalled, goading her to fight. She shook her head.

"Who the hell are you?" a deep voice behind her said.

She turned to see a man in a brown uniform, arms crossed, with a gray streak in his beard. Next to him was another soldier whose face appeared as if a mule had kicked it in long ago. Both had age and an air of authority on their side.

"Are you mute?" Gray Streak said. "I asked you a question."

"Shanti."

"Miss Shanti, you need to leave before I have you jailed for creating a disturbance. And you other women, go back to your knitting and leave these men to their work."

Shanti snorted. "Work?"

"Get out of my sight," Gray Streak said.

"I didn't start this. Your soldiers were making bets about who could beat me in a sword fight."

"Gambling? *My* men? Not only are you an instigator, you're also a liar."

Shanti had expected better of the leadership of the Willovian military. She stepped away from him, her chin held high.

Gray Streak left, and Flat Face moved closer. He spat a wad of tobacco next to her boot. "What is it ya want? I can see it in your eyes."

"A job."

He scrutinized her. "Leanna's been asking for help in the medical section. Ever use that thing on your back?"

"On occasion."

"Come on, Chief." A soldier pounded on the fencepost. "Let's see her fight."

Flat Face spat another brown cud onto the ground. "Tell ya what I'll do. Let me talk it over with the commander. I'm sure I can persuade him to see reason. An extra pair of hands 'round here comes in handy. Be here in the morning, Shanti, and you'll fight. If you win, you'll work with the other women in the medical section. Hell, I may even let you train with the men once in a while. The spirits know they need a dose of humility. If you lose, you'll be shoveling shit until next summer. Either way, you'll have a job."

"And the commander?" Shanti said.

"Is for me to worry about." Flat Face held out his hand, coarse hair covering the knuckles.

Success. Shanti shook his hand.

"Got a horse?" he said.

"Yes. Boarded at the stables."

"Bring her by tomorrow. We got plenty of stalls at the camp." He left, and a new round of betting enlivened the soldiers.

Ugly Chief Flat Face, with his vulgar habit of spitting brown crud where people walked, was now her best friend.

*

Mist obscured the sun rising in the field, and the hum of crickets filled the air. Shanti tied her horse to a fencepost. She wore pants under a skirt slit up both sides—not the best attire for fighting, but not the worst. Flies buzzed around piles of dung left by the horses during yesterday's activities. The lack of a crowd made her tense. Where were the men who had gambled on her? The townspeople?

Four horses, mounted by soldiers, clip-clopped down the road. Commander Gray Streak, Chief Flat Face, and two unfamiliar men tied their horses to a hitching post, then headed to the patch of dirt surrounded by timbers. Shanti joined them.

"Change of plans," Flat Face said. "You'll fight a soldier of the commander's choosing."

The black-skinned soldier was quiet and serious and solid as a stone wall. The other was wiry and so spastic, Shanti wondered whether he had been dropped on his head as a baby.

Flat Face gave her a thick leather vest to put on. "First one to contact his opponent's vest with their sword three times wins. No blows to the head, and stepping out of the pit is an immediate loss."

Gray Streak handed a protective vest to the spastic man.

Shanti twisted from side to side and jumped lightly up and down to loosen up. "I'd rather fight the dark one. He makes a bigger target."

"Toulley there's an honest man," Flat Face said. "Don't gamble; don't drink. He's here as a witness. Commander wants you to fight the Weevil. Listen, you ain't gonna tire the Weevil out, so don't try. He's got freakish arms with a long reach. Piss him off, and he'll go feral on ya."

Shanti unsheathed her sword and entered the pit with her opponent.

Flat Face chopped the air with his hand. "Begin."

"Here, chick, chick, chick." The Weevil crouched low, weapon at the ready. Acne scars pitted his face, and his hazel eyes were open far too wide. He advanced, then jerked backward, wiping away drool with his sleeve. "Here, chickie."

He jabbed at her knees in a style both unsightly and annoying, forcing her to defend her legs. She moved to strike his back. He parried, then slashed her vest, leaving a mark in the leather. *Damn, he was quick.*

"Point to Weevil," Flat Face said.

They continued to spar, and she studied the Weevil's technique: balanced, cocky, annoying. Despite his spastic movements, the man had training. His head twitched, but the rest of his body was relaxed. It was a manipulation, an act. Well, she could act, too.

Caravey's instructions dominated her thoughts. *Head over heart, brain over body.* Sword fighting entailed more than prowess with a weapon.

No women trained with these men. Perhaps she could use chivalry to her advantage. The sun hovered over the horizon. She took the defensive, countering his assault and conserving her energy while tracking the sun's position, careful not to squint and give away her tactic. When the sun's rays burst over them, her feet crossed and her shoulder dropped. His sword struck her side. Shanti cried out and forced herself to stumble.

"Point to Weevil," Flat Face said. "Ready, Shanti?"

She returned to the start position, elbows in, sword vertical, one foot in front of the other—and nodded.

The Weevil advanced. Their swords clashed, but his attack lost the aggressiveness it once had. Shanti breathed through her mouth and slumped as if in fatigue. She steered him around until the sun lit his face, and then overextended her reach. Her arm came in contact with the feeble swing of his blade. Shanti cried out and doubled over, pressing her arm against her chest and dropping her sword. A deliberate risk. The Weevil moved closer, weapon down by his side. Unguarded.

Caravey's voice echoed in her head: *surprise is a potent ally.* She clamped her hands onto his arm and turned. Using the strength of her legs, she flipped the Weevil over her shoulder and onto his back. His feet landed outside the pit.

"Ye're out of bounds," Flat Face said. "Shanti wins."

The Weevil jumped up and shrieked, "She cheated! This is a sword fight, not a grappling match. Commander, I protest."

Gray Streak closed in on Shanti. "Do you have anything to say?"

"I was given three guidelines: no head shots, three strikes on the *vest* wins, and stepping out of the pit is a loss."

"I didn't step out of the pit," The Weevil said. "I was thrown out."

"Did you lose those two points on purpose?" Gray Streak asked Shanti.

"The first point, no. The second, yes."

"How's your arm?"

She looked down and saw no blood, her sleeve intact.

"You're lucky," Gray Streak said. "A trick like that could have cost you your hand. You have no respect for the weapon and what it can do. You're reckless. But you do have skills. Who trained you?"

Caravey had warned her to conceal her association with the Nunqua from the Willovians, but she was no longer under his control. She lifted her sleeves, the parallel scars visible across the skin of her forearm. Gray Streak's brow furrowed. The others gathered closer for a better look.

"What happened to her?" the Weevil said.

"Nunqua." Flat Face's head bobbed as he counted the scars. "Seven. Seven losses. How? You're Willovian."

"What do you mean, 'seven losses'?" the Weevil said, his twitching less pronounced but still present.

"Seven losses in sword fights," Flat Face said. "The scars are a permanent reminder. A humiliation."

"No," she said. "The scars are the mark of a warrior, to be worn with pride. To win, a warrior must first know what it means to lose. Pain is our teacher, sacrifice our duty. And, Commander, I respect the weapon, though I do not fear it."

"If you have seven losses," Gray Streak said, "how many wins do you have?"

She crossed her arms. "Counting today?"

"I haven't given my verdict on today's match."

She had lost track of how many fights she won, so she made up a number. "Twelve."

"If the Nunqua trained you, why are you here and not with them?"

"Didn't fit in."

"And you want to work with us?" Gray Streak said.

"Yes."

Flat Face cleared his throat.

"Yes *sir.*"

"Shanti wins," Gray Streak said. "You'll report to Chief Emmins. And the less I hear of you, the better."

"I understand, sir."

Chief Flat Face planted a quid of tobacco in his cheek and walked with Shanti to her horse. "We'll get you a uniform and a place to stay. You'll work in the medical section with the women. How long you been with the Nunqua?"

"Five years."

"Ever married?"

"No."

"Any children?"

"No."

He inspected her horse's hooves, bridle, and saddle. "You'll maintain your own gear and train with the men when there's time."

"Thank you, Chief."

"Don't go thanking me yet, girlie."

3
A Hidden Agenda

BEDS, WITH BLANKETS and pillows folded on top, lined the infirmary. Open windows let in a breeze. Shanti wore a brown uniform. Made for a man, it bagged at the crotch and drooped about the waist. She perused the contents of a shelf: empty bottles, chipped mortar and pestle, dog-eared pages of a handwritten book.

I need supplies," Leanna said to Chief Flat Face, "not another worker."

"She can saw through a bone, restrain your rowdy patients. Give her a chance."

"Can she distill her own alcohol, make bandages out of nothing, forage in the woods for medicine?"

Flat Face sighed. "Commander Mossgail can give you your supplies."

"But he doesn't"

"I'll talk to him."

"Talking doesn't do any good." Leanna showed him a sheet of parchment. "I've documented his continued refusals—"

"Put that away, Leanna. You know I can't read."

"Then tell the camp commander," she said. "He can do something."

"I've never seen a commander accuse another of wrongdoing. I'm sorry, but you must deal with this yourself." Flat Face left.

"Men!" Leanna grumbled. "Out of my hands. Nothing I can do. You're on your own. Commanders protect their own and forget about the soldiers they're in charge of. Someone's going to die because we can't get the supplies we need, and they'll blame me." She pushed a loose strand of hair behind her ear. Dimples highlighted her cheeks, and she smelled faintly of perfume. "You, show me your fingernails."

Shanti did as instructed.

"Good. Keep your nails clean and your appearance neat. Can you read and write?"

"Yes."

"Chief would have been a commander by now if he could read. Are you here to find a husband?"

Odd question. "No."

"Most women are. No weapons in the infirmary. Lock your sword in the armory. You can get something to eat on the way back." Leanna stuffed the parchment into a box.

Shanti secured her sword in the armory, then hiked around camp. Smoke billowed out of a chimney connected to a kitchen. She got some food and went to an unoccupied table.

The bread was hard enough to chip a tooth, and sauce drenched the unknown meat. She took a bite and spat it out. Subdued laughter from the nearby tables reached her ears. Were they watching her? The men's plates contained the same fare. Shanti took another bite, swallowed, then swished water around her mouth to wash away the taste. She threw away the rest of her food and returned to find chaos inside the infirmary.

The black soldier, Toulley, hollered. He shoved the Weevil, who stumbled into a bed. Leanna raised her palms in an attempt to calm Toulley. "Let us give you the medicine to dull the pain. Settle down, please." She pointed to Shanti, and her tone changed. "You, get the nicidem, there in the bottle."

Shanti poured liquid into a cup and brought it to them.

Toulley smacked it out of her hand. "No tricks."

The Weevil moved next to Shanti. "Dislocated shoulder," he said. "The obstacle course."

"Why didn't you fix it there?"

"He wouldn't let anyone help him." The Weevil's head twitched. "Figured the situation needed a woman's touch."

"You have to let us help you," Leanna pleaded with Toulley.

These women had no understanding of military discipline. Perhaps they weren't given the authority they needed to do their job. The pain was making Toulley unreasonable. Time for action. Shanti rolled a bedsheet. "Weevil, take out his legs. Get him on the ground. I'll reposition his shoulder."

Leanna scowled at the sheet in Shanti's hands.

"Now," Shanti said.

The Weevil seized Toulley's thighs and wrestled him off his feet. Toulley hit the floor and writhed about.

Shanti shoved the sheet beneath his armpit. With his uninjured limb, he tugged at her hair, and strands pulled free from the warrior's knot on the back of her head.

"Someone hold his arm!" Shanti yelled.

"Your idea," Leanna said, sitting atop Toulley's knees while another woman sprawled across his feet. "Do it yourself."

Shanti wiggled the sheet into place and felt the abnormal lump near the collarbone. It must hurt like hell. "Take the pain, Toulley."

"Hurry up!" Leanna shouted.

Shanti pushed her boot on his uninjured shoulder for leverage and heaved on the sheet. "Stop squirming." She tightened her grip and used her body weight to pull. Toulley yelled. With a muffled *thunk,* the top of his arm reseated into its socket. Toulley wilted on the floor.

Shanti rolled away from him, breathing as if she had just run a footrace. Toulley's biceps was as thick as her calf. He could have crushed her. Good thing she hadn't realized that until after reseating his shoulder.

Weevil and the women helped Toulley into a bed as Leanna headed in the opposite direction. Shanti went over to her.

"Nicidem." Leanna held the bottle. "'Medicine' spelled backwards without the 'e.' It's sugar water. Damn that Mossgail." She handed Shanti a broom. "Fix your hair, and clean up."

You're welcome. Perhaps joining the Willovian military had been a mistake. She didn't want to end up like these women: disrespected, disregarded, desperate. Shanti straightened the beds and wiped up the sugar water with a rag.

*

After treating a bloody nose, wrapping a sprained ankle, and nursing a mysterious stomach ailment, Shanti left the infirmary. She bypassed the camp's kitchen and went to town for a real meal and sewing supplies. On the way back, she saw lamplight burning in the infirmary and heard voices.

She entered to find Leanna in a chair next to Toulley, who was sitting up in bed, his back leaning against two pillows and his arm secured in a sling and swathe.

"Come here." Leanna took a drink from a brown bottle. "Toulley tells me you were with the Nunqua."

"Show her your arms," he said.

Shanti lifted her sleeves, exposing the parallel scars.

"I knew there was something different about you." Leanna offered Toulley a drink, which he declined. "I bought this to help you with the pain," she said.

"You know I don't drink," he said. "Besides, the pain's not so bad now."

Leanna pointed to the small bundle in Shanti's hand. "What's that?"

"Needle and thread. My uniform needs to be taken in."

"She can sew *and* use a sword." Leanna chuckled, her eyes glassy. "How will I get anyone to notice me, with her around?"

"My name . . . is Shanti."

"I don't bother with names," Leanna said. "Most women aren't here too long."

"Don't pay attention to her, Shanti." Toulley repositioned the pillow with his free arm. "She's drunk."

"I *deserve* a drink after today," she said.

Toulley pointed to his shoulder. "Think *you've* had a bad day?"

"Sorry. It's just that bastard Mossgail."

"Talk to chief about it," Toulley said.

"I did."

"Everyone knows what Commander Mossgail's doing with the supplies."

"But no one will speak against him," Leanna said.

Shanti left them to their conversation. Working in the infirmary might be a thankless job, but watching Leanna keep Toulley company made her realize it was also an important one.

*

"She's the one, sir," Chief Emmins said. "Shanti speaks her mind, knows how to fight, and the men take to her. You saw the way she bluffed the Weevil. Hell, even *I* was ready to stop the fight."

Commander Edwyn sat behind a desk flanked by two flags. Three ceremonial swords hung on the wall behind him, tassels dangling from the grips. "As impressive as her skills are, I have concerns," he said. "She seems antisocial."

"Nah, Shanti's got friends—she just acts like she don't. Send a letter to High Commander Gy. Tell him we found someone to train Rega Bayla."

"How old is the heiress?"

"Seventeen," the chief said. "Maybe eighteen. She'll be ready for the test in a year or two."

The commander set one of the ceremonial swords on his desk

and buffed it with a cloth. "I had Shanti's room searched while she was working at the infirmary. We found a wristlet and darts under her mattress. The darts have hollow points filled with a greenish-gold substance. She's been trained by the Nunqua, who poison their enemies and—"

"She's as Willovian as you or I, sir. And what if she were a Nunqua, spots and all? Wouldn't that be better for the Guardians' plans? Scare the piss out of the princess."

"This isn't a joke. She knows how to use a sword, knows how to kill."

"Isn't that what we're teaching these men, sir: how to kill? You're better with a sword than anybody I've met; you have battle experience. Does that make you a murderer?"

"Why would the Nunqua trust a Willovian woman?" the commander said.

"Because they saw something in her. Look me in the eye and tell me Shanti ain't perfect for the job. It's fate, I tell ya."

"It's risky."

"So you'll send a letter to Commander Gy?" the chief said.

Commander Edwyn pushed the sword aside and took a quill and jar of ink out of the desk drawer.

"You're a good man, sir," the chief said.

"Yes, I know. Now, get out of here before I change my mind."

*

Rain pattered on the infirmary window, lulling Shanti to sleep in her chair. Her head bobbed, and she awoke with a start. Leanna was absorbed in writing at a table. Shanti stood and shadow boxed. Leanna glowered at her.

"Want to play cards?" Shanti said.

"No."

"Dice?"

"No."

"Arm wrestle?"

"I'm trying to finish a letter."

Shanti lifted one leg off the floor, raising both arms to shoulder height.

Leanna put down the quill and rubbed her eyes. "Do you mind?"

She closed her eyes, fought to keep her balance, switched legs, then leaned forward while grasping her ankle in the flowing exercise that Caravey had taught her. She repeated his instructions out loud: "Balance is the key to sword fighting. The wind is my offense, the rock my defense."

"And faking injury is your fallback, from what I hear," Leanna said.

She wobbled and lowered her foot to the floor. "Who are you writing to?"

Chief Flat Face entered with two other soldiers. They took off their hats, water dripping from their clothing. "Ready, Shanti?"

She had no idea what he was talking about, but hurried to the exit anyway, happy to escape the boredom of the infirmary.

"Do *I* have a say in the matter?" Leanna said.

Flat Face scanned the empty beds. "You can have her back in ten days or so. Get your sword, girlie, and saddle your horse. Someone needs to take Toulley's place and ride as a guard with the supply cart to the Outer Boundaries. His shoulder needs time to heal properly."

"Speaking of supplies," Leanna said, "Commander Mossgail still hasn't given us any."

"I already told ya," Flat Face said, "it's out of my hands."

Leanna huffed and returned to writing.

Shanti went to her room to pack, putting on a poncho and donning her wristlet of poisonous darts. Sleeping arrangements would be close and, most likely, out in the open. Wearing the darts would deter any overfriendly soldiers. Flat Face might not approve, but as the only female guard, she had to protect more than the supplies—she had to protect herself.

She rummaged around a sack for her comb and items used to secure her hair in the warrior's knot. Her hand came in contact with a velvet bag. Inside was the lock of hair attached to a necklace. The hair belonged to the Nunqua warrior she had killed on the night she was taken away from Willovia.

Defend yourself or be raped. Truth be told, it was a lucky swing of a blade, which surprised even her. She had forgotten many of the details of that night, but she did remember Caravey giving her the necklace made from a lock of the dead warrior's hair. He had put it around her neck and told her it would protect her from the dead man's spirit. Superstitious nonsense. The hair was a trophy, nothing more. Caravey could have healed the man but didn't. He sacrificed one warrior to train another: her.

She was the product of the unlawful union between the great warrior Shintar and his Willovian woman and could change her appearance from a spotted Nunqua to a monotone-skinned Willovian at will. Caravey had found out about her, kidnapped her, trained her, ridiculed her, cut her, stabbed her, burned her, loved her, and told her she was important.

The necklace was a Nunqua symbol of pride, meant to induce fear. That part of her life was over now. She was with the Willovians. Shanti returned the necklace to its bag.

*

High Commander Gy, his stomach distended from the previous three courses, forced down the last bite of bread pudding out of courtesy. He dined with other guests at a long, polished table in Commander Edwyn's manor house. Even though Gy outranked his host, Edwyn was wealthier due to an inheritance and an auspicious marriage. The house belonged to Edwyn's plump wife.

"Commander Gy," Edwyn said, "it's time for us to take our leave and retire to the study. We don't want to bore our dinner companions with business."

Gy excused himself and followed Edwyn to an oak-paneled

room. The glow from the hearth illuminated statues of statesmen and athletes. The opulence of the room made him uncomfortable. Edwyn came from wealth, whereas Gy had worked his way through the ranks to become a high commander. He was the son of a farmer, who had left to find glory in the foolishness of his youth. Glory—how fast that concept had faded! More rank meant more work, more responsibility, more worry. Was this woman Commander Edwyn had written him about after glory? Or were her motives nobler?

"Tell me about this Shanti," Gy said. "What's she like?"

Edwyn sat in a chair and crossed his legs. "She's different."

"Is she pretty?" Men outnumbered women at the camps by a hundred to one. Most women were married and gone within a year. It would be a waste to include Shanti in the Guardians' plans if she would be busy with a family at the time of Rega Bayla's training as a soldier.

"'Pretty' suggests a delicacy that Shanti lacks."

Gy chuckled to himself. Perhaps Edwyn wasn't the best judge of a woman's appearance. Although the man had a wife, he sought his pleasures elsewhere. "What about her skills?"

"Above average. That's what worries me. The scars on her arms . . . Why would the Nunqua train a Willovian woman using such brutal tactics? There are secrets in her past that go deeper than she's telling us about."

"We all have secrets," Gy said.

Edwyn shifted uncomfortably in his chair. "What if she's a spy?"

"Then she would have hidden her scars under her sleeves. Does she have the potential to lead?"

"Shanti's a natural leader," Edwyn said, "but arrogant."

Gy took a pipe out of his pocket. "May I?"

Edwyn nodded. "I need to discuss another matter with you. Rumors concerning the dealings of Commander Mossgail are rampant, and supplies for the camp are low. He's black-marketing our provisions. I'm sure of it, only I have no proof."

Gy lit the pipe, then sat in a chair next to Edwyn. "To accuse another commander of a crime is a serious matter. Defamation of character may cost you your command if your accusations are unjustified. Not to mention, it will put you, your family, and your lifestyle under scrutiny. Do you wish to request an inquiry?"

"Nothing so formal. An investigation into Commander Mossgail's affairs will suffice at this time. A *quiet* investigation. But Mossgail is well connected in this region. I request your assistance in sending an unfamiliar face to—"

Gy waved his hand. "I'll send a team." He puffed on the pipe, and smoke swirled up out of the bowl. If the rumors were true, Commander Mossgail was a major nuisance that needed to be dealt with: a commander stealing from his own troops. Disgraceful. But it was nothing compared to the training of the heiress and the fate of the kingdom itself! In two years, Rega Bayla would be taken away from the castle to work alongside the soldiers, to better her understanding of the military. The Guardians of Willovia would test her competence under pressure, according to tradition. And it worried him.

Rega Bayla was a princess. Motherless, the only child of King Magen, and the last of her bloodline, she had been coddled all her life. If Bayla failed as a soldier, the Guardians of Willovia would fight to ensure that she never wore the crown.

This woman Shanti might be just the person they needed to show Rega Bayla that a woman could command.

4
SCHEMING WOMEN

SHANTI RETURNED TO camp with one thing on her mind: a bath. The trip to the Outer Boundaries had lasted fourteen days. No bandits, no belligerent townsfolk, no equipment troubles—just the open road and endless questions from the other guards. The soldiers treated her with curiosity rather than disrespect and tried to get her to gamble away her money like some inexperienced newcomer. Nunqua warriors had done the same when she first joined them. Military men were the same everywhere, she supposed.

She put her horse in the stable, then headed to her room to unload her gear. A barrel-chested, broad-shouldered man intercepted her.

"So you're the woman everyone's been talking about." White teeth gleamed behind his bushy mustache. He radiated rank, but his demeanor was casual. Too casual by half.

Shanti straightened her posture. "Sir."

"No need for such formality. I'm Commander Mossgail. How was the trip? No problems, I assume. By the way, I have something for you." He showed her an armguard with an eagle and two flags punched into the leather. Holes perforated the edges in a decorative design. "I hear you're training with the men, so I thought you might need this for archery."

"I already have an armguard, sir."

"This one's made by the royal leather crafter."

Although handsome, the band was too wide to be practical. And "royal leather crafter" sounded like a load of manure. "No, thank you."

"I've heard about the darts you wear. May I see?"

Shanti raised her arm but did not remove the weapon.

"I know a fellow close to the king who would give good money for such an item. You could buy ten swords for the price he's willing to pay. What do you say?"

"The weapon has sentimental value, sir. I'll not part with it."

Leanna tromped toward them, and Mossgail grinned. "Aren't you looking pretty today?"

"Shove it, Mossgail."

Shanti's eyebrows rose at the defiant outburst.

"Don't be sore just because things didn't work out between us," he said to Leanna.

"Did you bring back any supplies?" she asked Shanti.

"A few things. They're in the cart."

"Where's the cart?"

Shanti gestured in the direction of a wooden building, and Leanna hurried away.

Mossgail's grin vanished, and he followed Leanna. "No, you don't. Those items need to be inventoried first. If you take anything out of the cart without authorization, I'll have you jailed."

Shanti returned to her room, then went to the bathhouse. Warm water never felt so good. She put her hair in the warrior's knot, donned her one clean uniform, and brushed dirt off her boots before going to the infirmary with a burlap bag slung over her shoulder.

Leanna sat beside a bed and scowled at nothing. Her plans to access the cart were obviously unsuccessful.

"You and Mossgail," Shanti said. "Now it makes sense. You're not angry about the supplies; you're angry about being rejected."

"Then why don't we have medicine?" Leanna said. "No bandages, no splints, no extra bedding—"

"And no respect," Shanti said.

"You're so stupid."

She lowered the bag from her shoulder and dumped the contents onto the mattress: dried herbs, strips of cloth, packets of seeds, bottles of medicine. "I may be stupid, but I'm not blind. Went to the infirmary at the Outer Boundaries. They were overstocked and willing to share. It's not much, but Mossgail can't claim this on his inventory."

Leanna sorted through the supplies. "Shanti, what are you doing tonight?"

Finally, Leanna had called her by name. "No plans."

"Come with me into town. I want to show you something."

*

Shanti's nose twitched as she entered the apothecary. The cloying aroma of incense turned her stomach. Spices lined the shelves, and black leeches squirmed in a bucket of water. Tobacco leaves hung from nails on the ceiling, and barrels of animal parts rested on the floor: sharks' teeth, bear claws, desiccated cougar hearts, bull scrota. A sign on the wall read "*Confidentiality Guaranteed.*"

Leanna took her arm and led her to a section with jars behind glass, labeled "hemlock" and "opium." Shanti picked up a tourniquet with a metal turning mechanism.

"Mossgail's been black-marketing our supplies," Leanna whispered. "This shelf represents a mere handful of the things he's stolen. He has buyers all over the kingdom. Never sells his stock to just one place—makes it harder to trace."

A woman emerged from the back room. Body paint of a moon

and stars accentuated her exposed cleavage. Designs of mythical creatures covered her feet and hands, and her hair was dyed an inky black. Her mannerisms and appearance were crafted to give the impression of a witch, as if power were something one could put on or take off like a robe.

"Good afternoon, ladies." The saleswoman smiled. "What are you interested in today: love, revenge, fertility?"

"Sleeping potion," Leanna said. "A very *strong* sleeping potion."

"Right this way."

Shanti continued to inspect the contents of the store, pausing at jars of snake venom.

"Hiet va shay." A Nunqua man came out of the back room and stared at Shanti. *"Hiet va shay."* Spots covered his skin, and he wore a black coat over a blue vest. His long hair was oiled and braided.

Leanna backed away from the man and bumped into a display of fortune-telling cards.

The saleswoman admonished the man, "Stay in the storage room. Customers aren't used to Nunqua. My apologies—he's one of my suppliers."

Shanti stood her ground, wondering what the medicine man sensed in her. *"Hiet tae,"* she said. The saleswoman had a seductive quality, and the Nunqua man was fine looking, though a bit thin for Shanti's tastes. A thought occurred to her. *"Isc taka no schira?"* (Is she your woman?)

The man laughed and answered in the Nunqua language, saying the saleswoman would rather die than take a Nunqua man as a mate.

Was Shanti truly the only half-breed? *"Deape na tey vuy a?"* (Do you know who I am?)

"Yes," he replied in Willovian.

He must have seen her fighting in the arenas during her time with the Nunqua. *Damn.* A Nunqua man in Willovia. If this medicine man could get here, so could Caravey. "May I see your arms?" she said.

He lifted his sleeves. Manly hair and spots covered his skin, but no scars made by the blade of a sword. He wasn't a warrior.

"Do not speak of me," Shanti said.

He gestured to the sign guaranteeing confidentiality and bowed before returning to the storage room.

Leanna bought a yellow powder. They left the apothecary and walked down the street to a tavern.

"Problems falling asleep?" Shanti asked.

Two other women who worked at the infirmary were already seated inside the tavern. They joined them at the table. "I need your help," Leanna said to Shanti. "I'm going to take the medical supplies that belong to us."

"This isn't my fight." Shanti said.

Men passed by and nodded, eyeing her companions. The waitress brought over a round of drinks from an admirer.

"You work with us," Leanna said. "You see what's happening. Mossgail tried to buy you with that armband. I've exhausted all legitimate means of getting the supplies we need. The soldiers suffer from this injustice."

"You're the only one who can help," the others chimed in.

Shanti sipped her drink. "I'm flattered, but I won't steal."

"It's not stealing if it's rightfully ours." Leanna traced the rim of her cup. "I see appealing to your integrity won't work. What were you and the Nunqua talking about? 'Do not speak of me.' Who are you hiding from?"

"Blackmail won't work, either. Why not leave, go to a different camp? Escape?"

"Because he controls supplies at the other camps, too." Leanna hung her head. "I trusted Mossgail. Thought he would take care of me, protect me, marry me. I was wrong to get involved with him. Now he won't give the infirmary the supplies we need, just to make me look bad. Nobody takes me seriously, because he's a commander and I'm . . . I'm just a woman."

"Did you practice that speech?" Shanti said. Mossgail was as slippery as a skinned eel—she had sensed it from the moment he offered her the armband—but she wanted to stay out of trouble.

"Haven't you ever made a mistake because of a man?" Leanna said.

A pang of remorse seized her as she thought of Caravey. Perhaps she should help. There was no winning a fight against a healer, but Mossgail was different. And the supplies did belong in the infirmary. "What's your plan?"

"Ladies." Four men pulled chairs around the table to join them. They wore sheepish grins on their clean-shaven faces. One, tall and bright-eyed, put an arm around her. Shanti stared at him until he pulled away.

"Thank you for the drinks," Leanna said, "but now isn't the time."

"Just looking for some company, nothing more."

"I'm sorry, but we're busy."

"Are you sure?"

"Yes."

The men left, and the two younger women waved and flirted. "Bye-bye, boys."

Leanna remained serious. "We take the medical supplies while he's sleeping. We'll go to jail if we're caught . . . or worse."

"And all of you are willing to take this risk?" Shanti said.

"Yes."

"Yes."

"Absolutely," Leanna said.

Shanti drummed with her fingers on the table. The more she thought of Mossgail, the more the idea appealed to her. "I'm in," she said, "on one condition."

"What is it?"

"Acquiring a few medicinal items will only annoy him. You must injure his pride. We take *all* of his supplies, his boots and clothing, too. Humiliate him. Mossgail will be seen as incompetent if his entire inventory is stolen from right under his nose. And if it's ever revealed that he was raided by a bunch of women while he slept, we may pay the price by going to jail, but he'll be laughed out of camp. The soldiers would be better off without him."

They clinked their cups together in agreement.

*

Shanti led the three women through the dark camp, avoiding the guards on duty. They padded around buildings and crawled through bushes until they reached the supply quarters. Leanna put a key in the lock on the door as Shanti held her breath. During festivities in town, she had taken the key and poured sleeping powder into Mossgail's drink while the fair-haired woman from the infirmary danced with him. What if it was the wrong key? The door opened, and Shanti tensed. So many things could go wrong.

An orange glow emanated from the hearth, and Mossgail snored in bed, his left foot sticking out from under the wool blanket. Pants and boots were strewn across the floor of the small room next to the supplies.

"Take everything you can carry," Shanti whispered.

They filled sacks with blankets, medicines, dishes, tobacco, and whatever else would fit. The fair-haired woman lifted a nest of hairless baby mice, then dropped it, stifling a squeal, when she realized what it was. They moved the nest to a corner of the chamber.

Shanti entered Mossgail's bedroom and filled a sack with his clothing. He grunted and turned over in bed. She froze. Drool dripped from his mouth, and his eyes were partly open. She waved her hand in front of his face, flicked her finger close to his eye. Nothing. She continued packing his gear.

Leanna entered the room, knife in hand, as if in a trance. She moved toward Mossgail.

Shanti intercepted her, grabbing her wrist and squeezing. The knife fell to the floor with a loud clatter. Mossgail snored away.

"What the hell are you doing!" Shanti hissed, a hard edge to her voice.

Leanna stammered, unable to answer.

Shanti picked up the knife. Standard issue. Leanna must have gotten it from the supply area. "If you want to show that bastard you can hurt him, that it's personal, then cut off a lock of his hair." She handed Leanna the knife.

Leanna went over to Mossgail, seized a finger-size clump of hair, and tried to saw through it. His head bobbed, and Shanti's stomach jumped. He would wake for sure.

She took the knife from Leanna, quickly sheared a lock of hair, and then stepped out of the room. "I need string." One of the women threw a ball of twine from inside a bag to her. Shanti worked at binding the hair with twine as the others finished packing. She hung the ornament from a nail so that it swayed in the doorway, sure to be seen.

Leanna picked up a sack the size of a gourd. It was heavy and jingled. Inside were gold and silver coins—more money than a commander made in two, maybe three, years. The fair-haired woman ran her fingers through the treasure. "We split the money."

"No," Shanti said. "This money is tainted, acquired from the illegal sale of goods. Only bad outcomes can arise from spending it. We take only the supplies. I need an anchor."

"A *what*?"

"A metal ring of some sort."

"How about a buckle?"

"That will work." Shanti cut a long length of twine. "Where's his sword?"

Leanna retrieved Mossgail's sword, still sheathed in its scabbard, and handed it to her.

Shanti knotted the twine around the neck of the money bag and the hilt of the sword, then threaded the two loose ends through the buckle. She balled up the remaining twine and threw it over the highest rafter in the storage area, catching it on its return. Pulling twine through the loop made by the buckle, she hoisted the sword and the money bag to the ceiling. With Leanna's help, they whipped the dangling ends around the rafter and out of reach.

Mossgail slept on.

Loaded down with sacks, they left the supply area. Leanna relocked the door, then pushed the key under the crack. They darted between buildings and sneaked around camp. Shanti lifted her fist in the air, and the women plowed into her.

"Stop, stop!" Shanti showed them her fist. "This means 'stop.'"

"Sorry."

Two guards passed on their rounds, oblivious to the deceit being perpetrated on their watch.

The other infirmary women went one way, Shanti in another. "I'm getting rid of his clothes," she said.

She trekked to the river. The water rushed past, swollen from the recent rains. She removed her boots and waded in to her knees, tossing the sack into the deep and hoping it would float far downstream.

Shanti put on her boots and returned to her room.

*

Shanti heard the commotion before she saw it. She finished putting her hair in the warrior's knot, left her room, and went outside. A crowd of soldiers had gathered around Mossgail. Wearing short pants, an undershirt, and stockings, he looked wildly about and shouted, "Where is she!"

Commander Gray Streak and Flat Face came out of the supply quarters, scratching their heads.

Mossgail caught sight of Shanti. "*She* did it. Shanti's the thief. The lock of my hair proves it. She . . . she threatened to poison me if I didn't give her my supplies."

Shanti crossed her arms and watched the antics of the thief who stole from the soldiers he was supposed to serve. He deserved what he got.

Two men in civilian clothes came out of the supply quarters.

One clutched a long stick with a knife tied to the end; the other man held Mossgail's money bag and sword. The tall one had a lean, muscular build and seemed familiar. Recognition hit, and Shanti's stomach sank. He had been at the tavern, bought her and the other women drinks, put his arm around her.

"*Shit,*" she said under her breath. If he had heard their conversation about the crime, the plan would be ruined. He could testify against them.

Commander Mossgail continued to rant. He stomped over to Shanti and stuck a finger close to her face. She suppressed the urge to bend it backward until it broke.

"Search her room," Mossgail said.

"A reasonable request," Commander Gray Streak said. "Come with us, Shanti."

She headed to her room with the others.

Chief Flat Face mumbled to her, "Inquiry."

Once inside, the men in civilian clothes searched through her possessions. Shanti felt the lump in her pocket from the velvet bag containing the hair of the warrior. Good thing she had remembered to take it out of her belongings. Some things she didn't want to explain. The men confiscated her money bag but did not open it. One of them took a cork out of her container of greenish-gold beetle innards.

"Careful," she said. "It's poison." She showed them the wristlet of darts strapped to her arm. "Hollow points."

"Take that as evidence."

The man who had put his arm around her at the inn lifted his hand. She unbuckled the wristlet and gave it to him. He also kept hold of her money bag and the jar of poison.

Mossgail's expression brightened, and he snapped his fingers. "She sold my supplies. I hear there's a man doing business in town, a Nunqua. Shanti's working for him, or with him. Everyone knows she's been trained by the Nunqua."

Flat Face, standing next to her, coughed, "Inquiry."

"Nothing else is of interest here," the civilian said. "I'd like to see the infirmary."

Taking control came naturally to the two unknown men. Judging by their youth and the way they ordered two seasoned commanders around, they were not intimidated by the hierarchy of rank. Constables, perhaps. Investigators. The style of their clothes, the cut of their hair, the way they carried things in the left hand to keep the sword hand free, suggested they were soldiers. Shanti went with them to the infirmary, feeling as if chains would bind her wrists and ankles at any moment. Once inside, she saw Leanna stocking a cabinet while the other women inventoried a trunk full of goods.

Flat Face mouthed the word "inquiry" to Shanti as Leanna gave the men a tour.

"Exemplary work on keeping the infirmary in such fine condition, Leanna," Commander Gray Streak said.

For the first time, Shanti wondered if the women had set her up for a fall. She had underestimated their scheming.

"Let's straighten this out in my office," Gray Streak said. "Shanti, Commander Mossgail, come with us."

They entered the office. Shanti examined the three ceremonial swords displayed on the wall. Gray Streak was a champion sword fighter. Really?

The investigators placed two piles on the desk. One pile contained her wristlet, the container of poison for her darts, and her money bag. The other pile contained Mossgail's sword, his lock of hair, and his money bag.

Between the two piles, the tall man set an antler of some sort, a bull's scrotum, and a vial of snake venom. "These and other goods were bought from the apothecary in town," the man said. "This apothecary also has military items for sale, and bottles of alcohol in the back, marked for military consumption." He picked up the jar of snake venom. "Do you know how much this cost?"

No one answered.

"I bought this for one silver coin," the man continued. He put the vial down, then picked up the antler. "All these and other items were bought with marked coins." He took a silver coin out of his pocket. "Coins with a unique symbol engraved across the back. If either of these money bags contains the marked coins, it would indicate the owner sold the military stock to the apothecary for their own personal gain."

"Who do you think you are!" Mossgail sputtered. "You're barely old enough to shave. I forbid you to go through my bag without permission from a high commander. I know my rights!"

"Shanti?"

"Go ahead," she said.

"Commander Edwyn, Chief Emmins, you are witnesses."

The investigators dumped out her money, checked each coin meticulously, and found no markings.

"Commander Mossgail?" the investigator said.

"Having one of those coins doesn't mean anything. It could have changed hands a dozen times. I could have picked it up in a tavern, perhaps, or from the seamstress in town."

"Which taverns do you frequent?" the investigator asked.

"I don't have to defend myself to you," he sneered. "I've served in the Willovian military ever since you were a baby on your mother's teat. Give me my things and let me be on my way."

Gray Streak seized Mossgail's money bag. "I'm aware that only a high commander can order a search of your property. But as commander of this camp, it is in my power to confiscate your money for the purpose of replenishing the goods that are missing. The supplies were in your care. Therefore, you are responsible. If the stolen items are recovered in usable condition, you'll be reimbursed."

Mossgail snatched up his sword and stormed out of the room with all the dignity he would muster while in his underclothes.

Gray Streak turned over Mossgail's money bag, the contents spilling onto the desk. They found three coins etched with inconspicuous squares that had loops at the corners.

"Why didn't you demand an inquiry?" Flat Face yelled at Shanti.

"What's an inquiry?"

He groaned and dropped his head. "A trial resulting in a formal judgment regarding wrongdoing. A high commander officiates over the proceedings."

"Will he be prosecuted?" she asked.

"That remains to be seen," said Gray Streak. "Shanti, you're free to go. Just remember, a humiliated man will always seek revenge." He regarded the wristlet of darts for a moment before returning it to her. "But I have a feeling you already know that."

She took her things, glancing quickly at the tall investigator on her way out. He had brown eyes, a ruddy complexion, and a confident bearing. She decided to make it her mission to find out his name and buy him a drink. Marked coins—it was brilliant. Mossgail's money really *was* tainted. The only thing left to do was have a long and unpleasant chat with Leanna.

*

Shanti swung open the infirmary door, slamming it against the wall. A bottle fell to the floor and broke. Her sword was sheathed on her back, and she wore her wristlet. "You—all of you—tricked me into hanging the lock of Mossgail's hair in the doorway, knowing I'd be accused!"

Leanna ran over and hugged her. "We *did* it!"

"You would watch me go to jail so you could reap the reward!"

"Don't be silly." Leanna fell onto a bed and giggled like a child. "Did you see Mossgail in his bedclothes, running around camp in high dudgeon? It was rich!"

Shanti loomed over Leanna. "Did you happen to notice that the men who bought us drinks at the tavern are the same men who are investigating the theft—the same men you gave a tour of the infirmary?"

"Don't be so mistrustful. It couldn't be."

"It is, and if they overheard us—"

Leanna got up from the bed and put her hands on Shanti's shoulders. "What are you worried about? You're here—exonerated, I presume. They'd never banish you or put you in jail."

"Banish?"

"They treat you like one of their own."

"Who are 'they'?" Shanti asked.

"The men. You're allowed to train with them. You're taken seriously, whereas we are not. By the way, why are you wearing your weapons in the infirmary?"

"Mossgail's ready to kill me."

"This is a place of healing. Put your things in the hole." Leanna plucked a key from a hook on the wall, then pushed aside a bed. Beneath it was a hatch. She unlocked and lifted the hatch.

Shanti peered inside. A portion of the stolen supplies and several weapons were in the hole—a roughly dug out pit with enough room left over for one person to crouch down and hide. "How long has this been here?"

"Years," Leanna said.

The hole below was bare dirt with very little wood shoring. Dangerous—could cave in without warning. Light from above shone off the warped blades of swords left exposed—passable as practice weapons but next to useless in a real fight. Shanti remembered her last conversation with Caravey before she left the Nunqua: how they had talked about the generals planning war with Willovia. It seemed unimaginable—the king of Willovia's impending death and the resulting conflict. Even though she didn't believe the prophecy of King Magen dying in his sickbed, better to be prepared. "Do any of you know how to use these weapons?"

They shook their heads. "If we're attacked, the soldiers will guard us and the wounded," said Leanna.

"What if *they're* dead?"

"Then you'll protect us."

"You sure about that?" Shanti's mind raced. She could teach

them sword fighting; there was plenty of time during the day. After all, the women wore the uniform, too, and they needed to defend themselves.

If no one was going to give these women respect, she would teach them how to take it.

5

TURNING THE SCREW

S HANTI PLAYED CARDS with a soldier named Deney, who had taken an unlucky fall off his horse and broken his leg. She knew most of the soldiers' names now, and life had settled into a daily rhythm: mornings in the infirmary, afternoons training with the men or teaching the women the more rugged skills of being a soldier. Commander Gray Streak had even taken an interest in her sword-fighting skills, teaching her different techniques to improve her advantage on various terrains.

The hole beneath the infirmary, where the supplies were kept, had been enlarged and shoring installed, and the extra dirt went behind the building for a medicinal herb garden. Yarrow, chamomile, horehound, bloodroot, poppy, and lavender soon flourished there. Everything was going smoothly, though Shanti never found the tall, bright-eyed investigator. No other men in the camp or town interested her for anything beyond friendship. Truth be told, it was getting lonely.

Commander Gray Streak and Chief Flat Face entered the infirmary, and the women, infused with a new sense of military bearing, stood at attention in the presence of their superiors.

"Shanti," Gray Streak said in an official tone, "I have something for you." He handed her a rolled-up letter.

She unfurled the parchment. She was being transferred to a different camp for . . . Did she read it correctly? She moved the parchment closer to her face for a better look. Yes, transferred to a different camp to undergo training for promotion to the rank of commander. It must be a hoax. Flat Face was a hellish prankster, but then, Gray Streak never joked.

"A commander?" she said. "Me?"

"What in the world?" Leanna lost all sense of bearing and snatched the parchment away to read for herself. "Commander Shanti."

"Not yet," Gray Streak said. She has to get through the training first. Not everyone who's nominated succeeds."

"Who nominated Shanti?" Leanna looked at Flat Face.

"Wasn't me. Only a commander can nominate a soldier for the training."

Everyone turned their attention to Gray Streak. He pulled on his collar. "It wasn't me, either."

"The only other commander I know is Mossgail," Shanti said.

Laughter erupted in the room, and she had to admit, it was funny.

A smile brightened Gray Streak's usually severe countenance. "I guarantee, Commander Mossgail didn't nominate you."

"Then who?" Leanna said.

"That's confidential."

"Someone must have figured you're gettin' soft," Flat Face said. "The letter lists the things you'll need for training: your horse, weapons, uniforms, boots, haircut."

"I won't cut my hair."

"It'll grow back," Flat Face said.

"To a Nunqua, it's a grave humiliation."

"Let me get this straight: getting scarred from losing sword fights is a mark of pride, but cutting your hair is a humiliation?" Flat Face shook his head.

"Better get used to humiliation, Shanti," Gray Streak said.

Flat Face punched her in the shoulder, hard. "I got money riding on ya, girlie. Don't let me down."

"I won't."

"Gray Streak put out his hand. "I have every confidence in you."

She shook his hand. "Thank you, sir."

The men left, and the women hugged her, except for Leanna, who moved away and wrinkled the parchment in her tight grip.

Shanti went over and carefully took the letter out of Leanna's hands. She was beginning to realize why commanders had few friends. "I didn't ask for this," she said.

"I've been in the military longer than you."

"The Willovian military."

"I made the plan to drug Mossgail," Leanna said. "I got the supplies we needed. I planted the garden."

"We all did that," Shanti said.

Leanna stared out the window, her jaw set in stone. "Why you?"

"Let me ask you a question," Shanti said. "Remember when I first came here and rode as a guard with the supply cart to the Outer Boundaries? Toulley couldn't go, because his shoulder needed time to heal. If Chief Emmins had asked you to take Toulley's place as a guard, would you have gone, knowing you'd have to sleep outside in the rain, use a rock for a pillow, and eat cold food for days? And if the cart was attacked by bandits, you'd have to fight, possibly kill someone, to save the supplies, or even get killed?"

"If Chief Emmins ordered me to ride as a guard, I would go."

"I didn't say *ordered*. If he *asked* you to go, would you have done it? Honestly?"

"No," Leanna said.

Shanti repeated Caravey's words: "*Pain is our teacher, sacrifice our duty.*" She'd been with the Willovians for almost a year, yet she sometimes found herself favoring Caravey's teachings. Was his influence really that strong? She moved aside the bed and retrieved her weapons from the hole.

"If you don't make it through the training," Leanna said, "if you quit, we'll never get the respect we deserve. And I'll kill you myself."

The attitude indicated a jest. Shanti pushed the bed back, relieved at the break in tension. Leanna wouldn't stay jealous for long. It was a momentary reaction, quickly overcome by reason. Their friendship would withstand the strain. "You can try."

"Shanti," Leanna said.

Considering how long Leanna had taken to say her name in the first place, it was a fitting send-off. Shanti bowed grandly and left the infirmary.

*

More than one person told her she had come to the wrong place. The soldiers weren't being rude; they simply had never encountered a female commander before. Of course, she wasn't a commander yet, merely a candidate.

Seventeen soldiers milled about the stone building in the main camp, waiting for instructions. Shanti spotted a tall one from behind, lean but not too thin, his hair cut short. Something about him jolted her memory. She studied his mannerisms, the way he walked, and caught a glimpse of brown eyes. It had been a long time since the Mossgail incident, but the investigator had made an impression. Was it him? She moved through the crowd to get closer. "Excuse me," she said, "but you look familiar."

"Hello, Shanti."

He remembered. So he was a soldier and not a civilian. "I'm sorry," she said, "but I don't know your name."

"Taran. Are you ready for this?"

"How do you know I'm here for the training? Everyone else thinks I'm lost. They keep pointing me back toward the infirmary."

He gave her the same sheepish grin from the night he had put his arm around her. Maybe Taran knew who had nominated her. He was an investigator, after all, with access to information.

"You know they'll probably make you share the same sleeping quarters with us," he said.

"It's not the sleeping arrangements that worry me," she said. "It's the humiliation." It was an attempt at small talk. After being stuck with knives by Caravey, humiliation wasn't so daunting. "By the way, what happened to Commander Mossgail?"

"I'm not at liberty to say."

A bear of a man came out of the building, catching everyone's attention. "All right, you worthless pond scum, grab your gear."

More men came out of the building, whooping and yelling. One headed straight for her. "If it isn't the freak!" he said. "Give me those darts."

"Sir?" she said, not ready to hand her weapon over to a stranger. His uniform bore no rank. Indeed, none of the men wore identifying insignia.

"Are you disobeying an order?" he said.

"Not that I'm aware of, sir."

"Give me the damn darts! I won't have you using them as a crutch. If you make it through this training—and you won't—it will be because of your integrity and not your ability to intimidate."

"And you are . . . ?" she said.

"Ignorant bitch. Don't even know who I am. I'm going to do everything in my power to ensure you don't become a commander. One last time: give me the darts. Disobey, and you can return to your pitiful life cleaning bedpans and wiping up puke in the infirmary. Don't belong here anyway."

Out of the corner of her eye, she saw Taran tilt his head, signaling her to give the man her weapon. She did as instructed.

He rolled up the wristlet and whacked the side of her head.

"Poison," she said. "Those darts have poisonous tips."

"Afraid of dying? I'd be doing the military a favor. You really are a maggot-infested pile of sheep shit—too foolish to know, you *never* give up your weapon. And you—are you the freak's woman?"

"No," Taran said. "No sir, Commander Gy, sir."

Commander Gy! *The* high commander, who took his orders directly from the king! Oh, hell, this wasn't starting well.

He hit Taran in the side of the head with the wristlet.

So it begins, she mused.

*

Taran punched her in the jaw, and she toppled on the dirt path. Shanti hooked his ankle with her leg, and he went down. She scrambled over the top of him, planting a foot in his back to push off. Sliding through his grasp, she raced toward the next obstacle. Spectators—soldiers who had come to watch the show—stood alongside the obstacle course, hissing and shouting obscenities while pelting the contestants with acorns and pebbles.

Watermelons were perched on logs at eye level. Shanti yanked her sword from its scabbard and ran to the right, cutting the first melon in two. She spun to the left and cut another, drooling at the sight of the juicy red meat. *So hungry.*

Taran cut his two watermelons and ran. They swung over piles of pungent manure, and Taran took the lead. Reaching the maze of ropes that stretched as long as a barn, he crawled through, entangling his sword in the web.

Shanti reached the ropes and, instead of trying to maneuver through them, stepped on them, gaining ground on her opponent. On her way off the maze, she hooked a loop of rope around his sword to slow him down.

Something hit her in the side and splattered. An egg. Another egg hit the top of her shoulder and sprayed her hair with viscous liquid. A quick glance to the right caught a grinning High Commander Gy. He flung another egg at her, and she ducked. A hand pushed her from behind, and she was once again off her feet. *Taran.*

She picked up a small stone and hurled it, hitting Taran in the back of the head. He staggered and put a knee to the ground—her cue to speed to the end. She caught up to him, but his long legs made him faster in the straightaway, and he reached the finish line first. *Second place.* Damn, she was close this time. Shanti leaned against a tree, hunger gnawing at her insides. She tried to wipe the egg out of her hair.

Taran came over, touched the back of his head, then showed her the blood on his fingers. "You bitch."

"You hit me in the face."

"It's an improvement." He took a step away. "What's wrong with your neck? It's . . . splotchy."

Her spots. Damn, she was losing control. Shanti swallowed, concentrated, softened her muscles. Willovian. She was Willovian.

"Freak," he said.

"Bastard."

Commander Gy marched over to her. "You don't deserve to be a commander. You're weak, you're worthless, and you'll never win. I expect a written report tomorrow morning analyzing your disgraceful conduct during the obstacle course, and I believe you owe Candidate Taran an apology."

Shanti faced Taran, pulled her shoulders back, and took a deep breath. "My actions during the obstacle course were regrettable. Jealousy and arrogance influenced my deplorable behavior. As a candidate, I must strive to control my base tendencies and conduct myself with integrity and honor. Please accept my apologies, and congratulations on your victory."

"A full written report," Gy said to her. "By tomorrow morning, and write small. And you"—he poked Taran in the chest—"go to the infirmary and get your head looked at. Lord knows what they'll find. Nothing but air." He walked away, grumbling. "*Stagnant* air, at best."

Shanti went to the sleeping quarters—an open room with

twenty beds aligned in two rows, and only four of them occupied. Her bed was on the opposite side of the room from the men's.

She was poison to them. If they showed any interest in her, befriended her, said one supportive thing to her, the instructors would make their lives hell. No fraternization allowed. None. Nobody being nice to her, nobody helping her, no camaraderie or working together to achieve a common goal—just an uncomfortable, silent coexistence with the other candidates. Commander Gy kept turning the screw, expecting her to splinter and break.

Not likely.

Her bed had been overturned, as usual, and her belongings dumped out. Probably Commander Gy's doing. She cleaned up and got ready for guard duty, hoping for enough moonlight to write one ridiculous report on assaulting a fellow candidate.

It was going to be another long night.

*

Shanti stood motionless inside a meeting room for one last interrogation, her breathing calm and her back straight. Today was the last day of training—the day she would find out if all the abuse heaped on her was for nothing. The instructors sneered at her uniform, boots, long hair in a warrior's knot, and the sword on her back. How she hated their collective disdain!

Commander Gy's presence dominated the room. "You ignorant bitch," he said. "Why should I promote you?"

Was it a trick question? She didn't want to seem overconfident, nor did she want to seem weak. What was the answer he was looking for?

"You're pathetic," he said.

"I have passed every test," she said, "both physical and mental, succeeded at—"

He smacked the side of her head. "Wrong!"

She swallowed the urge to open her mouth and rebuke the highest-ranking commander in the room—in the Willovian military, for that matter. Now was not the time for cheek. She straightened her posture.

"I would like to speak with Shanti in private," Commander Gy said. "Everyone else, out." The other instructors trickled out until only she and Gy remained. He closed the door—an unthinkable act. A man and woman alone behind closed doors started rumors. "Before we go further," he said, "I need to know about your past."

"I'm loyal to Willovia."

"Show me your arms."

Her breath stopped in her chest as she remembered being alone with Caravey in a similar situation. Caravey had given her an order to change for him, plunging a knife into her gut when she disregarded his command.

"Finally," he said, "a crack in your shield. Maybe now we can get somewhere. Show me your arms."

"And if I refuse, sir?"

"Why would you do that?" he asked, genuinely curious.

"I would like the decision concerning my promotion to be based upon my abilities, character, and actions during this training, not on my past."

"Don't shit me. You flaunt those scars for attention. Why refuse my request to see them now?"

Commander Gy wasn't Caravey. He didn't have healing power that made him invincible. She lifted her sleeves. Seven straight scars marred the flesh— seven memories of her former life. The scars got her noticed by the right people, but they could also ruin her chances of advancement.

The tone of his voice changed from loathing to frustration. "Do you understand how much I've risked by allowing you into this training? If you're loyal to Willovia, why do you bear the marks of a Nunqua? Why did they train you? You're Willovian. It's unprecedented."

Could she trust him? Shanti understood that his conduct toward her was not a true reflection of his feelings. Trainees were supposed to be treated with the utmost contempt. Her affiliation with the Nunqua was known among the soldiers, but she had concealed the depth of the connection. "They," she said, aware that the blink of her eyelids and the pause in her speech betrayed her emotions. "My father—"

"Stop shillyshallying."

"The Nunqua forced me out of Willovia after both my parents died. They trained me as a warrior, like my father before me." She rubbed the scars on her forearms, breaking her stiff posture in a moment of reflection. "But I . . ." She wanted to say "escaped," but that was too telling. "I left."

"What do you mean, 'trained you like your father'? Speak plainly."

"I'm not entirely Willovian. My father was a Nunqua warrior."

"*What!*"

"My father was—"

"I heard you," he said. "Just not sure I believe you. And your mother?"

"Willovian."

"You're *half* Nunqua?"

"Yes."

"How's that possible? There's no interbreeding between the two races."

She dared look directly at him. "Breeding is for horses and dogs . . . sir."

"You have no spots, no red lips," he said.

"I look like my mother."

"What was your mother's occupation?"

"Homemaker. Raised sheep, chickens, a few milking cows now and then. Whatever it took to survive."

"Did she entertain many guests?"

"My mother was not a prostitute," Shanti said. "I knew my father. He brought us money, food, gifts. He taught me the Nunqua language and how to read, told me stories." An unexpected spasm of grief hit her. She hadn't thought much about her mother and father for a long time.

"Why did you leave the Nunqua to join us?"

"Because their cruelty went beyond the cutting of my forearms."

He retrieved her wristlet from a nearby table and inspected it, touching the latches and coils. "I've never seen anything like it."

She smirked, unable to resist telling the tale that had entertained so many of her companions. "Bought it from a hag who was half mad and blind in one eye. Her teeth were greenish-gold from chewing beetle wings. The flecks of gold you see on the hollow tips of the darts are the poisonous innards harvested from the beetle. Guaranteed to kill a man in a day."

"Not much use in battle, then," he said.

"I don't harbor any delusions that I'm physically strong as a man, so I compensate for it in other ways."

"You have strength enough." He gave her back the wristlet, then paced in the room.

Shanti fastened the weapon to her forearm. Perhaps the beetle story had been too informal for the occasion, better suited to an inn than an inquisition. Besides, she didn't want him to think ill of the Nunqua. "I'd like you to know, Commander," she said, "not every Nunqua is brutal or addicted to beetle wings. My uncle and his family have always treated me well. They live honorably in—"

He waved his hand, indicating he wanted silence. She stared ahead, awaiting his decision concerning her promotion.

He laughed unexpectedly, mischievously. His condescending attitude disappeared, and a genuine smile warmed his face. It was as if the mask had disappeared and she was permitted to see the man. "You're perfect, Shanti—more than I could have hoped for. Your training is complete, and your secret is safe with me. For now."

Commander Gy didn't spurn her because of her Nunqua heritage. He had called her perfect. Perfect for what?

"Do you know who nominated you for this training?" he asked.

"I suspect it was Gray St—I mean Commander Edwyn—but I'm not certain."

"It wasn't Edwyn," he said. "It was I."

High Commander Gy, whom she had never met before her first day of training, had nominated her. But why?

*

Shanti lingered in an alleyway and watched people enter a crowded tavern. Through the open door, she saw a waitress balancing a tray of mugs over her head. A boisterous voice told indecent jokes, and someone sang off-key.

An autumn breeze chilled the air, and she tried to smooth the wrinkles out of her dress without success. Her clothing had been crumpled inside a bag for the duration of her training, when all she could wear was a uniform. The dress used to be nice, but now it smelled musty from being packed away. It felt good to let her hair down, although wearing the dress made her uncomfortable since she had gotten so used to the uniform.

A rat scuttled along the ground and stopped to sniff a discarded shoe. The crescent moon reflected in a rain puddle. It was getting late. The merriment might end before she even arrived. Had she forgotten how to relax and join in a friendly conversation? If only she didn't have to go in alone. But what the hell—she deserved to have a good time.

Shanti left the alleyway, crossed the road, and entered the tavern. Everyone cheered.

Men and women gathered around her, eager for adventure, wanting to hear grandiose tales full of bravado. One young man shoved a mug of ale into her hand. "I knew you could do it. How many started training with you?"

"Seventeen," she said, surprised by the attention.

"And how many were promoted?

The young man's smile was boyish, charming. Shanti couldn't help but smile back. "Four." She took a sip of warm ale.

The waitress tapped her on the shoulder. "They're waiting for you at the commanders' table."

"Too good for the likes of us now." The young man gave her a congratulatory hug and a quick kiss on the cheek. The crowd around her dispersed.

The tavern, popular with the soldiers, smelled like smoke, alcohol, and perfume. It was the first time she had visited the place or had a reason to celebrate since her training began.

There they were, at a table by the fire: commanders of the camp—respected leaders, pitiless taskmasters, the most feared men in the Willovian military. And there was nothing boyish or charming about them.

Commander Coda sat with his back to her. It was Coda who had given her a bloody nose when he tripped her on one of the obstacle courses. Next to Coda was the commander who had stolen her boots, tossed them up a tree, and made her train barefoot. Commander Gy was also at the table. He conversed with Commander Hajari, master of swords, whose unnerving stare made even the strongest soldiers want to crawl under a rock and hide.

Yet none of them had ever slashed her with a knife and calmly watched her bleed. Caravey's voice resounded in her skull. *The fires of combat do not burn in their bellies. They are soft—sheep ready for the shears or the slaughter. I made you greater than them all.* She shook her head to rid herself of the presence that often engulfed her thoughts. She supposed it was normal; Caravey had taught her first.

Commander Coda moved over to make room for her on the bench. "Have a seat." His tone was oddly pleasant. Shanti set her mug down on the best table in the tavern, reserved exclusively for the commanders. Coda put a shot of liquor in front of her. "You've earned it."

A compliment? She lifted the cup. "You didn't make it easy." The fiery drink filled her mouth and drained down her throat.

"It's not my job to make it easy." Coda lifted his own glass in a toast. "To the meanest woman I've ever met, who can give as well as take, and who's a hell of a lot of fun on an obstacle course. Congratulations, Commander." Coda gulped down his drink, then refilled his cup from a bottle on the table.

"I'm not mean," she said. The men at the table laughed. Even quiet, stone-faced Hajari cracked a smile.

"Do you know where you're going after this?" Coda asked.

"The castle," Shanti said. "I've been assigned as the princess's personal guard."

"I don't envy you."

"It's only for a short time. When spring comes, I'll accompany Commander Gy to a new camp."

Coda turned to Commander Hajari. "Who's in charge of the royal guards at the castle?"

Hajari answered in a voice that reminded Shanti of a snake, if snakes could speak. "I believe it's High Commander Kyros."

"Not good for you," Coda said to Shanti.

"Why not?"

Hajari spoke in his usual aloof hiss. "Kyros is not fond of women."

"Oh, he's fond of women, all right." Coda stopped a passing waitress and ordered another bottle. "As long as he can get under their skirts. You wear the uniform of a soldier, a female commander. He'll not like you. Unless . . ."

"Unless what?" she challenged.

Coda's hearty laugh drowned out the noise of the tavern. He smacked Shanti good-naturedly on the back, propelling her head and shoulders forward. Commander Coda didn't know his own strength sometimes. Or maybe he did.

It seemed strange to be talking with the same men who had treated her so terribly, told her she was a waste of skin. But she knew that their cruel games were just that: games to test her competence under pressure. Other soldiers quit rather than suffer through the ordeal. Shanti had learned to play the game long before she became a member of the Willovian military, and she was good at it.

"Don't let Kyros push you around," Commander Gy said.

"But he outranks me."

"And *I* outrank *him*." Gy took a pipe out of his pocket and stuffed the chamber with tobacco. "Remember, you work for me."

Coda drank another shot of liquor in one gulp and set the cup on the table without so much as a waver. "Where's home for you, Shanti? Are you going to visit your parents before starting work at the castle?"

"Both my parents are dead."

"Sorry. Brothers or sisters?"

"Only child."

"Family?" Coda said.

"I have an uncle. He lives far from—"

"You can stay with my family for a while," Gy said. "It's on the way to the castle."

Stay with the high commander and his family? As uncomfortable as that would be, it was an offer she must accept. "Thank you, sir."

"I'll expect you in a few days. It will take at least that long to get reacquainted with my wife." He puffed on the pipe with an air of self-satisfaction. "Give her what she's been missing."

"A few days," Coda said, "or a few seconds?"

Everyone except sword master Hajari laughed at the joke. He scrutinized Shanti with slanted eyes sunk deep in a weathered and serious face, like a serpent eyeing its prey. Hajari nodded once—a small gesture of approval that meant more to her than all the free drinks and backslaps of the other rowdy soldiers put together.

*

Shanti stayed three days with Commander Gy, his wife, Tova, and their two children at the family's farmhouse. She slept in a small room by the kitchen and helped Tova cook and gather food from the garden. Plenty of time was available to take her horse for long rides through the countryside and visit the town. The night before she was to leave for the castle, she sat alone with Gy before a dying fire.

"Do you know why I nominated you to undergo the training to be promoted to commander?" Gy said.

"No sir, but I've been wondering about it since you told me. I don't remember meeting you before the first day of training."

"That's because we had never met. Commander Edwyn told me about you. He considers you a natural leader and said your skills are above average."

"Really?"

"He also called you arrogant, reckless, and antisocial."

Shanti nodded. That sounded more like the Commander Edwyn she knew.

"I also reviewed the incident involving Mossgail, and although you were never officially implicated in the theft, we know you were involved. Hell, everyone knows it. You disregarded the law to expose—dare I say, humiliate—a corrupt commander and see that the medical section got the supplies they were entitled to. Although I cannot and will not publicly support your method of dealing with Mossgail, it's one of the reasons I chose you for this mission."

"The mission to guard the princess?"

"Those are your official orders. I have another mission for you—something far more important." He got up and pumped a bellows to feed the flames. "An untested leader is no leader at all."

"I don't understand."

"Before being promoted, you were tested to see how you handled pressure. I tried to get you to quit the training, made it so that every other candidate there hated you—even Commander Taran. I suspect he had great affection for you in the beginning. And you for him."

Was it that obvious?

"As much as the other candidates learned to hate you, they listened to you, and they would go into battle with you." Gy set the bellows down, then returned to his seat. "Your mission is not simply to guard Rega Bayla, but to test her as we have tested you."

"Test the princess?" she said.

"You're a commander now. You will lead a handful of soldiers, give orders, and expect those orders to be followed. One day, the princess, as queen, will be in command of the entire Willovian military, yet she doesn't know what it means to be a soldier. It's the duty of the Guardians of Willovia to train her. And to test her."

Shanti was more confused than ever. "The *what*?"

"The Guardians of Willovia. We're a secret society made up of select citizens and soldiers. Commander Edwyn and Chief Emmins are Guardians; so is the castle artist and the undertaker in town, and others you wouldn't expect. Our purpose is to ensure that the monarchy is capable of leading the military, and act in the best interest of the people. When winter's over, we'll take Rega Bayla away from her home to a camp in the Hedgelands, along with sixty other soldiers. Your orders, Shanti, are to train the princess. She must know what it's like to be a soldier, and show concern for those she will one day lead. When her training is complete, she will face one final task. Rega Bayla needs to stand against a traitor and put the needs of Willovia before her own safety. You are to play the part of a traitor."

You'll find a way, Caravey's voice said. *You always do.*

No! Her gaining access to royalty was a coincidence and not a path she had pursued. Her mission to spy for the Nunqua was irrelevant.

"I made you a commander," Gy said, "and now I'm making you a Guardian of Willovia. Not many know of our existence. You must swear an oath to do what's best for the kingdom, even if it means disregarding the law and turning out those too inept or corrupt to rule."

A commander *and* a Guardian. Pride swelled in her chest. "I swear it."

"I'm putting my trust in you, Shanti."

"I won't let you down," she said.

"During your time as Rega Bayla's guard at the castle, I want you to watch her closely, find out what she's like. It won't be easy."

"All I have to do is stand still, study the princess, and keep quiet. What's so difficult about that?"

"For you?" He raised one eyebrow, the pipe clenched between his teeth.

The embers in the fireplace burned red, popping and splitting, then cooling into piles of ash. She had heard rumors about the opulence of the Willovian castle: sumptuous feasts, fine wine, the best music, art in every room, beautiful gardens, and well-kept stables. It would be a relaxing break and much better than the meager accommodations she was used to. Besides, she was a commander now. How hard could it be?

6

THE DAUGHTERS OF
FORTUNATE BIRTH

S HANTI SPENT ALL winter working at the castle, guarding the princess and answering questions posed to her by the elites. The honored guests of King Magen were curious and cordial enough, and she had made friends with many of the royal guards. The castle and its grounds were painstakingly picturesque, but a heaviness pervaded everything inside the walls of the compound. She felt that she could never be comfortable, never be herself, in the restrictive environment. Day after day, this feeling darkened her mood.

For the second time since she arrived in autumn, Shanti climbed the spiraling stairs of the tallest tower for a private meeting with King Magen. Her first encounter with the king had set the rules concerning her interactions with Rega Bayla and served to establish his displeasure at Shanti's status as a Guardian of Willovia. Indeed, King Magen tolerated her presence only because he had endured the test of confronting a traitor himself, when he was a prince. He understood the Guardians' importance and, Shanti surmised, despised their purpose now that his only child, his petite and precious daughter, was due to undergo the rigors of a soldier's life.

Guards admitted her into the king's presence. She entered and stood motionless in front of a marble desk with an empty chair. On top of the marble slab rested parchment, a peacock quill, an inkwell, and three bars of sealing wax the thickness of a man's finger. The legs of the desk were sculpted in the shapes of lions. Floor-to-ceiling flags adorned the walls between the windows, the most prominent depicting an eagle on a field of blue.

King Magen gazed out of a window, his hands clasped behind his back.

"Your Majesty," she said.

He moved away from the window and stepped around her while inspecting her brown uniform, hair pulled back in a warrior's knot, sword strapped to her back, and darts strapped to the wristlet on her arm.

"You're wearing the wrong uniform, Commander. Why aren't you dressed as a royal guard?"

"Royal guard uniforms are made for men, sire. One is being made for me by the tailor." It was a small lie. *A lie to the king.* The tailor had finished the outfit some time ago.

The men's uniforms looked good on them, handsome and respectable. Hers was a blue and white mess. Clusters of scratchy lace embellished the collar, baggy pockets adorned the shapeless jacket, and the voluminous skirt trailed along the ground. She suspected that Commander Kyros had something to do with the design of the dress—a joke to him, an insult to her. She would do anything to avoid wearing her royal guard uniform, even if it meant lying to the king.

"You've been at the castle far too long not to be dressed in the proper attire," he said. "I have called you here to inform you of the plans concerning my daughter. You will train Rega Bayla to be a soldier. She will pass every test given to her. Do we have an understanding, Commander?"

Her training had taught her to be tactful when dealing with her superiors, even when given a corrupt command. "I'll do what's best for Willovia, Your Majesty."

Magen stroked his gray beard. "Are you aware of the seriousness of this matter? Bayla is my only child. If she fails, the Guardians of Willovia will try to prevent her from taking her rightful place as queen. Many of my loyal subjects will fight to see that Bayla wears the crown. Is that what you want, Commander Shanti? Revolution? War? Your duty is clear: Bayla will pass the trials, especially the final test."

Shanti avoided eye contact and remained still. The king smelled like alcohol. No, not alcohol—medicine.

"Know this. If your actions aren't in the best interests of Willovia, my punishment will be severe: I'll put your head on the chopping block."

She must show no emotion. An emotional soldier was a weak soldier. Shanti focused on the in-and-out of her breath.

King Magen moved behind the desk. He sat in the chair and waved the back of his hand at her. "Dismissed."

She lowered her head.

"Be prepared." He picked up the quill and dipped it into the pot of ink. "It is almost time. Ships are stationed offshore and awaiting orders to attack."

Shanti left the room.

The two royal guards who flanked the doorway outside the king's quarters wore blue uniforms with white trim and held spears decorated with gold filigree. No longer in the king's presence, Shanti turned to the familiar faces with a casual air. "Boys . . ." She bowed and spread her arms, playfully taunting their inability to respond while on duty. "I shall see you both after the feast." The royal guards stared into the distance, as she had done only moments before.

She descended the spiral staircase and stopped to look through an arrow slit built into the curved wall. The opening faced the city of Erbaut, with the sea behind it. Shanti leaned the side of her head against the stone to view rooftops and roads. Through the slit, distant figures of men, women, and children meandered in and out of view. The king's threat disturbed her thoughts. If Rega Bayla failed the trials or the final test, Magen would have her beheaded.

She imagined herself being paraded through the streets of Erbaut, with her hands tied behind her back and dressed in her ugly blue and white royal guard's uniform. A mob of people encircling her, pointing and laughing with their mouths open so wide she could count their bad teeth. The throng parting to create a path. A hooded man holding an ax, next to a bloodstained block of wood and a basket near his feet. The basket slightly larger than her head. Spectators cheering, pushing her toward the scrawny man wielding the blunt ax, his exposed arms wrinkled and thin like an old woman's.

How many blows would it take?

It wouldn't come to that, would it? The Guardians' mission would encompass one summer of her life, when she would teach the princess to become more than a princess. Her part in the plan would be justified, rewarding: push Bayla to the breaking point, pretend to be a traitor to Willovia, show everyone that Bayla would put the needs of her kingdom before her own safety, reveal the plan, congratulations all around, and move on.

Nothing was that simple, and plans had a way of unraveling. Shanti thought of Bayla and touched her neck. Even Caravey wouldn't be able to heal her if the king took her head.

No sense thinking too far into the future, though; now was the time to concentrate on the task at hand. She tore herself away from the arrow slit to continue down the staircase and find the princess.

The Daughters of Fortunate Birth lounged in an elegant room, waiting for the nightly feast to begin. The women stopped chatting when Shanti entered. With a sideways nod of her head, Shanti ordered the temporary guard to leave. She remained by the door, watching the princess, studying her in secret.

Rega Bayla sat near an open window looking out over the sea. A caterpillar crawled on the windowsill. Bayla stroked the bristles of the insect with her fingertip.

The princess wore a dark green dress that billowed in the spring breeze. Geckos, painted in emerald hues and garnished with small jewels, had been drawn on her wrists. Her hair cascaded down her back, and her long nose had a regal bump. She picked up the caterpillar, cupping it in her hands.

"Rega Bayla," said a woman with pink roses painted on her arms, "I don't see why your personal guard has to be near you all the time. Can't she stand in the hallway or somewhere less conspicuous?"

"Yes, Rega," said another Fortunate Daughter, reclining in a chaise. "She's too menacing. Perhaps she should dress more appropriately for the castle. Send her to the painter for some body art."

"I doubt it would help."

The Daughters of Fortunate Birth laughed—a practiced laugh sounding like the sweet chirping of birds. Shanti knew not to respond to their insults. She was a guard—emotionless, invisible.

Not for long.

Rega Bayla uncupped her hands to release the treasure within. The caterpillar, now a butterfly with bright blue wings, crawled to the tip of her finger. "I'll speak to my father tonight about her. After that, she won't be a problem."

Few were aware of Bayla's strange power—a well-guarded royal secret. Shanti had spent enough time with the princess to know. The Daughters of Fortunate Birth also knew. The young women acted entranced when Bayla displayed her unnatural skills. But Shanti detected fear. The Daughters of Fortunate Birth were frightened of Bayla, every single one. The princess, heiress to the throne of Willovia, was a witch. And many of the citizens of Willovia believed that witches were evil.

The butterfly, the tiny miracle conjured by Bayla, danced about the room and fluttered out the window into a sky of blue. Without moving her head, Shanti watched the butterfly escape the confines of the castle, and she, too, wished for wings.

*

Shanti followed Bayla into a chamber packed with guests after the castle feast. Atonal notes of instruments being tuned echoed off the high ceiling. Shanti stood by the entrance with her back to the wall and listened to the conversation between King Magen and his daughter—not difficult, since Bayla made no attempt to hide her venom.

"But, Father," Bayla said, "she doesn't even address me as 'Rega.' Due to her insubordination, I feel she must not be allowed to serve as my personal guard."

"Then whom do you suggest?" Magen said.

"The royal guards who have served me in the past."

"Half the royal guards, along with most of our troops, are at the Outer Boundaries, defending the country from attack. She will continue to be your protection."

"She's a misfit in this castle. You must—"

"Bayla, she stays. It is by my order as king that she is your guard." Magen's voice softened. "Stay close to her. The monks have warned me that enemies are preparing to invade Willovia."

"Thank you, Father, for respecting my opinions. Your belief in me means so much." She performed a quick curtsy, then left her father standing alone.

Shanti stood in surprised silence. Odd that King Magen should refuse Bayla's request. The Guardians of Willovia, it appeared, had stronger influence over him than his own daughter.

Joyful music began to play, and Bayla stormed out of the hall. Shanti glanced at her face when she passed.

Bayla turned on her toes and positioned herself in front of

Shanti, the top of her head level with the bottom of Shanti's chin. "Look at me again, and I'll have you flogged."

A hollow threat. No royal guard would punish her for glancing at the princess. Not even High Commander Kyros would obey such an outrageous command. The princess was so young, so naive. Shanti returned her attention to the guests, only barely managing to keep a smirk off her lips.

"Is something funny?"

"No, Rega."

"Careful, guard. You're not as important as you think."

Oh, but I am.

*

Shanti walked outside with the two royal guards who had earlier flanked the entrance to the king's quarters. The spears the men had carried were put away for the night. It was dark, and the three off-duty guards entered the castle's kitchen, where workers cleaned dishes and swept the floor. The guards asked if they could have a taste of the food left over from the feast.

A bald man in charge of kitchen inventory wrote in a journal. Shanti placed two coins on top on the journal.

"To toast the arrival of spring," she said.

He put the coins in his pocket and jerked his thumb in the direction of the wine cellar.

Shanti descended the steps to a cool, tidy underground room filled with bottles stacked inside crates. After examining several boxes containing all types of costly liquor, she chose an inexpensive bottle of red wine and brought it up.

A short, snaggle-toothed cook, his yellow hair slicked back with a heavy coating of grease, confronted her. "Who do you think you are?"

"We missed dinner," she said.

"Then go to the . . . wherever the guards eat, and leave us alone. This food is for the royals and their guests."

"It would take us half the night to walk there."

"And?" Stains from food and sweat discolored his once-white shirt.

"We've gotten food from the kitchen before. No one's ever complained." She looked for the bald man in charge of inventory, but he must have left. "Besides, I already paid for the wine."

"You didn't pay *me*. One silver coin, and I'll let you have it."

She inspected the bottle. "It's not worth that much."

"Then put it back."

Why was he being difficult? She had bought wine from the castle's stores before.

One of the guards approached, laden with an armful of food. "Commander Shanti," he said, "we're ready to go."

She bypassed the cook and headed for the door.

"Commander?" the cook said. "How many men did you have to pleasure to obtain the rank of commander?"

She stopped a few steps away from the exit. The Daughters of Fortunate Birth, Rega Bayla, and even this filthy cook had insulted her, and all on the same day. She was sick of keeping quiet, taking the verbal abuse, and swallowing her pride.

"Watch the door," she told one of the guards, handing the bottle of wine to the other guard.

The cook snickered. "Judging by your reaction, I'd say I'm right. I'll give you all the food you want if you satisfy me. *I'll* show you how to command."

Workers in the kitchen moved away as she walked toward the cook until they were an arm's length apart. "I'm sorry," Shanti said. "I didn't quite hear you. Can you repeat that?"

"He's unarmed and not worth the trouble," the guard holding the bottle of wine said. "We have enough food."

The lookout by the door whistled.

"Commander Kyros?" She kept her gaze locked on the cook.

"Yes," the guard said.

"You two, get out of here. Do not let Kyros see you, and do not drink my wine."

The royal guards made a hasty retreat out the back door.

"You," she said to the cook. "Pick your weapon."

His gaze alternated between the hilt of her sword, visible just above her shoulder, and the darts secured to the wristlet on her forearm.

"We're surrounded by knives. Pick one. You wanted to see why I was promoted to commander, didn't you?"

A deep voice behind her said, "That same question has come up in my mind—many times, actually."

She stepped back from the cook, who scurried away like a ferret that has seen a hawk.

"Outside," Commander Kyros ordered.

Although he was a soldier, Kyros didn't wear a uniform. His elevated rank and proximity to the king afforded him certain privileges at the castle. His fine breeches and coat accentuated his muscular frame. Dark skinned, with a strong jaw, he cut a respectable figure.

They walked away from the kitchen and any prying ears. "I should have expected as much from you, Commander Shanti. Attacking an unarmed cook—it's inexcusable. What do you have to say for yourself?"

"I'm merely teaching him some manners, sir."

"What Commander Gy sees in you, I'll never know. Always trying to prove yourself, trying to make everyone think you're so dangerous. Go ahead, pull your sword on me. Shoot me with a poisonous dart." Kyros leaned toward her and whispered, "Go ahead."

She knew better than to battle the high commander under such circumstances. It would land her in jail, exactly as he wanted. Or was he after something else? Kyros was popular with women, and many female admirers at the castle were trying to hook him into marriage.

"Scared?" he said.

"You flatter yourself."

"Where's your royal guard uniform?" An arrogant smile lifted the corners of his lips. "Still at the tailor's? Failure to wear the proper attire is a demotable offense."

Shanti did her best to keep a professional demeanor. She was a commander now, with some authority.

"A proper uniform would not hinder my ability to protect the princess, ride a horse, or fight with a sword. If I'm demoted for such an infraction, I'll demand an inquiry to determine the adequacy of the uniform that, I believe, *you* designed. I'll also insist that the uniform be presented as evidence."

"How very self-righteous for someone who threatens an unarmed man! You're a bully, Shanti, not a soldier." And with that, Kyros left and entered the castle.

She joined the two royal guards sitting on top of a wooden table. Succulent scraps of food left over from the feast were scattered about them, and wax from a single candle dripped onto the tabletop. She opened the bottle of wine and poured some into a cup made from staves of wood held together with tarnished metal bands.

"So," one of the men said, "do we still have to call you 'Commander,' or have you been demoted?"

"Kyros has no real authority over me. He can't take my rank away."

"Why not? He outranks you and has charge of all the royal guards, does he not?"

She sipped the delicious wine from the brutish cup that matched her brutish mood. Kyros couldn't take her rank away, because she worked for Commander Gy—a fact that she must conceal.

Red wine dripped from a loose seam in the side of the cup. Shanti placed her finger over the seam and took another drink, letting the dry, earthy flavor fall over her tongue. The princess would never use such a crude container. Why should she? Bayla had the best of everything without having to work for it.

That was about to change.

7
HEXED

SHANTI CREPT INTO the bedchamber where Rega Bayla slept soundly. The fire had gone out, making the room cold. "Wake up, Rega," Shanti said.

Bayla rolled away and nestled deeper in fluffy, warm blankets. Shanti snatched the covers off. "Wake up!"

Bayla sat bolt upright in her bed, hair obscuring her face. "You fool! The king will punish you for this."

Shanti seized Bayla's upper arm and dragged her out of bed. She opened the shutters of a window with a view of the water. The dark outlines of three ships could be seen. Smaller boats were rowing to shore on the moonlit sea. Enemy craft all. "We have to go now," Shanti said.

Bayla moved away from the window and squatted in her night-gown, her back against the wall, arms around her knees. "You must take me to the king. I'll seek refuge with my father."

"If you and your father are found together, you both could be killed, and the royal bloodline would cease to exist. We must go to the Hedgelands and seek refuge there." Shanti opened Bayla's wardrobe and rifled through the fine garments. She threw riding clothes onto the bed.

"Only three ships threaten the castle," Bayla said. "The royal guards will subdue the besiegers. I'll stay here."

"The guard is under half strength, and the monks warned the king of an attack already. No military would invade a city this large with only three ships. The ships are a diversion. We've received reports that more enemy troops are positioned along the coast and waiting to strike. The king ordered you to stay by me."

Bayla remained crouched against the wall.

Not the time to act like a damsel in distress—not tonight, when they were so close to leaving the castle. "Either you get your clothes on," Shanti said, "or I carry you out of here in your nightgown, kicking and screaming."

Heavy footsteps and the clank of weapons came from the hallway. Royal guards were preparing for the castle's defense. Distant bells rang in the city, alerting citizens to the bogus invasion.

"We don't have time for this, Bayla."

"You will address me as 'Rega,' guard."

Shanti took two steps forward and stretched out her hand, ready to haul Bayla out of the comfort of her lavish room.

Bayla lurched away, and her feet caught in the nightgown, tumbling her unregally onto her side. "There's no need for force," she said. "I'll follow my father's wishes." She changed into the riding clothes on the bed.

They hurried to the stables, passing men dressed in the same brown uniform as Shanti. They carried bows, spears, and battle-scarred shields without the Willovian crest. Helmets hid their faces, and heavy leather vests covered their torsos.

The stable, lit by a few lanterns, bustled with men saddling horses for combat. It was hard to see anything in the dim light. A man handed the reins of a horse to Shanti and gave her two crescent-shaped flasks of water. She gave one to Bayla.

"Where is Rega Bayla's horse?" Shanti asked.

The soldier shook his head. "Sorry, Commander. The princess's horse is too difficult to handle."

"Looks like you have to saddle your own horse, *Rega*."

At the far end of the stable, an animal snorted and kicked the gate of its enclosure. Soldiers flinched, keeping their distance from the unruly beast. The horse reared and whinnied, pawing the air with its forehooves. Bayla went to the stall, her back straight and head held high. She picked up her saddle and blanket, then entered the wild stallion's stall.

Shanti listened. All was quiet in the stall. It took Bayla only a few moments to return, leading the stallion, saddled and ready to ride.

The two women rode away from the castle. Bayla paused only once to look back at her home, silhouetted against the sea. Pinpoints of light from the city under siege spread out in a semicircle from the base of the castle.

They continued on their way and traveled in silence until dawn, stopping on a hill that overlooked a farm. A thin line of smoke rose from the chimney of a two-story cottage of dark stone with a red roof. Freshly turned plots of soil surrounded the abode.

"Is *this* where my father wants me to stay?" Bayla said.

Shanti rode closer to the cottage and dismounted.

Bayla kicked her heels into the sides of her horse and trotted down the hill.

"Dismount, Rega," Shanti said.

A woman emerged from the cottage with a basket. Upon seeing the two women, she retreated inside.

"It's disrespectful not to dismount," Shanti said. "We seek their help."

"You have no cause to speak to me of disrespect, *guard*."

A man came out of the cottage. Commander Gy held the hand of a girl about four or five years old—his daughter, Donora. The young girl's hair was the color of corn silk. Gy shooed her back into the house, then came toward them.

Under her breath, Shanti again ordered, "Dismount."

Bayla got down from her horse. "For his sake, not yours."

"Hello, Shanti," Gy said. The wool shirt on his broad shoulders looked warm enough to keep out the crisp morning air, and his sandy-brown hair seemed grayer around the temples than she had remembered. "What's the reason for your visit today?" he asked.

"Commander Gy," Shanti said, "the castle was attacked last night."

His brow creased in concern. He was quite the actor. "King Magen has been expecting an invasion." Gy bowed to Bayla, "This must be the princess, Rega Bayla."

Bayla wore no royal insignia, no finery to signify her status. Her hair wasn't even combed. Yet she curtsied to him in a proper royal greeting.

"You must be hungry. Please come in and have some breakfast." Gy called out, and a freckle-faced boy rushed out of the cottage. "Jonas, take care of the horses, and don't be slow about it."

"No!" Shanti snatched the back of the boy's shirt to stop him from taking the reins of the stallion. "My apologies, but Rega Bayla's horse is hard to control. Only the princess can manage him."

"Nonsense." Bayla smiled shrewdly at Shanti while speaking to the boy. "You'll find that my horse is no trouble at all."

Shanti let go of his shirt, and Jonas led the horses to the pasture.

Gy ushered the women into the cottage, which was warm from the cook fire and filled with the smells of breakfast. Shanti took her sheathed sword off her back and handed it to Gy. She also removed the wristlet of darts so he could place the weapons on a shelf. She pushed up her sleeves, giving Bayla a chance to glimpse the long scars that marred the skin of her forearm.

Donora tugged on the hem of Shanti's jacket, and Shanti pulled a length of hard candy from her pocket and broke off a piece for the girl. Gy's wife was busy making breakfast. Shanti gave her a welcoming hug, then sat in a chair with her feet up on a stool, glad to be free of the strict rules that governed conduct at the castle.

"Rega Bayla," Gy said, "I'd like you to meet my wife, Tova."

"Rega Bayla . . . the princess?" Tova lowered her head in an appropriate gesture for greeting royalty, then continued to cook, banging bowls of food onto the table. "I guess this means I'll have to do without my husband for a while. Royalty does not visit our home without a reason. What is it this time?"

Tova didn't know? "The castle was attacked last night," Shanti said. "The princess and I were able to escape before any fighting began."

Gy set plates and silverware on the table. "Did you see the attackers?"

"No," Shanti said. "Three ships approached from the east. They were unmarked."

Gy spoke to Bayla, "Commander Shanti and I will go to the village and send word to assemble your guard at the Hedgelands. I suggest you stay here and get some rest. We can't risk your being seen until we know what's happening at the castle. We leave tonight."

Bayla pushed on the frayed cane seat of a chair with her hand before sitting down. The chair wobbled under her weight. She wiped her hand along the table and inspected it for crumbs. "My guard?"

"Of course," Gy said. "You didn't expect the only protection for the heiress to the Willovian throne to be an old man and one worn-out soldier."

"Worn out?" Shanti said.

The old man chuckled.

"Jonas, come in and eat," Tova called out a window. The boy came in. "Donora." The quiet girl climbed onto a chair and sat on a block of wood that allowed her to see over the table.

Shanti mounded food on her plate while Bayla took only a ladylike portion of bread and fruit.

"Rega Bayla," Tova said, "we've been blessed with much food here. Please feel free to eat all you like."

"Thank you for your concern, but I do not eat meat."

"Are you sure?"

"Yes." Bayla returned her attention to Gy, "Exactly how many guards will there be?"

"Sixty," he answered between bites. "Did your father mention the plans for your protection?"

"No." She pushed the food around her plate with a spoon.

"Understand that King Magen has provided for your safety ever since you were born."

"Do you know my father?"

"Very well. Believe it or not, I commanded the entire Willovian forces at the Outer Boundaries until I returned home a few years ago to be closer to my family."

Tova pounded a spoonful of potatoes onto her plate. "Not that it makes a difference. You're hardly ever here—always off with the soldiers."

"I thought you liked it that way. Why, just last night she wanted to kick me out of the house, and now she's complaining that I'm leaving?"

Tova frowned at the jest. "Another invasion, another war. When will it end?"

Gy put his hand on top of hers and stroked the skin with his thumb while speaking to Bayla. "We'll set up camp in the Hedgelands, a four-day journey from here. Messengers will be sent to collect news of the invasion. When it's safe to return, your guards will escort you back to the castle. These are the king's orders."

Shanti filled up on ham, eggs, biscuits, jam, and potatoes, knowing it might be her last home-cooked meal for a long time.

*

Commander Shanti, Commander Gy, and six other Guardians of Willovia discussed the princess in a closed-off room at an inn. Sunlight filtered through shades the color of burnt umber. Cheap carpets, ripe with the odor of alcohol, hung on walls to muffle the noise within the room. Mugs and half-empty pitchers of cider sat on a table.

"Not once did Rega Bayla ask who was invading or why," Shanti said. "Nor did she ask about the defenses of her people. For all she knew, the citizens of Willovia were in grave danger, yet Bayla seemed to care more about her horse."

"Is it possible she knew the attack was fake?" said the village undertaker, a slim man smelling of strange spices. Two hoop earrings adorned each of his earlobes, and his fingers were long and graceful. "Someone might have informed her of our existence. Perhaps King Magen told her what to expect."

"There was no indication she had any knowledge of the plan," Shanti said.

Another man, a stout landowner dressed in finery, spoke. "I've been to the castle and have seen the princess on occasion, although I've never talked to her. Do you think she'll want to join the soldiers? It's such a different way of life from the one she's used to."

"Rega Bayla is very competitive," Shanti said. "I believe it will be only a matter of days before she asks to train."

A woman with a thick, white braided chignon asked, "What was she like at the castle while you were her guard? Was she happy?" An angora shawl, soft and pink like the petals of a rose, draped her shoulders.

Shanti covered her mouth and yawned. She hadn't slept in over a day. The question was interesting—something she hadn't thought about until now. "Rega Bayla always seemed depressed unless she was riding her horse."

"In your opinion, is she intelligent enough to lead?" the woman said.

"Bayla is very intelligent, but manipulative and self-centered." Shanti yawned again.

The white-haired woman stood up from her chair and motioned to Shanti. "Come with me. You must be tired. A bed is upstairs. You can rest before you leave tonight on your journey to the Hedgelands. You've told us all we need to know."

Shanti followed the woman, grateful for the chance to sleep. "Thank you."

They entered a clean room with dark quilts covering the bed. "By the way, my name is Madiza."

"Do you own this inn?"

"No." She took hold of Shanti's hand.

Stunned by the unexpected contact, Shanti tried to jerk free of the woman's touch but couldn't. Indeed, she couldn't move at all.

Madiza's warm hands enclosed Shanti's hand. On her wrist, a bracelet of dark opals shimmered in multicolored hues. "I'm a fortune-teller."

She wanted to shout, but her voice was gone. Her vision faded, and her muscles relaxed.

"Let go, Shanti. Sleep."

The room disintegrated into blackness, and Shanti melted into a pool of soothing heat. She tried to stop her body from falling, tried to stop the fortune-teller from casting the sleeping spell and looking into her future, but the quiet chanting overwhelmed her. She floated farther and farther downward. Beams of light broke the darkness. Shanti landed, soft as thistledown, in a forest next to a river.

She was only vaguely aware of being lifted onto a bed. Her body was so weary, all she wanted was sleep.

8

THE THRILL OF THE RACE

THE CLICK OF the door latch woke Shanti.

Her weapons rested on a table near the bed. She unsheathed the sword and pointed the blade at the door as it swung open.

Commander Gy entered the room. "How are you feeling?"

She returned the weapon to the table and relaxed, falling backward onto the dark quilt and flat pillow. "Violated."

He closed the door for privacy. "It wasn't my idea. The other Guardians wanted to ensure that your intentions are honorable."

"It isn't right," she said. "Reading someone's future without permission."

"Is it right to take Bayla away from her home under the pretext of an invasion and test her competence without her knowledge? We do what we believe is best for our country."

Her boots lay on the floor at the foot of the bed. Someone must have removed them while she was under the sleeping spell.

Gy leaned against the wall with one hand in his pocket and looked through a window. "Would you like to know what Madiza said?"

She swung her legs over the edge of the bed and sat up, pulling on her boots. "No."

"I'm going to tell you anyway. Madiza said you're like a string pulled so tight, it's bound to break."

"That's my future?"

"Many paths lead to the future. Our choices determine the way we go there. At this juncture, your future is linked with Rega Bayla's. Madiza said that your path is intertwined with hers. If you don't train her properly and she fails, then you also fail."

"Magen," she breathed. "If Bayla doesn't succeed, King Magen said he will have me beheaded."

Gy laughed at the revelation. *Laughed.* "He's bluffing, trying to protect his daughter. I've known Magen for a long time. He wouldn't do such a thing. The Guardians won't allow it."

"What if she doesn't pass?"

His expression turned serious. "You understand the consequences for Willovia."

"Would there be a war?"

"In all probability, yes. Shanti, I believe you've already made up your mind about Rega Bayla. You're determined to fail her. Give her a chance. Teach her. You yourself said she's intelligent."

Shanti touched the side of her head and grimaced. A painful lump had formed there.

"When Madiza put you under the spell, you fell and hit your head rather hard."

She remembered no discomfort, only the opal bracelet and the forest. "How long have I been sleeping?"

"All afternoon," Gy said. "I must tell you something else about your future. Nunqua warriors dressed in black, with spots on their skin and marks like yours across their arms, will come looking for you."

Caravey. Why couldn't he just leave her alone? Or maybe it wasn't him. It had been almost two years since she last saw Caravey. Perhaps the Nunqua warrior looking for her would be her uncle, wishing to convey important news of the family. Or perhaps Madiza was wrong, just like the old hag who foretold King Magen's death.

A washbasin rested on a table. Shanti rinsed her face and dried it with a thin towel. She viewed her reflection in a mirror: hair disheveled from sleep. She twisted it back into the warrior's knot.

"I'm going to give you an opportunity," Gy said. "Here and now, you may reject the task that has been assigned to you, with no unfavorable repercussions. You can walk away, go back to a regular military encampment, and have nothing more to do with the princess. You are free to choose a path separate from hers."

Walk away? Give up? Accept a lesser position because the responsibility was too great? The other soldiers would think her weak. They would never respect her if she walked away from duty in the face of hardship. "Gy," she said, "I'm looking forward to showing the princess what it feels like to be ordered around."

He stopped leaning against the wall and stood tall. "Do I have your word that you'll be fair in your treatment of Rega Bayla?"

"Fair?" Shanti said. "You mean, like you treated me when I was training? Every time we played the game of war, you changed the rules of engagement so that my team would lose. You tied my ankles together with rope during sword practice—a burden no other candidate had to endure. You sabotaged my equipment—"

"That's not what I meant," Gy said. "Will you give Bayla a chance to prove herself?"

"I'll tell you the same thing I told King Magen," Shanti said as she put on her sword and wristlet. "I'll do what's best for Willovia."

"I expect nothing less from you, Commander."

*

During the first night of her journey, Bayla left the cottage under the cover of darkness, in the company of Commander Gy and her guard, Shanti. They did the rest of their traveling in the light of day. The weather was cool but not cold. The summer's heat would be upon them soon enough, though. The princess ate outside or in inconspicuous taverns, and Commander Gy and Shanti never once called attention to her royal identity. After four long days, they reached a place where the road entered a forest of bare trees. The woodland sloped upward into rocky, mountainous terrain, and snow capped the faraway peaks. The Hedgelands.

"Finally," Shanti said. She and Gy galloped up to a group of mounted men in brown uniforms, milling about the edge of the tree line.

Bayla saw no castle, no houses—just fields and trees and the distant mountains. The soldiers congregated around her traveling companions, leaving Bayla alone. The dust of the road felt grimy on her face, so she decided to dismount and rinse off in a nearby stream. Kneeling on a rock, she splashed her face with the frigid water.

A dragonfly with iridescent wings flitted about. Bayla lifted her arm, and the creature landed on the back of her hand. More dragonflies flew over to greet her. The insects swooped about and rested on her until she was half covered with their gossamer wings.

Bayla looked up to see only strangers. Commander Gy and Shanti were gone. Panic lumped in the pit of her stomach, and the skittish dragonflies, sensing her distress, zoomed away.

One man stood apart from the rest, giving orders. She had no choice but to grab the reins of her horse and approach him. To her relief, she did not have to speak first.

"Rega Bayla," the man said, "I'm Commander Jun."

"But . . . where is Commander Gy?"

"He and Commander Shanti have gone ahead to camp."

"Isn't this where we'll be staying?" Bayla immediately regretted asking the question that exposed her inexperience.

"This place is out in the open and vulnerable to attack. The camp is farther down this road."

A dirt path disappeared into the forest. Brown branches the same dull color as the soldiers' uniforms arched over the pathway. The entrance to the woods reminded her of an entrance to a cave.

All the soldiers except Commander Jun were mounted now. Men hollered in excitement, and restive animals fidgeted and snorted. Even her stallion pawed the ground.

"Rega Bayla!" Jun shouted to be heard over the clamor of the men. "When entering a newly established camp, it's customary for those on horseback to race."

Twelve riders waited astride horses eager to run. Commander Jun walked in front of them, lifted his arm, then dropped his fist. "Go!"

The horses bolted for the woods, kicking up divots of sod as they strove for the lead. Bayla's whole body vibrated in response to the pounding of hooves.

Commander Jun put his hands around his mouth. "Bayla."

The sound of her name pulled her out of the trance.

"What are you waiting for? Go!"

Bayla's horse, a gift from her father for her sixteenth birthday, was the foal of the two fastest horses in Willovia. He whinnied and pranced about, tugging the reins in the direction of the racers. After the slow pace of the past four days, he was ready to run.

"Go!" Commander Jun yelled.

Bayla jumped onto the prized horse and raced into the woods.

The straight path slit the woodlands like a long scar on a hairy scalp. Bits of sunlight filtered through the bare branches. The riders and their horses focused only on what lay ahead of them in the dangerous chase. Bayla and her steed passed the men with astonishing speed. She leaned low in the saddle, weaving through the pack.

Bayla arrived first at the clearing in the forest where Commander Gy and Shanti stood with several others. Coming in second was a well-built soldier with dark hair and eyes.

Bayla dismounted and put her arms around the stallion's sweaty neck. She could feel its satisfaction at competing and winning. It truly was a horse bred for speed.

The young man who had come in second put his hand on the flank of Bayla's horse. "Congratulations, Rega. My name is Zindar."

She nodded politely. "Zindar."

Other racers entered the camp. They, too, got down from their horses and commended her victory.

Commander Gy put his hand on Bayla's shoulder. "The winner is Rega Bayla."

She felt awake and alive as the men cheered her victory. The exhilaration of the race still quickened her blood. Her status as a leader, the future ruler of all Willovia, was now firmly rooted in the minds of her guards.

Shanti's stern expression contrasted with the cheerful countenances of the others in the crowd. "She didn't win."

The noise of the soldiers quieted as everyone waited for an explanation. Fear rose in Bayla at the thought of what Shanti would say: *it wasn't fair for her to race; she's not a soldier; her horse is worth more than all the others put together.*

"She didn't win . . . because she cheated."

"Commander Shanti," Gy said, "how could Rega Bayla have cheated?"

"Trust me, she cheated." Shanti walked away from the group.

No one spoke a word in Bayla's behalf. The thrill of the race vanished. The men left to pitch tents, their previous exuberance destroyed.

Although Bayla appeared calm, a storm raged inside her. Shanti knew that she hadn't needed her power to win, but she had embarrassed her in front of her new royal guards anyway. Was it in retribution for the shabby treatment Commander Shanti had received from the Daughters of Fortunate Birth? Or was it out of jealousy? It was a bold move—a move that she would make Shanti regret.

9
INFESTATION

DRIED LEAVES AND twigs crunched beneath Shanti's boots as she approached a soldier checking a list of provisions in a cart. The cart contained blankets, soap, lanterns, oil, tent pegs, tools, and various other necessities for the camp. Larger items, such as storage cabinets and cots, were neatly stacked in piles on the ground. Wagons must have delivered the supplies before she and Commander Gy had arrived at the Outer Boundaries with the princess.

"Commander Jun?" she said.

He stopped inventorying the goods. "Yes."

"Are you in charge of supply?"

"Why? Is there something you need?"

Commander Jun had short hair, a cleft in his chin, and he wore the uniform well. "I . . . I need a map of the area."

"There is only one map. You may look at it if you want."

"I need it *with* me to set up the guard posts—along with shovels and pickaxes."

He pointed to the road leading into camp. "Just put one of the guard posts there, one by the horses, and one at the rear of camp.

It's simple, really; even someone like you can figure it out without a map."

"Someone like me?"

He grinned. "A joke."

Her face flushed in embarrassment, or was it something more? "Map, shovels, pickax."

He took a bag out of the cart and shook out a scroll. "This is the only map. Be sure to return it to me when you're done. Shovels are by that tree."

Shanti took the scroll and put it in the jacket of her uniform. A shovel and a pickax leaned against a nearby tree. The pickax had a broken handle, and the shovel was cracked.

"You can't be serious."

"The other tools are in better condition. They're being used now."

Shanti grabbed the worthless gear and left, wondering whether Commander Jun was married. He had to be or, at least, had to have a significant woman in his life. She glanced in his direction once more, and her legs collided with the thorny branches of a low-growing shrub. She untangled her feet, feeling stupid and hoping he hadn't seen.

While soldiers were putting up tent poles, Shanti dropped the broken shovel next to a functional one and picked up the good one without anyone noticing. She tapped a soldier on the back. "Come with me."

By the time she left the camp accompanied by four other soldiers, Shanti possessed the map, three serviceable shovels, and a pickax in excellent condition.

They climbed to a stony promontory jutting low from the mountain, with a good view of the area. It was the perfect place for a guard point. No digging would be required, and cover was plentiful. The four men examined the map while Shanti scanned their surroundings. Below them were roads, grasslands, a town, and a winding river. The sound of a rip caused an icy spasm to rush up her spine.

"It's his fault, Commander Shanti, he—"

"I don't care whose fault it is." She carefully took the map away. A gaping tear ran down its center. "It seems I have four volunteers for guard duty tonight."

Maps as detailed as the one in her hands were hard to come by. And expensive. Commander Jun was going to be angry.

*

Bayla watched the soldiers work together with speed and efficiency. Strong youths in the service of her father—the backbone of the Willovian forces, doing what needed to be done. And she would rule them one day.

Brown and green tents nestled among the trees—a small one for each of the commanders, and larger ones to accommodate twelve soldiers each. Men hammered nails into the roof of a wooden pavilion. A tree stump marked the middle of camp. Beyond the tents, horses grazed in a roped-off enclosure.

Several men were cooking something in pots over a fire. A scrawny fellow plucked feathers from a headless chicken. He was the only person besides Bayla not wearing a uniform.

Food was set out, and the soldiers gathered for their meal. Commander Gy went first, and the rest followed. The men sat on rocks and timbers, chatting and eating. Gy came over to her, carrying a plate of food that contained no meat.

"Rega Bayla," he said, "let me show you where you'll be sleeping."

They entered a tent the size of her stallion's stall at the castle. It smelled of mildew. Gy gave her the plate and excused himself, saying that much work needed to be done.

The tent was the color of mud and altogether unfit for the daughter of the king. She usually ate from plates rimmed in gold, not from a wooden trencher. It would be understandable if her stay was to be short, but the pavilion indicated otherwise. Something was wrong here.

Bayla wondered about her father, and for the first time, she worried about his safety. She knew that the king was alive. If anything should happen to him, the monks would find her immediately.

The monks, forever the servants of Willovia's rulers, were soothsayers, prophets of doom. If her father died, they would take charge of the fallen king's body and march it through the city of Erbaut before burial in the royal catacombs. Then she would be queen, and the monks would become her advisers, inexorably by her side, telling her strange things about the future. She hated them more than she hated Shanti.

"Rega . . ." Someone was standing outside her tent. "May we come in?"

"You may enter."

Two soldiers carried a cot, blankets, soap, and a storage cabinet into her tent, then left her alone.

Bayla touched the lumpy pillow and the coarse, woolen blanket—so different from the fine bedding she was used to. The gritty soap smelled like sawdust. What was going on? Why hadn't she been informed of the measures put in place for her safety in case Willovia was ever attacked? Even Shanti had known of the plan to take her to the Hedgelands should an invasion occur at the castle. Damn her father for never telling her anything! She was almost twenty, the future queen, yet voiceless when it came to matters of importance.

Angry power surged around her like a whirlwind. She was trapped in this secluded camp with her guards, just as she was trapped at the castle. A slave to the will of her father, a pathetic princess to be protected under the command of others. The tent felt like a cage. Bayla pointed her hand at the plate of food sitting on the ground and splayed her fingers wide.

"Baylova." She spoke her formal name with a mix of pride and pain. "Queen of Willovia, sovereign of the people, supreme commander of the military, unquestioned leader."

The plate shook. Her hand clenched into a fist, and the plate cracked in twain with a loud crunch. Food scattered across the tent.

"Someday," she whispered.

"Rega?" Men gathered outside her tent. "Are you all right?"

Commander Gy barged in, followed by three others. They saw the broken plate and food strewn across the ground, the canvas walls, and Bayla's boots.

"What happened?" Gy said.

"I dropped my plate."

He looked around at the mess. *"Dropped?"*

"It slipped from my hand." Bayla pulled her shoulders back as she had been trained to do since she was a child. How many hours had her governess made her walk around with a book on her head, teaching her never to lower her face to others?

"You're bleeding, Rega." Commander Gy pointed to her hand.

Blood trickled down her fingers from a cut in her palm—the price for using her power. "Oh." Her shoulders hunched in surprise. She hadn't noticed the pain until now.

"Where's Commander Shanti?" Gy asked one of the soldiers with him.

"She's setting up the guard posts."

"Rega Bayla," Gy said, "see Commander Shanti when she returns. She should have some bandages." Commander Gy and the others left as abruptly as they had entered.

Bayla could hear the men's conversation through the cloth walls of her tent.

"Not even here a day, and the princess is already having tantrums."

"Really! Throwing plates of food around . . ."

She strained to hear more, but the soldiers had moved too far away. Using her unbloodied hand, she wiped the food off her boots and riding pants. She removed a sheet from the mound of bedding and ripped a strip of cloth off the end. Taking the improvised bandage to the stream near camp, she washed the blood from her hand in the cold water, exposing a shallow cut. She wrapped the wound with the cloth but had trouble securing it with only one free hand.

She wouldn't lower herself to ask Shanti for a bandage, but she did have an order in mind. Shanti was her guard, after all—her servant. It was time to start exerting her authority.

*

"Do you know how much this cost?" Commander Jun inspected the torn map on a table inside the pavilion. Dinner was being prepared in the fading light, and oil lamps hung low from the rafters.

"I'll pay for the replacement." Shanti pretended to look down at the map. Instead, she looked at his hands: strong, with clean fingernails and a small scar between the left index and middle fingers.

"This is one of a kind." He rolled up the damaged map and returned it to its leather pouch. "I hope you're a good artist."

"What do you mean?"

Bayla entered the pavilion. "Commander Jun," she said.

"Rega."

"Shanti, my tent needs to be cleaned. I want you to see that the bed is made every morning and the storage cabinet organized."

"What's wrong with your hand?" Shanti said.

"It's just a scratch." Spots of blood darkened the bandage.

"Let me see," Shanti said.

Bayla moved her hand behind her back. "It's nothing. I expect my tent to be taken care of in the manner I'm accustomed to." And with that, she left the pavilion.

"And I expect you to make me a new map," Jun said. "Better yet, four identical maps: one for each of the commanders."

"That would take weeks."

"Are you going to make the soldiers clean her tent?" he said.

"Of course not. She can do it herself."

"What about the map?"

"The map was in my care and, therefore, my responsibility. Do you have any glue?"

He laughed. Apparently, he didn't approve of the idea.

"All right," she said. "When I have time and you've provided me with the proper materials, I'll attempt to make a single copy to replace the map that was damaged."

"Three copies, and you keep the torn original."

"One copy."

"Three." He smiled. "Now I understand why everyone says you're so difficult to work with."

"And why is it that everyone who works in supply is motivated by greed? One copy is fair."

"Two." Laugh lines deepened around his eyes.

"I'll not haggle with you. Who says I'm difficult to work with?"

"Everyone," he said.

Soldiers were lining up for dinner just outside the pavilion. The aroma of roasted chicken filled the air. She looked at his short hair. "Commander Jun, I may have to borrow scissors from you. Looks as if you'll need a haircut soon."

The smile left his face. "Are you threatening me?"

"What's so threatening about a haircut?"

"Only Nunqua warriors are known to cut the hair of their enemies. I believe that Commander Mossgail found that out the hard way."

"Mossgail? I think I've heard of him. Wasn't he in charge of supply, just like you? Weren't all his provisions stolen in the middle of the night while he slept, and a lock of his hair found hanging by a string in the doorway? I wonder if they ever found the culprit."

Jun's voice was as cold as his stare. "I'd advise you to be careful, Commander Shanti. I'm not as stupid as Mossgail."

"Nor are you as fat."

Men entered the dining area, holding plates of hot food and sitting at tables.

"One copy." Shanti pushed her way to the front of the line of soldiers waiting to get their dinner.

Damn him. He was just like the others, regarding her

authority as insignificant. Bayla wanted her to clean a stupid tent, and Commander Jun wanted her to make four copies of the map when one copy was fair. No male commander would be treated in such a demeaning manner. Shanti slammed her plate down and put a hunk of bread on it.

The more she thought of Jun—the harsh look on his face, the coldness of his stare, the breadth of his shoulders—the more she felt a delicious rage swarm over her senses.

The food smelled good. She spooned the hearty chicken stew with carrots, peas, and potatoes onto her plate. A familiar laugh grated on her ears like a rusty blade scratching glass.

"I knew it. Knew you wanted to see me again. I have that effect on women."

In front of her stood the scrawny cook who had insulted her at the castle. Smears from a dozen meals discolored his shirt, and his greasy yellow hair was tucked behind his ears. "But I didn't think you were desperate enough to follow me all the way to the Hedgelands. Are you ready for your first lesson on how to command?" His gaze traveled over her body. "Perhaps I should teach you some submissive positions. You'd like that, wouldn't you?"

Shanti set down her plate, ready to haul the cook out of the pavilion, tie him to the nearest tree, and leave him there until morning. A hand squeezed her shoulder.

"My compliments on the food, Mr. Pascha," Commander Gy said. "It's excellent. Don't you agree, Commander Shanti?"

She picked up her plate and walked away from the cook.

"I don't mind plain women," Mr. Pascha called out after her.

"Ignore it," Gy said. "I know he's an ass, but he's the best cook I could find. Try to be friendly."

They sat at a table in the corner of the pavilion. The stew and bread on her plate did look appetizing. She took a bite. "Needs salt," she lied.

"Shanti . . ." His voice was stern.

"Okay, I'll try to be civil for the sake of the camp."

The food was good. Shanti decided to do her best to avoid Mr. Pascha and even returned for a second helping of stew.

*

Shanti slept soundly that first night, lulled by the singing of crickets and frogs. The smell of sausage enticed her out of bed. Taking a bar of soap, she headed out into the misty morning as most of the soldiers still slept. She washed in the river, fixed her hair, put on her uniform, and went into the pavilion for breakfast. Men emerged from their tents and tightened tent ropes or groomed themselves for the day.

Bayla came out of her tent, dressed in riding clothes and with her hair pulled off her face. Dark circles outlined the skin around her eyes, and her shoulders slumped. She looked as though she hadn't slept. Was she worried about her father? About Willovia? Or was it merely the change of scene that had kept her awake?

Shanti walked over to Bayla, feeling more comfortable in their new surroundings than she had ever felt at the castle. "Rega," she said, "Commander Gy wishes to speak with you after breakfast, concerning your stay."

"What about my tent? Why hasn't it been cleaned? The bed needs to be made and the food needs—"

"More important matters need to be attended to, Rega."

"You have no intention of following my commands. We'll see what my father has to say about this."

Shanti crossed her arms. "Your father's concern lies with the enemy invasion, not with a tent you're too lazy to clean yourself."

"My orders will be obeyed."

"If you want to be obeyed, then start giving orders that make sense. You'll clean your own tent while you're here. Every soldier is responsible for his area."

"I'm a royal," she said, "and as such, I have expectations that need to be addressed in order for me to fulfill my responsibilities."

"I heard your father was an excellent soldier before he became king," Shanti said. "You can discuss your living situation with Commander Gy after breakfast. I'm certain he'll find it interesting."

She watched Bayla enter the pavilion and wander about like a lost traveler. The princess stood amid the soldiers, a peacock among eagles. The greasy cook headed straight toward her, rubbing his hands together. Time to intervene.

"Well, well, well, if it isn't the princess, come to grace us with her presence!" The cook bent at the waist so his nose almost touched his knees. "What will it be today, Your Highness? Roast beef with red wine sauce, or maybe poached pears with a hint of cinnamon?"

Shanti moved behind Bayla, diverting the cook's attention.

"Mister Pascha," Shanti said. "Is something wrong?"

He looked up, a snaggletoothed smile contorting his face. "Of course not, Commander Shanti. I'm just getting breakfast for our guest and making her feel welcome." Using his shirt as a hand towel, he scrutinized the two women. "Beauty . . . and the beast," he chortled.

"Pascha, you scum!" one of the soldiers said. "Give us our food and shut up."

Mr. Pascha's left eye twitched. He went about his business in the kitchen.

"I can't believe you let him treat you like that, Commander Shanti." The soldier scooped eggs onto his plate and paid no attention to Bayla.

"Yeah, well, I told Commander Gy that I would *try* to get along with the cook," Shanti said. "It's proving difficult."

She watched Bayla take her food to an empty table and inspect her spoon, polish it with the folds of her shirt, then polish the knife in the same manner. Conversation in the pavilion died down, and Bayla's ears turned red, as if she had suddenly noticed the soldiers regarding her with odd expressions on their faces. She stopped cleaning the silverware and ate.

*

Shanti, Commander Gy, and Commander Jun stood around the tree stump at the center of camp and informed Bayla of the details concerning her stay.

"Sixty-five soldiers are assigned here for your protection," Commander Gy said. "The king is alive but with the Willovian forces at the Outer Boundaries. It has been determined that the castle is not safe for your return."

"How long will I have to stay here?" Bayla asked.

"Until we have written word from your father," Gy said. "While we're here, four commanders have charge of this camp. Commander Jun is responsible for supply. Please see him if you need anything. Commander Shanti is responsible for your protection. Guard posts are situated around the camp and continually manned. Commander Vittorio will arrive in a day or two. He's in charge of training. To be effective, the soldiers need to continue training or their skills will grow rusty. I want you to know, Rega, the men here were *chosen* to be your security; they didn't volunteer. Most would rather be fighting at the battlefront. As for me, I'm in charge of the commanders."

"Commander Gy, I was wondering if I could go for a ride this afternoon."

"That would be up to Commander Shanti."

Shanti put her hand on her chin and narrowed her eyes in thought. "I'd like to patrol the area first to determine that it's safe for the princess to leave the camp. Perhaps, tomorrow we can spare some personnel to escort Rega Bayla on a ride."

Bayla thanked Gy for keeping her informed, then went moping into her tent.

Gy chuckled. "Shanti, don't you think you're being too hard on her? Breaking her spirit too soon?"

"I haven't even begun. Besides, both of you would be treating Bayla differently if she were a man. I've seen you make men cry with your cruelty, Gy. You weren't so nice to me when I trained."

"Bayla hasn't started training yet," Jun said. "I doubt she'll want to. She doesn't seem the type."

"Don't underestimate her," Shanti said. "There's more to Bayla than can be seen on the surface. If she's to lead the Willovian forces as queen one day, she must first learn what it's like to follow. Only then can she appreciate the sacrifices these men make."

"Remember who she is," Gy warned. "If you push her too far, it may cause the plan to fail."

"She might try to return to the castle," Jun said.

Shanti shook her head. "She won't go back there . . . Commander Jun, Bayla will probably ask for some things soon: books and paper and such. I request that you wait to give them to her. For this to work, she has to be absolutely bored, and it's imperative that she watch the men train."

"That can be arranged, but I don't think it will make a difference. The princess will never want to join the soldiers."

"Are you willing to wager?" she said.

"A silver coin," Jun said. "Bayla will never of her own accord ask to train."

"A silver coin it is," Shanti said. "In five days, she'll be begging to join us."

With his right foot on the stump, Commander Gy reached into his pocket and pulled out a silver coin. He placed his bet with confidence. "I believe it will take only three days."

*

Shanti hiked alone on a barely discernible trail winding near the river. The terrain was rocky and steep. Remnants of old buildings and ruined bridges dotted the landscape. She sat on a boulder near water that babbled over a stony stream bed. Removing her wristlet and boots, she placed them on a rock and rolled up her sleeves to expose the scars on her forearms. She waded into the clear stream, stopping at knee depth and submerging her arms.

The cold water and solitude were a soothing balm for her soul. A gray heron stood downstream, spearing fish and frogs in the plentiful river, and birds chirped high in the trees.

It would have been easy to take Bayla for a ride this afternoon, even without a large security detail for her protection, for the danger was minimal. But she wanted Bayla to feel trapped, powerless, without control. Even more importantly, Shanti needed time away from people, especially after enduring the suffocating atmosphere of the castle.

The earthy smell and springtime luxuriance of the woods sparked her memory. The dream! It was the same forest, the same river, from Madiza's spell. The fortune-teller's prediction returned to her thoughts: if Bayla failed as a soldier, Shanti, too, would fail.

The babble of rushing water calmed her. Shanti was grateful for the opportunity to be alone and unwind. And it was only with great reluctance that she put on her gear and headed back to camp.

*

In the fading light of day, Shanti practiced slow-moving sword drills. A group of barefoot soldiers with soap in their hands headed to the spot where the river ran deepest. "Going somewhere, boys?" she said. Before they could answer, Bayla emerged from the trees. Wet hair hung down her back, and she carried a bar of soap. Shanti and Bayla left the men to splash and clean up in the river.

She escorted the princess to her tent and turned to leave. A black snake as long as her arm slithered out from beneath a bush and coiled into a threatening posture. A rat eater, not poisonous. It hissed and bared its fangs. Bold behavior for a snake. Bayla must have used her power to summon it. Another hollow threat?

With her boot, Shanti lured the serpent to strike. Then she stepped on its outstretched head. Its tail wrapped around her leg. She unsheathed her sword and cut the snake in two. Out of the bushes came two new snakes, larger and more aggressive than the first. Not rat eaters, these. Gray, water-loving, deadly.

So the princess was ready to play. Shanti released a latch on her wristlet to activate the darts. Twisting her torso, she pointed the weapon at Bayla.

"Toy arrows—how precious!"

"More venomous than your slithering friends there," Shanti replied.

"I don't think so. No monks are here to chronicle my death."

"The toxins on the tips of these darts will not end your life right away. It takes a day for the poison to eat away your brain and stop your heart. If I die, so will you. I have every right to defend myself. *Anaya say midea.*"

"What?"

Shanti repeated the phrase and continued to speak to the princess in the language of the Nunqua.

With clawlike hands, Bayla raked the air. The snakes slithered closer to Shanti.

"You would cripple or kill me for *what*? Not cleaning your tent? Such is the folly of nobility."

"You'll hold your tongue, guard, and show the proper respect."

"We're not at the castle anymore, Princess."

Bayla's expression remained aristocratic, emotionless, cold. She dropped her hands and retreated into her tent as the snakes returned to the bushes.

Shanti took her foot off the black serpent's head and kicked it into the vegetation. Then she picked up the long tail and went inside the pavilion. "Mr. Pascha."

"Eh?" Clumps of hair drooped down the sides of his face. "Oh, it's you. Come to take me up on my offer?"

An involuntary shudder ran through her shoulders, but she needed Pascha's assistance. "I have a request. The princess asks that you prepare a rare delicacy for her." Shanti stretched the body of the snake in both hands. "I believe you'll have no problems impressing her with your culinary abilities. Rega Bayla is eager to savor such an unusual treat."

"Woman," he said, taking the snake away and inspecting it, "I like your style."

Shanti rinsed her hands in the river while the cook skinned, gutted, and then cooked the snake and set it on a platter. He even garnished the meal with edible green leaves. With a wicked chortle, he placed the dish on the ground in front of Bayla's tent.

Bayla came out of her tent and bent low to get a closer view of the long coil of meat on the serving platter. Realization struck, and her hands clenched into fists. She shrieked and kicked the platter, and the roasted snake tumbled into the dirt.

Men inside the pavilion snickered quietly. Shanti watched the princess from the shadows, studying her. But she didn't laugh like the others.

"How's that supposed to help?" Jun said from behind her.

"I'm showing her she's not truly in charge, no matter who her father is."

"And I'm telling you, she has no desire to be a soldier. Bayla's going to run to the nearest castle to be with her own kind."

"She'll train," Shanti said. "I'm sure of it. Though I'm not so sure she'll pass the trials or the final test."

"You don't think Bayla will put the needs of Willovia before her own, fight a traitor, face death?" he asked.

"She wants all the glory and none of the pain. Bayla knows nothing of sacrifice."

*

A dozen soldiers stood around two carts that had arrived at the camp. A squat man in uniform gave orders to unload. The carts contained swords of every size, as well as bows, arrows, battleaxes, lances, shields, and other weapons.

Commander Gy greeted the trainer. "Commander Vittorio! I was beginning to think you weren't coming."

Vittorio, in his brown uniform, looked like a thick tree trunk. His black hair was cropped short, and a luxuriant mustache divided his square face into upper and lower halves. Curly chest hair rose above the collar of his uniform.

"Looks like I arrived just in time. These weaklings obviously need my help." Vittorio's robust laugh carried across the camp. He lowered his voice for only Gy to hear. "Is it true what they say? Shanti's here, promoted to commander and in charge of the princess's security, no less?"

"It's true."

"I don't know, Commander Gy. I've heard some strange stories about that one. Do you think it wise to have her here?"

"Why don't you ask her yourself?"

Vittorio turned to find Shanti standing behind him.

"Commander Vittorio," Gy said, "meet Commander Shanti."

"Of course." He rocked back and forth on the soles of his feet. "I've heard some good things about you, too."

"I'm sure you have," she said.

*

Jun ate lunch with his fellow commanders at their usual corner table in the pavilion. He saw Bayla come in, pick over the food, put a few scant morsels on her plate, then sit alone.

"She seems so young," Vittorio said. "And small. I have my doubts that this will work."

"Some of the soldiers here are younger than the princess," Gy said.

"I'd no more put a sword in her hands than give one to my own daughters."

"Your daughters are free to live a simpler life," Gy said. "They don't have to deal with the pressures of ruling a kingdom."

"True enough." Vittorio turned to Shanti. "I hear you're good with a sword."

"Not good enough to defeat such a formidable opponent as you, Commander Vittorio."

"Indeed." He beamed at the compliment. "Still, I wouldn't mind if you found time to join us on the training field. I hear your methods are, um, unconventional."

"Who would I fight?" she said. "I can't beat Commander Gy in a fair match without the risk of being sent back to the castle—or someplace worse. And since you're the trainer, all you do is fight. I doubt I could defeat you. Jun, on the other hand . . ." It was the first time she dropped the formality of calling him by his rank "Jun is merely in charge of supply. I'd hate to embarrass him in front of everybody by winning."

Jun looked up from his plate, noting the other commanders' amusement. "I guarantee, you'll *never* beat me in a sword fight."

"Ha!" Vittorio's laugh reverberated through the dining area. "That sounds like a challenge. Maybe this place won't be so boring after all."

Bayla approached their table. "I'd like to ask Commander Jun for some things," she said.

"I was finished anyways." He picked up his plate and dropped it off in the kitchen, leading Bayla out of the pavilion to the tree stump, where their conversation would be private.

"I need parchment, quills, and ink to correspond with my father."

Shanti was right: here was Bayla, asking for writing materials. "Rega, has anyone explained to you how the camp communicates with the king?"

"Commander Gy said there would be messengers."

"That's not what I'm talking about," Jun said. "All official correspondence is written in code. No regular soldiers, and only a few commanders, know it. The code is a safeguard against information falling into enemy hands. If messengers are captured, they'll be tortured for information. Riding as a messenger is one of the most dangerous jobs a soldier can do. An intercepted letter from the heiress of Willovia to the king would, in all probability, expose both your and his location."

"As the future queen, it would make sense that I know the code. Commander Gy can teach me."

"Commander Gy has the responsibility of running this camp. He doesn't have time to teach you."

"Then Shanti can show me."

"She doesn't know the code," Jun said. "I'll teach you, but I have to leave for a few days to get supplies. Your lessons can start when I return. Under no circumstances is the code to be revealed to others at this camp."

"I'm aware of the seriousness of this undertaking," she said.

"Until you've seen the mutilated body of a messenger who was captured, I doubt you'll ever understand."

*

In the afternoon, Bayla took her stallion for a long ride with twelve other riders. On the return trip to camp, she saw soldiers setting up an archery range. A short distance away, men dumped shovelfuls of dirt into a ring of stones and spread pine needles over the dirt.

She entered the pasture used for grazing and asked a soldier for a brush to groom her stallion. He went to a canvas bag at the base of a tree and found her a brush. "That truly is an exceptional horse you have, Rega," he said.

"Thank you." But before Bayla could tell him it was a birthday gift, or how she had raised him from a colt, or that she was the only person ever to ride him—before she could tell him anything at all—the young man left to join the other soldiers.

Bayla brushed the knots out of her stallion's mane and watched the guards converse. Even Shanti, who had seemed so stiff and severe at the castle, was more relaxed here at camp.

The horse pushed her gently with his nose.

"At least *you* like me." Bayla glanced at the pasture and then back to her horse, giving him permission to leave.

The stallion whinnied and galloped away.

*

Shanti awoke early, as usual, and put her feet on the ground. Something tickled her left toe. In reaction, she jerked both feet back onto the platform and thin mattress she used for a bed. Her eyes adjusted to the dim light. Centipedes and millipedes infested the tent. The creatures made her want to shriek.

No, she must control herself. Where were her boots? She saw them on a crate at the opposite end of the tent. Shanti would rather confront the snakes outside Bayla's tent than walk with bare feet across the bug-ridden ground. Centipedes the size of daggers clung to the cloth walls of her tent. One of the many-legged creatures crept up the platform and onto her blanket.

Shanti jumped from bed to table to crate, her feet never touching the ground. She picked up her boots from their resting spot as a black scorpion scrambled toward her, its tail poised to strike. A prickly sensation flooded her nervous system. Scorpions were not native to this area. Shanti smashed it into a crunchy mess under her boot heel.

She went outside wearing short pants, undershirt, and boots, with her hair still untied, and beat the sides of her tent using the flat of her sheathed sword. Soldiers coming into camp from their late-night guard duties eyed her curiously. More men emerged, but none dared speak to her. Shanti rolled up the sides of her tent, squishing any errant bugs.

She shook the jacket of her uniform and inspected it for inhabitants before putting it on, then went into the pavilion to find the other commanders. "Do any of you have bugs in your tent?"

"Bugs?" Vittorio said.

"Spiders, ants, centipedes, scorpions?"

They shook their heads.

"No scorpions are around here," Gy said.

"Exactly." Shanti stomped away, muttering to herself.

"Bayla!" She stepped into the princess's tent.

Bayla sat on the ground and said nothing, not even to rebuke Shanti for failing to use her title. Written in the dirt in front of the princess were symbols: numerous lines crossed by short dashes, and one arc with a dot on the end.

A momentary fear pierced Shanti like a pin pushing through

flesh. Bayla was a witch and the heiress to the Willovian crown—a powerful combination. Shanti should warn Gy. It would make her sound weak, though—a commander unable to cope with the difficulties of the task given to her. "If anything happens to me," Shanti said, "I guarantee, your guards will leave you without protection."

"You must be careful," Bayla said. "Scorpions are everywhere in these lands."

"No, Rega. They're not. And if I have to, with my last ounce of breath, I'll tell them who's to blame. If I die, your protection leaves."

"I never asked for sixty guards. I don't need them to keep me trapped here."

"Don't you understand? What you do affects all Willovia. If you hurt me or kill me without justification, the soldiers at this camp will tell other soldiers in your father's army. When it comes time to rule, no one will follow you. Why should the guards risk their lives for you? No more surprises." With a swipe of her boot, Shanti destroyed the drawings in the dirt.

"So what am I supposed to do while I'm here?"

"Am I your governess? Your jester? Your maid? Shall I dress you in the morning, bring you your meals, pull down your covers at night?"

"I'm merely implying . . ."

"Implying what?" Shanti said.

"I would like to . . ."

Shanti waited. The plan was working.

Silence.

Come on, say it.

"I'd like to participate in the activities of this camp." Bayla said.

Shanti exhaled and continued with the charade. "But you said you're a royal and not a soldier."

"I know what I said." Bayla returned to creating symbols in the dirt with her finger. "My father spent many years with the Willovian military in his youth before he was crowned king. He speaks fondly of that time in his life. You're a woman and allowed to work along-side the men. I see no reason why I cannot do the same."

"Certain rules must be adhered to for you to train with the soldiers. All commanders of this camp must agree to your request."

"I'll ask Commander Gy to—"

"Don't be mistaken," Shanti said. "Just because you've seen Gy with his family doesn't make him less a soldier. I'll tell the others so we can review this matter."

"I will not sit here any longer without a purpose."

"Rega, for you to train, all commanders must be in agreement." Shanti once again obliterated the symbols on the ground, leaving nothing visible but the outline of her boot. "Including me."

With her tent now free of bugs, Shanti dressed, put her hair in the warrior's knot, and pulled the covers over her bed. She joined the other commanders inside Gy's tent, planning the day's events. Taking a silver coin out of her pocket, she handed it to Gy. "Bayla has requested to join the soldiers. It's been three days since we made the wager."

"I don't believe it," Jun said.

"Rega Bayla has asked to train of her own free will," Shanti said.

"So it begins," Gy said. He held his hand out to Jun and received another coin. "Tomorrow morning, Shanti. The princess starts tomorrow."

10
AN UNHOLY BAPTISM

"WAKE UP."

Bayla lifted her head to find Shanti inside her tent.

"Hurry up and get ready. I'll be waiting." Shanti went outside.

At least, Shanti hadn't pulled the blankets off this time when waking her, as she had done at the castle during the invasion.

Bayla emerged from her tent into the quiet camp. Light came from the pavilion, where breakfast was being prepared.

"All the commanders have agreed to your training," Shanti said. "You will be treated like the others, and to protect your whereabouts, no word of this shall pass out of the encampment. You'll perform the same duties as the rest of the soldiers, except for one: you will not have guard duty. Do you consent to these conditions, Rega?"

"Yes."

"Then follow me."

They went into the pavilion and passed the cook, who was busy chopping mounds of potatoes and mushrooms.

"Ah, Commander Shanti, I see you've brought me more help."

"Mr. Pascha," she said. Shanti stopped near two soldiers who were carrying dishes for the morning meal. "Names?"

"Aiden."

"Pirro."

"Rega Bayla will be working with you for a few days in the kitchen, after which she'll be joining us in training." Shanti left the pavilion and returned to her tent.

Both men stared openmouthed at her.

"What can I do to help?" Bayla asked.

"Um, Rega," Pirro said, "it's not fitting. The heiress to the Willovian crown shouldn't be waiting on soldiers."

"It's fine. I want to help. Honestly."

Pirro's head bobbed twice, rather too quickly for a proper salutation to royalty. "This way, Rega." He showed her to vats of mush that needed to be set out.

Bayla didn't mind the work. In fact, she was relieved to be doing *anything* after the boredom of the past few days. When the soldiers came to eat, they were surprised to see her laboring in the pavilion—all except the commanders. Mr. Pascha would bark out orders but generally left his helpers alone as long as the work got done. Aiden and Pirro treated her kindly, carrying the heavier burdens or stealing her work out of kindness. The job was easy, and there was often time for breaks.

It took all Bayla's courage to go to the table where Pirro and Aiden were talking.

"Rega?" they said in unison.

She joined them. "Please call me 'Bayla' while we're here at this camp. Why is it that neither of you seem upset about working in the kitchen? Wouldn't you rather be with the others?"

"Working here is great," Pirro said.

"I don't understand."

"I must tell you, Rega," Pirro said, "helping in the kitchen is better than some of the other duties at camp. I won't go into detail. Anyway, we'll return to training in a few days."

"Besides," Aiden said, "the company has vastly improved since you arrived to help."

Pirro nodded in a gesture of approval. "Nice." He had red hair and a wide grin that never left his face.

"Thank you," Aiden said.

"How long have you two known each other?" she said.

"This drunken pig?" Pirro pointed to Aiden. "Too long."

Bayla smiled in relief. It was good to finally talk to someone.

*

Aiden's arms were submerged in dishwater to his elbows, and he laughed at Pirro, who sang a dirty tune about loose women. "You probably shouldn't sing that in front of the princess." Upon saying it, he realized that Rega Bayla wasn't with them. Mr. Pascha had cornered her at the other end of the pavilion.

The cook looked her petite figure up and down. "You can ride with me on the wagon to get food today."

"Mr. Pascha," she said, "you know I have to ride with a guard. I cannot leave camp without one."

"It's okay, I'll take care of you."

Pirro and Aiden rushed to her aid.

"Rega Bayla," Pirro said, "we need your assistance."

Aiden took hold of her arm and escorted her away from the cook.

Mr. Pascha called out, "You forget about these boys. They can't show you nothin'. I'll treat you like a queen." He smacked his thigh, amused at his own wit. "You ride with me today, Rega. It won't take long."

Bayla faced Mr. Pascha, her head held high. "If you wish for me to go, you must ask Commander Shanti since she's in charge of my protection. I'm sure you won't mind discussing the matter with her."

Upon hearing Shanti's name, Pascha scowled and retreated to the food wagon.

"That shut him up," Aiden said. He decided to keep better track of Bayla's whereabouts. Despite their working together, they were still her guards. He just hadn't expected to be protecting her from the cook.

*

Aiden kept a close eye on Bayla for the next two days, and his friend Pirro thanked her for making them famous at camp. "Everyone's been asking about you, Rega—I mean, Bayla," Pirro said.

"They have?"

"Of course, especially Zindar."

Zindar was the soldier who had come in second place in the horse race. Aiden gave Pirro a harsh look for that revelation. He wished his friend hadn't mentioned Zindar, who boasted constantly about all the women he had known. Bayla would never fall for someone like that. At least, he hoped not.

"But I told them you were only interested in redheads."

Bayla laughed, making Pirro's face turn nearly the same shade as his hair.

Commander Jun returned to camp with a laden cart. He entered the pavilion, and Mr. Pascha avoided his presence like a deadly disease.

"Rega Bayla," Commander Jun said, "see me after you've finished for the day. I have some things for you. Aiden?"

"Yes, Commander."

"I hear you have a talent. Come with me."

Aiden hummed good-naturedly as he took off his apron.

Bayla looked to Pirro, puzzled at Commander Jun's comment. Pirro shrugged.

*

Commander Jun gave Aiden carving tools, brushes, and paint and told him to craft a symbol on the stump in the middle of camp.

Aiden went to the stump and thought about what he should

make. Perhaps the Willovian crest, depicting a noble falcon? Too obvious. Something barbaric would be better.

He carved a dragon into the stump: long, lean, and bloodthirsty. The dragon's forked tail encircled the stump, and he emphasized the mythical beast's fangs and claws. Three bottles of dye waited on the ground for when he was ready to paint the creature.

Bayla came over and knelt next to him, quietly watching him work.

"You do have a talent," she said. "I daresay your skills rival the castle's own artist."

Aiden laughed at her comment and the proper way in which she spoke. It was endearing.

"What?" she said.

The castle artist was his father—a fact he wanted to conceal for now. As much as he enjoyed spending hours lost in artistic endeavors, it was better that she think of him as her guard. "I'll tell you later."

Zindar approached, and Bayla stood up to greet him.

"Hello, Zindar," she said.

"You remembered my name, Rega."

Aiden mistakenly gouged a large chunk of wood out of the dragon. The last thing Zindar needed was encouragement.

"Of course," Bayla said. "I should get my things from Commander Jun."

Zindar crouched next to Aiden and watched her leave. "Pretty, isn't she?"

"Don't even think about it," he said.

"I wouldn't be dumb enough to go after the heiress to the Willovian crown, no matter what she looks like."

"Right. Besides, Commander Shanti would cut you into tiny pieces if you did."

"But she's so . . . pretty."

"You've said that already."

Shanti entered Commander Jun's tent to find him handing the princess a uniform. "Where are her boots?" she said.

"It was hard enough to find a small enough uniform without everyone thinking we're inducting children. Look at her *feet*."

Shanti considered the princess's small feet. "As nice as those boots are, they won't last out here. She needs thicker boots with a better grip, able to withstand the conditions—"

"Commander Shanti," he said, "I have it under control. It will just take time. Rega, you may go."

Bayla left, and Shanti softly kicked a crate covered with cloth. Glass clinked inside. She kicked the crate again and raised her eyebrows at Jun.

"Go ahead," he said.

Shanti removed the cloth and let out a whistle. "Where did you get these?" She lifted a dusty bottle from the crate. The alcohol inside was expensive and much sought after, and Jun had managed to get a whole crate. "I'll never doubt your skills in supply again."

"Take one."

"How much would I owe you for one of these?"

"I'll think of something."

She froze at the suggestive tone of his voice.

"All the commanders get one."

"Oh," she said. "Even Commander Gy? He doesn't drink."

"They can be used for other purposes."

She took a bottle and replaced the cloth over the crate.

Jun handed her a roll of parchment, a straightedge made of wood, writing utensils, ink, and the torn map.

"One copy," she said, with her arms full, "and don't expect miracles."

"How's Bayla doing?"

"She seems more comfortable. I've even seen her talking with the soldiers—something she wouldn't condescend to do while at the castle. I'm not sure, though. We'll know more when she starts archery tomorrow."

"*That* I'll have to see."

*

The old monk joined his brothers, draped in robes of blue. They gathered around a copper tub the length and width of a casket. Embers burned red in blackened pans beneath the tub, heating the water inside. Steam rose to the ceiling, which was originally painted a deep blue but had faded and chipped over time. No windows graced the room deep within the bowels of the monks' domicile. Candles brightened ancient plaques on the walls. The old monk dipped his fingers in the water: hot, relaxing, *ready.* He nodded to his brothers, who took away half the pans to keep the water from boiling. The old monk picked up a crystal beaker with clawed feet of silver. Black liquid inside the beaker gleamed bluish-purple when struck by the light.

A middle-aged monk lay on the floor, naked except for a strip of cloth bound tightly around his hips. The brother's skin seemed to glow in the candlelight, the bones of his ribs discernible beneath the membrane of his pale flesh. Short hair conformed to the shape of his skull. Other monks tied a metal chest plate to his torso and weighted his ankles with rings, then helped him into the tub.

The old monk removed the stopper from the beaker. "Are you ready?"

The brother expanded his lungs with a final breath, then plunged into the water.

The old monk emptied the inky elixir into the tub, creating shadows in the clear liquid. He waited for the potion to pass through the skin of his brother monk, enter his bloodstream, and travel to his brain. The submerged brother writhed within the watery confines. His body convulsed, became calm, then convulsed again. One hand reached out of the water, its veins darkened by the potion.

Just a little more time, the old monk thought.

Another hand reached out, searching, splashing.

A few moments more.

The surface of the water became increasingly turbulent with the man's spasms.

"Now," the old monk said.

The brothers lifted him out of the water, blue and black and subhuman. They removed the chest plate and ankle weights. The brother gulped in great lungfuls of air and opened his eyes. The water in the copper tub had become transparent, the spell fading. Only lingering effects remained.

"Tell us the future, my brother," the old monk said.

"Invasion. I saw invasion . . . fire . . . death."

They already knew of an invasion. What they couldn't foresee was the fate of the House of DeyTrudi. "What of King Magen?"

Eyes blinded to the present stared into the future. "The king of Willovia will die."

"When?" one of the other monks asked.

"As leaves fall to nourish next year's growth, so, too, will he."

Autumn. The king would die in autumn.

"His death is the catalyst," said the brother still experiencing the aftereffects of the spell.

"The catalyst for what?"

"War."

"King Magen will die *before* Willovia is invaded?" the old monk asked.

"Catalyst. War."

"What of Rega Bayla?"

The half-naked monk lay on the floor and closed his eyes, unresponsive to all stimuli. His skin gradually regained its normal pallor. Water dripped from his body.

The brotherhood of monks waited in the candlelit room, circling like vultures around the carcass of an animal, hungry for the future.

The man emerged fully from the vision and squinted in the dim light.

The old monk knew he had to ask questions quickly while the memory was fresh. "Who will attack Willovia?"

Someone put a blanket around the visionary's shoulders. An ordinary cup of water was placed on the floor in front of him, and he took a drink. "I saw the Nunqua. They consider the death of King Magen an opportune time to strike and seize the lands of Willovia. The Nunqua believe the country is weakened from his passing."

"What will be the outcome of this attack?"

"This I could not see."

"What about Rega Bayla?" the old monk said. He received no answer. Picking up the cup of water, he flung it against the wall. Shards of pottery and droplets of water flew across the room. One of the ancient stone tablets cracked. "Tell us about Queen Baylova!"

The visionary held his head in his hands, his body trembling with the potion's aftereffects. "I don't know. I cannot see her future. I never could."

The monks talked among themselves. "Is Rega Bayla's power and hatred for us so great that she can influence our minds, block our vision? Why can't we see her future?"

"Do you think she knows? Is that the reason she despises us?"

The old monk gently picked up the silver-clawed beaker, empty now. "Let us hope she never discovers the source of our power—or what happened to her mother."

The visionary swayed, putting one hand on the floor for balance. "What about the invasion? The king must know that the Nunqua will attack, so he can prepare the Willovian forces to fight."

"We will not reveal that information until the king dies and Rega Bayla is crowned," the old monk said. "We must convince her of the necessity of our continuing presence." A drop of black liquid clung to the side of the beaker. The old monk lifted the vial, letting the drop fell onto his outstretched tongue.

"If we cannot see her future, how can we convince her of our indispensability?"

Another monk warned, "It is possible the Guardians of Willovia will not endorse her as queen. They may fight to place someone more suitable on the throne."

"Rest assured, my brothers, our order shall prevail as it has for centuries. The royal bloodline will continue." The old monk put down the beaker, then lifted his hands, watching them turn to bones and then to dust before his eyes. It was amazing how one drop of liquid held such power. "Perhaps a new perspective is needed—a young scholar who hasn't become immune to the potion. We'll search for a pupil with a strong mind, who can overcome this blockage of our visions concerning Rega Bayla. It's been a long time since a new monk entered our hallowed profession."

"But our ranks have always numbered twenty," the visionary said. "Inducting an apprentice now would fly in the face of our traditions."

"Have I ever told you what a great service you've done for us?" The old monk turned away from the visionary. "Truly, you're a fine and outspoken member of our family. Your mind is so focused on seeing the future of the royals of Willovia, you haven't tried to see your own future. Aren't you at all curious?"

"To look into my own future would cause insanity. You taught me that."

"Yes," the old monk said. "I want you to know you'll be buried in a place of honor, among kings and queens, your name resounding to the highest heights, your sacrifice a glorious example to us all."

Monks swarmed about their brother. The visionary sprang up from his knees and ran for his life, slipping through feeble fingers. The blanket fell from his shoulders, and his bare feet encountered sharp shards of the broken cup strewn across the floor. A trail of blood followed the visionary. He pushed on the door to escape, but it was locked.

"Do not be afraid, my brother," the old monk said. "It has been foreseen."

Monks seized the visionary and refitted him with the chest plate and ankle weights. Then they forced him back into the tub, where they left him until the next day.

The visionary's death came from unexpected hands—hands committed to ensure the continuation of the royal line of Willovia, whatever the cost.

*

Magen wheezed inside the dusty tent at the edge of the Outer Boundaries. The wheeze turned into a rattling cough that shook him to his core. He had endured the cough, the sickness, for over a year now: night sweats, swelling under his armpits and in his neck, an ache in his chest. He wiped his lips with a cloth. Pink froth splotched the material. How much time did he have left? Death didn't scare him. His main concern was Bayla.

"A messenger to see you, Your Majesty," one of the guards announced from outside his tent.

King Magen stepped into sunshine. On the grassy valley of the Outer Boundaries were hundreds of busy soldiers wearing blue armbands. Weapons and horses stretched across the field. A flag emblazoned with a falcon soared above Magen's tent.

Among the royal guards and advisers prowling about was a monk dressed in robes of blue. The dark eyes in the monk's gaunt face gave the appearance of evil. A necessary evil.

High-ranking commanders surrounded a young messenger who looked ready to soil his underclothing in the presence of so many superiors.

"I hope you've brought me good news," Magen said.

The messenger blurted, "It's from Commander Gy at the Hedgelands, Your Majesty." He lifted the parchment, his hand shaking.

Poor fellow. Magen took the letter and patted the young man's shoulder to calm him. "I've been waiting days for this. Commander Kyros, please show our friend where he can find some food and rest. He is to be commended for his service to Willovia."

Magen returned to the privacy of his tent and tore open the letter. It had Commander Gy's mark on it, and a symbol indicating that all was well. The body of the letter was short. The encoded script stated only that Bayla had asked to train. He needed no more information than that. Magen cursed to himself. Everything was going according to the Guardians' plan.

If only his wife had lived! If only he had sired other children—sons to bear the burden of leadership. Magen remembered when he had undergone the training: the aches and pains, the undignified treatment, the last test. How could he put his little girl through such an ordeal? There was one hope. Bayla was reaching marrying age. Perhaps she would find a suitor during her training—a strong soldier able to lead the military in her stead.

Magen destroyed the letter and returned outside. He moved away from his guards and advisers, motioning to them to keep their distance, and listened to the sounds of soldiers as they worked. Men in the distance trampled fields, raced horses, practiced with swords, and marched with spears. Some sat alone with their backs against rocks, reading or writing letters.

Commander Kyros approached and bent his head. "My king."

"Kyros, forgo the niceties, if you please. I've made a mistake. I should never have let her leave. Bayla is vulnerable. She's not ready."

"Your concern is admirable but unwarranted, sir. Commander Gy is at the camp. Surely you trust him. Sixty guards protect her."

"Sixty guards prepare her . . . punish her. I have not forgotten what it's like."

"Rega Bayla comes from a hearty lineage. She is certain to excel in her training."

"Always the flatterer, you are." How he wished to speak with Gy. Gy would tell him the truth. "What about *her*?"

"Who?"

"Shanti," Magen said.

"She is no threat. If Shanti shows even the smallest sign of treason, she'll be eliminated. It's taken care of."

"Is it enough? Do you have children, Kyros?"

"No, sire."

"A wife?"

"I'd rather have the pox," Kyros said.

"You prefer men?"

Kyros scoffed at the idea. "Women serve their purpose for a night or two. But a lifetime? That's too long."

"I see. You've never known love."

"Your loyalty to your wife is commendable, even after her death. My sincerest condolences. But love is not for me. Lust will suffice."

Magen laughed, then coughed. He pulled the cloth from his pocket and wiped his mouth. "A rare moment of honesty from you. How extraordinary! My doctors say I'll see her soon, my Sera. The monks tell me we're due for an invasion. A *real* invasion."

"You believe this, sir?"

"Yes, though I will not be here to see it."

"The monks have predicted this?"

"I don't need them to tell me everything." King Magen cleared his throat as Kyros looked away from the unregal display.

How could his daughter handle such pressure alone? Magen had asked the monks for an idea of what would happen to her after her training. Would she marry and have heirs? Would she rule?

Those damnable monks had given him no answer.

11
QUEEN OF THE BUGS

AFTER BREAKFAST, BAYLA waited with the soldiers in the archery field. She wore the same brown uniform as the others. The sleeves of her jacket were rolled up to her wrists, and the breeches sagged at the knees. By contrast, Shanti's uniform fit like a second skin. Both Pirro and Aiden had finished their time in the kitchen and were also in attendance.

What would her father say if he knew that his daughter was training with common soldiers? It was thrilling to do something so inappropriate for someone of her station. She was glad her father wasn't here to overprotect her.

Commander Vittorio barked out the rules of the archery range, adding that anyone who disobeyed his orders would suffer dire consequences. He paired Bayla with a soldier she had never met. They took bows from the many lined up on the ground. The soldier chose a bow for himself, then one for her. "Try this, Rega."

"Please call me 'Bayla' while we're here," she said.

He also selected arm and finger guards and quivers for them both. They headed to their target. Hanging from a thick tree branch was a stuffed burlap bag with a crude red circle painted in the middle.

"Done this before?" he said.

"No."

"I'll go first." He positioned his feet perpendicular to the target, nocked an arrow, drew back the string, aimed, and released. The arrow hit the side of the bag and caromed off into the woods. "Damn . . . Oops, sorry, Rega. Now you try."

Bayla mimicked his stance and pulled an arrow from her quiver.

"Just aim down the length of the arrow," he said, "and try not to be nervous."

It took all her strength and a couple of tries before she pulled hard enough on the string to bend the bow. The arrow fell short of the target. She expected to hear laughter. No one laughed.

"It just takes practice," he said. "Try again."

Two more attempts, and Bayla was still no closer to hitting the target. Her shoulder muscles hurt. The commanders were behind her, no doubt scrutinizing her lack of skill. Bayla drew back the string again, ready to shoot another arrow.

Commander Vittorio moved next to her and pushed firmly on the middle of her back. "Stand straight," he said. "Don't lock your knees. Move the index finger of your drawing hand to your cheek." He lifted her elbow. "Let the arrow do the work, Rega. The key is to be calm and relax."

She released the arrow. It hit the side of the burlap bag and caromed off to join her training partner's arrow in the woods.

Vittorio crossed his arms and glowered at the commanders standing behind them.

Gy, Jun, and Shanti moved away.

"They're gone, Rega. It's just you and the target. Concentrate. Clear your mind of everything else."

Bayla ignored the ache in her shoulder. She aimed, held her breath, and released the arrow. It struck the bag inside the target, and she jumped for joy. *Like a girl.* Vittorio watched her antics and sneered. She stopped jumping and put on a serious face.

"Better," Vittorio said. "Not great, but better."

She and her partner each took several more turns. Archery was much more fun than working in the kitchen. Lunchtime drew near, and the soldiers took a break.

"Rega Bayla," Commander Gy said, "it's time for you to see a small portion of what it takes to become a commander." He shouted over the heads of resting men, "Commanders up!"

Jun, Shanti, and Vittorio each had their own bow, quiver, and arm guard. They moved in front of the targets, and soldiers gathered around as the commanders awaited instructions.

"Fifteen paces," Gy said. "Three arrows."

They walked away from the targets as instructed. General laughter ensued as the soldiers realized that Vittorio's short legs gave him an unfair advantage.

"Four more paces for you, Commander Vittorio," Gy said. "Any commander who misses the target will retrieve every arrow from this field, and the soldiers will be free to go back to camp." Gy directed his next command to the spectators. "All right, men, let's hear some noise."

Bayla cringed as an onslaught of curses and verbal abuse spewed forth from the soldiers around her. Her face flushed with astonishment at the cruel words that the men directed toward Shanti, Jun, and Vittorio. All her life, she had been shielded from such language. These men were her guards, chosen from the ranks for her protection. The bloodthirsty dragon painted by Aiden now made sense. No longer sheltered with the privileged, she stood among soldiers now.

All three commanders were calm in the presence of the cursing men. As Shanti prepared to shoot her first arrow, they turned their venom on her, bellowing that she was an insignificant woman and had no right to wear the uniform. They howled and hollered that she was forced to be a soldier because no man would have her. They called her "mangy bitch," "hard-riding wench," and every other name unfit for polite society. Shanti's arrow flew quick and straight to strike the burlap target, low and left but inside the circle.

Commander Jun prepared to launch his first arrow, and the soldiers' malice turned on him. They called him "half-wit," "donkey dung," and "bastard son of an infectious whore." His arrow also struck inside the target, high and right.

Commander Vittorio faced the insults. He raised his arms, bow in one hand, arrow in the other. "Is that the best you've got, ladies?" Even with the profanities heaped upon him, Vittorio managed a perfect shot.

Shanti's next arrow plunged deep into the target. Commander Jun hit the target's center, while Commander Vittorio's second arrow landed almost on top of the first.

The foul language of the soldiers intensified. On her last try, Shanti drew back on the bowstring and took aim, oblivious of the soldiers cursing her. Bayla wondered how she could ignore such an intense berating. How could *anyone*? Shanti released the arrow, and it sank into the target. A perfect shot. The men's jeers turned into cheers. Soldiers now ridiculed the male commanders for letting Shanti outdo them. As Jun's and Vittorio's third arrows landed close to center, the insults changed to praise.

The soldiers' hostility evaporated like steam. Now Bayla understood why the verbal abuse from the Daughters of Fortunate Birth had not affected Shanti. For the Fortunate Daughters' words were nothing compared to what she had just heard. The commanders walked among the others as if nothing out of the ordinary had happened, and the soldiers showed no ill will toward the commanders.

Bayla helped retrieve arrows from the archery field, noting that the Commanders were exempt from this duty. A devious smile lifted her lips as she thought of calling Shanti a few obscene names at a later opportunity. If the men could do it, why shouldn't she?

*

Shanti joined Commander Gy, who leaned on a tree at the edge of the horse pasture. A wisp of smoke curled above his head. She breathed in the smooth vanilla aroma of the pipe—his sole weakness. A short distance away, Bayla held the reins of her stallion and argued with Commander Vittorio. Vittorio seized the reins from her and gave them to Zindar. The stallion reared.

"Is Vittorio doing what I think he's doing?" Shanti asked Gy.

"He wants to see if the princess's talent in riding is because of her horse or because of her skill."

"But even I wouldn't be so mean as to let someone else ride her horse."

Gy looked at her.

"Okay, I probably would. But Bayla has a special attachment to her horse. From what I understand, she's the only person ever to have ridden him."

They watched Zindar try to calm the spirited stallion. It swung its head in an attempt to yank the reins out of Zindar's hands.

Shanti yelled across the field, "Bayla!"

The princess now held the reins of a tame roan. She glared at Shanti. The stallion stood still and snorted, its ears pointed backward. It pawed the ground once.

"She does have a gift," Gy revealed.

"You know? Why, you've known all along that Bayla's a witch!"

"Her mother had the same gift," he said.

Shanti viewed the odd scene with amusement. Petite and proper Bayla expertly handled the roan, while muscular Zindar bounced astride the menacing stallion, who was unaccustomed to the weight of the stranger. The horse bucked as though it had never been broken.

"You realize," Gy said, taking a puff from his pipe, "that she's just like you."

"I'm no Daughter of Fortunate Birth," Shanti said.

"I think 'fortunate daughter' is an inaccurate description of Bayla. Even you said she was unhappy at the castle."

Zindar fell from the stallion and got up, patches of dirt clinging to his uniform.

Gy continued, "You both have been put into situations you did not choose. You both have put up tremendously thick walls to hide your true selves, and you both have a certain power."

Power and madness—two sides of the same coin. "I have no power," Shanti lied.

"It's not easy to command, yet the soldiers listen to you. They wouldn't follow a fool."

The stallion ran past Zindar and sideswiped him into the trunk of a tree. Zindar dropped to his knees. He stood, wiped the dirt from his clothes, and then chased after the reins of the horse.

"Why did you choose me to train Bayla?" Shanti said. "To test her?"

"Because I believed that the princess could have easily manipulated the men, but not an obstinate, spiteful woman such as yourself," Gy teased.

"Thanks a lot," she said.

"More importantly, I wanted to show Bayla that a woman can command."

*

Bayla headed toward the roped enclosure for the horses, with two carrots as a peace offering for her stallion. Someone touched her arm.

"Zindar."

"Rega Bayla, I'm sorry about today. I was just following orders."

"I know," she said.

"If it makes you feel better, I'm sure I'll have many bruises from being pushed around by your horse."

Bayla cast her eyes demurely to the ground. "He can be unmanageable at times."

"You seem to handle him well."

"I raised him from a colt."

"I just wanted to say I'm sorry, Rega."

"It's all right."

Zindar left, and Bayla entered the horse enclosure. The stallion didn't come over to retrieve the carrots she held out. He was holding a grudge. Not wanting to force her horse's actions, she tossed the treats to the ground. It was ironic that the stallion should snub her just as the soldiers finally stopped ignoring her. She assured herself that the grudge was merely temporary.

*

Shanti drew wavy lines on a sheet of parchment. The torn map rested on the table in front of her, and men looked over her shoulders as she worked.

"Is that a valley or a ridge?"

"It looks like a valley," someone answered, "only it's supposed to be a mountain."

"Where's the river?"

Having them criticize her efforts was infuriating, especially since they were right. Her copy was a poor imitation of the original.

The soldiers continued their appraisals. "That's not how to draw a road. Aiden should make the map."

"Aiden's a good artist. Let him do it. That way, we won't get lost."

"Where is Aiden?" she said.

They pointed to some men playing cards at a nearby table.

"Aiden!" Shanti shouted across the pavilion.

He put down his cards and came over, wincing at her pathetic effort. "The proportions are all wrong, Commander Shanti," he said. "You need to draw guidelines first."

"You could do better?"

"Yes."

"How long would it take you to duplicate this map?"

"Two days, maybe three."

Shanti rose from her seat. "Aiden, you're exempt from training for four days, after which I expect you to hand me a copy of the map. If your work is substandard, if you rush, I'll require *four* perfect copies of the map, and you'll perform your regular duties plus guard duty every night until all copies are finished. I'm being more than generous."

A soldier hit Aiden with his elbow. "Four days without training. Take it."

"I was having lousy luck with the cards anyway." Aiden sat in Shanti's place and drew guidelines onto a blank sheet of parchment.

What a relief to have someone else tasked with drawing the map.

Bayla leaned on the waist-high wall of the pavilion, tucking her arm close to her body in an awkward position.

Shanti strode over to her. "How are you feeling, Rega?"

"Excuse me?" Bayla said.

"*How* are you feeling?"

"Fine." Bayla stared into the woods.

"Is your shoulder sore from archery?"

"No."

Shanti moved behind the princess. "Raise your arm so I can see for myself."

"No."

"I'm trying to help. Hold out your arm."

Bayla lifted her chin, then her arm.

Shanti grasped the elbow with one hand and pressed her fingers into Bayla's shoulder with the other.

"*Ow!*"

A few men looked their way as Bayla cringed at the pain. This didn't deter Shanti from kneading the tenderest areas. "The muscles of your shoulder are knotted."

"All right, I admit it. It hurts. Now will you please stop? Ow!"

Shanti dug her fingers deeper into the sensitive flesh. "Afraid of a little pain? This is nothing, Princess." She continued rubbing the knots.

"Stop it, Shanti!"

She moved her fingers underneath Bayla's collarbone and pushed upward on the nerve located just under the skin.

Bayla bent forward and shrieked, but no soldiers came to her aid.

"Quiet," Shanti whispered. "Take the pain and stop whining. When I ask you a question, I expect an honest answer. Do you understand?"

"Loathsome bitch," she said loud enough for only Shanti to hear. "Get your hands off me."

"Such pretty language, Rega! You think you have everyone fooled, pretending to be so proper."

"Let go of me."

"As long as you wear the uniform, you'll address me as 'Commander.'" Shanti took her hand off the pressure point and twisted Bayla's arm. Bayla squirmed but did not cry out. A rustling came from the bushes. Then growling.

A snarling animal licked its snout, cornered but not ready to come out of hiding and fight. Shanti didn't see the beast. Rather, she felt it, was part of it. It was a wolverine, hair standing on end, claws digging into the pine needles and dirt. Shanti wanted to bury her fingers in the fur of the wolverine, touch the rough bark of a tree, prick her skin on the thorn of a bush. What was going on? The smell of soil was intoxicating. Life teemed around her; heartbeats echoed in her head. Worms crawled through the dirt, and ants gathered food for their colony. Shanti was no longer an observer, but a worker ant with jaws ready to puncture the queen ant buried deep in the ground. Other ants scurried around her, oblivious to her murderous intent.

An ivory ant inside the ebony colony touched antennae with Shanti. *Killing the queen will kill the colony. Your paths are linked.*

She released Bayla, silencing the ivory ant and the heartbeats in her head. The pavilion came back into focus. Shanti placed the heels of her hands on her forehead, dazed at the sensations coursing under her skin. A hidden world had broke open. It felt like solving a difficult puzzle for the first time.

The ivory ant was Madiza, the white-haired fortune-teller who had put her under a spell at the inn. Madiza communed with that magical world, as did Bayla. Shanti had merely stumbled upon the dimension as an outsider, a thief taking power from another.

*

Shanti watched Vittorio and Jun play a board game inside the pavilion. Smooth white and black stones were strategically positioned on the board between them. Jun moved two white game pieces, then leaned back in his chair, smiling smugly.

"You cocky son of a bitch!" Vittorio slapped a coin on the table. "I'll beat you yet." He stomped away, his hands balled into fists. Soldiers parted to give the commander a wide berth.

"You realize that Vittorio is trying to trick you," Shanti said to Jun. "He let you win. Now he will double or triple the bet, then play you in earnest."

Jun pointed to the board. "Are *you* up to the challenge?"

"Not today. I wanted know if you could get some medicine, a salve for sore muscles. You can get it at any encampment with a proper medical section."

"For you?"

"For Bayla. Her shoulder's strained from overuse. I'm sure she's hurting in other places, too, although she's too proud to admit it."

"I can't believe you'd allow that. You're going out of your way to be nice to her?"

"I'm trying to prevent bigger problems. Besides, Commander Gy has saddled me with taking care of the sick and wounded. One of them just happens to be the crown princess."

Jun slid the stones off the wooden board, into a tightly woven basket. "I wasn't planning on leaving, but I suppose I could. There's a larger encampment two days' ride from here."

"Thank you. It's a yellow ointment. Make sure the jar is full, and don't accept any used medications."

"I really wish you'd stop telling me how to do my job."

Shanti hadn't intended the remark to sound patronizing. "You might not want to mention my name, either."

"Afraid I'll run into Commander Mossgail?" he said.

"How do you know Mossgail?"

Again Jun pointed to the game.

"We'll play half the board, usual stakes." She picked the black stones out of the basket.

"I've been a soldier longer than you," Jun said. "It's inevitable I would hear something."

Others inside the pavilion conversed or played cards. No one was paying any attention to the two commanders. Shanti moved a black stone across the board. "There was an investigation, and my name was cleared."

"I heard." He moved two white stones. "Commander Mossgail was in charge of supply. He woke up one morning to find all his provisions gone—stolen in the night. Even his clothes were taken. Is that right?"

Shanti chuckled at the memory of Mossgail running around and looking ridiculous in his underclothes. He was so angry, he didn't care what he wore as he screamed, "She did it! Shanti's the thief!"

"How come you know so much?" she said.

"I happen to be friends with one of the investigators."

"Then you should also know Mossgail was black-marketing medicine to fill his own pockets. The medical section was low on supplies—supplies he wouldn't give to us. Mossgail didn't demand a proper military inquiry, because he knew it would expose his own criminal activities."

"Ah, yes, you used to work in the medical section with the other women. Still, it was pretty daring. You stole everything from Mossgail's supply area *while* he was there."

She studied the game board before making a move. "Who said it was me?"

"Commander Mossgail."

"From what I hear, he was asleep at the time."

Jun leaned forward. "You can tell me."

She wanted to tell him. She wanted to brag and laugh and tell him the whole story of how that bastard wouldn't give them the supplies they needed. She didn't regret the robbery, but she had to be careful. "Since you're friends with the investigator, why should I tell you?"

"If it makes you feel any better, Commander Mossgail wasn't popular. My friend thought what you did was hilarious: securing his weapon and moneybag out of reach on a rafter, cutting off a lock of Mossgail's hair, and tying it with twine to hang in the doorway. Personally, I think it was dumb. The hair confirms that you stole his supplies. Only Nunqua warriors cut the hair of their enemies. I'm curious, though: how does a Willovian woman find herself in such brutal company? How come the Nunqua let you stay with them— as a warrior, no less? More importantly, why did they let you leave?"

"Who says the Nunqua are brutal?"

"They're not like us, not human."

"The Nunqua are . . ." A question popped into her thoughts. Jun was friends with one of the investigators." Do you know Commander Taran?"

He moved two pieces across the game board. "I win."

He had answered her question by not answering. Jun knew Taran, who, according to protocol, was unable to talk about what happened with Mossgail. Why would he discuss the incident with Jun? *Because Jun's an investigator, too.* He didn't act like any quartermaster she had ever met. Supply was his cover. So a spy lurked inside the camp, but who was he spying on?

Shanti pulled a coin from her pocket and placed it on the table. "You've certainly done well tonight, Commander."

He took the coin. "I think you let me win."

Bayla jogged to keep up with the men as they headed deep into the woods toward the mountains. By the time they reached their destination, she was out of breath.

"Rega Bayla," Aiden said.

"Please, drop the 'Rega' and just call me 'Bayla' while we're at camp. Besides, I don't feel very regal at the moment. Do you know why we're here?"

"Obstacle course."

"Fantastic." She frowned.

"It's not so bad. In fact, it can be fun."

Commander Vittorio put his hand against the rocky side of a cliff. "The obstacle course begins here on this path, marked by orange ties on the trees. Do not deviate from the course, do not skip any obstacles that stand in your way, and do not be careless. Nobody gets hurt. That's an order. Any questions?"

Only the birds chirped in the trees.

Vittorio pointed to two men. "Go."

Soldiers watched their comrades climb the steep slope. When the men reached the top and disappeared from view, Vittorio pointed to two others. "Go."

What had she gotten herself into? She couldn't compete with the men physically.

The next two disappeared over the hill. Vittorio pointed to Aiden and Bayla. "Go."

Rocks jutted from the cliff, creating small handholds and footholds. Bayla climbed to the top and gazed down at her accomplishment. It had gone easier than it looked. Perhaps she could do this.

Along the path marked with orange ties was a shoulder-high wall of wood. Behind it stood another wall, taller than she was. She shook her head. "There's no way . . ."

Aiden tugged on her arm to get her to move.

Bayla climbed over the first wall without much difficulty. The second proved impossible on her own. Aiden balanced horizontally on the topmost beam, held out his hand, and pulled her up and over. They ran toward narrow logs lying on the ground—easy to navigate. Next, they scrambled over a net. Two soldiers passed them, but Aiden stayed with her.

Bayla jumped, swung, climbed, and crawled through the dirt on the long path marked with orange ties. She crossed a shaky rope bridge positioned high above the ground and ran around a bend in the road. She stopped.

"Keep going!" Aiden said. "We're almost at the end."

She stared straight ahead.

Shanti stood on the trunk of a massive fallen tree blocking their path. The dark roots, no longer buried in the ground, spread out in an ominous circle at the tree's base. "Ready to take off that uniform, Princess? You know you can't handle it."

"I'll distract her." Aiden focused his attention on their next obstacle. "You're going down, Shanti."

"Mapmaker, is that you?" Shanti moved to the center of the trunk. "You don't have what it takes to push me off. And it's 'Commander Shanti,' you worm."

They ran toward the uprooted tree with Shanti on it, blocking their way. Aiden hoisted himself up and kept low, but Shanti kept her distance from him and waited for Bayla. He crept forward, positioning himself lengthwise on the tree, and clutched the ankle of Shanti's boot.

Her head swung around to face him.

Aiden didn't let go.

Shanti bent low, putting her hands on the rough bark for balance. She clenched the back of his shirt and maneuvered her body on top of him. Her knee dug into the center of his back, and Aiden released her boot.

Bayla climbed over the tree trunk without confrontation.

"How chivalrous," Shanti said. "Remember my order, mapmaker."

Others on the path gleefully called Shanti's name as they drew near the fallen tree.

She released her hold on Aiden. "Don't ever touch me again, and get off my tree."

He rolled off the trunk and caught up with Bayla.

"Thanks," Bayla said.

"It was nothing. As a matter of fact, I rather enjoyed having Commander Shanti sit on me."

"I noticed."

"Jealous?" he called out as he ran to the next obstacle.

Yes. Bayla chased after him, and they finished the remainder of the course.

Sweat dripped down her face, and someone handed her a flask of water. She was back at the beginning of the obstacle course. It must have been set up in a circle, winding up and down the steep hills. Bayla stayed near Aiden and tried to calm her breathing.

Pirro joined them. "So, Rega, how was it."

"So much fun, I'm ready to do it again." She wiped her face with her sleeve. "What's wrong?"

Pirro held on to his hand. "Shanti stepped on my fingers. Oh, I mean *Commander* Shanti."

When all the soldiers had finished, Commander Vittorio hopped onto a rock and announced, "Now we race." He divided the soldiers into four-man teams.

It couldn't be. Bayla was so fatigued, she felt like falling flat on her face. One thought kept her going: Shanti's insult about her being ready to take off the uniform. She wouldn't be intimidated.

Vittorio split Aiden, Pirro, and Bayla into different teams. At least she knew somebody in her group, and Zindar didn't even seem tired. Commander Shanti joined the soldiers and was also placed on a team. Vittorio put himself in another. Apparently, the commanders would join in the competition.

It was inevitable that Bayla's team should be paired against

Shanti's. Perhaps, Commander Vittorio believed it fair since they were the only two females.

The race began. Bayla watched her opponent climb the cliff, and her spirits sank. Shanti was a natural athlete.

"Rega!" Zindar yelled from halfway up the slope.

She followed him up. Her group was fast and worked well together, but Shanti's team was faster. Bayla realized she was slowing her teammates down. She had to do something about it. She didn't want to lose.

*

Shanti jumped across a succession of parallel timbers positioned high above the ground. She stabilized herself with ropes stretched across the path, above her head. A black spider scuttled toward her. More spiders followed—hundreds more. Cave crickets with long legs and thin antennae joined the spiders on the log. Shanti squashed the bugs with her boots, but there were just too many. The log cracked but did not break, and she lurched downward. Despite the roughness of the bark, her feet slid on bug innards. She tightened her grip on the ropes above.

Spiders jumped onto her legs; crickets hopped onto her sleeves; fat beetles and ants crawled out of the log onto her boots. She tried to shake the insects off. The log collapsed, and Shanti lifted her feet, entangling them in the ropes above. The knots loosened instead of tautening as they should have, and the ropes gave way. Shanti dropped through the air. Putting her hand out to break her fall, she ripped through a sticky spider web. Her thumb hit the ground first, bearing her weight and bending painfully backward.

Shanti shrieked. She pulled the web out of her hair with one hand while cradling the injured thumb close to her body. "That witch!" She saw the princess on the trail behind her, eyes cold but triumphant. The insects retreated. Swallowing her pain, Shanti bypassed the parallel timbers with her teammates.

"Are you all ri—"

"We finish it!" Shanti avoided using her throbbing thumb the best she could as they raced to the end. She and her team crossed the finish line first, and Bayla's team finished shortly after. The brooding princess leaned against the cliff.

Shanti tromped past Vittorio. "Parallel logs are unsafe. That obstacle is off limits." She went over to Bayla. "You pull a trick like that again, and I'll recommend your training be stopped."

"No one will believe I conjured those bugs to attack you, especially out here in the wilderness."

Shanti towered over the princess. "How many soldiers went through the course before me? Fifty? Sixty? It's interesting that such a delicate spider web could have survived all those people running over it. Not to mention that the bugs chose to jump on *me,* and the log broke at the exact moment I was on it. The ropes came unbound when I hung in the air—not a coincidence. I've seen you change a caterpillar into a butterfly back at the castle, so don't play innocent."

"It wasn't fair for you to race," Bayla said. "You weren't tired from going through the obstacle course once already."

"I've been through a hundred obstacle courses worse than this one." Shanti's voice grew louder, and heads turned in their direction. "Do not think I'm the only one at camp who knows about you. You cheated at the horse race, and you cheated here. No more tricks."

"One day I'll be queen, and you'll have to follow my orders."

"Do you actually believe I'm going to stay in Willovia for the short, incompetent reign of Queen Bayla?"

The princess mumbled something.

Shanti softened her voice into something sinister. "What did you say?"

"Baylova. It's Queen Baylova."

"Not yet." She walked away from the soldiers, filling her lungs with air and hiding the pain in her thumb, which made her want to retch.

Jun strode across camp, carrying a box. He handed it to Shanti and noticed her swollen and discolored thumb. "I thought this medicine was for Bayla," he said. "What happened to you?"

She groaned as the weight of the container aggravated her injury. "Don't ask." Shanti moved the box so it rested on one hip, and rummaged through the contents.

"By the way, I did mention your name," he said.

"Really?"

"I didn't go to the normal medical supply area, but straight to the medical section at the encampment. They gave me the medicine you requested, and more. Leanna says hello."

"Leanna—I haven't seen her in a long time." Leanna was the one who had bought the concoction to knock out Commander Mossgail. Two jars of muscle relaxant were in the box. She gave one to Jun. "It would be better if Bayla got this from you and not me."

He took the jar from her bruised hand and walked away as she watched him. Leanna was her friend and in her debt because of the Mossgail incident, but Shanti realized that the women who worked in the medical section were more than happy to give Commander Jun the supplies he requested. They were probably falling all over themselves to find out who the good-looking commander was. No, the box of supplies the camp received was not on account of her friendship with Leanna.

Jun gave her more medical supplies than she had asked for. He also gave her a bottle of expensive alcohol. Generosity in commanders who controlled supply was unheard of. They always wanted something in return. So what was Jun after?

A group of soldiers passed by and caught her staring at Jun. She immediately changed her face into a menacing mask and put the supplies in her tent.

*

Late that night, Shanti sat on her bed and opened a small pouch filled with aromatic herbs. She untied the pouch, added white powder to the contents—medicine for her throbbing thumb—then retied it and took the spiked tea bag to the pavilion. The stars were hidden, and it smelled like rain. Shanti hoped it would storm. In the kitchen, she used a stick to stir coals from the fire used to cook dinner. She found a cup, filled it with water from the nearby creek, then returned to the kitchen.

Mr. Pascha blocked her from getting near the hot coals. "What the hell do you think you're doing?" he growled.

What was he so mad about? "Boiling water."

"Boiling water!" Pascha took a metal pan and filled it with clean water from a barrel. Shanti dumped the river water out of her cup. He began heating the pan on a rack over the hot coals while muttering to himself. "Damn woman eats more than anyone I know. Thinks she owns the whole camp, too. Well, not my kitchen."

As much as Shanti disliked the cook, he did keep his area clean and orderly.

"My kitchen." He filled her cup with hot water. "Not yours."

She remembered Commander Gy's order to ignore Pascha for the sake of the camp. Dunking the sachet of medicine and herbs into the cup, she went outside to find somewhere to drink her tea alone. There was a place to sit on a low tree branch where she wouldn't be bothered. After inspecting the area for insects and snakes, she sat and watched the quiet camp while enjoying her hot brew. The wind blew, and she could feel the storm's approach. Thunder rumbled in the distance.

A light penetrated the dark. The flap to Commander Jun's tent opened, but it wasn't Jun who came out. It was Bayla, carrying a pair of boots and the jar of medicine.

What was going on? The flap should have been open the whole time Bayla was inside. Doors were always left open in mixed company. It prevented problems. Why was Bayla in Jun's tent so late, anyway? She should have gotten her supplies at a more appropriate time.

With Bayla's training in mind, Shanti had given the soldiers an order that no relationship with the princess be pursued while at camp. But she didn't have the authority to command Jun. Could he and Bayla be lovers? If a romance was going on between them, there would be no point in training the princess. Bayla would use Commander Jun to breeze through the training.

Like I used Caravey.

No, that was different. Caravey had tormented her, stuck knives into her, burned her, taught her self-reliance, taught her to push away the pain and fight. She had completed her training with the Nunqua. Only after they won the competition in the Grand Arena had she gotten involved with the famous general Caravey Delartay. And he still abused her.

Her cup was empty, and rain pattered sweetly on the canopy of leaves overhead. Shanti tilted her face to the black sky, enjoying the feel of the first cool drops on her skin. The throbbing of her thumb receded to a dull ache. She thought of the scars on her body, and her tarnished past. Bayla was young, beautiful, and rich—every man's dream. Whoever courted and married her would be king, and Jun had been a soldier long enough to know that the tent flap should have been open.

*

The commanders of camp waited inside Gy's tent for the meeting to start. Gy entered and paced in front of them. "I've asked all of you here to determine how the princess is progressing. Commander Vittorio, what's your assessment?"

"Rega Bayla is doing well. I've never seen a better rider, and her archery skills are much improved. I believe strength, speed, and confidence will come with more training."

"Commander Jun?" Gy said.

"Learning the code will be no problem for her. She's intelligent enough to lead in time. I see no problems."

Gy stopped pacing and exhaled loudly. "Commander Shanti?"

She rested her chin on folded hands. The code! That explained why Bayla was in Jun's tent with the door closed. He was teaching her the code—a task that required the utmost secrecy. To protect the encryption of messages, only the king and a select few knew the code. It was one of the most important skills for Bayla to learn.

Shanti wanted to kick herself for jumping to conclusions. The fact that Jun knew the code only solidified her belief that his occupation, his true profession, entailed more than managing supplies.

"Please be honest," Gy said.

"Bayla has a lot of determination," Shanti said, "but she doesn't understand what it means to rule. She thinks only of herself." She lifted her thumb, wrapped tightly in a beige dressing. "She sabotaged the obstacle course so her team would win and I would take the blame for the loss."

"Do you have proof?" Gy said.

"No."

Gy paced in the small tent. "I was wondering if Rega Bayla has asked any of you about what has happened, or is happening, at the castle."

They shook their heads. Bayla never inquired about the castle or the "invasion" that was a ploy to lead her away. She never asked who had attacked their lands or what was happening to her people, and she never asked about her father, the king.

"I've devised a plan to test Rega Bayla." Commander Gy looked at Shanti. "I also believe it's time we inform the other commanders of her unusual abilities. They'll need to know."

She nodded.

"Good. Commander Shanti, tomorrow I want you to determine just where Rega Bayla's loyalties lie: with herself or with the people she will serve."

12

APPRENTICE MONK

TOBIAN CLEANED THE lenses of his spectacles with the folds of his new blue robe. He followed the old monk through the main monastery. The brothers' complex of buildings skimmed the edge of a cliff overlooking the sea, near the castle.

They entered a brightly lit room with tall windows and bookcases lining the walls. Hard cider had been set out on a table, along with nuts, fruit, and thin slices of meat. Life at the monastery was more comfortable than he had imagined. He had initially believed that the monks were so devoted to their craft, they must sleep and work in the tiniest of cells, with only meager rations of food for sustenance. How wrong he was!

"What troubles you, my brother?" the old monk said.

Tobian wasn't a true brother yet, but merely an apprentice. For he had yet to submerge himself in the future, the true source of the monks' influence in royal society. "I'm not so sure you chose wisely."

"Do not doubt yourself," the old monk said. "You've proved to be a brilliant scholar even before joining us. Your desire for wisdom is great. It's why you were chosen. Understand that your presence among us has been foreseen."

Tobian took a book out of the bookcase. He opened it to a random page, breathed in its scent, admired the delicate lines of the words. Meticulous illustrations adorned each page.

"Beautiful, aren't they?" the old monk said. "Much more than words, they are works of art. These books will tell you the history of Willovia and its royals, but it's not the same information you will find in other sources. It's much more truthful. I must warn you, though. You are about to read of the past *and* the future. Remember to keep this knowledge secret and discuss it only within our order. Information can be a powerful thing." He smiled and bowed like a servant instead of a master. "If you need anything—more food or candles—it will be brought to you. Take your time, my brother. Very few people are privileged to read these rare treasures." The old monk left and closed the door behind him.

"Tobian." He poured himself a glass of cider. "My name is Tobian." It was an odd custom for the monks to abandon their names. Tobian reclined in a chair and took off his spectacles, not needing them to read. The monks' appearance— withered bodies, eyes rimmed in red—made him uneasy. Maybe that was the reason he thought the order forbade extravagances beyond what was necessary to sustain life. Collections of books, sculptures, and historic artifacts decorated the rooms, giving the impression of a museum rather than a monastery. Servants prepared meals, cleaned the buildings, and tended the gardens. He detected no evidence of self-denial in the monks. So why did they seem so sick? Perhaps they lived longer than most due to their scholarly existence.

Tobian opened the book. Drinking in the well-crafted words, as intoxicating as any wine, he lost himself in the pages of Willovian lore.

*

Shanti, her hand wrapped in a bandage, with fingers exposed, led

Bayla to Vittorio's tent before sunrise. He was dressed and waiting for them. Vittorio handed them each a quiver of arrows and directed them to the bows. Shanti got her bow, then headed into the dark forest wet with dew. Bayla followed.

"Where are we going?" Bayla said. "The archery field is the other way."

"I know."

"What's this about?"

Spiky twigs arched over the path and tugged at her uniform. "We're going hunting."

Bayla avoided a branch that Shanti had pulled back and let swing at her head. "I will not kill an animal. I don't eat meat; you know that."

"We'll find deer in the field up ahead."

Bayla stopped. "I won't do it, Shanti. You can't make me."

She stopped and faced Bayla. "It's '*Commander* Shanti.' Even your father had enough respect for the military to call me by my rank." She continued down the narrow trail. "You're a soldier. Soldiers hunt. There's a field up ahead where we'll find deer."

They concealed themselves behind bushes and waited for the sun to climb over the horizon. Three adult deer, along with two fawns, came out of the trees and bent their heads to graze in the meadow.

"Take the shot," Shanti whispered. "Aim behind the shoulder."

Bayla stood and nocked the arrow, then drew back the bow. Her technique had improved since the first day of archery practice. She released the arrow and missed. The frightened and confused deer looked up, too stunned to move.

"Do you think I'm stupid?" Shanti said.

The deer bounded into the woods.

"I will not kill an animal."

"Still the little princess? Still think everything's about you?"

"You're asking too much," Bayla said.

"These men are willing to give their lives in your father's army, and you won't lift a finger to give them the food they need. Do you believe every soldier, every servant, is there to fulfill your childish wishes? You'd rather they starved?"

The bow dangled loosely in Bayla's hand. "Enough food is at camp. I'll not kill a deer to satisfy you."

"*I'm* not asking you to do this. Commander Gy gave the order for you to hunt."

"I'm Bayla dey Valrise DeyTrudi, Heiress of Willo—"

"Your birthright doesn't make you a better leader than Gy."

Bayla held the palm of her hand toward the pasture. A medium-size deer with velvet stubs for antlers emerged. She pulled another arrow from her quiver, took aim . . . then lowered the bow.

Shanti quickly shot an arrow into the deer's hindquarters, grimacing from the sting in her sore thumb.

Bayla sank to the ground and groaned.

The deer sprang away from them with the arrow buried in its haunch. Another arrow flew from the trees and sank deep into the deer as it ran into the woods. It wouldn't get far. Two soldiers jumped down from their perches and awaited instructions. One of them carried a knife.

Bayla had failed Commander Gy's test of self-sacrifice. Failed! Did she expect any different? Bayla's failure meant Shanti's failure. Their paths were linked. Shanti wished she had never met Madiza. The fortune-teller's predictions were clouding her judgment.

"You must act without hesitation," Shanti said.

"I don't eat meat. I shouldn't have to kill for food."

"When you wear that uniform, you are no longer an individual, but part of a group." She sent the soldiers to find the deer."

"It's too soon, Commander Shanti," one of the soldiers said.

"Leave us," she said.

Bayla rocked back and forth on her knees in the tall grass and put her hands over her face. Shanti wanted to touch her, feel what she was feeling. She wanted to hear the deer's heartbeat thundering in her ears, racing for life, silenced for the good of the pack.

"The pack," Shanti said.

"What?"

There was hope. Bayla was still young, unable to fully control her powers or know her true potential.

"Go back to camp, Rega."

As Bayla left the meadow, Shanti signaled two soldiers waiting in the trees to discreetly follow the princess. The last soldier emerged from the bushes. She ordered him to stay close to her and be careful.

"Careful for what?"

Shanti scanned the idyllic pasture. "Retribution."

The soldier looked around as she had done, his face screwed up in uncertainty.

The pack—the Willovian military! The princess would be able to understand the basic survival instincts of predatory animals hunting in groups. She could be leader; she could learn responsibility.

Could she?

Shanti went to find the dead deer, all the while feeling like a string pulled so taut it was bound to break.

*

Far behind Commander Vittorio's tent, Zindar and Bayla worked at a table littered with feathers, sticks, and arrowheads. They made arrows to replace those that had become too damaged to repair.

Zindar thought the princess looked sadder than usual. "What's wrong?"

"It's been a long day." She sighed. "Where's everyone?" Only a few soldiers wandered around the camp.

"They took a trip to town to get a hot bath and . . ." Zindar pretended to concentrate on gluing feathers into the end of the shaft. He had almost told the Willovian crown princess that her guards were out looking for cheap alcohol and even cheaper women.

"And why didn't *you* go to town?" she asked in a proper, mocking voice while sharpening the point of an arrow on a whetstone.

Her fingers, so much smaller than his, made the task easier to manage without getting a cut finger.

"I have guard duty."

"A hot bath would be nice," she said.

"Not even if we cut your hair would we be able to disguise who you are, Rega."

"Call me 'Bayla.'"

A bat darted across the darkening sky. The princess didn't even flinch when it dived close to the table to catch an insect in its jaws. They were almost done making arrows for Commander Vittorio. Instead of hurrying to finish, Zindar worked at a slow pace and enjoyed the pleasure of her company.

He told her about his family, his four brothers and sisters, and growing up in a small house where everyone fought for the chair by the fire or the last morsel of meat. Still, they were happy memories. She told him about the castle and how she would sneak away from her governess and explore the many rooms. Her governess would be livid when they found her, but her father didn't mind.

The woods got darker, and their work slowed to a snail's pace. Bayla leaned her head against his shoulder.

Just one kiss, he thought. They hadn't seen anyone for hours. No one would know. One kiss, and that would be it. Unable to deny his feelings, he put his arm around her. Zindar bent his head to hers, giving her a chance to pull away. She didn't. His lips touched hers softly.

One kiss became many long, deep kisses as they sat at the table in the woods, surrounded by arrows and flitting bats. Never in all his time as a soldier had Zindar been so happy to have guard duty and miss a trip to town.

*

Two men heard a noise behind Commander Vittorio's tent. They went to investigate and saw the outline of a couple sitting close together. The two soldiers left the pair alone and complained about not being able to leave camp for a bit of recreation.

"Who do you think won the bet?" one of them asked.

"Not me. I was sure Commander Jun and Shanti would have gotten together before this." The men in their tent had collected a pile of coins going to whoever guessed the correct date the two commanders would get together. Shanti wasn't bad to look at, and Commander Jun was unattached. It was only natural to expect something to happen in such close living conditions.

"Wait. I thought Commander Jun went to town with the others." They entered the pavilion and saw Commander Shanti there, with food in her hand, as usual.

"What?" she said, swallowing a morsel of bread.

"Nothing, Commander." It must have been Bayla, the only other female at camp, sitting in the dark and kissing somebody. All the men knew that the princess was not to be touched.

"What!" she said.

They had to tell her. It was only a matter of time before she found out anyway.

Shanti stormed out of the pavilion and into the night.

*

"I'm sorry." Bayla said to Zindar.

"This would be so much easier if you weren't the heiress to the Willovian throne."

Bayla had needed to feel comforted after having to go hunting that morning, but she didn't want Zindar to get into trouble. More importantly, she wanted to prevent the monks from peering into his future. The monks were always worrying over the affairs of Willovian royalty.

He held her hand and squeezed it. "Don't worry, no one will know."

"I wish things could be different," she said.

"So do I." Zindar kissed her hand. Picking up the bundles of finished arrows and placing them in front of Commander Vittorio's tent, they went their separate ways.

As Shanti watched from a distance.

*

The men returned to camp late at night, full of alcohol and good cheer. Most were asleep when Zindar, tired from his early-morning guard duties, entered the pavilion to get breakfast.

Shanti didn't eat with the other commanders, as she usually did. She walked past their table as they kidded her, saying they had never seen her skip a meal.

Zindar looked up and watched her approach. She placed her fingers underneath the edge of the table he was sitting at and flipped it. Food and tableware crashed to the floor. Then Shanti left the pavilion as if she had done nothing wrong.

Zindar's hands clenched into fists. Mr. Pascha spat on the ground and shouted obscenities. Young men stared in silence at the upturned table.

The other commanders, the calm eye of the hurricane, continued eating breakfast. Gy took a bite of bacon, sipped his tea, wiped his chin with a cloth, then spoke to Jun and Vittorio. "Meeting in my tent after breakfast."

*

"You jackass," Aiden said to Zindar, who was lying on his cot inside their tent.

"I didn't tell anyone."

"You didn't have to. Macvee and Trey saw you and Rega Bayla together. Commander Shanti saw you and Rega Bayla together."

"It was just one kiss," Zindar lied, smiling to himself and thinking of the previous night. He sensed his tentmate's hostility and guessed that Aiden had feelings for her, too. Zindar wanted to provoke Aiden and boast about his time with Bayla, but he was in trouble enough, and getting into a fight would make matters worse. "What could Shanti possibly do to me?"

"Commander Shanti can have you banished for disobeying an order. Royal guards are not supposed to get involved with the people they're protecting. Not to mention, Shanti has always been Commander Gy's pet. Commander Gy has good connections with Bayla's father—oh, that's right, who happens to be king. What do you think King Magen will do when he hears about you two?"

Hearing the king's name terrified Zindar. Things were spiraling out of control. Still, he didn't regret it. "She started it. What was I supposed to do, say no?"

"Shut up, Zindar," Pirro spat from three beds away.

"Jackass," Aiden said.

*

Shanti sat in a chair in the middle of Gy's tent as Gy, Jun, and Vittorio stood around her.

"Why did you give the order?" Gy asked.

"Because she has to do it on her own," Shanti said. "Nobody should do it for her."

"She's not you," Vittorio said.

"Do you consider her weak?"

"That's not it," Gy said. "You have to expect this sort of thing to happen. It's normal."

"I know that," Shanti said. "I understand."

"Then why did you give the order?"

"Because I don't want the men to use Rega Bayla for their own personal gain, and I don't want her to use any of the soldiers to make it through this training. She has to learn to trust in her own abilities and not lean on someone else, like her father or Zindar, to do things for her. Whatever happens after she's completed the training is of no consequence to me, but until that time, I request that the order stand."

"What about Zindar?" Gy said.

"He disobeyed my order."

"I'll not have him banished. He's a strong soldier."

"So any order I give can be ignored?"

"Damn it, Shanti, that's not what I said! You handle this, but Zindar will not be banished." Commander Gy left the tent.

Shanti rested her head on her hands, remembering how Commander Gy had tormented the male candidates for merely trying to talk to her, much less kiss her, during her training for promotion to commander. Why was Gy so hard on her and so easy on Bayla?

She sat up straight. "Vittorio, when's the next time you plan on having sword practice? I could use a little exercise."

"For you, I can arrange to have practice this afternoon." He bent toward her. "Zindar is strong but inexperienced. He prefers to attack from the right to overpower his opponent. If you force him to defend his left side, he'll lose focus and can be easily defeated."

At least, she had one ally in this matter. "Thanks," she said.

Jun's allegiance remained a mystery.

*

Shanti joined the large crowd gathered around the ring of stones where the sword fights were held. The soldiers' spirits were high as they enjoyed the one-on-one sport officiated by Commander Vittorio. Several pairs had fought already when Vittorio pulled Zindar out of the crowd, seemingly at random.

Zindar put on a protective vest. Shanti also put on a vest and picked up not a dull practice sword, but her own sharp blade. She twirled it by the hilt in her hand—a trick taught to her by one of her Nunqua colleagues. The weapon was more than an extension of her physical body; it was an extension of her will, her spirit.

Soldiers enthusiastically placed bets as they waited for the contest to begin. Bayla stood among them—emotionless, cold, imperial. Zindar stepped into the ring of stones, and Shanti did the same.

"You know the rules," Vittorio said. "No head shots, nothing below the waist. First one to get three shots to the body wins. Begin." Vittorio backed away.

Zindar yelled and sped toward Shanti with his weapon held high. She dropped to one knee and blocked the overhead strike. He swung at her again, and she jumped up, moving away from the blow. With a two handed grip, she came at him from the left. His sword stopped hers from touching his protective vest. Their sparring lasted only a short time before Zindar got through her defenses to point his blade downward through to her torso.

Vittorio motioned to Zindar with one finger held up. Zindar had won the first point. Cheers and groans came from the audience, depending on how they had bet.

Shanti had only pretended to be ineffective, to learn Zindar's technique and make him overconfident—a trait easy to exploit in the young.

Round two began, and Shanti took the defensive, blocking blows and sidestepping Zindar's attack. His power increased with each swing of the blade, as did his temper, but his technique was predictable and lacked control. Once again he tried to overpower her with an overhead swing. Before he could start on the downward motion, she made a slashing move to his unguarded gut, winning the point.

A shadow passed over the ground. Directly over the circle of stones, two large vultures flew around and around in a dizzying spiral, eyeing the possibilities for a meal below. Shanti continued to battle Zindar as more vultures joined those circling above. Even Vittorio momentarily took his attention away from the match to glance up at the eerie sight.

Shanti repeatedly struck at Zindar's left side. He backed away, but she did not let up. Zindar's left hand clenched into a fist. He hit her in the face, and the spectators groaned. She grasped the neck opening of his protective vest as Vittorio stopped the fight.

The tip of her sword touched his leather-clad abdomen.

"Point goes to Commander Shanti," Vittorio said. "Any more blows to the head, Zindar, and you'll forfeit."

She pushed him backward. Blood dripped from a cut in her eyelid. The noise of the crowd disappeared, and she heard Caravey's instruction resound in her head. *Finish it.*

"Match point," Vittorio said. "Begin."

Striding toward him, she made a lateral move to the right, and a stab of her sword beneath his shoulder pitted the leather of his protective vest. As soon as Vittorio declared her the winner, Shanti seized Zindar's wrist and sliced through the skin of his forearm with the sharp edge of her sword.

"You bitch!" Zindar said.

Vittorio snatched the weapon out of Zindar's hand, positioning himself in front of Shanti. "It's fair," he said. "You spilled her blood; she spilled yours. Let it go. I said let it go, Zindar."

Disappointed vultures circled low in their fruitless search for meat. One of the creatures landed, folding its wings to its sides. It's orange eyes glared at Shanti. Bumpy red skin covered its head and neck. Bayla must have been controlling the vulture—an odious show of displeasure. So be it.

Shanti stepped out of the ring and swung her sword harmlessly at the vulture. It smelled of decay, as if it had just fed. The bird flew away. Shanti removed the heavy vest. Picking up a cloth, she wiped the blood off her face and sword.

Zindar sat on a boulder at the opposite side of the ring, holding his injured arm. The cut would heal, as would his pride. A scar would remain.

Shanti went over to him. "By the way, Zindar, you have guard duty tonight."

*

Shanti sat on the cot inside her tent, holding a rag gingerly over one eye. It hurt to blink. But at least, her eye wasn't swollen shut. Her vision was intact—a good sign.

Jun came in and sat beside her. "Let's see."

She removed the white rag spotted with blood.

"It's not so bad," he said.

"I really hope I don't get a black eye." She put the rag on the bed, next to the bandage used to wrap her injured hand.

Jun took her left hand and inspected the thumb. The inflammation had gone down, and the purple bruise had turned yellow as it healed. "Why are you always getting hurt?" He pushed her sleeve up to expose the parallel scars, then pushed the other sleeve up to see more scars, all made by the blade of a sword. He traced the lines with his thumb.

"Seven," she said. "Seven losses from sword fights."

"Nunqua?" he asked.

"Yes."

"It is . . . cruel."

"It's an incentive to win."

"Is that what you were trying to do: teach Zindar how to win?"

"No." A faint smile played on her lips. "I was just being cruel."

He gave her a disapproving look.

"Zindar will forgive me in time. I'm not so sure about Bayla, though."

Jun pulled her sleeves down to hide her past, then held her hands. It was hard to look at his face. Her feelings for him were unmistakable.

He left the tent, and Shanti fell backward onto her bed, lamenting the bad timing. She was finally alone with Jun, but dirty, sweaty, not to mention bleeding, with the possibility of a black eye, and her scars exposed for him to see and touch.

*

Thousands of stars shone in the moonlit night. Shanti trekked through the woods alone to the farthest guard point. Zindar sat on a rocky perch overlooking the land cloaked in shadow below. She handed him a bandage for his arm. "You understand why I did it, don't you?"

He held on to the bandage and said nothing.

She sat next to him. "I'm not mad at you for showing interest in Bayla, but you disobeyed an order. I cannot allow my authority to be challenged without repercussions. If Bayla is crowned queen, she must learn to do the same." She gazed at the stars, waiting for Zindar to respond. "Bayla's purpose at this camp is not simply for her protection or to train her as a soldier. She's being tested, studied, analyzed by those who have the power to overthrow her if she fails. Bayla must put the needs of Willovia before her own. Many individuals, many groups, want to know if she's worthy to become the next ruler of Willovia."

Zindar undid the loose end of the bandage and rolled it back up.

She thought of Taran: his brown eyes, sheepish smile, and how he hit her in the face and called her a freak when they were both training for promotion to commander. Shanti had hoped to start a friendship—more than a friendship—with Taran before Commander Gy ruined it and turned him against her. Zindar and Bayla shouldn't have to suffer the same fate. Still, she had had a purpose in giving the order. Shanti tried to reason with Zindar. "If you want to continue to see Rega Bayla and she feels the same way about you, you must wait until this camp is torn down and her training is complete. If I find you two alone together while this camp is running, I'll have you transferred with a letter of reprimand. Or banished, depending on the circumstances."

The muscles of his jaw tightened.

"Zindar?" she said.

"Understood, Commander."

"Good. You have guard duty for three more nights and will continue training during the day."

She slipped back into the forest.

13
THE SWORD AND
THE SWARM

INSECTS HUMMED IN the woods, and birds chirped in the trees. Soldiers waited under a canopy of leaves to begin training for the day. Bayla sat on a stone, surrounded by morning mist. A black spider crawled from her back, over her shoulder, and onto the bare skin of her arm. She controlled the creature, ignoring those around her, knowing that the men watched. Bayla lifted both arms, palms facing up. Dozens of spiders roamed over her fingers, uniform, and neck.

Shanti walked out of the pavilion with long strides and hopped onto a rock. "Who's ready to climb?"

Silent soldiers started their hike to the cliffs.

"Do you all hate me that much?" she asked, her tone light-hearted. Her eyes met Bayla's, and her liveliness disappeared.

Good. Shanti didn't deserve to be cheerful after belittling Zindar and besting him in a sword fight. It wasn't a fair fight, anyway.

Spider legs tickled Bayla's flesh. She could make them creep all over Shanti, too, sneaking into her mouth, nose, and ears as she slept.

"Let's go, Rega," Shanti ordered loudly enough for everyone to hear. "And leave your little friends behind."

Spiders jumped, climbing in midair on invisible silken threads. Bayla joined the men on their march.

The sun hid behind gray clouds as they reached the cliff. Shanti pointed to a ledge on the side of the mountain and spoke to Bayla. "We'll climb to that area. It's not a race, so use caution. You'll find a rope you can use to pull yourself up in the most difficult places. Trey. Pirro. You two stay with the princess and help her, but only if she needs it. And, Rega, if I so much as see a snake, spider, or rabid animal, we'll tie a rope around your waist, strand you on a ridge, and leave you there until tomorrow. That's a promise."

Bayla climbed at a moderate pace, followed by Pirro and Trey. The narrow passageway twisted over and around giant rocks. Rivulets flowed downward, wetting the trail, which was slick as ice in places. Halfway to the top, her lungs burned and her leg muscles cramped. She pulled herself up a rope. Her boot slipped, and her knee bashed against a rock. Loose pebbles tumbled downward, and she skidded toward the land below, unable to find secure footing.

Pirro snagged her by the back of her uniform to stop her fall. "We're all feeling it, Rega," he said.

Her hands burned from the rope. How she missed her fluffy bed back at the castle, watching the sunset over the sparkling sea from her bedroom window. She wanted to ride the familiar trails on the castle grounds with her stallion, smell the wonderful scent of honeysuckle in the summer, eat delicious feasts, and dance to glorious music. She had longed to get away from the castle, but now it seemed so good there, so easy. What was she doing on this rock?

Bayla glanced up. They were close to the top. Relief and a new energy spread through her.

"We're almost there," Pirro said.

She peered down to see how high they had come, and her legs

trembled. The treetops spread out like a green blanket, with the silver ribbon of a river curving through it. Bayla clung to the side of the mountain and squeezed her eyes shut. She would not survive a fall from here.

No monks. Why was she frightened? For no monks were present to chronicle her death.

"Never look down," Pirro said. He grabbed her hand and pulled her up until they reached the safety of the ridge. Soldiers ambled about, recuperating from the climb.

Commander Shanti was the last one up. She turned to Aiden. "Count?"

"Everyone's here," he said.

She bent forward and put her hands on her knees. Her cheeks were red from exertion. She rested on a boulder near the edge of the cliff and gazed at the countryside. A cool wind blew. She took her hair out of the warrior's knot, letting it blow in the breeze.

Bayla tried to hide the shaking of her legs. She joined Pirro and some other soldiers. He told her some jokes in an attempt to make her laugh, like always. Didn't he see the spiders? Didn't he consider her abnormal, odd? Others talked to her, too—perhaps more cautiously than before, but they did not ignore her. Only Shanti sat alone, taking in deep breaths of fresh mountain air.

*

Jun scanned the camp to make sure he wasn't noticed. He went through the back flap into Shanti's tent. She would be gone all morning on the climb. Her bed was made; otherwise, things were not organized. In fact, they were a bit messy.

He found the box of medical supplies he had given her, searched through the contents, and picked up a bottle of strong medicine. Jun opened it to see that most of the powdered white drug was still there. He expected it to be gone. It would explain a lot. The medical supplies looked as they should: used but not used up.

He also found the alcohol that he had supplied her

with—unopened. Jun felt under the blankets of her bed and inside her pillow, taking care not to disturb them from their original positions. Still nothing.

Many of her personal supplies were on a crate in the corner of the tent, along with a small box that was locked. Jun took a thin metal rod out of his pocket. He picked the lock to see what was inside. He found a few extra darts for her wristlet, and a vial of something he'd rather not touch. The darts had hollow points.

Only a crazy woman would wear poisoned darts. Why did Shanti wear them? Was she afraid of being killed, or were they part of some sinister scheme? He relocked the box, then continued to look through her things.

He found a bar of soap that smelled like almonds—girl soap—and a bag containing a brush, the things she used to put her hair up, and something else, which he almost missed. It was a smaller bag, made of black velvet with the pile worn away in spots. Jun opened it and pulled out a lock of hair tied with a string. It pretty much proved she was involved in the Commander Mossgail incident. She had stolen his medical supplies, cut his hair, and hung it by a string in the doorway as Mossgail slept—but Jun didn't care about that.

He just couldn't figure her out. Should he take the bag and force a confrontation? She would be beyond angry when she realized it was gone. Though he took a certain liking to the idea, he returned the hair to the velvet bag.

He scanned the contents of her tent again. She was always pretending to be so tough, it made him want to break through her defenses and have his way with her. Jun knew she had feelings for him; he could sense it instinctively. Bayla was just a child; he had no interest in her. Shanti, though—now, there was a challenge. But work before pleasure. He had a job to do.

*

Carvings covered the walls of the strange cavelike chamber buried in the depths of the monks' residence. Tobian touched the stone etchings, which he guessed to be of ancient origin. He could not understand the writing, but the pictures depicted battles and royalty. One of the carvings had a crack in it. Images of celestial bodies floated high on the walls; the blue paint on the ceiling was faded and chipped. The place reminded him of a tomb. A tub positioned over a blackened pit occupied the center of the room. Along the wall, beakers with silver clawed feet were displayed in a case. Only one beaker containing the mysterious, black potion remained. "Is this all there is?"

The old monk, his mentor and master, answered, "Our supplies are low at the moment." He continued to instruct his apprentice. "You have read about the future, the king's death, and the attack on Willovia?"

"Yes." Tobian traced the carvings with his fingertips, trying to soak up the information through his skin.

"Understand the power of your knowledge. You cannot inform King Magen of his imminent demise. To know the manner of one's own death can be tragic. Men have gone mad knowing. I'm sure you have read of such events in our history books, which you so cherish."

Tobian often found himself returning to the comfortable room where he had first read the leather-bound books. He studied the chronicles of Willovia in his spare time. Its history was so much darker than commonly believed. "I understand." He inspected the potion. No light filtered through the liquid. "What's it like?"

The old monk lifted the container. "It is like entering a tunnel, entering death itself. To see the future mapped out before you is exhilarating. To take information from a superior power and return to the land of the living is an immense experience. Nothing compares."

Tobian frowned at the one surviving sample in the case.

"I'm afraid you won't be able to experience the future until the potion is replenished."

"If I may ask, when will that be?"

"Soon. Making it is not an easy process. Until then, I have arranged for you to meet the princess. She is detained for now, training with the Willovian soldiers in the Hedgelands. As soon as she completes this training, you can see her. Rega Bayla is quite beautiful. You'll find her easy to talk to. I encourage you to get to know her, to help you in seeing her future . . . for the fate of Willovia."

"Empty myself of self." Tobian had heard the saying so many times, it was practically the monks' motto.

"Not necessarily. We're in the service of the king, chosen for our intellectual superiority, and have given up our names, but we're not immune to certain pleasures."

What was the old monk hinting at?

"What have you read about Rega Bayla?"

"Not much. Her birth, the future death of her father, and the death of her mother."

"Ah, Queen Serova." The monk hung his head in remembrance. "Unfortunate."

Tobian recalled reading, in the true history of Willovia, that Rega Bayla's mother, Queen Serova, was poisoned. The monks could foresee no justice for her murderer. No one outside the monks' order knew the true fate of the queen. The people of Willovia had only been told that she died in childbirth along with the son she was to bear the king.

"Her power was great and terrible," the old monk reminisced. "Serova used her gift to control the castle and the king. She even tried to get rid of our order once or twice." He sniffed oddly, like a hound picking up the smell of a skunk. "Rega Bayla has inherited her mother's power and a hatred for our order. She does not understand our importance to her enduring reign. She will not hate you, though. In fact, she will have a certain fondness for you, a weakness. Your friendship with the future queen had been foreseen. Our success depends on you."

Upon hearing the old monk's words, Tobian felt a damp chill

in the underground room. Nowhere in the pages of Willovia was he mentioned. All dreams of the future were supposed to be written down. The monks informed him of things that had been foreseen but not recorded. He wondered if another book existed—one he wasn't allowed to see. One thing was clear: his brother monks had secrets.

*

"Damn it, Pirro," Shanti said. "Swing at her like you mean it."

Pirro apologized to the princess as he repeatedly chopped at her with a dull practice sword. They were back at the encampment, and Shanti decided that it was time Bayla learned how to use a sword.

Bayla blocked him but nearly lost the dilapidated weapon, which had seen better days.

"You wouldn't hesitate if it were me," Shanti said.

"You, Commander, I wouldn't mind fighting."

Pirro continued striking harmlessly at Bayla.

"Rega, that sword is too light for you." Shanti went to the practice swords lined up in the tall grass, and selected a heavier one. "Try this."

The princess held out the weapon to make the switch, but before Shanti's hand touched it, she dropped it for Shanti to pick up.

The sword lay on the ground between the two women's feet.

"Oh, hell," Pirro said, backing away.

In her most convincing voice, Bayla proclaimed, "I am Bayla dey Valrise DeyTrudi, descendant of the great Valdant DonTrudi, heiress to the throne of Willovia, and will be treated with the respect that my title merits. Your continual defiance of my authority is inappropriate for a commander of the Willovian forces. I will not hesitate to prosecute such insubordination."

Shanti took two steps forward and squeezed Bayla's neck in a viselike grip.

Bayla's fingers clawed at the hand around her throat.

Shanti let go and shoved her to the ground. "Get your swords," she commanded the soldiers. "Take up a perimeter. Kill any animal, anything, that crosses the perimeter."

"No sword can defeat the swarm," Bayla said.

Buzzing from unseen insects made Shanti's skin prick.

"You're no match for me, *guard.*"

Shanti knelt and held the bare skin of Bayla's forearm. Abnormal power over animals infused her senses. "Think again, Princess."

The beating of wings in Shanti's head was invigorating. Her skin no longer pricked. She zoomed through the air with her brothers, an army of wasps armed with poisonous stingers ready to penetrate supple human flesh. Two figures wrestled on the ground: one friend, one foe. But which was which? Bewildered insects soared through the air and dived into a green pond of muck in a strange other world.

Shanti's wings were wet, too heavy to move. Her body flipped and contracted under the slimy water. She did not know which way was up and struggled to break through the surface of the pond, to breathe.

Hands shook her shoulders. "Say something. Can you hear me, Shanti? Shanti?" Someone slapped her face.

She opened her eyes. "Pirro?" He hugged her in relief. Shanti no longer touched Bayla. The princess lay on the ground, her lips blue.

"She's not breathing," Pirro said.

Bayla was still submerged in another dimension. Her eyelids flickered, and she began to choke.

"Turn her over," Shanti said.

The men rolled her facedown and pounded on her back, following Shanti's command to clear her lungs. Green-tinged water spilled from Bayla's mouth, and she began to breathe.

Hundreds of wasps in the throes of death encircled them. Short bursts of buzzing could be heard as the insects tried to fly, only to fall back to the ground.

"She tried to kill me," Bayla coughed. "Everyone saw it, saw her push me to the ground and choke me."

That sly witch. Shanti grasped the wings of a dying wasp with two fingers and picked it up to view the stinger. "There shall be an inquiry. Everyone here is a witness and cannot discuss this matter until the inquiry is complete. You can bring your case before Commander Gy, Rega, or another commander if you so wish."

"You're too close to Commander Gy. High Commander Kyros will officiate."

"Who's Kyros?" Pirro said.

Shanti tossed the dead wasp to the ground. "A message will be sent to Commander Kyros."

"And to my father," Bayla said. "So the king can know of your murderous intentions."

"Any message must only state that there is an inquiry of conduct at the camp. No specific details shall be revealed until both parties have had a chance to defend themselves. These are the rules of an inquiry, unless royalty is now above the rules."

"You shall rot in jail for what you've done."

"And you shall hold your tongue until the inquiry is over." Shanti stood, and a feeling of wooziness came over her. Wings once there wouldn't respond, and she had to walk on awkward, rubbery legs.

"Pick up that weapon, Princess." She barked to the soldiers, "Clean up the site so we can go back to camp."

14

CHAMELEON

THE HEAT AND humidity of summer enveloped the camp like a thick, steamy blanket. Shanti took a long soak in the river, but moments after getting out, she was again bathed in sweat. She sat on a log near the soldiers' tents and wrung the water out of her hair.

"My favorite commander!" Mr. Pascha plopped down next to her. "I do believe you owe me for breaking my table and making a mess of the dining area."

She would sooner sit by a dung heap. "I owe you nothing."

"You also owe me for the snake I prepared for the princess." He leaned toward her, his breath reeking of onions.

Shanti remembered her promise to Gy, to ignore Pascha.

"Come on, Shanti. Let's be friends."

Ignore it.

"I've been in the woods too long. Even *you're* starting to look good," the backs of his fingers stroked her arm."

"Mr. Pascha, I'll give you this one warning. Do not touch me."

"Just having a little fun." A shock of greasy yellow hair half covered his eyes. "You owe me," he cooed. His hand reached up and felt her breast.

Silence hung heavy in the oppressive heat. She looked at the man, not in anger but in disbelief. Had he actually just *groped* her?

"You sure are somethin', woman." He cackled and slapped his knee. "All talk. I knew the only reason you made commander is because you slept your way to a promotion. Mr. Pascha ain't so dumb."

A strange coolness enveloped her. She blinked, and her pupils dilated. An ominous sneer darkened her blood-red lips, and mottled spots like a leopard's emerged on her skin. Her face remained clear, drained of all color except for a few small spots around her left eye.

Pascha's mouth opened and closed like a fish's. Only one word squeaked out of his throat. "Nunqua . . ."

She grasped his ankle and lifted his leg as he kicked feebly at her with the other. His head hit the log with a low *thunk*. Pascha twisted onto his belly, but her grip remained firm.

"Nunqua!" he yelled. "She's a Nunqua!"

Shanti walked backward, dragging him easily along the ground. His hands raked leaves and dirt and broke twigs off bushes as he reached for something, anything, to hold on to.

Soldiers emerged from tents and followed at a prudent distance. Bayla came out of the pavilion with Aiden and Pirro. Everyone stared dumbstruck at the spectacle. Shanti—hair wet, skin mottled with spots, lips red on a pale face—continued hauling her victim through the camp.

Pascha's hands grasped at a tree root the thickness of his finger, with both ends trapped in the soil. Seizing it, he held fast as Shanti yanked on his leg. She stopped her efforts long enough for him to get his whole hand under the root.

She unsheathed her sword.

"No-o-o-o-o!" Pascha yowled.

The sword blurred in a swift downward arc next to his face,

severing the root at one end. She chopped the other end of the root, freeing Pascha from his anchor. Returning the sword to its sheath, she continued to haul him over the ground.

Commander Gy blocked her path, along with Vittorio, Jun, and even High Commander Kyros, who seemed out of place in a clean brown uniform that hadn't seen a day in the field.

"Commander Gy, you let a Nunqua in the camp!" Pascha spat. "A Nunqua! Worse than an animal." He tried to stand, but Shanti put her boot on his back.

Kyros smiled in a superior manner. "Commander Shanti."

"Commander Kyros, so good to see you again!" A subtle change came over her voice, and her speech grew slower and more deliberate.

"Explain," Gy ordered.

"Mr. Pascha took certain unwelcome liberties," she said.

Brown leaves stuck to his hair, and bits of dirt clung to his sweaty face. "I ain't done nothin'. You hear me? Nothin'!"

"What exactly did he do?"

"He made advances that couldn't be ignored, Commander Gy."

"Stop talking in riddles, Commander Shanti. What did he do?"

"Nothin', I said." Pascha lay on the ground and attempted to pull his leg out of her grip.

One of the soldiers, a witness to the incident, spoke up. "He grabbed her . . . ah . . . chest, then laughed like it was funny."

Others nodded in agreement with this statement.

"Mr. Pascha," Gy said, "you're a fine cook but a sorry excuse for a man. Commander Shanti, do as you wish."

Shanti continued to haul the kicking, squirming man to Vittorio's tent, where she found some rope. Slinging the rope over her shoulder, she scanned the area till she found a thick tree. Then she tied Pascha securely to the trunk as he shouted obscenities.

"Nunqua scum! Worthless animal!"

Again she unsheathed her sword in the blazing heat, standing before her assailant.

"Come on, Commander Shanti. It was just a joke." His tone was sugary and thick as syrup. "I didn't mean anything by it! You know I really do like you."

Her changed face was expressionless.

"I mean, respect you. I *respect* you."

She clutched a fistful of his hair and pulled, slicing it close to the scalp with her sword.

"Hellcat! Spawn of demons!"

Glancing at the oily shock of hair, she put away the weapon, then wiped her hand on the shoulder of Pascha's stained shirt.

She left him there, tied to the tree, with a chunk of his hair missing, for everyone to see.

Pascha's confinement lasted until the middle of the night. Shanti, looking once again like a Willovian, wordlessly cut him free. He scampered around camp, tripping over tent ropes in the dark and collecting his gear. Soldiers guarded the pavilion, cooking supplies, and horses so he wouldn't steal anything on his way out.

*

"Were you aware that Shanti is a Nunqua?" Kyros asked Gy. A medium-size tent was put up for his temporary stay at camp, and all four male commanders were inside.

"Actually, she's a half-breed."

"Willovians and Nunqua do not breed," Vittorio said.

"I'd advise you not to say that to her," Gy said, "unless you want to be tied to a tree."

"Did you know she could alter her appearance?" Kyros asked.

"Not until yesterday."

"Commander Jun," Kyros said, "you may bring in Rega Bayla for the inquiry."

Bayla entered and faced the commanders.

"Rega Bayla," Kyros said, "you claim Commander Shanti tried to kill you. Exactly how did she do this?

"She pushed me down and squeezed my neck until I couldn't breathe. I passed out."

"Can you tell us about the wasps?"

She did not respond.

Kyros rubbed his forehead. "Rega, your power is known to us."

"I summoned the wasps for my protection."

"Tell me again, Rega, so I can be certain. How did Commander Shanti try to kill you?"

"I was on the ground, and she choked me."

"I want you to know that any decision made in this inquiry is my own. The other commanders are here to bear witness to testimony only. They will not influence my judgment. You may go," Kyros said.

"That's it?"

"Yes."

Bayla frowned and left the tent.

"Commander Jun," Kyros said, "can you please get Commander Shanti."

Shanti entered and faced Kyros.

"Commander Shanti, did you attempt to kill Rega Bayla?"

"No."

"Where was your hand when Bayla was on the ground before she passed out?"

"It was on her arm."

"But witnesses say you seized her neck," he said.

"Yes, but only to push her down. After she fell, I held on to her arm."

"So Rega Bayla passed out because you were holding on to her arm?"

"No," Shanti said. "Passing out was the price she paid for using her power to summon the wasps."

"And how do you know this?"

"I've known Rega Bayla for some time now, studied her. When she uses her power, it creates a burden that can sometimes overwhelm her—a cut on her hand for shattering a dish, for example. It's my belief that when she gains more maturity and more control over her emotions, these repercussions for using her power will cease."

Kyros nodded and leaned back in his chair. "Relax, Commander Shanti. The princess lied. Every witness I've talked to confirms your version of events: you were holding on to her arm when she passed out. No bruises are on her neck. The inquiry is over."

"You seem disappointed," she said to Kyros.

Gy answered, "You're not thinking like a Guardian. What's the punishment for lying at an inquiry?"

Suddenly, Shanti felt no joy at proving her innocence. The ramifications for Willovia were terrible. "Punishment for lying at an inquiry is banishment. Bayla's no longer a soldier. The Guardians won't support her as queen. The princess is the last of her bloodline. Infighting among the Willovians will occur to determine who rules the country. Civil war."

"Bayla will not be banished!" Gy said, his usual composed demeanor gone. "We must give her another chance. Shanti, I gave you an order to teach her to be strong, teach her to be a leader. You failed."

To have King Magen or Commander Kyros admonish her was one thing, but Commander Gy's words were like a slap in the face, a knife in the heart.

"Madiza warned you: your failure is her failure." Gy's face burned red in anger. "You want her to fail. You're jealous of her power, her potential. You would throw away Willovia for your own overstuffed pride."

She couldn't respond. Gy had been her main supporter. He

was the one who recommended she be trained and promoted to commander.

"I will not banish Rega Bayla," Kyros said. "Neither will Shanti be punished. The princess will be given another chance."

Gy picked up a short sword encased in leather. He wrung the supple sheath in a strangling motion, then carried the sword out of the tent, followed by Kyros.

"Commander Gy is under a lot of pressure," Vittorio said. "Don't take it personally."

"I guess royalty *is* above the rules." Shanti turned away to hide her emotions. An emotional soldier was a weak soldier. She did not want to seem weak.

15
BANISHMENT

B AYLA WOKE TO the sound of someone entering her tent
in the middle of the night. It was Shanti. Her sleeves were
pushed up, and she was not wearing her wristlet of darts—
just a braided orange band that encircled her upper arm. Black
paint was smeared across the skin under her eyes. Shanti threw an
orange armband onto the bed, then left the tent.

Bayla jumped out of bed and tripped on the sheets wrapped
about her legs. She dressed in the uniform and tied her hair behind
her. In her rush to see what was happening, she buttoned the shirt
wrong. *Damn!* Now she had to unbutton and rebutton the uniform. She raced out of the tent, pulling the orange band around her
upper arm.

Shanti was waiting for her just outside the tent. They went to
the tree stump with the dragon on it. Other soldiers, also wearing
orange armbands and with black paint smeared across their faces,
were gathered at the stump. Shanti took a map out of her shirt and
unfurled it. More black paint darkened the skin of her arms, and
the full moon shone overhead, giving enough light to read by.

"Eight members of our team are spread out in a defensive

position around our flag . . . here." She pointed to an orange triangle on the map. "Two advance teams have gone ahead to determine the location of the blue flag, which should be in this area." Blue shaded a large portion of the map, but no blue triangle could be seen.

"You five, take the left flank," Shanti said. "We'll take the right. If you see the blue flag, do not strike unless you're sure you can take it. We need as many people as possible to get through their defenses.

"When a flag is captured, Commander Gy or Commander Vittorio will sound a horn indicating the game is over. If you get close enough to a member of the blue team to kill him, take his armband. If he gets close enough to kill you, he will take your armband to signify you're dead. If you're killed, you stay in that spot, silent as the grave. No help is to be given to your teammates. Remember, this is a game of stealth and honor.

"There are three targets. The primary target is the flag. Capture their flag, and we win. Secondary targets are their map, which shows the location of their flag, and Commander Jun. I have a bottle of very expensive brandy in my tent I will trade to whoever gives me Commander Jun's armband."

The men around her quietly expressed their approval.

Shanti rolled up the map and handed it to Bayla. "Keep it hidden." She opened a canister containing a solid block of black paint and rubbed two fingers along its surface. Turning to Bayla, she placed one hand on the side of her head and stroked her fingers across Bayla's cheekbones and the bridge of her nose. She also covered Bayla's arms with paint.

Bayla was used to being touched by strangers: hairdressers, seamstresses, artists. Having Shanti touch her without the usual disdain felt . . . peculiar.

"Since you hold the map," Shanti said, "you stay behind with me. You"—she put her hand on a soldier's arm—"take the lead. Let's go."

They walked slowly. A short way into the wooded area, the man in the lead noticed someone leaning on a tree in the open. He motioned with his fist to take cover. Shanti signaled Bayla to hide. They waited in the dark forest, heavy with the scent of pine. The lone figure wore no armband. Crouching low, Shanti and another soldier crept up to him. The dead man handed her his sword. She brought it to Bayla, who swung the weapon in its sheath across her back. Its weight on her body was actually comforting.

"He's one of ours," Shanti said. "The blue team must be half-way to our flag by now. We don't have much time."

They continued toward blue territory and encountered a group of soldiers from the orange team. "We think the blue flag is here," one said, "just beyond that hill. Three men are guarding it."

"How many have you lost?"

"Two of ours . . . killed three of theirs."

"Bayla, come with me and keep low." The two women crawled through the bushes. Peering over a hill, they saw soldiers with blue armbands lying on the ground. They backed down to the orange team. Shanti asked Bayla, "What do you think?"

"There are eight of us and three of them. We should attack."

"You think the blue flag's behind them?"

"It would make sense."

"It's not there." Shanti said.

"Why not?"

"Because they're purposely showing themselves to us. If they were protecting the flag, they'd be hidden."

An orange-team soldier approached. "Commander Shanti, we lost four of our team members to the west. They have the area booby trapped with noise-making snares."

"Booby trapped?"

"I think it's Commander Jun, but I didn't stay to find out."

"When in the hell did he find time to make traps?" She asked Bayla for the map. "Let's see, we are here." She put her finger on blue territory. "Where are the traps?"

"About here."

"My guess is, their flag's somewhere behind those traps. We might be able to hit them from behind—take everybody along this ridge." Her finger slid along contour lines. "It may be here or just south. Let's hope we outnumber them."

"What about the blue team over this hill?"

"Leave them; they're a decoy." She handed the map to Bayla. "Stay with the group."

Bayla put the map in her shirt. "Where are you going?"

"After Jun."

*

She saw it only because she was looking for it. If her head had been up and searching for the enemy, she would have missed the trap. Shanti bent down to examine the contraption made from things commonly found in the woods. The noisemaker, if such it was, was simple yet ingenious, though she had no idea how it worked. Leaves rustled behind her. It was too late to defend herself. The blade of a sword lightly touched her back.

"You of all people know not to be out here alone."

"Nice trap . . ." She spun about to face him. ". . . for someone who works in supply."

"The dead do not talk." He put his hand on the orange band and caressed her arm as, ever so slowly, he pulled the armband off. Jun stood closer than was proper, and whispered, "It's not like you to show so much skin."

He was mocking her. Shanti would have pushed him if only she weren't enjoying the warmth of his breath on her cheek, her neck.

"Map." Black stripes were painted across his face.

She didn't move.

"Do you want me to search you for it?"

Yes! A rigorous, thorough search, please! But the woods were too full of eyes—soldiers playing the game. "I don't have it."

He put her orange armband in his pocket and headed north-ward to defend the blue flag.

She studied the strange trap again and realized that Jun didn't need to cheat. He was just that good.

Shanti picked up a stone, threw it at a tree, and missed. She threw another and another, hurling a great many stones at the tree before the horn sounded. It came from blue territory.

Soldiers, wearing either orange or blue armbands, congregated on the crest of a rolling hill. They stood around Bayla, who held the blue flag. Commander Gy was with them.

"I swear, Commander Shanti!" Someone leaned on her shoulder and laughed. "You should have seen it."

"Seen what?"

"Squirrels. She had them chasing after squirrels."

"Looks like I missed all the fun." Shanti went over to Bayla and crossed her arms. "Squirrels?"

"We won, didn't we?" A smile lit her black-smudged face.

"You torture me with snakes and scorpions and spiders, and the best you can come up with now is *squirrels*?" She held out her hand. "I'll take that sword back to its owner."

Bayla gave her the weapon.

"I believe Commander Gy is waiting to congratulate you, Rega."

"Rega Bayla," Gy said in a voice loud enough for everyone there to hear. "It's time you knew that we're more than your royal guards. We are guardians of the kingdom, proud protectors of the people of Willovia." Gy took the short sword in its sheath off his back, held it horizontally in front of his chest, and gave it to Bayla. "And now you are one of us."

Bayla, the heiress to the Willovian throne, bowed upon receiving the gift. She unsheathed the sword and lifted it to show those around her. It was a simple soldier's sword, not an elaborate show-piece normally given to impress royalty. The only decoration on the weapon was an engraving of a dragon on the blade.

"Thank you, Commander." She bowed again as the men cheered.

"Commander Shanti wanted to put a snake on it," Gy said. "For some reason, she's very fond of calling you 'the snake eater.' I insisted on the dragon."

"I truly appreciate it." Bayla swung the gift onto her back and strapped it in place.

"The schedule will be light today. Food and drink await us back at the camp. Enjoy yourselves and get some rest."

The full moon had sunk low in the sky. Shanti leaned on a tree, away from the crowd, reluctant to join the revelry. The princess had lied at an inquiry and was given not only a sword but also a party. It just wasn't right.

They assembled in camp, except for the unfortunate men on guard duty and those taking over the cooking duties in Mr. Pascha's absence. Torches blazed around the food. One soldier wore a purple hat; another played a fiddle. Men clapped in time to the spirited tune. Some sang. Bottles of wine and a keg of ale were set out for the soldiers.

Bayla sat next to Shanti. *"Snake eater?"*

Shanti chuckled and wiped paint off her face with a damp rag.

"I need to ask you . . ." But before Bayla could utter another word, a group of soldiers whisked her away to celebrate.

Shanti's arms felt grimy as she rubbed paint off them. Jun sat down beside her.

"I hear you placed a bounty on my head with the brandy I gave you. That's low." He watched everyone having a good time. The atmosphere was cheerful, not rowdy.

"Doesn't matter," she said. "It didn't work." Jun still wore the blue armband, although he had taken most of the black paint off. "So you weren't involved in the great squirrel deception?" she asked.

"No, I missed it. Didn't get there in time."

Shanti threw the dirty rag on the ground. "Where did you learn to make traps like that?"

"Quartermaster training," he said. "Standard procedure."

Vittorio joined them, and they talked until the woods lightened with the approaching dawn. By the time Shanti made it to her tent, she could barely get her uniform off before falling into bed, exhausted.

*

Bayla washed away the last traces of paint in the river. She emerged from the trees to find Shanti surrounded by men.

"Let's see you change, Commander," one of the soldiers said.

"No."

"That was smashing, the way you scared Pascha!"

"Can you transform into a Nunqua whenever you want?"

"How do you do it?"

"Finally!" Shanti said when she saw Bayla. "What took you so long?" She handed Bayla her new sword as the men went to bathe.

Bayla went into her tent and found a kit for cleaning and sharpening her weapon on the bed—probably put there by Commander Jun. She unsheathed her new sword and touched the smooth metal of the blade, making a few slashes through the air. The weapon was neither too heavy nor too light.

Someone entered the tent from the back.

"Zindar?"

He lifted the palms of his hands toward her. "I just wanted to see you. Don't be worried."

Worried? It was only the strange remark that worried her.

He took her sword and swung it in a half circle, showing off. "Nice. A little small, but perfect for you. Why have you been avoiding me?"

"I haven't . . . I'm not avoiding you."

"Yes, you are." He slid the sword into its sheath. "I thought we had something."

His strong body, once so desirable, now filled her with dread. Zindar kissed her, his breath smelling like ale. She went limp in his arms. How could she tell him she didn't want a relationship, without hurting his feelings?

"I watched you washing in the river," Zindar said. "Had to sneak away from Shanti. When you two aren't fighting, she's guarding you like a damn mother hen."

Hands moved up and down her back. Bayla squirmed and tried to move away. "This is too fast," she said. A stupid thing to say, but she wanted him to stop.

Zindar moved her hair, kissed her neck. His wet tongue slid inside her ear. "Don't be afraid. I would never hurt you."

"No." Pushing him was like pushing a rock wall. Unwanted hands caressed her everywhere. "Stop!"

"You're so beautiful," he whispered, undoing the topmost button on her jacket. Then another. Only the thin wet undershirt beneath her jacket served as a flimsy barrier between them.

"No. Please . . ."

"Please what?" Zindar pressed himself against her, and Bayla shrieked. This couldn't be happening. How could this be happening?

"Don't be such a tease." Hands reached up and felt her breasts. She tried to shove him away, but Zindar wrapped his arms around her.

"No. Stop!" she cried out.

But he was twice her size, and drunk. He ripped open her jacket, causing the bottom buttons to pop off.

The flap to her tent opened. Three soldiers wrenched Zindar away from her and wrestled him to the ground, pummeling him with fists. They forced him into a standing position, arms locked behind his back.

Aiden cocked his fist back and punched Zindar in the face. "Jackass."

They hauled him away.

Everybody had gathered outside her tent. Everybody knew. *Everybody.*

Bayla pulled the sides of her jacket over the wet undershirt, arms over her chest. She went outside, weaving through the crowd, until she stood beside Commander Gy.

"I will not allow such an act to go unpunished at this camp," Gy said. "Commander Vittorio, get the whip."

Vittorio nodded and moved away.

"Commander Shanti," Gy said, "Rega Bayla will stay with you in your tent."

Shanti ordered four soldiers to bring Bayla's cot and things into her tent.

"Inquiry," Zindar said. "I demand an inquiry."

"There will be no inquiry," Gy said, "no investigation. I command this camp. I decide your fate. Your punishment is to receive four lashes, one from each of the Commanders. Plus one from Rega Bayla."

Vittorio returned with a rope and a whip.

"Commander Jun, take charge of this matter."

Commander Jun ordered Zindar to take off his shirt. He tied Zindar's wrists together in front of him, then forced him to kneel.

Vittorio said with disgust, "You brought this on yourself."

The whip arced high in the air, then slashed down on smooth flesh. Drops of blood flecked the ground.

Zindar screamed and bent forward until his head hit the dirt.

Bile filled Bayla's throat, and she wanted to run, to hide in embarrassment. She shuffled backward until she bumped into someone. Shanti.

"You must be present for the punishment," Shanti said. "You're the one he wronged. These are the rules."

Jun held the whip, and Zindar lifted his torso for the next strike. The spike split swollen and bleeding skin for a second time. A cry of agony escaped Zindar's lips.

Jun handed the whip to Shanti, and she left Bayla's side.

"I made a mistake trusting you," Shanti said to Zindar. She opened his flesh for a third time. Blood streaked down his ribs.

Zindar lay in the dirt, in too much pain to rise into a kneeling position. Commander Jun ordered two soldiers to hold his arms and position him for one last blow.

Shanti held the whip out to Bayla.

Bayla still shielded her chest with the jacket pulled tight. The forest spun about her. "I can't."

Shanti went over to Zindar and sliced through his flesh once more. The two soldiers let go of his arms, and he fell facedown in the dirt. Shanti returned the whip to Vittorio.

"Zindar," Gy said, "you are hereby banished." His command echoed through the quiet woods.

No birds sang in the trees, no insects buzzed through the air, and no animals came to Bayla's aid. No soldiers murmured or shouted, and Zindar did not speak in his defense.

"Your actions are unbecoming of a soldier," Jun said to Zindar. "You are no longer a member of the Willovian military and will be escorted out of camp."

Watching the awful scene play out before her was like descending into the darkest depths of hell. Bayla slipped away from the group. The bright blue sky and green foliage hurt her eyes. She tried to use her power to search for signs of life, grasp hold of something she could control. But nothing answered her call.

Shanti caught up with her.

"We had to do it. It's a commander's job to enforce the rules. We must act without hesitation."

She wiped the cool sweat from her forehead.

"You'll stay in my tent until further notice."

Bayla ducked under the flap to Shanti's cramped tent and dropped to the ground. She welcomed the feel of the cool dirt against her face, but it couldn't quell the queasiness sloshing around inside her stomach. She ran out of the tent and into the woods and vomited.

16
THIEF

"I'LL BE LEAVING tomorrow." Gy sat on a log at the edge of camp with the other commanders and puffed on his pipe. "Commander Jun is in charge while I'm gone. I'll notify the others of Zindar's banishment and have him tracked."

Shanti drew in the dirt with a stick. It had been a colossal mistake to confide in Zindar while he was on guard duty and tell him about the plan to test the princess.

"I'll return with another cook and a soldier to replace Zindar."

Shanti didn't want to tell them of her mistake and incur yet another reprimand from Gy.

"That's all." He tapped his pipe against the butt of the log, knocking out the ash, and left.

"I wonder who'll be next," she said to Jun and Vittorio.

"What do you mean?"

"First Pascha, then Zindar. Things like this always happen in threes."

"Superstitious Nunqua," Vittorio said. "Speaking of which, can I see you change into—"

"No." She could feel his breath on her face. "Stop it, Vittorio. Who do you think will be next?"

"It's not something we should bet on," Jun said.

He was probably right. Shanti went into the pavilion and got two cups, then went back to her tent.

Bayla lay on her cot, one arm covering her face.

Shanti opened the bottle of expensive brandy from Jun and poured two drinks. She hit Bayla in the shoulder with a cup. "Here."

Bayla ignored her.

"It'll help you sleep." The elixir coated Shanti's throat with a smooth, satisfying burn. "I don't understand. This area is full of animals. You could have used your power. Why didn't you defend yourself?"

Bayla lifted her other arm and draped it over her face.

Shanti sipped her drink. "You fight me and not Zindar?"

"Zindar was drunk. I was with him behind Vittorio's tent that night."

"You kissed him that night. He wanted a good deal more today. You said no. Hell, we could hear you screaming across camp."

She uncovered her face and sat up. "It's your fault!"

"Of course." Shanti held the drink to Bayla. "Why shouldn't it be? Everything else is."

"You humiliated him, upended the table where he ate, beat him in a sword fight, cut his arm. Zindar was emotional, drunk. He wasn't thinking straight."

"Being drunk is no excuse! What he did was wrong. Don't blame me, and don't blame the ale."

Bayla took the drink and swirled it in the cup. "I need to ask you something."

Shanti removed her sword and darts, then put them under her cot. Lounging on her cot, she scratched the place usually covered by the leather wristlet.

"I've seen you in my dreams before I met you," Bayla said.

"Only I didn't know it was you. A leopard with spots like yours chases me."

"It's just a dream."

"It's not always a leopard. Sometimes it's a bird or a dog or a fox, but always with your spots."

"You've never seen a Nunqua?"

"No. They say you're half Willovian and half Nunqua."

Shanti swallowed the rest of her drink. "My father was Nunqua, my mother Willovian. Both are dead now."

"Who is the white wolf?"

"The white *what*?"

"Wolf," Bayla said, "the polar bear, the ivory ant. Who is it?"

The white wolf was Madiza, the fortuneteller. Shanti thought it best not to reveal her name. "She's the hidden witch."

"A woman." Bayla sipped her drink. "You've met her?"

"Yes."

"Is her power great? Greater than mine?"

Shanti poured herself another drink. "*Different* from yours." She rummaged through her things, found a sewing kit, and tossed it to Bayla. "You need to fix your uniform. The buttons are still in your tent."

"I don't know how to sew."

"You . . . *what*?" Shanti sighed. "Give me your jacket. I'll start it; you finish it."

Bayla put down her cup. She flung the jacket to Shanti, then lay back on her cot with her arms over her face.

*

Commander Gy returned with a new cook and a soldier to replace Zindar. The brown uniform hugged the woman's ample chest, and she smelled faintly of perfume. Soft ringlets framed her round face.

Shanti greeted the new addition to camp. "Leanna!" It was her old coconspirator in drugging Commander Mossgail and recovering the stolen medicines.

"Commander Shanti."

"Leanna volunteered to come," Gy said. "Her responsibility is to take care of any medical emergencies, and she'll be the princess's new tentmate."

"Volunteered?" Shanti said.

"Anything to help."

"I believe you two know each other," Gy said. "Shanti, please give her the medical supplies and show her around."

Gy left, and Jun came over. "Leanna, is that you? I'm surprised to see you here."

"I'm not," Shanti said.

Leanna smiled and blinked twice. "Why, Commander Jun, I had to come. After all, we can't very well trust Commander Shanti to take care of the sick and wounded, now, can we?"

"How can she take care of the wounded when she's always getting hurt herself? I have some things to do now. I'll see you later."

Leanna and Shanti watched him as he walked away. "I can figure out why you're here," Shanti said, "at this camp, in the middle of nowhere. It's not like you to leave a more comfortable encampment to come to a place like this. Don't get too interested."

"Why? Is he married?"

"And by the way," Shanti said, "the princess snores."

Leanna laughed, and a dimple appeared on her cheek. Shanti hated that her friend was so pretty.

"I've been hearing rumors about you," Leanna said. "They say you can transform into a Nunqua. Is that true?"

"It's been known to happen."

"Can you show me? I'd like to learn how your skin changes. What makes Nunqua so different from Willovians?"

"I won't be your experiment."

"I thought we were friends. Let me see you change." Leanna looked at Shanti as if she were examining a sick patient.

"No."

A tall man with brown skin pulled on something hanging from the roof of the pavilion.

Shanti jogged over to stop him. "Stop. Leave it be."

"It's not right, not clean." The new cook tugged on the tuft of yellow hair hanging by a string from the rafters.

"It's a custom," Shanti said, "and I request that you leave it alone."

The lock of hair remained.

*

They ran through the obstacle course twice with swords drawn. The covering of leaves offered shade but little relief from the heat. All four commanders had positioned themselves on the course as obstacles. Each soldier sparred briefly with each of them on the way to the finish. It was an exhausting ordeal.

Bayla gasped for breath after completing the course. Salty sweat stung her eyes, and the constant buzz of cicadas irritated her ears like the scratching of metal on metal.

The participants drank from floppy goatskin bags of water. Too thirsty to care about the communal nature of the drink, Bayla gulped the water down. If only the Daughters of Fortunate Birth could see her now, they would snicker behind her back and call her a filthy brute. How long had it been since she felt clean?

She returned to the boulder where she had left her sword propped in its sheath, and her muscles tensed despite their fatigue. It wasn't there.

The sword wasn't on the ground or near the bushes. It wasn't anywhere. Of all the things that could have happened, she would rather have broken a bone from falling on the obstacle course than lose her sword. Vittorio announced that it was time to return to camp.

Her panic increased with each step toward the formidable trainer. "Commander, I don't have my sword."

"Where is it?"

"I—I don't know."

You left your sword *unattended*?" he yelled.

"No. I mean, yes. But only to get water, I—"

"I don't need to hear how you lost it, Rega. Just find it." He ordered two soldiers to stay with her until the weapon was recovered.

She searched and searched until the events leading up to the sword's disappearance became jumbled in her mind. Had she left it somewhere else? Her body slumped from despair.

"Rega," one of the soldiers said, "we've been out here forever, and I'm starving. Besides, it's getting dark. You can look for it tomorrow."

The three soldiers dragged back into camp. Bayla ate very little before retreating into her tent. Losing the sword upset her more than leaving the castle, her home, on that night long ago.

Leanna entered, and Bayla feigned sleep. When she finally did sleep, bizarre dreams filled her head. No leopards chased her, and no white wolf watched her. Instead, she fell down a black hole while hands tried to stop her—hands unable to halt her dizzying plummet. She hit the ground. The thin mattress compressed upon impact, waking her from the dream.

*

"Do you have any idea what we went through to get that sword?" Vittorio said. "It was specifically designed for you."

"I'm sorry, Commander."

Her apology fell on deaf ears. "What would happen if you lost your sword in battle? That's what we're training for: battle. War. Do you expect one of the soldiers to give you his sword because you're the crown princess?"

"Isn't that what they're supposed to do?" she said. "Isn't that what they're doing now—protecting me even at the risk of their own lives?"

His face showed his revulsion at her comment. "Stop thinking like a spoiled child! If you lose your weapon in battle, these men will fight for you, protect you. But don't expect a soldier to give up his sword. It would be like asking him to become a eunuch. It isn't right. Never leave your sword unattended. Never drop your sword in battle."

Vittorio selected a practice sword from the many at his disposal and gave it to her. The weapon was dull, chipped, and ugly. It embarrassed her to carry it on her back.

"We guard you only because you represent Willovia. Or *do* you?"

Her spirits could sink no lower. She hated carrying the old blade, a testament to her stupidity. What had happened to her sword? She was determined to find out.

Bayla stomped over to Shanti, who leaned against the wall of the pavilion, eating a peach.

"What do you want, Rega?"

"Where is it?" she said.

"Where is what?"

"My sword, *Shanti*."

"First, you will address me as 'Commander.' Second, don't blame me for your own ineptitude. Your sword is your responsibility."

"I know it was you. You took it . . . *Shanti*."

"Failure to address me by my rank is a punishable offense."

"And how does an insignificant, low-ranking half-breed punish royalty? What are you going to do? Cut my hair? Tie me to a tree? Shoot me with a dart? Those darts aren't poisonous, anyway. Everyone knows they're fake. I doubt you could even hit a target with that useless wristlet of yours."

Shanti threw the half-eaten peach into the bushes. "Let's find out, shall we?" She left the pavilion.

Bayla jogged to keep up with Shanti's long stride. They stopped in front of the pasture. Horses grazed on the tall, luxuriant grass. Shanti bent beneath the ropes and entered the enclosure. She lifted her arm and pointed the darts at Bayla's stallion.

Gy stood close by, puffing on his pipe and watching the two women.

Bayla allowed her anger to infuse the stallion. The horse lifted its head, ears pointed back. Even if the darts were poisonous, they couldn't stop the heavy steed from charging Shanti and trampling her into a mangled, muddy mess.

"Careful, *guard*. That horse is worth more than your pathetic life."

"Exactly." Shanti lowered her arm and left the pasture. "Baylova, queen of the animals, commander of insects, and to hell with everyone else." Shanti bowed to the princess as several soldiers viewed the demeaning performance. "We're merely your pathetic guards, Rega—your servants. Insignificant. What shall be your first decree as ruler? No deer shall be killed in Willovia? Eating of meat shall be forbidden? Or will you put me in jail for speaking the truth?"

"Enough," Gy said.

Shanti's head snapped in his direction.

The soldiers turned away from Bayla. It was a mistake to call her guards pathetic. She had meant to say *Shanti* was pathetic. Shanti had baited her, manipulated her. It was Shanti's fault. It was *always* Shanti's fault.

*

"Why are you trying to be something you're not?" Jun's legs stretched out on Shanti's cot. In his hand was the black velvet bag containing the hair tied with string. He had gone through her belongings. "You're still one of them, aren't you? Still loyal to the Nunqua. They sent you because only a woman could get this close to the princess."

Shanti closed the flap of her tent. "Why are you here?"

"Commander Kyros sent me to spy on you. You've known what I am for a long time. You know my purpose. What's yours?"

"Give it to me."

He closed his hand over the bag. "Take it."

"It doesn't mean anything to you. Give it back."

"Whose hair is it?" He waited for a response. "I'll shut down this camp and put you in prison. Not even Commander Gy could save you if I tell King Magen you're a threat to his daughter. And I have the authority to do much worse than send you to prison."

She shook her head. "And people say *I'm* arrogant."

"Does it belong to Bayla? The king? Commander Kyros? Whose hair is it?"

"The hair is from a dead Nunqua warrior," Shanti said. "I killed him when the Nunqua took me away from Willovia after my mother died. Caravey Delartay gave me the hair, saying it would protected me from the warrior's spirit."

"Enough of your lies. Not only did you kill a man, but the infamous General Caravey Delartay made you a gift from the hair of one of his dead warriors? I don't believe it."

"Believe what you want," she said.

He got up and threw the small bag on the bed. "I have every authority to end your life if I even perceive that your intentions are not in accordance with the plan." His words were harsh, but his eyes were anything but cold.

"They forced me out of Willovia—kidnapped me. I didn't know what was happening. I surprised the warrior, took a knife—or was it a sword?—and . . . My memory of that night is vague."

"You stayed with the Nunqua willingly. They cut your arms to teach you to overcome pain. You can change your appearance. You're the perfect spy."

Jun stood close, smelling of soap. He lowered his head, his voice soft and low. "You're trying to scare me with your stories. It's not going to work. You may have everyone else fooled, but not me." He touched the spots emerging above her left eye.

Shanti morphed gradually, unwillingly, into the natural state of her birth. She was not Willovian, nor was she a full-fledged Nunqua. She was different, a hybrid with faded spots and dark lips.

"Tell me you're not loyal to the Nunqua," he whispered, fingers moving down her cheek.

Her body flooded with warmth. "I'm playing the part of a traitor."

"You're not answering the question."

Was Jun pretending to be interested to get information? "Is this an interrogation?" she said.

"Willovian or Nunqua? What are you?"

"Both."

17

A RUBY RING

"I'VE RECEIVED A message," Gy informed the commanders inside his tent. "As you know, Mr. Pascha and Zindar have been trailed since leaving camp. This message states that Mr. Pascha has found a position as a cook for a mining camp in the southernmost part of Willovia. Zindar is now working as a sailor on a merchant ship laden with trade goods for the Merulians."

Gy unrolled the map drawn by Aiden on top of a small table. Black lines on beige parchment illustrated detailed features of the terrain. "Now, to other business. We shall leave during the next full moon, over these mountains and to the east, for a game of war. When we reach this area"—he pointed to a blank spot representing a flat section of land—"the soldiers will split into two teams. Vittorio, you're in charge of the red team. Jun, you'll lead the yellow. The goal is to capture the enemy and confine him temporarily. You may also try to rescue members of your own team if you choose. Whichever team has the most prisoners after two days will visit the town when we return."

Gy rolled up the map. "Commander Shanti, I need to speak with you alone."

Jun and Vittorio left the tent, slapping each other on the back and bragging about who would win the game.

Shanti was excited to get away. The same scenery and day-after-day routine of camp were getting dull. Playing war was just the change she needed to work off some frustration.

He avoided her gaze, walked around the small space, and pulled the pipe out of his pocket to inspect it. Finally, the words came. "You'll not be going. I need you to stay at camp."

"I protest."

"I knew you would. Protest away."

"Why am I being excluded? You're purposely prohibiting me from interacting with Bayla, not to mention undermining my authority."

Gy rotated the pipe in his hands. "You're not being excluded. Someone's needed to watch the camp."

"May I speak openly, Commander Gy?"

"Yes, but I already know what you're going to say."

"Please allow me to say it anyway. There was a time when you called me a useless and weak woman, a freak, a maggot-infested pile of dung, and that was when you were feeling charitable. You smacked me in the back of the head every time I did or said something wrong."

He nodded in agreement.

"And squeezed my arms so hard they bruised. You sabotaged my equipment, overturned my belongings, made Taran and the other candidates hate me. You did all this to train me to be a commander. Bayla will be queen, if the Guardians allow it—in charge of the commanders and the entire Willovian military. And you have never once raised your voice to her, not even when she lied at an inquiry."

"The consequences for the kingdom are great if she fails."

"The consequences are even greater if she's allowed to succeed without proving her worth. You taught me how to shoot an arrow into a target at a hundred paces, surrounded by chaos and insults and hate."

"I taught you how to fight in battle," he replied. "Bayla is a royal. She can, and will, choose to stay at the castle in times of war. Control of the military will be given to the commanders."

"There are far fiercer battles being waged inside the castle than on the battlefield. She must be strong and learn to rule Willovia surrounded by chaos, insults, and hate. She must not be manipulated. You're a Guardian, Gy. You made me a Guardian. I don't understand why you're spitting on the plan."

"I'm not spitting on the plan! Let me ask you: who do you think will rule Willovia if Bayla *doesn't* become queen? She's the last of the royal bloodline."

"I don't know."

He slipped the pipe back into his pocket. "You'll stay here with the cook, go to town, relax. That's an order. We return in seven days."

"Am I still to play the part of a traitor?"

"Yes."

"Do you think Bayla will pass the final test?"

He gazed into the distance. "Yes."

She could tell it was a lie.

*

Pirates captured the Willovian merchant vessel after a brief skirmish. While the ship was being looted, Zindar stood in the brig, hating his bad luck. Two Nunqua guards conversed outside the cage.

"Spots," a skinny Willovian sailor sneered. Tattoos of skeletons and sea creatures covered his skin, and multiple gold loops pierced his eyebrows. "Have you ever seen anything so ugly?"

"I have." Zindar leaned against the bars with his arms crossed. "Met a half-breed once. Her name was Shanti."

The Nunqua guards turned toward Zindar. *"Tuv condelettka Shanti?"*

Zindar lifted his sleeve and showed them the scar across his forearm made by Shanti after the sword fight.

The Nunqua men hooted and hit each other on the shoulder. One said, *"Eh, cov Shanti sus mak,"* and left.

The Willovian captain, imprisoned in the brig with his crew, came over to Zindar and whispered, "Boy, if you get out of here, I want you to bargain for our lives. They're ignoring protocol and refusing to speak with me. You seem to have their attention. They can keep the goods. Tell them we want the ship and enough food to get to land."

The guard returned with a Nunqua sailor wearing golden earrings and a necklace with an emerald stone. "You know Shanti?"

"Are you the captain?" Zindar said.

"I'm the interpreter, but I can take you to the captain."

"Then yes, I know her."

Pirates escorted Zindar out of the brig and brought him up on deck. A Nunqua sailor, his gray braids dyed blue, inspected a silver mug, furs, a case of Willovian wine, and bolts of cloth. Gemstone rings adorned each of his stubby fingers. The captain looked over Zindar in the same appraising way he looked over the goods. *"Tuve wah condelettka Shanti?"*

"How do you know Shanti?" the interpreter said.

"I was a royal guard responsible for the princess's protection. Shanti . . . worked for me."

The captain spoke directly to Zindar; the interpreter stood to the side and translated. "If you're a foot soldier, how come you're on this ship?"

"Because I had a relationship with the princess. Shanti and the commanders didn't want a commoner to become king, so they conspired against me. I was banished from the military and given this." Zindar lifted his shirt to show them the four stripes across his back.

The two Nunqua men conversed. The captain slid a ruby ring off of his finger and gave it to Zindar.

"He asks that you come with us to Nunqua territory," the interpreter said. "The captain can guarantee your safety."

"I'll go only if the crew and captain remain unharmed and enough food is left on the ship for them to reach land."

The interpreter translated, and the captain nodded. *"Kreha."* He lifted his bejeweled fingers.

Zindar shook hands with the captain, then put the ruby ring on his finger. It was worth more than he would ever make swabbing decks, mending sails, and tying knots. The Nunqua weren't so bad after all. Maybe his luck was changing.

*

The interpreter examined the ship's logbook. "They intended to sell their cargo to the Murulians at far below market price," he said.

"The Willovians are trying to forge an alliance," the Nunqua captain said. "It's good we intercepted this ship."

"What about Zindar? You know what those marks on his back mean: he's a criminal."

"Aren't we all?" the captain said.

The interpreter frowned. "He can't be trusted."

"Zindar has connections to the royal family and Shanti."

The interpreter looked up from the logbook. "You believe his story, then?"

"No, but he may be valuable. We'll bring him to land and let the military extract information from him."

"Torture?" the interpreter said.

"Torture, money, drink, soft words, women cooing over him—whatever it takes. Tell the men that our guest is to be treated well. We're ready to sail back home with our newfound wealth."

18
SCAPEGOAT

BAYLA WORE A yellow armband as she searched the woods for the enemy. Lightning flashed, offering a temporary view of trees swaying in the wind.

They had been away from camp for three days, with little rest and even less to eat. Commander Jun, leader of the yellow team, was a different person when playing war. The game excited him, as did the storm. He insisted on making the yellow team hunt for prisoners in the bad weather. The storm would mask their movements, he said, giving them the advantage of surprise.

Twigs scratched her arms, and her stomach growled. Bayla leaned on the trunk of a dead tree that had yet to fall, and realized she was alone. She must have wandered away from her partner, another soldier with a yellow armband. Should she stay here? Thunder rippled across the sky. Spending the night in a downpour by herself would not be wise.

The sound of water rushing over rocks perked her ears. A creek ran alongside her team's site. If she could just find the creek, she could follow it back to where guards watched over the prisoners wearing red armbands.

Bayla moved toward the sound, arms up and protecting her face from branches.

She had just found the creek when someone jumped out of a tree and landed in front of her. The soldier wore a red armband to match his red hair.

"Hello, Pirro," she said.

"Hello, prisoner."

She smiled. "Not without a fight." Bayla pulled the ugly sword from its tattered sheath as raindrops pattered on her skin.

"Fine with me." Pirro unsheathed his sword.

She swung at him again and again, forgetting the rain, her heartbeat quickening.

He blocked her efforts but did not fight in earnest. "You're getting much better, Rega. Really, you are." Pirro's boots splashed in the ankle-deep water. He tripped her, and she plunged into the creek, her pants soaked through. "But I'm still taking you prisoner." Pirro offered his hand and helped her to a standing position. Lightning struck close, distinguishing the shadow of a figure watching them. Thunder cracked.

Did the soldier belong to the red or yellow team? Her eyes strained to see who approached. Features came into view: long hair, dark lips on a pale face, and spots on mottled skin. "Shanti?" But this man's girth far exceeded Shanti's, and he held a broad sword.

Pirro pushed Bayla away from the Nunqua warrior dressed in black. "Who are you? What do you want?"

The warrior cracked his neck from side to side, then ran toward Pirro. He attacked—his skill with the blade evident at once.

Watching the warrior duel Pirro was like watching a bear fight a dog.

"Find the others," Pirro said to her. "Stop the game!"

"Pirro!"

He turned to look at her. "Get out of here now!" Pirro bellowed, and collapsed into the creek. He tried to stand, but the stranger sliced his neck.

Wolves howled in the distance. The pack raced to her aid, but they were too far away. She planted her feet on the ground, held the worthless sword in front of her, ready to . . . to what?

The warrior glanced at her, then returned his attention to the body. "You are joking." His accent was thick. He bent over and cut off a lock of Pirro's red hair, putting it in his pocket. He disregarded Bayla while rummaging through Pirro's uniform.

Five soldiers emerged from the bushes and converged on the Nunqua warrior. Commander Jun carved a deep gash across his leg, but he broke free from the soldiers and limped into the trees.

"Stay with the princess," Commander Jun ordered. He chased after the warrior, disappearing into darkness.

Rain fell in sheets as thunder split the air. Two men lifted Pirro's body from the creek. More soldiers arrived at the scene and positioned themselves around Bayla and their fallen comrade.

A pack of growling wolves reached their position. Wet hackles rose stiffly along their spines.

"Do not touch the wolves," Bayla said.

She knelt next to Pirro. Red muscle blossomed out of the hole in his side, blood pouring out and mixing with the rain. A gaping wound split the flesh of his neck. Pirro's eyes were unblinking; no groans of suffering escaped his lips. He was gone.

Bayla wanted to touch Pirro's blood; it would connect her with him somehow. She wanted to lie on the ground next to him, die with him. Funny, wonderful, perfect Pirro had given his life to protect her.

*

The Nunqua was large, and he was wounded. He crashed through bushes and clambered over boulders that stood in his way. Jun followed the noisy warrior's trail.

The warrior stopped running and spun around, ready to fight.

The clanging of their swords mixed with the crashing thunder. Wind bent the treetops. Jun stabbed the warrior's abdomen. The

Nunqua buckled onto his hands and knees and made a hacking noise, his back hunched.

Jun's sword, in a two-handed grip, arced high above the head of his enemy.

An arrow whizzed under Jun's armpit. He dropped flat on the ground in the thick underbrush. The murmurings of men speaking a different language reached his ears. Their voices grew louder.

"You think you've killed me?" The large Nunqua warrior chortled. Then he moaned, gurgling blood and holding the skin of his belly together with one hand. "Eh, Willovian?"

Unfriendly figures came into view among the trees. They hefted swords, bows, and spiked maces. Their eyes shone silver in the dark. Jun crawled through the foliage, away from the Nunqua and toward the creek. He changed directions, not wanting to lead the warriors to the princess and his Willovian cohorts, and stopped when he reached a jumble of smooth boulders, some as big as houses. Jun concealed himself amid the boulders and listened. Pounding rain tapered to a steady drizzle. He stayed in that spot, shivering from cold, anger, and fear, until the sky grew lighter and the clouds dispersed with the first rays of dawn.

*

Commander Gy spoke with Jun, Vittorio, and Bayla in a sodden field, their uniforms muddy. A pink and red sunrise adorned the no longer stormy sky. A short distance away, Leanna wrapped Pirro's body in a cloth, and the soldiers lashed it onto two poles to be dragged behind his horse.

"I saw ten Nunqua at least," Jun said. "I say we find them before they find us."

Gy scratched the stubble on his chin. "What are they doing here?"

"They're after Bayla," Vittorio said. "They want to kidnap her."

"They had their chance," Gy said. "The warrior could have taken her but didn't."

Bayla, with a wolf sitting obediently at her feet, said, "It was Shanti. She's alone at camp. She went to town and sent a message telling the Nunqua where we'd be."

Gy closed his eyes. Only when Bayla mentioned Shanti's name did he realize the Nunqua's purpose. "I don't know how they found us, but I know why they're here. They're not after you, Rega. They're after Shanti."

"But she's one of them," Bayla said.

"She's a traitor to them!" he spat. "Madiza, the fortuneteller, predicted it. I should have figured it out sooner. Madiza foretold of warriors with marks across their arms like Shanti's, who would come looking for her."

"Madiza." Bayla's eyes narrowed "The hidden witch . . ." She straightened. "Commander Gy, Shanti is a threat to the safety of the men at this camp. Pirro is gone because of her. She will be removed from our presence."

Gy wanted to hit her for that remark. "Camp is over, you stupid woman. I'm tired of listening to you make her the scapegoat."

"You must see—"

"Shut up, Bayla!" Gy ignored the wolf growling at him. "Pirro died honorably in the service of Willovia. I'm in charge. His death is my fault, my responsibility. Shanti was right, only I didn't want to listen to her. You are selfish. I've waited a long time to hear you ask about the invasion at the castle, to show concern for your people, to take responsibility for your actions. We've given you too many chances. Camp is over." Gy faced Vittorio and Jun. "The trials are over. No final test is needed."

"What test?" Bayla said.

"Your guards will bring you back to the castle, Rega. I will take ten men and return Pirro's body to his family, offering my deepest, sincerest condolences for their loss."

The wolf lowered its head, yellow eyes fixed on Gy.

"What test?" Bayla said.

"It's my utmost wish, Rega, that you marry, soon, to somebody who cares more about Willovia than you do. And if that wolf bites me, may the spirits help you. I'll not constrain my actions any longer because of your gender or your privileged status as heiress to the Willovian throne.

"Commander Jun," Gy said, "you're in charge of the princess's protection. I know you have the skills to keep her safe. Do not think for one moment that you have fooled me. I know the reason you're here."

Jun nodded.

"Commander Vittorio, you're now in charge of supply and taking down the camp. The tents and other equipment will be returned to the permanent encampment. I believe you know the way. Commander Shanti will go with you, and you may take six other soldiers. Protect her and be on the lookout." He glared down at Bayla. "Although Shanti's quite capable of defending herself, a true leader always does his best to protect those under his command."

It felt liberating to finally say what needed to be said. Gy mounted his horse, feeling terrible about Pirro but better about himself. He was no stranger to combat. Young soldiers under his command had died before, and he had long ago learned to channel his grief into determination. He rode in front of the princess, fifty-eight soldiers, and one fallen corpse, over rough, mountainous terrain. Gy only hoped the Nunqua hadn't raided the camp already and found Shanti alone.

*

Shanti hiked away from camp, eventually reaching the peaceful river—her sanctuary as foretold by Madiza. She dug a hole in the ground. Beside her was a blanket, and Bayla's sword with the dragon carved on it. The edge of the barely used sword was still sharp. She sheathed the weapon, wrapped it in the blanket, and placed it in the hole. Then she covered the sword with dirt and stacked four rocks on top of the mound. The sturdy cairn of stone reached her knees. The ground near the river made a much better hiding place than the earlier location at the camp. Shanti rinsed the dirt off her hands in the river, then removed the warrior's knot from her hair.

Taking the sword after Bayla finished the obstacle course had been easy. No one saw her hide the weapon in her jacket, then slip away from the group to conceal it in her tent.

Shanti strolled through the woods at a leisurely pace. She touched the rough bark of trees, inspected wildflowers, and climbed the crumbling rock walls of abandoned buildings. A patch of black-berries grew along the trail. She picked a handful to eat, in no hurry to return to the empty camp. The earthy aroma of the woods filled her senses, and the lush forest radiated a calm serenity.

Two more days, and the soldiers would return from playing the game of war. Being excluded wasn't so horrible. She went to town and bought sweet-smelling soap, a local wine, and sugared cookies. She took a long soak in the river, cleaned and organized her tent, and even, purely out of curiosity, walked through the men's tents, trying to figure out who slept where. At night, she played cards with the cook. Still, a tiny annoyance, like the buzzing of a solitary fly on a beautiful summer's day, distracted her thoughts. Gy didn't trust her.

She returned to the campsite, and goose bumps rose along the back of her neck. Scanning the area, nothing appeared amiss. The cook had left for the afternoon to gather provisions from the town. Her intuition screamed that someone or something lurked close. Shanti drew her sword, alert to every sound: the babbling river, gently rustling leaves, singing birds, chirring insects. Out of the pavilion they came, bizarre specters from a forgotten dream, two men in billowing blue robes. Monks.

The monks were royal advisers, definitely not dangerous. She returned the sword to its sheath and headed toward the servants of Willovia. Although dressed the same, the two monks were complete opposites in physical appearance. Skin like wet parchment clung to the older monk's frail bones. His hair was thinning, and his eyes were rimmed in red. The younger monk looked healthy, wore spectacles, and observed the camp with great interest.

"We need to speak with Rega Bayla," the old monk said.

Shanti bowed to the scholarly monks. "She's not here."

"Not here? What, then? Training with the soldiers? Where is she?"

"Aren't you supposed to know?" Shanti asked.

The din of voices, rattling equipment, and horses' hooves sloshing over wet ground reached their ears. Commander Gy led the soldiers into camp. The storm must have caused them to end the game prematurely. A two-pole drag behind a horse carried a body wrapped in cloth. Leanna, somber faced on a dappled-gray mount, rode beside the corpse.

Shanti clasped her hands near her mouth and bit her knuckle. What had happened? What could have gone so wrong? She searched for Jun. He sat astride his horse. And Bayla and Vittorio were both alive. So who was swathed in the sheet?

She moved toward the body, the forest and soldiers fading from view, and pulled away the top of the sheet. Red hair peeked out of the covering. "Pirro."

Gy dismounted and stood beside her, the reins of his horse still in his hand.

"How?" was all she could say.

"Look again," he said. "The hair."

She uncovered more of the top of his head and noticed a tuft of hair cut away.

Shanti caressed the cold forehead. Her skin itched. She wanted to tear the flesh from her bones—the dichotomous flesh that made her such a freak. A Nunqua warrior had killed Pirro and made a trophy of his unusual red hair.

Madiza had predicted that the Nunqua would come. How had they known where to find her? She scratched the exposed skin of her arms until bright red patches formed. Two lines of tears rolled down her cheeks for Pirro.

19

AN INTERROGATION

BAYLA LISTENED TO the old monk speak without sentiment, his fingers interlaced over his chest. "Your father is dying of sickness, Rega. If you wish to see him one last time, you must return to the castle. He lies in bed waiting for you. His reign is at an end."

The commanders of the camp stood around the snarling dragon, carved by Aiden on the stump near her feet. She swayed and grasped Vittorio's arm for support. The wolf that she possessed paced back and forth in the trees. First Pirro, and now her father. Death was a reasonless, unstoppable wind.

"We leave tonight for the castle," Commander Gy said.

"We can't leave tonight," Shanti said. "Nunqua attack at night. We're safer here. Guards can be positioned around the perimeter of camp, twenty men at a time. No guards will be at the far posts. It's better to leave in the morning. The men can get some rest and food."

"This area is crawling with Nunqua," Jun said. "If we stay here, we're easy targets."

"Nunqua see ten times better in the dark than Willovians,"

Shanti said. "If we travel at night, we're dead. They probably followed you back to camp and are waiting."

"Which is why we have to leave. Tell me, Shanti. I cut open a warrior's stomach, and he laughed as he was dying—said I didn't kill him. What did he mean? And why are they after you?"

She closed her eyes. "It means Caravey is with them."

"General Delartay?" Gy frowned.

"Yes." Shanti said to Bayla, "I suggest you keep that uniform on. They won't expect the crown princess of Willovia to be wearing the dirty uniform of a soldier. Switch horses with someone, Rega. Your stallion is a sure sign of your status. If we're lucky, they don't already know you're here."

Bayla looked at the monks. She wanted to run from the robed ghouls, her demonic blue shadows, her escorts to the grave. She must know. "Are you here to chronicle my death?" she asked the monks. "Is my father really dying, or is it a story concocted to disguise the real reason you're here: to witness my demise."

An inscrutable smile played on the old monk's lips—a show of sympathy that seemed patently false. "We're here to take you to your father, that's all."

Commander Gy took the pipe out of his pocket and rolled it over in his hands. "We stay at camp tonight and leave tomorrow morning. That's final."

*

Tobain clasped his hands behind his back and wandered around camp as an outsider. Soldiers hid in bushes, behind rocks, and up trees in anticipation of an attack. He carried no weapons, yet devices of death were everywhere: bows and arrows, swords and shields, knives, and fatal traps to ensnare anyone attempting to enter the camp by stealth. Quiet tension permeated the woods. Tobian remained a serene oasis clad in blue, like a stream of water passing through a thicket of thorns. He was a student of life, not a combatant.

What did the Nunqua look like? Were they hideous beasts with cloven hooves, cats' eyes, and burnt skin? Storytellers scared children and adults alike with tales of the Nunqua: half-animal, half-devil atrocities that collected souls by cutting off the hair of their victims. God had cursed the wicked Nunqua with spotted skin and lips red as blood—the sadistic Nunqua who tied their prisoners to trees, inflicting a thousand cuts with poisonous blades. The poison did not kill immediately; it took days for the toxin to eat away the victim's brain and slowly stop his heart. Tobian wanted to see a Nunqua face to face, to know if the stories were true. A wolf, lying on its side in the shade of the pavilion and panting, watched him.

Are you a soldier dressed to look like a monk?" Bayla asked.

He turned toward the princess, whose face was clouded by sorrow. "Excuse me?"

"Are you a soldier, or a monk?"

"I'm a monk, Rega Bayla." He bowed, glancing at her dirty boots and scruffy uniform.

"You don't look like a monk. You look like a soldier. What's your name?"

She was testing him. "I have no name."

"Then what shall I call you when I see you at the castle?" No animosity tainted her words.

"You may call me your humble servant." They must have made an odd pair, he thought: the princess in the uniform of a common soldier, and him in the robes of a learned man.

Her eyes darted behind him, seeing . . . something. She took a step backward. The wolf sprang to her side. "I shall see you at the castle, then."

"Rega." He bowed again as she hurried away. The crown princess of Willovia was not what he had expected. The old monk slunk next to him, glaring greedily at Bayla.

"You've done very well indeed," his mentor breathed. "I've been in the presence of the princess many times at the castle. I watched her grow up. Rega Bayla has never approached me, talked with me of her own free will, asked my name." The covetous look on the old monk's face turned to spleen. "Never."

Bayla was quite the combination of sweet and dangerous. Tobian wondered what would be recorded about her in the history books for generations of monks to come. Why was so little of her future recorded, anyway? Would Baylova be a beneficent ruler or a tyrant? Would she be queen at all?

War with the Nunqua was coming to Willovia. The young man killed in the Hedgelands would not be the last to die. Tobian wanted to tell Rega Bayla about the future, the things he had read in the leather-bound books. But he was just an apprentice, sworn to secrecy, with no control over the timing of the revelations. His mentor was right: information could be a powerful thing. But the old monk had forgotten to mention that it could also be a burden.

*

Darkness slithered into camp, the threat of danger riding its back. Shanti didn't join the soldiers on guard. They viewed her warily because of her half-breed status and her absence from the game when the Nunqua attacked. She watched Jun command the men to ensure that the area was secure. He gestured in silence, his orders harsher than normal. Jun entered his tent and left the flap open. Now was her last chance. She might never see him again. Her desire for Jun exceeded her fear of rejection. She went into his tent and closed the flap. He stopped packing things into a bag and faced her.

Last chance. She had to know, even if it meant making a fool of herself. Shanti removed her sword and wristlet and placed them on the bed.

"You're full of secrets," he said.

"So interrogate me."

"You're a spy."

She shook her head. "They asked me to . . . but I chose to disregard those orders."

"The Nunqua won't attack tonight, because you're here. All our efforts are in vain."

"I don't know if they'll attack." She wanted to wrap herself around him like a blanket, but did he feel the same way? He had to. Even in this awkward situation, the pull between them was unmistakable.

"You call him Caravey; everyone else calls him General Delartay. He did more than train you to be a warrior. You're different, unique. You had a relationship with him."

Time for the truth, no matter how painful. "Three years ago," Shanti said. "It was a mistake. I was naive, stupid. Caravey demanded I return to Willovia to gather information for him. Tricking him into thinking I would follow his commands was the only way I could escape. After spending all that time training me, Caravey wouldn't permit me to leave without a reason that suited his purposes."

"So you are a spy?"

"That was never my intention," Shanti said.

"Willovian or Nunqua? What are you?"

"Both. I had nothing to do with Pirro's death, I swear it."

"If they're after you," Jun said, "why kill Pirro?"

She could think of only one answer. "Gitonk. Caravey wouldn't have given such an order unless the war was already under way. Gitonk's more thug than soldier. He idolizes Caravey and wants attention. I suspect Gitonk murdered Pirro."

"War?"

"If the monks are correct and King Magen dies, the Nunqua plan on invading Willovia."

"War?"

She nodded.

"You knew about this and didn't tell anyone? You're making it very hard for me to trust you."

"A woman addicted to beetle wings foretold the death of King Magen years ago, and I didn't believe her. Until now."

"What about this warrior Gitonk?" Jun said. "I cut open his stomach, and he said I didn't kill him."

She didn't want to tell him, didn't want to talk about Caravey now that she was so close to Jun. "Caravey has built a reputation for himself as a ruthless and cunning warrior, but in reality, he's a healer. He will heal Gitonk, as he has done before. Warriors under Caravey's command do not fear death; they fear only Caravey."

"How do I know you're not tricking me?" Jun said.

Shanti lifted her hands. The skin of her fingers changed as she remembered the cruelty she had endured: the flesh, blistered and cracked until it resembled the wood of a tree with the bark peeled off. "He forced my hands into a fire until I screamed, and then he healed me." She made visible a scar that ran from her cheek to her chin. "He cut my face with a sword when he thought I was using him to advance my own intentions, and then he healed me." She pulled up her shirt to show him the scar on her abdomen. "He stabbed me with a knife the day before I left the Nunqua to come to Willovia, and then healed me yet again, giving a warning that some fates are worse than death." She pulled down her shirt to cover her scarred belly. "Why would I be faithful to Caravey?"

Was it compassion she saw in his expression, or pity? She took a step toward him. "Are you going to put me in jail?"

"No."

She took another step closer to him. "Are you going to tell Commander Kyros what I've just told you?"

"Yes," Jun said.

"Don't," Shanti said. "Not everything. Tell Kyros about the invasion and the war but not about Caravey and me. That's personal information meant only for you. I'll inform Commander Gy and the Guardians of Willovia of the Nunqua's plans to invade."

Shanti took a final step until she was as close to Jun as she could get without touching him. "Will I see you again?" she asked.

He opened his mouth as if to say something, but no words came out. His chest rose and fell with each breath, and his eyes no longer had that hard, questioning look about them. Shanti closed her eyes and pressed her lips to his. Their first kiss might very well be their last, but she didn't care.

Jun put his arms around her and deepened the kiss.

Relief intermingled with other feelings that swirled in her system. Time had no meaning; her will was lost in a sea of emotion. Footsteps passed by the tent.

"You need to go," Jun said. "We can finish the interrogation at a better time."

"Is this how you interrogate all your informants?"

"Just you," he said.

"Where are you going after this?"

"After what you've just told me about invasion and war, I really don't know. I'll find you, I promise." He kissed her until they were once again pressed together in a prolonged embrace.

A twig snapped outside the tent. More footsteps. Hushed voices.

Jun released her, and Shanti gathered her weapons. She left the tent, not caring who saw. No lamps lit the darkness, and she dilated her eyes. Bayla, Gy, Leanna, and the monks sat inside the pavilion with other soldiers. Men crouched under bushes or lay prone on the ground, prepared for the worst.

Shanti went to her tent and stretched out on the cot. Sinful, sweet thoughts centered on Jun: the feel of his body, arms holding her tight, mind-numbing kisses. Jun wasn't pretending to care about her in order to get information. Was he?

It couldn't be.

*

No Nunqua attacked, and morning brought a sense of relief and discontent. Aiden, a leather pouch of coins strapped over one shoulder, and sword strapped to his back, approached Bayla. She sat alone on a log, feeding the wolf scraps of raw meat. Tents were being struck all around them, and soldiers stowed bundles in carts.

The wolf padded around Aiden's feet and waited to be petted like a tame dog.

"Did you win a bet?" she asked, her voice flat.

He jingled the heavy pouch. The money from the wager would go to whoever guessed the correct date Commander Jun and Commander Shanti got together. The bet seemed tactless now, insignificant. This money was going to a far worthier cause. "I'm taking donations for Pirro's family." Every soldier had contributed to the fund, the commanders giving a larger share.

She laughed and wiped away a tear. "I'm the richest person here—in all Willovia, for that matter—yet I have no money to give. They took me away from the castle with just the clothes on my back and my horse. Tax collectors and advisers handle the royal funds."

"It's okay." He longed to put his arm around her, but she was the crown princess—and a witch. "I just wanted to say good-bye."

"I can have him buried in the royal catacombs in a place of honor, wrapped in silk winding sheets, in a tomb carved by the finest craftsmen, with rare incense burned at the funeral."

"It's a generous offer, but I'm sure Pirro would rather be buried near his family." He watched her toss a piece of meat into the air. The wolf caught it in its jaws and gulped the morsel down. Aiden could hardly believe she was touching the remains of a dead animal—something she would not normally do. Her father was dying, and Bayla seemed hollow, on the edge of insanity. More than ever, he wanted to comfort her but kept his distance. Something dark seethed inside Bayla—a blackness that she needed to spit out before it grew and swallowed her whole.

"Good-bye, Rega."

"Aiden, please, you can call me Bayla."

*

Caravey touched the mythical dragon carved into the stump. Willovians—even out here in the middle of the woods, they managed to flaunt their presence with artistic flair. It was one of the things he admired about them. He picked a yellow leaf off the ground and gazed upward at the canopy of leaves soon to color themselves in autumn splendor. Warriors dressed in black explored the Willovian encampment. Holes in the ground served as markers to show where tents were placed; dirt paths gave clues to the soldiers' daily activities; guard posts had been hastily covered with brush. The pavilion remained. The Willovians hadn't burned it, because a fire would have exposed the camp's location sooner.

"General Delartay," Tracker said. Bands of leather circled his spotted biceps. "They have split into three groups."

"Is Shanti with the princess?" He twirled the yellow leaf in his fingers.

"No."

"No?" Caravey grunted.

"There's a town nearby, practically defenseless. We can take it to get food and something to drink."

"Shanti had better be doing her job," Delartay said, "or she'll suffer the consequences. I'll show her the true meaning of pain. Then again, she always liked that sort of thing."

The warriors around him snickered.

"What are your orders, General?" Tracker said.

Delartay dropped the leaf. "It's almost time. We'll go to the Outer Boundaries and join the other warriors waiting to invade. I know you boys are itching to fight."

"What about Shanti?"

"I'll deal with her later."

Caravey went inside the pavilion and pushed on a beam that held the roof in place. Sturdy construction. Walls were built waist high, and benches flanked each table. Blackened stone cooking structures bordered the pavilion. The facilities were big enough to feed perhaps fifty or sixty people. A lock of greasy hair hung from a string tied to the rafters. Caravey touched the odd ornament. "Shanti, my sweet." So she'd made an enemy at the encampment. It was good to know that Shanti, even when surrounded by

Willovians, retained her Nunqua culture. He had taught her well. She was bound to reveal her real self even though he had ordered her not to. Her biggest fault was a propensity for the truth. Shanti spoke her mind no matter how much trouble it got her into.

Gitonk lay wounded on a table inside the pavilion and tied a lock of hair onto a string, a multicolored necklace of blond, brown, black, and now red. "You brainless maggot," Caravey said. "You ruined our chance at surprise." He examined Gitonk's wound, crusted with blood and in the process of healing. "Next time, we leave you to die. You're slowing us down. One day, maybe two, and the cut will be closed."

"Sorry, General," Gitonk said. "The Willovian who injured me had some skills. I was surprised, that's all."

Gitonk and every other person he had ever cured recovered in a matter of days. Shanti's wounds healed within the space of a few breaths, the scars left as reminders—scars that she could easily make disappear. Caravey doubted that she even comprehended the extent of her powers. If only Shanti would acknowledge being a witch, her greatness would be legendary.

A peculiar yelp echoed in the woods. Caravey left the pavilion to investigate. Warriors lingered about a dead animal—a wolf with an arrow buried in its gut. "Your dinner?" he said to the Nunqua holding a crossbow.

"It was watching us, General, I swear." The warrior pointed two fingers to his eyes. "It had the look of a demon. The wolf was possessed. Not a good omen. I don't like it here."

Caravey wedged his boot under the wolf's snout and lifted its limp head. The animal's eyes opened, and its ribs heaved. A squealing inhalation contorted its chest. Startled warriors jumped away from the solitary creature.

*

Bayla, surrounded by soldiers, clutched the saddle horn of the roan mare she rode. She leaned on the mare's neck for support. A sharp stitch in her side made it hard to breathe. Through the eyes of the wolf she possessed, she watched Nunqua warriors meander around the camp in the Hedgelands. They searched the grounds, reclined inside the pavilion. Spotted faces of men stared down at her—no, at the wolf. A crossbow came into view, fired another arrow. A sharp pain, then nothing.

The vision vanished as the wolf closed its eyes, dead.

20

WAR

"THE NUNQUA DESIRE Willovia," Shanti told several Guardians inside the inn. Neither ale nor food was on the table, and the ashes lay cold in the fireplace. Somber faces took in her words. Gy was present, along with the village undertaker, the wealthy landowner and his teenage son, the innkeeper, a farmer, and Madiza, her hair a white crown, and fine wrinkles softening her pleasant face.

"Food and resources are abundant here. Willovia is bordered by the sea, with access to other lands." Shanti stared into the flame of a candle. "They've been planning a large-scale invasion for years. As soon as King Magen dies, they'll attack at the Outer Boundaries."

"We must try to stop an invasion with diplomacy," the landowner said. "Lord Argu rules the Nunqua. Talks can be established."

"Lord Argu is a coward and a fool," Shanti said. "The military rules the realm. The warriors consume the resources. They cut down the harvest to feast but do not plant seeds for future growth. That's why they want Willovia."

"We fight!" Gy said. "My children will not grow up ruled by the Nunqua."

"What about Rega Bayla?" Madiza said.

"She didn't pass the trials or face the final test," Gy answered. "She failed."

The farmer's jaws clenched and unclenched as he gnawed a quid of tobacco. He spat into a cup. "Then we cannot endorse her as queen. The Guardians must unite to seat another on the throne— someone more suitable to the task. Gy"—he spit again—"you shall be king."

Shanti's jaw dropped. It was so obvious! Why hadn't she seen it before? If Bayla, the last of the royal bloodline, failed, Gy would become king!

Madiza pulled an angora shawl tight around her shoulders. "There are those loyal to the monarchy who will fight to put Bayla on the throne. Willovia cannot withstand two wars at the same time: civil war and war with the Nunqua."

"I agree," Gy said.

"I must protest." Shanti viewed Gy with a new understanding. He did not want Bayla to fail, because then he would bear the heavy weight of the crown. "It's a Guardian's duty to do what's best for Willovia. She failed. Bayla is not what the kingdom needs now that we're facing war."

"If we take her from power," Madiza said, "the country is conquered by the Nunqua, or worse. I tried to warn you, Shanti. She has potential."

"You would let a girl of not even twenty years command the military?"

"No," Gy said. "*I* command the military. Commander Kyros will take charge of matters at the castle. Bayla will be crowned Baylova, a queen in name only."

Shanti spread her hand over a burning candle and put the flame out with her palm. "The puppet queen, false monarch of Willovia, a lie to the people. Tell me, Gy, do you plan on informing Baylova that her royal decrees are to be the ravings of a worthless monarch? She's a mute, dressed in fine robes with precious jewels glued to her skin. Body art to cover her flaws. Lips sewn shut with a golden needle and thread."

Gy rubbed his forehead and groaned. "We fight the Nunqua first! Then we worry about Baylova. Hopefully, by the time hostilities with the Nunqua have ended, she will have married, and we won't have to oust her from power. Willovia will have a new king."

"Then she'll be a married puppet, mute and blind, her only purpose to breed—"

"Damn it, Shanti!" Gy glanced around the room. "What are the opinions of the Guardians present?"

"The threat of the Nunqua is greater and must be dealt with first." The farmer spat in the cup for emphasis.

The wealthy landowner agreed. "Baylova will be crowned queen. Gy will lead the military."

"I concur." The undertaker nodded his narrow head.

Madiza spoke to Shanti. "Please, you have to believe. She can help Willovia. She's the only one who can help you. Bayla can sever the ties that bind you to him. Power is given for a reason."

"Give us your vote, Shanti," Gy said. "What are your thoughts?"

Her thoughts centered on Jun and his constant badgering. Was she Willovian or Nunqua? She reached out her hand and snuffed the flame of another candle with her palm. Quiet faces watched her, waiting for a response. She stood, brown uniform hugging her like a second skin, hair bound tight in the warrior's knot, the sword given her by General Caravey Delartay strapped across her back, the wristlet of poisoned darts buckled to her scarred arm. Shanti breathed deeply; a suffocating ache crushed her spirit. "I resign," she said.

"Don't do this." A measure of pleading infused Gy's voice.

"I will no longer serve as a commander in the Willovian military or as a soldier. I refuse to fight under a false queen."

"You gave an oath to do what is best for Willovia!" Gy shouted.

"So did you!" Her fist hit the table like a hammer. "What did we accomplish at camp? Nothing! Never have I felt so useless!"

Shanti's chin quivered. "I'll stay in Willovia and find other work. And remain voiceless." She banged open the door and stormed out of the room.

Madiza trailed, trying to catch up. "Wait, Shanti. Wait."

Shanti got on her horse and galloped away from the inn, the village, Gy, and Madiza. She returned to her temporary room at the encampment, collected her money and belongings, put on a riding skirt, with pants underneath, and a warm sweater, and let her hair fall loose down her back.

Alone in the forest with only her horse for company, Shanti built a bonfire. The brown uniform burned. Her life as a Willovian soldier no longer existed. She picked up an orange leaf, realizing that time was short. The Nunqua would soon attack. The scars on her arms vanished as she willed the skin smooth. She was ready to build a new life.

*

Monks covered the body of King Magen with a red blanket. They carried the corpse, withered from disease, out of the bedroom, through the castle, and into their domicile. A stately room draped in red awaited the entourage. Tobian stood beside his master, ready to learn about this most important task. Only monks were permitted to participate in the funeral preparations. One of the brotherhood examined a table covered with red velvet and the king's garments. He picked lint off the splendid uniform, shined the black boots, polished the king's one bejeweled ring to be entombed with him. The king was stripped, and a red cloth placed over his manhood. Monks washed the body. After cleansing, a tube and a large glass container were brought to the body to siphon out fluids.

Tobian gazed uneasily at the equipment that used negative pressure to suck out the liquid. He lowered his eyes, unable to watch the knife cut open the king's side, or the tube being pushed through flesh and muscle. The brothers worked quietly, speaking only when necessary. Blood and other body fluids dribbled and sloshed inside the container. A lock of the king's hair and a fingernail from his right hand were also put into the vessel.

The old monk turned to his apprentice. "Do you need to sit down, my brother?"

"I'm fine." He did not want to appear as weak as he felt.

"Go with the vessel," the old monk said. "It's important to see that part of the ritual, too."

Tobian followed three of his brother monks into an adjoining room. He found a chair and sat, trying not to faint dead away. Someone asked if he was all right. He lied with a nod.

The men in charge of the vessel shed their blue robes to work in blue breeches and white shirts, with sleeves rolled up. For all appearances, the room was an organized and well-stocked apothecary. Expensive jars filled with unknown substances lined shelves on the walls. A monk poured a clear solution into the vessel containing the king's blood. The liquid sizzled, then darkened. The container was placed on a hot stove. Jars of strange herbs were added. The brew bubbled thickly. Empty glass beakers with silver clawed feet waited nearby to be filled with the morbid concoction. Royal blood was the essential ingredient of the potion enabling the drinker to journey into the future—the dark science of the monks.

The old monk approached. "It's being boiled to take out the impurities, the sickness. The process will not be complete until tomorrow, and the potion will not be ready for consumption for several days."

Tobian removed his spectacles and rubbed his eyes.

"The relationship is symbiotic," the monk said. "The royals of Willovia derive their power from our knowledge of the future, and we derive our power from them. It's been this way for two centuries. We follow the traditions of the monks who came before us."

"So our knowledge comes at a price," Tobian said.

"King Magen was destined to die. We couldn't save him. Our actions are justified."

"Are the royals aware? Did King Magen know? Does Baylova

know? If our actions are justified, then tell Baylova. See if our presence is still desired at the castle."

"You'll understand soon enough." The old monk interlaced his fingers over his chest. "The fate of Willovia resides with us."

*

Jun moved deep beneath the castle. Water dripped and echoed in a series of natural caverns in the hard rock of the seashore. Oil lamps lit the underground labyrinth. Graceful formations, carved by flowing water, smoldered in hues of copper, amber, beige, and pink. Drops fell from stalactites into a pond, the ripples fanning outward in perfect circles. High-level advisers and royal guards used these caves to conduct secret meetings. The rooms of stone were comfortable, dry, and well stocked for emergencies.

Jun spotted Baylova in a red dress of mourning. The young queen's arms were folded across her chest, her posture putting off anyone who wanted to get close to her. One painted dragonfly shimmered on her wrist, and a blue sapphire adorned a black satin choker around her neck. Elaborate braids decorated her hair. She walked with Commander Kyros and seemed out of place in the caves, like an expensive doll mistakenly placed among tin soldiers.

"She's still a threat," Kyros said, "especially now that the Nunqua have invaded the Outer Boundaries and occupy the region."

"Where is she?"

"No one knows, not even Commander Gy. It's essential for the security of Willovia that we find her and bring her to the castle. We can observe her here, watch for signs of treachery."

"I agree, however . . ." Baylova noticed Jun and stopped walking.

Jun bowed to the newly appointed queen.

"Commander Kyros, will you excuse us for a moment." Kyros left them alone. "I should have known. No one who simply manages supply is allowed in these caves. Did my father send you to camp to spy on me?"

"No. I was sent by Commander Kyros to spy on Shanti, Bay-y-ylova." He had almost slipped and called her "Bayla." She was no longer Bayla, but Queen Baylova. Back at camp, he had said she would make a good leader someday, but now it upset him that she had the power to banish him from the Willovian military with only a word. He had served Willovia with honor and distinction for many years, paid his dues to become a commander, sacrificed much, only to answer to her now? She was too inexperienced to make decisions overriding his own.

"Is something wrong, Commander?" she said.

"Sorry. It's hard to believe." Her imperial facade could not hide how tired she looked. Jun tried to remember that she hadn't asked for this responsibility.

"Have you seen Shanti?" she asked.

"Not since camp. I don't know where she is." He stared at the sapphire nestled in the hollow of her throat. "I'm sorry about your father."

"Thank you." She left and returned to continue her conversation with Commander Kyros.

Jun pondered the reality that Bayla was now the commander of his commander. It just wasn't right.

*

Shanti cleaned the newborn babe, then wrapped her tightly in a woven blanket. The infant smelled powdery fresh. She stroked the soft head. The healthy baby closed its eyes, and Shanti laid the bundle next to the exhausted mother. Old Geyas, the village midwife, entered the room with a tray of food. Shanti worked as her apprentice, helping deliver three babies so far under Geyas's supervision. No longer did she feel useless.

Gray clouds drifted low in the sky. Shanti stoked the fire in a hearth to warm the bedroom. Winter had reached Willovia, although no snow blanketed the ground—merely an icy frost. War seemed far away. The Nunqua had invaded the Outer Boundaries, killing soldiers and creeping farther into Willovian territory. Casualties befell both sides, with no frontrunners in the conflict. Shanti held her tongue and refused to speak of the war, knowing she could never choose sides. She turned away from conversations about the accursed Nunqua, swallowing her anger at the hardhearted remarks. The townspeople fed on lies and spread them with abandon. Cloven hooves? Bestiality? Nonsense!

"A soldier is here to see you." Geyas's face furrowed with a grin, and she winked. "Quite handsome."

The mother's eyes shone brightly.

"No, my child." Old Geyas gently patted the new mother's arm. "Your husband's still fighting in the war. This man wishes to speak with Shanti."

Jun! Jun had said he would find her. Shanti raced outside into the freezing air, sliding gracefully on ice just outside the door. Her joy faded at the sight. Commander Kyros and six royal guards were waiting for her.

Flourishes of gold embellished the sleeves of his blue and white uniform. He removed a scroll from his jacket but didn't unfurl it. "Queen Baylova requests your presence at the castle."

Old Geyas listened at the door. Her hand touched her throat. "Queen Baylova!"

"Requests?" Shanti said, a mist visible with each breath.

"You're being summoned as a royal adviser. Your knowledge of Nunqua customs is essential to Her Majesty in conducting the war."

"What if I refuse?"

He tapped the scroll in the palm of his hand. "You cannot refuse. It is a royal decree with the seal of Her Majesty. If you do not comply, you'll be sent to prison as a Nunqua conspirator."

Shanti took a step backward and dug the ball of her foot into the frozen ground. "Six guards to escort me to the castle, not to mention such a high-ranking commander. I'm flattered. How honorably you serve the queen. Or is it, perhaps, the other way around."

"The position of adviser pays quite well, I assure you. Why wouldn't you take it? Unless, of course, you're not loyal to Willovia."

"I'm needed as an apprentice to Geyas," Shanti said.

"A midwife?" Kyros laughed. "Do you think these good people would let you touch their children if they knew what you are?"

A tiny baby's cry came from inside the home. Shanti came out of her fighting stance. "I cannot leave."

"You will leave." He moved toward her and held out the scroll. Shanti hesitated before taking it. Kyros seized her wrist, squeezing hard. He pushed her sleeve up with an odd look on his face. No scars marred her forearm. "Get your things. My men will accompany you. There's a carriage at the stables, better traveling accommodations than you're used to, I'm sure. You can hook your horse to the carriage." He dropped her wrist and moved toward Geyas, still standing in the doorway and listening to every word. "My dear woman, you shall be compensated for the loss of your apprentice. May I inquire where my men and I might find some food?"

Kyros, respectable in his uniform during time of war, charmed Geyas and the whole village. The soldiers were given a hearty meal for free. Unmarried ladies flirted and smiled coyly at Kyros, who only nodded politely to them.

Guards watched Shanti pack her possessions into two bags. She lifted the mattress of her bed to retrieve her sword and wristlet and stow them away, then threw a woolen cloak over her shoulders and lifted the hood over her head. She hugged Geyas, saying good-bye, and hooked her horse to the carriage for the long trip. The guards rode on horses, leaving her alone inside the covered carriage, which felt like a cage. She willed the scars on her arms to reappear—the markings of a warrior.

It surprised her to see the castle in the distance, the capital city of Willovia, and the sea. She had expected to be transported to a dreary camp surrounded by fences and armed guards, shoved inside by a laughing Commander Kyros to join other Nunqua as a prisoner of war.

The carriage passed through the heavily guarded gate and stopped in front of the main doors of the castle, reserved for royalty and dignitaries. Servants quickly attended to Shanti's horse and belongings. Kyros escorted her into the grand reception room, where a maid took her cloak. How peculiar to be treated like an honored guest! All her plans to avoid drawing attention to herself, while still performing meaningful work, for the duration of the war had been sabotaged. Something foul was afoot—something foul indeed!

21
A LUXURIOUS CAGE

OUT OF BOREDOM, Shanti investigated the oak armoires and cabinets in her posh room in the castle. She found nothing interesting. The fire burning in the hearth kept the cold away. The room had bare stone walls, blue overstuffed chairs, thick carpet, and ivory-colored drapes. A hawk flew onto the ledge of a closed window and tapped with its beak on the glass pane. Shanti banged the window frame with the heel of her hand and yanked it open. Cold air blew in, but the hawk flew away. Perhaps it was an authentic creature, not under Baylova's control.

She reclined in a chair with her feet tucked under her skirt. The brown hawk returned and hopped inside. Shanti took a cloth from one of the drawers, and folding it over her arm to make a pad, she whistled. The bird twisted its head.

"Come on, come on . . ." She whistled again. "Just sit here on my arm. I won't bite if you won't."

The hawk bobbed up and down. It spread its wings and glided to her outstretched arm, filling Shanti with awe. Sharp talons clenched the cloth and pinched her skin. The hawk was the size of a pullet hen but lighter. Shanti extended her fingers toward the feathers of its breast to touch the brown plumage. Someone knocked on the door, and the hawk flew off her arm, touched down on the windowsill, and soared away from the castle. A servant brought in food: cheese, meats, and a decanter of wine with a cup. Shanti sat in the chair and folded her feet beneath her once again, thankful for the grub. She fell asleep waiting for the hawk to return, or the queen to enter.

"Wake up."

Her head snapped off the chair, and she snorted softly. "Bayla?"

"Please, stay where you are. I'm tired of everyone treating me so . . . nice. You look different. I've never seen you wear anything other than the uniform."

Shanti had seen Bayla clothed in the expensive attire of royalty many times. Now she wore a red dress with a silk sash. Barrettes sparkled with diamonds in her glossy hair, and a painted golden snake wrapped around her wrist. Shadows dimmed the skin around her eyes. A wisp of wind could have blown the fragile queen down, shattering her into a thousand pieces.

"How are you?" Shanti said, stunned by Bayla's sickly pallor.

Bayla took pieces of meat from the tray and went to the windowsill. "Do you want the truth, or shall I recite the official version?"

"I can guess the official version for myself. Let's see, you're still very emotional over the loss of your father but are easing nicely into your new duties and thank everyone for their support at this most difficult time."

The hawk returned to the window. It came inside and grabbed bits of meat out of Bayla's hand with its hooked beak. "I've been giving him food for a few years now," she said. "He's quite tame." She scratched the top of the bird's head.

"Why am I being asked to serve as an adviser?"

"Because of your knowledge of Nunqua culture," Baylova said. "You'll stay at the castle. A room is prepared for you."

"Whose idea is this?"

"Mine." She stared out the window.

"And what if I leave?" Shanti asked.

"These are dangerous times. Women are being urged not to walk the streets or ride alone. It's unwise for you to leave the castle grounds."

"Just great," Shanti sneered.

"Would you prefer other accommodations?"

"Why can't I stay in the village as a midwife? It's far from the fighting."

"Because of who you are." Baylova finished feeding the hawk. "You'll join me for dinner tonight at the feast. The tailor will have something appropriate for you to wear. Please be sure to see him. No need to worry about money. Your pay as a royal adviser is substantial."

*

Shanti visited the tailor, who fashioned a simple dress with a gathered bodice, form-fitting sleeves, and a smooth lining that felt cool on her skin. The dress was beautiful and comfortable—much nicer than the hideous blue and white uniform they wanted her to wear as Bayla's personal guard.

She dined with the Daughters of Fortunate Birth, in the all-important place next to the queen. They sat at a round table decorated with flowers. Shanti ate tender meat drenched in rich gravy, with buttered potatoes. Nothing green touched her gold-rimmed plate. A carafe of red wine sat in front of her, her goblet over half full. The Fortunate Daughters wrinkled their noses in disgust as they watched Shanti enjoy the meal. Only a small amount of vegetables, along with a tiny morsel of bread, graced Baylova's plate. The other women's plates mirrored the queen's, and they drank the same white wine.

"Your name is Shanti, is it not?" someone asked.

"Yes."

"You look familiar," a golden-haired woman said, her eyelids narrowed in scrutiny.

"I'm surprised you don't remember me," Shanti said.

Her eyelids narrowed even further into slits. "How do I know you?"

"Perhaps I'm dressed more appropriately for the castle now." Shanti wiped dark gravy from her lips with a white napkin.

"Although you still haven't visited the painter for body art," Baylova said.

"Not like it would help." Shanti scooped a spoonful of potatoes off her plate and into her mouth.

A scowl twisted the face of the golden-haired woman. "Baylova's personal guard. So you do speak. Personal guard to royal adviser in one year—impressive!"

"You haven't changed a bit." Shanti gulped down wine and smacked her lips.

"You ought to be careful eating like that," said a woman with red ringlets tumbling down the sides of her face. "A man doesn't appreciate a woman who eats as if she were famished."

Another Fortunate Daughter, with small butterflies painted just above the neckline of her dress, decided to join in. "Or drinks as if dying of thirst."

The laughter at the table did not upset Shanti in the least. "From my perspective, a man appreciates a woman with an appetite. And a mind of her own."

"Ah, yes," the golden-haired woman said, "I understand you're popular with the soldiers. It is easy to see why—*very* easy, from what I hear."

A server came by holding a tray of desserts. "Oh, cake!" Shanti said. She took a plate and thanked the server. Baylova refused the sweets being offered, and the Fortunate Daughters followed the queen's lead. Several of the women all but drooled as they watched Shanti enjoy the sugary treat.

"So, Shanti," the golden-haired woman said, "where are you from?"

"A small, impoverished village far from here." She glanced slyly at Bayla before continuing. "Raised by a hag. When I was old enough, she sold me to the Nunqua to work as a slave. Before I left, though, the hag gave me poisoned darts. You remember the wristlet I wore as Baylova's guard, don't you? The poison is so powerful, only the most minuscule amount under the skin is enough to kill. The hag also taught me"—she took another bite of cake—"incantations for my protection. I was forced to work as a sexual slave to a cruel yet powerful military leader."

The Fortunate Daughters sat in silence, caught up in Shanti's lurid tale.

"But I grew tired of the Nunqua and decided to return to Willovia—change sides. As I left, out of jealousy, I made sure my master would never find another slave to pleasure with his nightly biddings." The women at the table leaned forward, and Shanti lowered her voice, "No other would yield to the painfully sweet, forbidden desires he demanded so patiently and skillfully. I made certain I was the last woman he would tie up, undress, and leave exposed, shaking with anticipation before warm hands—"

"Shanti," Bayla said.

"What?" She ate her last piece of cake, then licked the spoon. "You don't want to hear the details?"

"Perhaps not at the dinner table."

"Some other time, then," Shanti said.

The Fortunate Daughters regained their sense of decorum and sat straight in their chairs once more, busying themselves with napkins or silverware and trying to hide their disappointment at missing the rest of Shanti's story.

*

Shanti saw him conversing with a group of people after the feast. He was wearing a wool coat, black pants, and fine boots. Jun's eyes met hers from across the room, his face expressionless. He turned his back to her in an unmistakable signal: *keep away.*

All around her, castle guests enjoyed each other's company. Shanti felt out of place, ignored, a chicken among peacocks. Royal guards stood like statues at doors. She was no longer one of them, but neither did she fit into high society. Somber music played in the great hall—a melancholy air to match her mood.

She watched Jun, waiting for a sign of acknowledgment. Nothing. Meanwhile, the Daughters of Fortunate Birth hung on his every word. They stood close to him. *Too* close. He put his arm around the waist of the golden-haired woman, lowered his head, and laughed. Were they laughing at her? Maybe it had been a mistake to lie to the women about being a sex slave. The foulest of all jail cells would be preferable to this hell.

She retreated to a balcony overlooking the sea. The salty smell reminded her of fish and clumps of rotting seaweed washed up on a beach, but the frigid breeze consoled her spirit. Someone joined her on the balcony. Her hopes soared, then sank.

"What, may I ask, are you doing out here?" Commander Kyros said. "I believe the party's inside."

She gazed out at the stars, the half moon, the lights from Willovian ships docked in the distance.

He leaned on the stone barrier, swirling a cup of caramel-colored brandy. "I suppose this isn't your type of party. You prefer less civilized accommodations."

"Who requested I be assigned as an adviser?"

"I convinced Baylova to bring you here." Sipping his drink, Kyros watched the people inside the castle. "Do you actually think Jun cares for you, Shanti? Your feelings for him are obvious. He was doing his job, that's all. I've known Jun for a long time. He has a way of getting women to do whatever he wants—even you. It's the reason I chose him to spy on you in the Hedgelands."

A shiver ran up her spine at the way Kyros looked at her.

He moved the hair out of her face with his hand. "Jump," he

whispered. "End it. The Nunqua are hunting you, Baylova hates you, Commander Gy distrusts you, Jun doesn't love you, and I control you." He lifted a lock of her hair and pressed it to his lips. "Jump."

"You first," she said.

He stroked her hair gently. Anyone glancing out the window at the balcony would think them lovers. "Still so defiant? If you leave the castle grounds without an escort, the guards have orders to bring you back using any force necessary. It would save us the trouble if you just ended it now. Jump."

"Trying to plant the seeds of doubt in my feeble mind, Kyros? Think you can manipulate me as you manipulate Bayla? Shall I lean on you for strength? Or do you just wonder what it's like to be with a Nunqua woman?"

Kyros leaned in close. "Don't flatter yourself." He pulled away, tasting his drink. "You should join the party. You're missing all the fun." He left her alone on the balcony to digest his malicious words.

"Some fun." Shanti returned inside and walked away from the noise and the crowd. Exploring some of the castle's many empty rooms, she investigated a long, quiet portrait room, where faces of past monarchs stared down on her. Life-size paintings of men, women, and children, in elaborate frames, covered the walls of blue. Some rulers held branches; others held swords. All appeared grim.

A king with red-rimmed eyes, in old-fashioned attire, looked like a ghoul ready to whisper atrocities into innocent ears. He clutched a book in one hand, an empty glass beaker with silver clawed feet in the other. Next to him was a lion of a king: brawny, with a bearskin cloak on his shoulders. Trees and mountains graced the background. The small letter "g," secret symbol of the Guardians of Willovia, decorated his shield, and a hawk perched on his gloved hand.

She viewed the portrait of King Magen. He appeared vigorous, without any sign of the sickness that had ended his life. A gold chain weighted his shoulders, and clouds loomed in the shadowy background. Many symbols were hidden in the portraits. Shanti wished she knew what they meant, wished she knew the names and stories of the royals.

Next to the picture of King Magen was a portrait of a young queen, Baylova's mother, Serova. A barely noticeable skull was concealed in the folds of Serova's skirt, and a wolf rested at her feet. The queen held a bundle signifying the baby boy she had lost in childbirth. A dark opal bracelet adorned her wrist.

Madiza's bracelet! It had once belonged to Queen Serova. It was the bracelet shimmering on Madiza's wrist when Shanti was put under the sleeping spell and her fortune read. How did Madiza get it? Gy had said that Bayla inherited her power from her mother. Queen Serova was a witch. Why, then, didn't Bayla inherit the bracelet?

Shanti investigated other rooms of the castle: a trophy room with stuffed animal heads on the wall and exotic pelts on the floor. She doubted that Bayla ever entered such a space. There was also a library, lined with dusty books. It might be an interesting place to spend an afternoon. Shanti roamed the confusing passages of the castle, trying to find her own room. She finally located the correct door . . . and found Jun waiting inside.

"What the hell were you doing with Kyros on the balcony?" he said.

Kyros, that snake. He had wanted Jun to see them together. He wanted to make Jun jealous. And Jun was jealous! Shanti quickly closed the gap between them.

He kissed her like a man starving, and she knew at once that he had no interest in the Daughters of Fortunate Birth. "Sold as a sex slave to the Nunqua?" he said.

"It was a joke."

"This isn't camp. People here are different, more devious than you can imagine. They're watching you. Even the smallest sign of treachery will get you killed."

"If I have to stay here against my will, I might as well have some fun."

"You need to be careful. So what did Kyros say on the balcony."

"He said he loved me and wanted to marry me."

"Seriously, what did he say?"

"He told me my life wasn't worth living and I should jump off the balcony."

"I had every intention of finding you. Kyros knows I'm keeping secrets. If I tell him the Nunqua sent you here as a spy, you're as good as dead. Does Commander Gy know about you?"

"I'm sure he suspects."

"Gy might be the only one who can get you out of this mess . . . I have to leave tomorrow."

An odd lump of emotion formed in her throat—a new phenomenon she had never felt before.

"Kyros is sending me to the Outer Boundaries. I'll find you when I get back." He touched the spots emerging above her eye. "I promise." Jun pushed up her sleeves to see the scars. "I've heard a rumor," he said.

She willed the scars to disappear.

"You're a witch."

"No."

He questioned her with a look.

"My skin changes, that's all."

"You can touch Bayla and control animals."

"Coincidence," she said.

"Denial," Jun countered. "Be careful. Watch what you say, and don't trust Kyros."

Locked in each other's arms, they whispered words of longing kept hidden for too long. Jun stayed late into the night. He said a final farewell, opened a window, and hoisted a leg outside.

She grabbed his arm to stop him. "What are you doing!" They were on the third floor.

He jumped, his head and torso visible in the window. "There's a ledge. It goes halfway around the castle. You're being watched, remember. I can't go out that door."

Shanti stuck her head outside. Jun's heels hung off the icy edge. He shuffled along the rock wall two stories above the ground, in the dark, showing no hint of fear.

22

BLOOD ON HER HANDS

B AYLA LIFTED A paintbrush from a bench and felt the bristles with the palm of her hand. She had always loved the organized chaos of this room, with every hue of paint splashed about and different projects yet to be finished on work stands and easels. The artists' workshop, located in an informal wing of the castle, was so much messier than the rest of the castle, and a great place to explore.

"Hello, Baylova."

She blushed upon seeing that the old painter, the talented craftsman who had worked at the castle for years, was gone. "Aiden! What are you doing here?"

"I work here. What will it be today, Your Majesty?"

"I thought you were fighting at the Outer Boundaries."

"I was. Commander Gy sent me here. Consider me part of your royal guard. Besides, working conditions are better at the castle than at the Outer Boundaries."

"Royal guard?" He wore the clothes of a commoner.

Aiden opened a drawer, and there, behind pots of powdered dye, was his sword. A bow and several arrows were hidden inside a cabinet. Bayla's eyebrows rose when he picked up a large brush and pulled off the end to expose a wickedly sharp blade.

"I see," she said, astonished at the arsenal. "I never realized what a dangerous job the castle artist has."

They sat on three-legged stools separated by a paint-spattered table.

"Well?" he asked.

She put her hand on the table. "Surprise me."

"Hmm . . . A wolf would take too long. I know . . ." He took her hand.

Watching him draw the lines of the picture onto her skin, she reflected back to the time he carved the dragon into the tree stump at camp. "Will you be joining us for the castle feast tonight?" she said.

"Not today." He kept his eyes on his work.

"Why not? The castle artist is a respected position."

"I know." He laughed. "My father told me."

"Your father?" She examined him closely. "I've been so blind. Your father's the castle artist."

"My father's the castle artist and a Guardian of Willovia," he said. "And will you please stop moving."

"A *what* of Willovia?"

"Nothing. I mean, he's a soldier, a royal guard."

"How come I've never seen you at the castle before?"

"I guess I haven't come here much." He changed brushes. "My father did tell me a few things about you, though. He said that when you were very little, you liked to run away from your governess and visit him here when your parents were busy. He would cover the floor with rags, give you brushes and paint, and let you spend hours making a colorful mess of yourself."

Bayla gazed into the distance. "I don't remember that. Clearly, you have inherited his skill."

Aiden finished. He held her hand, trying not to smear the paint. "I'm sorry about King Magen."

He had nice hands: calluses, a smudge or two of paint, and a few scratches. She wasn't sure whether she should ask him about the war. "I will see you later, right?"

"I'll be here."

She took her hand back and got up to leave.

"Baylova," he said, and nodded. She retreated to her large bedroom and locked the door. Once inside, she dropped her noble facade, ran across the room, and concealed herself in a tight corner. Two red rosebuds were drawn on her wrist to match the red of her dress. Green leaves and thorny stems intertwined and extended up her forearm. She hoped she interpreted its meaning correctly. She kissed one of the rosebuds.

It had always been Aiden.

*

Baylova watched Shanti—in plain riding clothes and without her wristlet and sword—walk past some training soldiers. The men recognized Shanti, called out her name, and taunted her to join them.

"Not today, boys," Shanti said.

"You're not so tough," one soldier said. He stood near a ring of bricks where the sword fights were held. "In fact, I think you're *weak*."

She continued to walk, letting the comment go unanswered. Two guards with serious, sour faces trailed Shanti wherever she went.

Baylova wore a brown uniform and sat on top of a wooden table. She did not look very regal at the moment, though she felt much more comfortable. Aiden sat beside her, along with a soldier she didn't know.

Some of the men involved in fighting the Nunqua had come to the capital city of Erbaut. A few soldiers wobbled about on crutches or canes; others had bandaged arms or legs. She tried not to gawk at a man with a patch barely covering the wound from a gouged-out eye. The spires of the castle could be seen from the training center often used by the castle guards. The men here treated Baylova respectfully but did not trip over themselves to gain her good graces. It was a relief to be surrounded by soldiers again.

"That's not Shanti," the young man sitting with Baylova and Aiden remarked.

"Yes, it is," Aiden said.

"From what I hear, Shanti would never refuse a challenge. I guess all the stories I hear about her are false."

Aiden winked at Baylova, then said to the soldier, "I'll give you a gold coin if you go over there and pat Shanti on the bottom."

"What?" His eyes bulged at the indecent remark.

"One gold coin is worth getting yelled at, don't you think? She's not so dangerous. Go over there and see for yourself. She might even be grateful for the attention—want to see you again."

Baylova suppressed a laugh. "Or maybe she'll tie you to a tree."

"I can't believe you would talk like that in front of Baylova," the soldier said, bowing to her. "I apologize for his rudeness."

They watched Shanti stop in front of the many practice swords lined up. "A gold coin is a lot of money," Aiden said. "Think of what you could do."

"I'll give you *two* gold coins if you go over there and smack Shanti on the bottom," Baylova said.

Aiden snickered.

"I assure you, I have the means to pay."

"Your wealth is not in question, Baylova," the soldier said.

They watched Shanti pick up a sword and run her fingers along the blade. She swished it through the air, practicing against an invisible foe. Before putting it away, she twirled it in the palm of her hand.

"She would cut you and spill your blood on the ground before you had time to react," Aiden said. "And after she was done with you, Commander Jun would find you, gut you like a fish, flay your carcass, and make a saddle of the skin."

"I'm still not convinced." The soldier nodded to Baylova, then left.

"Why would Commander Jun gut him like a fish?" she said.

"Because he and Shanti are . . ." He scratched his head. "Never mind."

"Commander Jun and Shanti?"

"I can't believe you didn't know. I spoke with him as I was coming to the castle and he was leaving for the Outer Boundaries. He made me promise to send a letter to him or Commander Gy if anything bad happens to her—getting put in jail because she's a half-breed, that sort of thing."

A letter. "Do you know the code?" she said.

"Yes. Commander Gy taught me. For some reason, he made me his personal assistant at the Outer Boundaries. He also taught me military maneuvers and tactics. I don't understand why he showed me so much, then sent me to the castle, so far away from the fighting."

"Perhaps, it's because you were a terrible pupil." She smiled.

"You have me at a disadvantage, Baylova. I cannot respond to your insults."

Her smile widened. She felt happy just sitting beside Aiden.

*

Baylova was clothed for the castle, in a black dress fringed with lace. She strolled through the majestic hall with vaulted ceilings and thought of Aiden. The only red she wore was a ruby necklace. She did not feel like wearing the red of mourning from head to toe, for it brought nothing but sympathetic nods and hushed, reverent voices full of pity. Being near Aiden gave her hope, made her happy.

She reached a door that was closed and locked. In all her years at the castle, the door had been open. A loud bang reverberated through the hall. The door behind her slammed shut. Another door shut . . . then another. She was trapped in the large space. Five men emerged from the shadows: not Willovian, but Nunqua in black uniforms.

"Not as safe as you think, are you?" A warrior with blond braids and skin the color of buttermilk with tan spots moved toward her with his sword drawn. The others remained by the doors. What could she do? She couldn't run, couldn't fight a man twice her size, and no animals were here to come to her aid in the closed-off room.

The Nunqua man seized her wrist. "Baylova." This warrior was not a hideous-looking monster. He was handsome, with a straight nose and black eyes, but his bearing was filled with contempt. She looked at his spotted forearm, covered with fine blond hair and marred by two scars—the marks of a warrior.

"Willovia belongs to us," he said. "You're no match for the Nunqua." The guard lifted his sword to her throat. "Concede defeat."

She shook with terror but found the courage to speak. "If you're going to kill me, make it quick."

The weapon dropped a hairsbreadth, and the pupils of his eyes constricted. The doors to the majestic hall clicked. He moved behind her, the cold metal of the blade pressed against her throat. His hand twisted in her hair. "Let them in," he said.

Commander Kyros and royal guards rushed in to save her, only to realize her predicament.

"Put your weapons down!" the warrior ordered. He pulled her hair, and she cried out in pain. They did as he commanded. "Where's the queen? Where's Baylova?" He must have thought she was a decoy.

"She's safe," Commander Kyros said, "far away from the castle."

"Where?" He pulled her hair again, but she did not cry out.

"Baylova is well protected with the Merulians." Kyros took a step closer to them.

"The impostor goes with us," the Nunqua warrior said. Someone moved in through the open door, partially hidden by Willovian guards. "Stop, or her blood is on your hands."

A woman emerged. It was Shanti, arms down by her sides and palms facing forward. "You want to fight? Fight me."

"Stop, crazy Willovian!" the warrior said.

Shanti changed her appearance. She became a Nunqua with

spots, pale skin, and red lips. "Go ahead, kill me," she told the warrior.

"Shanti . . ." The weapon dropped from Bayla's throat.

"Some fates are worse than death," she said. Foreign words rattled out of Shanti's mouth, and Bayla wished she understood.

The Nunqua man let go of Bayla's hair and shoved her away. Willovian guards picked up their weapons. Fierce fighting began.

Commander Kyros ran toward the blond Nunqua, sideswiping him and pushing his nose hard into the marble floor. The man's sword fell out of his hand and clanked across the room. Kyros locked the Nunqua's arms behind his back. Shanti stood over the weapon and reached down to pick it up.

"Whom do you plan on killing with that sword?" Kyros said. "Who are you loyal to, Shanti?"

She backed away, changing her appearance to Willovian and leaving the weapon on the floor.

The fighting ceased as the Willovian guards subdued or killed all the attackers. The screaming and the dead were taken from the room. Shanti went with the wounded.

"Wait!" Baylova's command echoed off the high ceilings. She stopped the prisoners, the ones still alive, from being escorted out of the hall. The royal guards who surrounded her moved away. She ordered Commander Kyros to line up the intruders. Only three of the five Nunqua warriors stood in a row before the Queen. Blood streaked the floor. She questioned Kyros about the casualties.

"I believe two intruders were killed. One Willovian guard is . . . injured."

"Will he survive?"

"There's a chance . . ."

Baylova glared at him.

"No, he will not," Kyros said.

It all had happened so fast. The death of her father had been slow, agonizing. The lives of the men today had been quickly and unpleasantly snuffed out. Bayla felt responsible. She still heard wounded men screaming in the recesses of her brain and thought of Pirro's body falling limply into the water. She had never asked for this life, living in the vast castle, with strangers wanting to kill her and willing to kill those who protected her.

"Which blood belongs to the Willovian?" she said.

Commander Kyros pointed to an area by the door. The prisoners and guards watched her walk to that spot.

"Are you certain, Commander? It would be a grave mistake if this blood is not from a Willovian wounded by the enemy."

"I'm certain," Kyros said.

She dipped the tips of her fingers into the red ooze. Baylova lifted her hand and clenched it into a fist. "His blood is on my hands now. Commander Kyros, do what you have to do."

"It is you," the attacker who held her hostage said. "Baylova." Blood from his once straight nose flowed down onto his lips, chin, and neck.

A brown hawk flew in through the open doorway and perched on an exposed timber of the vaulted ceiling. The bird screeched at the Nunqua.

Kyros led the prisoners away, and Baylova's composure vanished. "Where are those wretched monks?" The marble floor cracked at her feet. She stormed out of the majestic hall, now stained by battle, followed by the brown hawk. War had reached the castle.

*

Shanti sat on the floor of an undecorated room containing a cot, bandages, herbs, and powders. The blood of the Willovian guard covered her hands because she had tried to stop his bleeding as they rushed him here. Now he was attended by workers much more capable than she would ever be. They closed his eyes and lowered their heads. He was gone.

23

NEWLY ORDAINED
BROTHER MONK

COMMANDER KYROS, TWO monks, and several high-ranking officials waited in a cave beneath the castle. Baylova had called them together to discuss castle security. She entered, with Shanti behind her.

Shanti's hands caressed the rock formations. She acted like a child discovering a secret world for the first time. Because of her previous association with the Nunqua, she had not been allowed in the secret caves. Judging by her actions, Kyros assumed that neither Jun nor Baylova had told her about their existence.

The sight of Shanti in the caves filled Kyros with rage. She didn't deserve to be here. Realizing that the queen was in trouble, he had commanded the guards to rescue Baylova, and he stopped the Nunqua warrior who had taken her hostage. But it was Shanti's foolish actions—arrogantly facing the enemy unarmed and thereby distracting them from Baylova—that ensured her fame. A good soldier would never have taken the chance. She got lucky. Women should stay out of men's business. Now Shanti and Baylova roamed the caves where previously only men had trodden. Soon they would be putting up decorations, having tea parties, inviting the Daughters of Fortunate Birth down to revel in the superiority they felt at being allowed into the men's domain. But they couldn't handle this domain. Shanti had used people to gain her status, and Baylova was born into her position. Neither had earned the respect they demanded as their due. Baylova should marry and give control of the kingdom to someone better suited to deal with the responsibility, and Shanti should just go away.

The bickering at the meeting accomplished nothing. Nobody knew how the Nunqua had gotten into the castle and so close to the queen. Arguments ensued among the officials when Baylova approached the sickly old monk with red-rimmed eyes, and the young monk in spectacles.

"How is it that you did not foresee the attack on the castle?"

The squabbling stopped as everyone in the cave listened for the answer.

The old monk's deep voice echoed in the cavern. "These are dangerous times for many. The attack on the castle was not foreseen, because you were never in danger of being harmed."

"One royal guard dies on the floor of the great hall, along with two Nunqua warriors, and you cannot foresee it?"

"Your safety was never in question. The guards are to be commended for their brave deeds in the service of Willovia."

"Why didn't they kill me when they had the chance?" she asked the old monk.

"Because they needed a hostage."

Baylova hung her head in thought, then lifted her chin. "Because of your failure to predict the attack on the castle, the presence of your order is no longer needed. As of this moment, I hereby declare that your status as royal advisers of Willovia be revoked. Correspondence with me or with dignitaries in the castle will be routed through proper channels. Upon my death, or the death of any royal, the castle guards will take control of the arrangements and burial."

The old monk's nostrils flared. The young monk unexpectedly stepped forward and bowed. "Baylova."

She nodded, agreeing to hear him.

"The Nunqua did not kill you, because they have orders from their highest command not to harm you. Even as a hostage, they still believed there was a chance you were the queen. *You* are the reason the Nunqua invaded Willovia."

Several sharp intakes of breath occurred at the monk's uttering of the words, telling the queen she was responsible for the war, responsible for all the death.

"Explain," she said.

"Nunqua spiritualists predicted years ago the date your father would die of sickness. The warriors planned the invasion to correspond with the death of King Magen. They believe you are too inexperienced to handle the pressures of ruling Willovia. You are being kept in power as an ineffective leader. You are not a target. The military commanders and village leaders are the targets."

"If I'm not a target, why did they come to the castle and hold a sword to my throat?"

"Baylova, I do not know," the young monk said.

"Your order has been reinstated." She looked at the young monk. "You will act as my liaison. If relevant information cannot be provided to aid in our decision making, I will disband the order without regrets."

"It is we," the old monk said, "who informed you of the upcoming war with the Nunqua in the first place."

"Then tell us how to win!" Baylova snapped. "Tell us how to defeat the Nunqua and drive them away."

He had no answer for her. No one did.

The queen spoke to Shanti. "How long have you known about the invasion?"

Shanti watched colors on the rock wall shift in the light of the oil lamps. "Years."

"You shall be put to death for withholding such vital information. You're a traitor to Willovia. Commander Kyros, take—"

"Withholding information?" Shanti said. "It was a prophecy by some crazy old hag looking for gold to fill her pockets. I didn't believe her when she spoke of the King of Willovia dying of sickness in his bed. And I did tell someone when I realized the prophecy was true—Commander Gy, leader of the Willovian military, who fights at the Outer Boundaries for the kingdom. Give him a death sentence for not telling you. And while you're at it, give the monks a death sentence for not telling you sooner."

"I'll summon Commander Gy to the castle to confirm your statement. We shall have an inquiry."

"Baylova," Kyros interjected, "we're at war. Commander Gy is needed to lead the fight against the Nunqua. I suggest we detain Shanti in the castle's prison until a more practical time is determined to send for Commander Gy."

"I thought I was already being imprisoned at the castle," Shanti mumbled, her face toward the wall.

"Commander Kyros, you *will* summon Commander Gy immediately, by official decree with my seal. Shanti will stay in the same room and still enjoy the privileges of the castle while we wait for Commander Gy's arrival. I'm not unreasonable. Once your betrayal is proven, you shall be beheaded in the town square."

"You sound just like your father," Shanti said.

Kyros frowned. Baylova would take Commander Gy, her most experienced leader, away from the battle for an inquiry and risk losing the war? He thought back to the inquiry at the camp in the Hedgelands. Baylova had lied, saying Shanti choked her in an attempt to kill her, and he had done nothing to punish her perjury. According to witnesses, soldiers who saw Bayla and Shanti half-dead on the ground with wasps raining down upon them, Shanti had told the truth.

He suddenly felt no joy at having his wish come true: Shanti was going away. Forever. Beheaded. And it would be his duty to observe her final moments and the deathblow.

The inquiry would not be fair. Baylova didn't know the meaning of a fair inquiry, and it was his fault, his mistake. The Guardians of Willovia should never have allowed Bayla to be crowned queen.

*

Aiden's hands and arms were in a soapy bucket of water. He was so busy trying to clean gray clay off his arms from a project he was working on that he didn't notice Baylova's entrance.

"Aiden," she said.

He jumped at the sound of her voice. "Baylova. I'll be with you in a moment."

"My royal guard, my protection," she teased, "should be more aware of his surroundings."

Aiden continued scrubbing as Bayla looked at an unfinished circular plaque depicting a Willovian eagle. She touched the moist clay with her fingertip and disfigured the curved beak into an unnatural shape. Aiden didn't see her inartistic contribution to his project. She wiped the muddy goop from her finger onto the folds of her skirt to conceal her mistake.

"I need to ask you something," she said.

"What is it?" An icy attitude replaced his usual easygoing manner.

"You were up near the fighting. How does the war go?"

He dried his hands with a cloth. "Not well."

Baylova picked up a brush and felt the soft horsehair bristles. "Nobody tells me the truth. All my advisers say is that we're keeping the Nunqua from advancing. They're being optimistic for my sake. I don't know what's going on. Even you keep secrets from me."

Aiden remained silent.

"Did you send a letter to Commander Jun?"

"Is there something you want done today?" he asked.

"I had to do it. You must see that she's a Nunqua."

"She was born a Nunqua; that doesn't make her a traitor." He covered openmouthed jars of pliable plaster and submerged dirty tools used for shaping the plaster in bowls of gray water.

Baylova moved next to him and touched his arm. "Shanti let the warriors into the castle. It's the only explanation. She told the Nunqua where we would be in the Hedgelands. She's responsible for the death of the royal guard. And Pirro."

He yanked his arm away from her. "Have you ever witnessed a beheading? Are you going to be there to hear her scream as they drag her to the platform for everyone to see, and when they chop off her head simply because you requested it? Are you going to dip you hands into her blood, too? They will bury her in a grave under a stone marker with the word traitor on it, her head beneath her feet. Then Commander Gy will become your enemy, as will Commander Jun, as will I. The royal guards, the soldiers, see how she's treated here. I expect many of them will leave."

"I never asked to be queen." Baylova squeezed her eyes shut. "I'm doing what's best for Willovia."

"Shanti never asked to born half Nunqua and half Willovian. From what I hear, she came to the castle against her will because *you* ordered it so. Condemning her without proof makes it nothing more than your personal vendetta against her."

"Aiden," she whispered, opening her eyes and looking into his face, unable to say the words she wanted to say.

"There was a time," he sighed, "when I would have done anything to be with you. I was so mad at Zindar, so jealous."

"I never cared for Zindar," she whispered. "It was one mistake; it meant nothing. They made me go hunting that morning. I was upset." She leaned her head against his shoulder and said the painful words. "I love you."

"Bayla . . ." He pushed her gently away. "It can't be now. It just can't be."

The old monk gleefully watched his apprentice.

Tobian, shirtless, held the glass beaker with silver clawed feet in his hands and knelt on a silken pillow. Several monks surrounded him in the sparsely decorated room with carved walls. The copper tub had been removed. A faster, though riskier, method of taking in the potion existed. This time, their order would be assured of gaining a clearer view of the future.

Not one of them pushed him to drink. All waited patiently for the apprentice to make his own decision. Tobian lifted the inky elixir to his lips and swallowed. "For the fate of Willovia." He coughed.

His apprentice had done it: drunk the potion resealing the ancient contract between the order of the monks and the royals of Willovia. The young man's transformation had begun.

The monks observed the body of the apprentice—a mere shell connected by a thread to his spirit as it roamed the future. His skin turned bluish-gray, and his veins became like blackened spider webs just beneath the skin. The young monk no longer appeared human, yet his countenance was filled with wonder. It was always that way for first-timers: wonder at the gift of knowledge they were being given. His face contorted, and he panted. Those who surrounded him became fearful. They could not interfere while he was under the potion's power.

Tobian muttered incoherently, collapsed to the floor, convulsed. The old monk inserted a hard wooden slat between his teeth, big enough so he wouldn't choke on it. Chroniclers leaned closer, straining their ears to hear, to understand what was happening, but Tobian muttered no more under the spell. The invisible thread pulled him back into the heavy body, and the newly ordained brother monk awoke. He spat out the wooden slat and looked around in confusion. "Am I dreaming?"

"No." They knew they must be gentle, for his mind would still be confused by his first foray into the future.

The old monk knelt on the ground. "Did you see Baylova?"

"Yes."

A breath of relief escaped his lips. His apprentice had done it, had seen the queen whereas they could not. There was hope.

Beads of sweat emerged on the young monk's forehead, and his blackened veins faded to gray. "Baylova will ride with the Willovian forces to battle the enemy."

"What!" a monk said. "The queen cannot take such a risk."

"What about heirs?" the old monk asked. "Will she have children?"

"I saw only the battle."

"Did you see her death?"

Tobian started laughing, or perhaps sobbing, crazily. Remnants of the potion still circulated in his system, magnifying his emotions. "I saw only glimpses of the battle. The sky grew black, there was a strange noise, and then I was pulled back here." He stood on shaky legs and walked over to the vials in organized rows. His spectacles lay near the potion. Tobian put them on his face, then donned his robe.

Even now the old monk could perceive his apprentice's desire to return to the future, but it would be too dangerous to attempt another drink for days. The invisible string that connected body and spirit could break, and they would lose the only monk with the ability to see the queen's future. He would encourage the young man, teach him how to probe deeper into the murky realm. They had to know if Baylova would have heirs. She had to, or their order was doomed.

Tobian stared at the vials.

"Powerful, isn't it?" The old man said.

"I wish to speak with Baylova as soon as possible, tell her about the battle."

"Do you think it wise?"

"It's something I must do," he answered.

The old monk nodded in agreement, although he didn't agree. "You should wait until the aftereffects of the potion wear off. You're quite a sight. Tell the chroniclers what you saw, and then get some rest. After that, you can see the queen."

The young monk gave the chroniclers details of the battle, then went to his room.

*

Alone in his room, Tobian reached into his robe and pulled out a single glass beaker filled with black potion—the one he had stolen and hidden in the folds of his robe after retrieving his glasses.

The ceiling swirled overhead. He placed the beaker in a drawer, then pulled out a mirror. His skin had lost all color. He placed the mirror on top of his nightstand, then crawled into bed with his robes on. He would tell Baylova that she would ride out to battle, and so much more. The power of the monks was about to be obliterated.

Tobian fell into a long sleep without dreams. When he woke, he picked up the mirror to find he had resumed his normal shade of tan. But his eyes were rimmed in red.

24

POISONED

JUN LIFTED HIS mug from a table sticky with spills inadequately wiped up. He tasted his drink. It wasn't watered down as he had expected. Only a few men were in the dirty tavern tonight, playing cards and losing their daytime troubles in strong liquor.

The barmaid, bored by the lack of customers, sat next to him. "You look like you could use some company." She had almond-shaped eyes, short hair, and none of the silly body paint that women wore. It was easy to see that the exotic beauty was not hired for her ability to serve drinks and keep the place clean. "Business has been slow ever since the war started," she said. "Are you a soldier?"

"Yes," he said.

"So's my husband. He left at the beginning of winter. Haven't seen him since."

They talked to pass the time. She would occasionally get up to wait on the other men absorbed in their game or their troubles, but would always come back to continue her conversation with Jun.

When the bar had emptied, the barmaid invited him up for a drink. "Just a drink," she said, "nothing more."

Jun looked into those pretty almond eyes and knew she was lying. He followed her up the stairs. She poured them some wine while he examined her room. The bed, wardrobe, desk, table, and chairs were much nicer than the furnishings in the tavern. Cleaner, too. She brought him the drink and remained close. He watched her lips as she lifted the cup to them but didn't swallow. Her face tilted upward, enticing lips wet with wine, wanting him to take a taste, but he knew better.

"Stupid girl," he said.

She backed away, still playing the game. "I'm sorry. I thought you wanted to. I'm sorry."

Jun locked the door, certain he didn't have much time.

"What are you doing?"

He opened the drawers of her desk and rummaged through the contents, searched through everything in the room.

"What's going on?" she said.

He found nothing of intelligence value, nor any traces of drugs. He hoped she hadn't put something in his drink earlier while they were downstairs.

"I made a mistake," she said. "Please leave now."

Jun knew that if he left through the same door he had come in by, his throat would be slashed. The men in the bar had never *looked* at the beautiful waitress. Hell, he was involved with a woman who wore poisonous darts and knew how to handle a sword, and *he* had looked. Jun had known he was in trouble the moment she sat down with him. Three Willovian soldiers had disappeared from this inn, and she was the obvious bait. The barmaid dressed too expensively, acted too haughty, to be working in such a squalid establishment. The one window in the room opened to a deserted street below. If he jumped, he could break a leg.

"I can save you." Her face took on a look of superiority that detracted from her beauty. "Just stay with me tonight, tell me what you're doing here, and they'll leave you alone."

"Who are they?" Jun said.

"They're only interested in information."

Jun thought about taking her hostage but didn't think it would make any difference. He searched through her clothes and quickly found a few thin scarves. She ran for the locked door. He stopped her from leaving and covered her mouth. She bit the palm of his hand. Jun bound and gagged the woman with her clothes, tying her to the bed. Then he opened the window and jumped down to the hard cobblestones below.

He wrenched his right knee, causing a sharp pain that increased with every step. Limping down the street, he sought the safety of a crowd. The silhouette of a man came into view. Other men came out of the dark recesses of the buildings. Jun took a knife out of his coat and hid it in the palm of his hand, the blade against his forearm.

Spotted Nunqua advanced toward him, swords hooked to their belts. "Trying to escape a jealous husband?" someone said.

"Willovian!" a familiar voice with a thick accent shouted enthusiastically. "He's the one who cut me in the Hedgelands. Disappointed to see me, eh? Perhaps you thought I was dead."

Jun couldn't take on all the men who surrounded him, but he might survive a fight against only one. "Let's finish it now," he told the warrior. "Just you and I. A fair fight." It was a ploy to stay alive. His vision blurred. "Jus' you an' I." He crumpled to the ground, the knife still clutched in his hand.

"You're in no condition to challenge me, Willovian."

Hazy faces of warriors looked down at him.

"So you were at the camp in the Hedgelands," a voice said. This warrior had no accent but spoke Willovian perfectly. He removed the knife from Jun's limp grip. "Later, Willovian. You'll have your chance to fight."

How could he be so dumb to be drugged by the woman and trapped by the Nunqua? Why weren't they killing him? Maybe they were, and he couldn't feel the pain of death because of the drug. Nunqua were renowned for their expertise in alchemy.

His thoughts turned to the home where he had grown up and his mother, father, brother, and sister. Jun thought of his misspent youth, the many fights and conniving ways, and serving as a spy for Willovia. He thought of the secluded cabin left to him by his grandfather, and the times they shared there. He thought of taking Shanti to the cabin someday. Then he thought of the war and realized he would never see his family or Shanti again.

Darkness replaced his thoughts.

*

Lifelike images of Baylova's ancestors lined the walls of the portrait room. The long-dead royals of Willovia peered down upon the living. Baylova and her advisers waited for the monk who had much-needed news of the war. The young man in blue robes entered, followed by his loathsome mentor. Only the liaison approached; the elderly monk remained by the door.

"Baylova . . ." The man with spectacles bowed.

She backed away and blinked. She had thought him a soldier once, when they first met at the camp. Then he was strong and healthy. He was different now—gaunt, sickly. *He's one of them.* She tried to shake off the unexplained feeling of revulsion she felt for the young monk. "You have something to tell us?"

"I have come . . ." He struggled to speak. ". . . to apologize."

From the door, the old monk stretched out his hand.

"I saw the future. I drank a potion containing the blood of your father."

"No!" the old monk cried.

"This potion allows us to journey into the future." The young monk stared down at the simple pattern embroidered on the hem of her dress.

"He's crazy," the old monk said. "My young brother has had a bad reaction to our medicines."

"I will hear it!" The queen's commanding voice did not fit her tiny frame.

"Lies! Just lies . . ." He stepped away from the door.

Baylova turned to Commander Kyros. "Shut him up."

At Kyros's command, strong hands gripped the parchmentlike skin of the monk's spindly arms.

"Continue," she said to the bespectacled young man.

"The bloodline of the royals of Willovia has been bartered to protect the country. This ancient agreement has been tainted. The blood is taken without consent, and only twisted outcomes arise. The monks serve not Willovia but only their own selfish interests."

"Why are you telling me this?" she asked.

"Your mother was powerful, as are you. She was chosen by the order so that the heirs of King Magen would inherit Serova's power. Your blood—the blood of royalty combined with the blood of a witch—is coveted by the order, as will be the blood of your heirs."

"You say you see the future, but you tell me only of the past."

"The other monks cannot see your future. Their visions are being blocked. I saw Queen Serova in my vision. Her spirit protects you still."

"So my future cannot be seen?"

"The monks have peered into the future of those closest to you. Serova permitted me to see only a little into your future. You will ride with the Willovian forces to battle the Nunqua." His head remained bowed, red-rimmed eyes downcast.

"You have my protection," she said.

"He's lying," the old monk said. "Baylova, you have to believe me."

"Put him in a cell," she told Commander Kyros, referring to the loathsome old monk. Then Baylova put her back to the old man and ignored his pleas. "I hereby disband the order of the monks. Block off their residence—"

"Impudent brat," the old monk said. "You're nothing without us. Nothing!" His screaming rant could be heard as he was dragged away. "You have no case against us. Our order has done nothing wrong. You, Baylova, have wrought the downfall of Willovia. The

Nunqua were right: you are unfit to rule. Witch. Pestilent, venomous witch!"

Baylova spoke to the young monk. "Those robes do not suit you. You may stay at the castle if you wish." She was grateful yet troubled by her aversion to his presence.

"Tobian. My name is Tobian." He looked into her face. "Baylova, you may disband the order, but the monks will try to kill you as soon as you have an heir."

She nodded, then walked regally out of the portrait room.

*

Baylova sat behind her father's marble desk, in her father's velvet-covered chair. Six flags hung from the walls of this room in the tallest tower of the castle, a noble falcon on a field of blue decorating the largest and most prominent.

The crushing burden of ruling Willovia weighed on her shoulders now. The Nunqua warrior had held a sword to her throat, the monks wanted to kill her and then drink her blood, Aiden didn't want to be with her, and nobody told her anything concerning matters of importance. Everyone still treated her like a child.

She placed her hand over a piece of parchment on the desk. It bore the names of fallen Willovian soldiers and those wounded in battle. Commander Jun was listed as missing. Aiden must have sent a letter, telling Commander Jun that she had ordered an inquiry into Shanti's actions of withholding critical information concerning the war. Jun was probably rushing to the castle to rescue Shanti now, to speak in her behalf at the inquiry.

How did that half-breed, that traitor to Willovia, manipulate everyone to come to her aid? Commander Jun, Aiden, the soldiers, and the royal guards all liked Shanti better than they liked their own queen. Even the Daughters of Fortunate Birth were captivated, eager to hear more of Shanti's lurid tales of being sold as a sex slave. Killing Shanti would turn everyone against her. What could she do to make everyone love her? How could she end her troubles, find admiration and sympathy?

She removed a small container and dart from her pocket, both acquired from a seldom-used cave. Her funeral would be a grand, sad event. She envisioned the people of Willovia throwing flowers at her coffin, the whole kingdom wearing red in her honor. They would speak in hushed tones of their beloved queen, poisoned by one of her own advisers. And Aiden would be heartbroken. He would paint her portrait to hang next to the paintings of her mother and father. Two beautiful red rosebuds would be drawn on her hand, with thorny stems to signify what could never be between them. Aiden would love her again.

She opened the container and dipped the tip of the dart into the poison. Shanti would be blamed for her murder. After all, Shanti used darts as weapons, and she was part Nunqua.

Bayla poised the dart over her wrist. The monks had it wrong. They could not foresee her future, because she had no future. It would hurt, though, plunging the dart into flesh, suffering sickness, dying. *Damn it.* She laid the dart on the desk. Cold sweat seeped from her pores. Blood pounded in her ears. An odd coo sounded. No, it was a *whoo*—the hooting of an owl. A snowy white owl perched on a beam above a window. She could not control the animal with her power.

"Hidden witch," Baylova said. "Madiza."

The owl flew down to the desk, wings spread and talons open, ready to snatch the dart. Bayla hit the bird, causing it to drop and skid on the desktop. Documents and quills scattered to the floor. Bayla lifted her hand, clenched it into a fist in midair, and twisted. The owl's screech sounded like a scream as it fell, its wing broken by Bayla's power.

"Baylova," royal guards yelled in the hall.

Bayla picked up the dart and jabbed the poisonous tip into her hand. The guards arrived just in time to see her pull it out of her palm. The white owl struggled to fly, but it tumbled off the desk, losing a feather as it crashed to the rug.

"Kill the owl," she told the guards.

They scanned the room for signs of real danger.

"Kill it!"

The guard's lance embedded into the owl's breast, staining the feathers red. Baylova lifted her hand to her face. "What have I . . . ?" The pupils of her eyes rolled backward, and she fainted.

*

Five royal guards escorted Shanti through the halls of the castle: two guards in front of her, two behind her, and one beside her, squeezing her arm. They pushed her into a room and closed the door. Antlers, animal heads, and pelts decorated the trophy room. Two elephant tusks hung crossed over the mantel. Commander Kyros sat in a stuffed leather chair and stared at the fire.

"Baylova will survive." He reached into an inside pocket of his coat and pulled out a white cloth. Kyros set the cloth on a table, opening it carefully. Inside were a dart, a lidded container, and a white feather with brown stains. "You're the only person I know who uses darts as weapons."

"I was not in the room when she was poisoned," Shanti said.

"True, but there are windows in the tower, and a ledge for you to stand on." He lifted the dart, holding it between his finger and thumb.

"That's not one of mine."

"It's Willovian." He put the dart down then picked up the small container. "There's an entire crate of these darts, and more of this particular poison, located in the caves. You've been in the caves. Baylova brought you there to discuss castle security. You have a reason for killing the queen, and the means to do it." Kyros returned the container to the white cloth, then picked up the feather. "But this? I don't understand this. Why would Baylova order the guards to kill an *owl*?"

Kyros walked around the trophy room. "Where are your sword and darts? Your room has been searched, but they're not inside. I remember you had them when we brought you to the castle. My guess is, you used the ledge one night to come to this room, then hid your weapons in here to keep them safe." He touched the head of a stuffed zebra. "But where? Where are your darts?" he asked.

"If I wanted to poison the queen," Shanti said, "she'd be dead."

"Tell me where the darts are."

Shanti went over to the padded leather chair. She grasped the armrest and braced it with her feet, pulling the chair onto its side. "Knife." She held out her hand, palm up.

Kyros reached into his boot and slid out a knife. He hesitated, then gave it to her.

Shanti cut the cloth covering the bottom of the chair, then returned the knife. She removed some of the stuffing, reached inside up to her elbow, pulled out a box, and gave it to Kyros.

Opening the box, he took out one of Shanti's finely crafted darts with hollow points and compared it to the ordinary dart that had poisoned Baylova. He inspected the wristlet that was also in the box, along with a lock of hair tied with string.

"The hair is from a Nunqua warrior. It's not Willovian." She reached inside the chair again and pulled out her sword. "Am I to be beheaded?"

"I'm giving you your freedom." He returned the box to her. "Jun's missing. I have word that he's being held as a prisoner of war inside Nunqua territory." Kyros took the sword from her and unsheathed it. He read aloud the words engraved on it. "*Anaya say midea*—strength of will."

"You know the Nunqua language?" she said. "It was *you*. You let the warriors into the castle."

"I speak four languages, and I did not let them into the castle. Why were the warriors afraid of you? You were unarmed at the time."

"It's not me they're afraid of. I have influential friends."

He gave her the sword. "Baylova wants to make everyone think you tried to kill her."

"Yes," Shanti said. "Baylova hates me, Jun doesn't love me, and you control me. Or so you said on the balcony."

"And your big mouth gets you into trouble. I'm giving you a chance to leave the castle and convince your warrior friends to let Jun out of prison."

"Right," she said.

"Once a Guardian, always a Guardian, I believe. You took an oath to act in the best interests of Willovia."

"You're not a Guardian. How would you know?"

"It's my job to know things." Kyros moved uncomfortably close. "Baylova tried to kill herself and blame it on you. I don't hate you—anymore, that is. I'm recruiting you. I will let you escape; then you will help Jun escape."

"You want me to go back to the Nunqua and just ask them to release one of their prisoners?"

"Yes."

He smelled like brandy and spice—a pleasing scent. "What about the inquiry and Commander Gy?" she said.

"Use your brain. I didn't send the letter to Commander Gy, telling him to leave the battle to come here for a stupid inquiry."

Shanti smiled, feeling empowered, energized. "You disobeyed a royal decree . . . for me."

"Leave tonight." He looked at her lips. "Use the ledge. Your horse will be saddled and waiting for you. As soon as you're off castle grounds, conceal the scars on your arms. There is some risk. When Baylova realizes you're gone, I'm sure she'll issue an order to find you and kill you, no questions asked. I don't control all the royal guards."

Shanti went to the table and picked up the feather. "May I have this?"

"What for?"

"It's important," she said.

"Take it, then."

"I have another favor to ask." She put the feather into her pocket, then knelt by the overturned chair and shoved the stuffing back inside.

"I *am* doing you a favor by letting you leave the castle. If I'm caught, we both lose our heads."

Shanti heaved the chair back upright. She took the wristlet out of the box and strapped it to her wrist. "Let me see the queen."

"You're as crazy as she is."

She swung her sword onto her back. "I'm a Guardian, and I will finish the task given to me."

"You're going to kill her now? Act in the best interests of Willovia?"

"I'm not going to kill her."

"Baylova's still in bed," Kyros said. "Sick from the poison."

Shanti picked up the container of poison, smelled it, and gave a short laugh. "Doubtful."

"I'll never understand what Jun sees in you."

"Also doubtful." It was so good to have a purpose, a goal, again. She would have kissed Kyros, that master of mind games, if she weren't in love with Jun. She knew that Kyros wouldn't reject a soft, slow kiss from her. Neither would he reject a hard, passionate, full-body kiss. The thought filled her with a sense of a power mightier than the sword! How fast things had changed!

"At least you're never boring," he said.

*

Commander Kyros opened the door to the queen's bedroom. Leanna sat in a chair next to Baylova, who lay in a massive four-poster bed overflowing with fluffy pillows and white blankets. "Leanna," he said, "may I see you for a moment?"

Leanna rose and put her hand on Baylova's forehead, smoothing the hair back from the pale face. Kyros led Leanna out of the room.

They passed Shanti, who was armed and waiting. Shanti entered the room, and Kyros closed the door.

"Poor, pitiful princess." Shanti strolled toward the bed.

"Guards," Baylova's weak voice croaked. Shanti jumped onto the wooden footboard and leaned against a post carved with clouds and stars. Baylova's purple and blue hand lay on the white blanket, fingernails black from the poison. She sat up in the bed and bellowed, "Guards!"

"Yell all you want. They're not coming."

"You turned everyone against me," Baylova sniffed.

"You did that to yourself. Such a big bed and no one to share it with—what a shame!" Her hand caressed the carved pole. "I can think of a lot of things I'd like to do in a bed like this. Has Aiden ever been in here with you? Any stories you'd like to share."

"You really are sick."

"*I'm* sick? I'm not the one in bed trying to make everyone feel sorry for me, *Princess.*"

"It's 'Queen Baylova.'"

"You want people to respect you as queen? Then prove you're worthy to rule. Win the war. Stop caring so much about yourself. Do what you know is right. And, please, invite Aiden up here and put this bed to good use."

Bayla's purple and blue hand with blackened fingernails reached upward. Invisible power surged around her, and tendrils of her hair lifted. Shanti jumped onto the mattress, near Bayla's feet, which were buried under the covers. "All I have to do is touch you to steal your power, Princess." Shanti crawled on all fours toward Bayla. "Just like I stole your sword. You made it so easy. Nobody saw me take it while we were at the Hedgelands on the obstacle—"

Bayla seized a handful of Shanti's hair and wrenched it hard. Shanti grabbed the arm and rolled out of the bed. She threw Bayla into a table, knocking a green pitcher of water over and soaking Bayla's nightgown. Enraged, Bayla picked up the glazed pottery pitcher and hurled it at Shanti. It hit the wall and shattered. "You bitch! Where's my sword?"

"Not so sick now, are you?" Shanti said.

Bayla threw a cup, glazed the same green color as the broken pitcher.

Shanti ducked, and it, too, smashed against the wall. She opened a window, and a gust of cold air blew in. "You want to be queen? Then find me, take back your sword, and win the war for Willovia." Shanti disappeared out the window and onto the slippery ledge in the dark night.

Bayla slammed open the door and walked briskly out of her bedroom.

"You're certainly feeling better, Baylova." Kyros said. "Quite an amazing recovery, I must say."

"Shut up." She continued toward a window and looked outside. "Damn, it's too dark. I can't see her."

Kyros moved beside her, watching out the window. "They say Nunqua can see in the dark."

Leanna was with them. A black blur flew past the window. "Baylova, no!"

Another blur—a large bat—swooshed past.

"They also say Nunqua know powerful spells to protect themselves," he said.

"Whose side are you on?" Baylova spat.

Kyros bowed to her. "I serve Willovia, as always."

"Stop this, Baylova," Leanna said. "Please. Leave her be."

Baylova stepped away from the window in a trance, using the bats to search for Shanti.

*

Shanti focused straight ahead, never looking down. With her belly pressed against the wall, she crept along the ledge, maneuvering three stories above the hard ground. Something hit her in the head. Tiny squeaks and squeals hurt her ears. A bat swerved near her face, and Shanti flattened her cheek against the wall. Another black bat, with repulsive ears and glossy eyes, hooked itself onto her skirt and climbed upward. Unable to swat it with her hand for fear of falling, Shanti bent her knee and moved it back and forth to knock the flying vermin off her. The other bat grasped strands of her hair, pulling them from her scalp as it continued to fly in a dizzying pattern around her.

A window was nearby. Just a few more steps on the ledge, and she would reach it. Shanti moved slowly, ignoring the attacking bats as best she could. She must get to the window. The bat crawling on her skirt reached her waist.

Shanti tried to open the window. Locked. She unsheathed her sword. The bat squeaked as it climbed upward, nearing her shoulder. The creature flying about her head entwined itself in her hair. Shanti screamed and whacked the handle of her weapon against the window. The glass cracked but did not break. Once more, channeling all her emotion into the blow, she struck the window with the butt of her sword, this time breaking a hole in the glass. She reached inside and unlocked the window.

Shanti tumbled onto broken glass inside, aware of only two things: the bat in her hair and the one crawling up her dress.

"Get off. Get off!" She yanked the bat out of her hair, flinging it to the floor and cutting it in two with her sword. Long strands of her hair were still clenched in its claws. Two tiny fangs bit into the soft flesh just beneath her collarbone. She wrenched the creature off, its teeth and claws scratching her skin, and threw it down and stomped on it. Blood dripped down her chest. *Her* blood. The bite from a bat carried a disease that caused the most painful death known to Willovians or Nunqua, and it was untreatable. She had to clean the bite wound as soon as possible, but she was back inside the castle, in an empty room on the third floor. She sheathed the weapon and sprinted out of the room and down the hall.

"Shanti!" an otherworldly voice shrieked. Baylova, dressed in her nightgown, leaned on the wall for support and shuffled toward Shanti in a fury.

Killing the bats must have weakened Baylova. A crack split the floor, and dust rose out of the fissure. *Or perhaps not.* Shanti ran into the great hall, the crack following the same path as her feet. She descended stairs, two at a time, as people who had gathered for the feast watched in stunned silence. Shanti tripped and rolled down to the bottom of the stairs.

"Are you all right?" Two men, honored guests with graying hair and flawless manners, lifted her to a standing position. Seeing the sword, the wristlet of darts, and the blood on her neck, one said, "What's going on?"

Baylova stood in the hall, white as a phantom in her nightgown. She did not shriek or dash into the room with the respectable royal guests, who believed her to be sick in bed from poisoning. Baylova moved backward into the shadows. Shanti ran out the massive front doors and into the night, bewildering everyone at the feast.

Her horse was saddled and waiting. "Thank you, Kyros," she said. Several paths led away from the castle grounds. Shanti hitched her skirt up to her thighs and swung up onto her horse. She raced through open gates into the city. A wolf howled in the distance. Another wolf answered. Shanti kicked her heels into the horse's sides as growling wolves emerged from behind buildings to chase her.

The city was empty, everyone inside their cozy houses enjoying warm fires. Her horse ran at a dangerous pace on the uneven cobblestone road. A wolf bit at its hind leg. The horse bucked, stopped. Shanti gripped the reins tight. The horse's ears lay back as it snorted in anger.

"Not fair, princess!" She jumped off the beast—now under Baylova's control—as it attempted to bite and kick her. Shanti tried to unbuckle the saddle and remove it, while staying clear of the horse's hindquarters. A snarling wolf tore her skirt as the pack circled her there in the street. A door opened, and a man holding a lantern peered out. The wolves lowered their heads. Other doors opened, and men and women came out of their homes. They used torches to scatter the pack of wolves. Shanti's horse foamed at the mouth and reared. Ropes were thrown around the animal's neck.

Someone pulled her away from the wild horse and placed a dark cloak over her shoulders. "Come with me, Shanti," a man said. A hood shaded his features so she could not see who it was. She lifted the hood of her cloak. Shanti followed the man down a deserted alley and away from the crowd, into a musty cellar.

A single lamp lit a space filled with old furniture and useless junk. He heaved a large desk aside and opened a secret door half as tall as she was. The hooded man picked up the lamp, pulled her inside the small opening, and closed the door. The walls were dirt with wooden shoring. Shanti took off her hood and stood up, banging her head on the ceiling timber. She looked under the man's hood. "Aiden."

He crouched in the tight space with her. "You certainly made her angry this time."

"Your girlfriend has quite a temper."

"She's not my girlfr— Your hair . . . and your neck!" He gaped at the two deep scratches on her collarbone.

"A bat bit me."

"No." His brow furrowed with concern.

"There's only a small chance it carried disease. Where are we?"

"Tunnel," he said. "Used by the Guardians of Willovia. They're waiting for you at my parents' house. Let's go." Aiden crawled into a hole in the dirt wall. Shanti stayed in the small room. He crawled back out. "I can't believe it," he said. "The infamous Commander Shanti, trained by the Nunqua, a woman who wears poisonous darts as jewelry and cuts men's arms in sword fights, who battles a witch . . . is afraid of a *tunnel?* You realize I'm going to tell everyone."

"Tell whomever you want; I'm not going in that deathtrap."

"It's harmless. I've traveled in these tunnels for years, since I was a kid."

"Then it's an *old* tunnel, which makes it even more of a death-trap," she said.

"Do you want me to hold your hand?"

"And upset your girlfriend further? I'll wait here until things have settled down, then go back into the city. She's weakening; she can't control the animals all night."

"Shanti, get in the tunnel."

The caves didn't scare her; neither did the ledge. But the tunnel was different. The tunnel was a cramped, convenient grave. "Don't leave me in there, Aiden."

"I'm not going to leave you. Relax." He crawled into the hole, holding the lantern.

Shanti, terrified, lifted her torn skirt and crawled in behind him.

25
WOMEN'S WORK

"YOU'VE BEEN CHALLENGED, Willovian," the Nunqua warrior said to Jun. They were alone inside a tent large enough to sleep ten men, but on this night, twenty-three men crowded the cold space, snoring, shivering, and starving. Threadbare blankets were folded on the floor, and small baskets of personal items held down the cloth edges of the tent to keep the wind out. The baskets contained combs, soap, extra socks, and letters. A rusty metal firepot in the middle of the shelter warmed the space. Smoke rose through a metal flue in the top of the tent.

"Do you know who I am?" the warrior asked.

Jun, with a scruffy beard and worn clothes, only gazed at the fire, which gave little comfort.

"Like I said, you've been challenged to a sword fight. This town has a small arena. Gitonk tells me you're quite good. If you win, extra food will be given to the men in your tent. The one who challenged you wants a fight to the death—not a normal request, I assure you. Fighting in the arena is a sport. Winners are always treated well. If he wins, he will kill you. You may do the same according the rules of the arena, or you may show mercy by cutting his arm." The warrior made a slashing motion across his forearm with the side of his hand. He turned to leave the tent.

"I will not fight for you, General Delartay."

"So you do know who I am. It's a challenge, Commander Jun. You cannot refuse." Caravey Delartay inhaled deeply. "I'm curious. You were at the camp in the Hedgelands. Whose hair hangs from a string in the pavilion? Who made Shanti so mad that she cut his hair?"

Jun continued to stare at the firepot, his stomach growling in hunger and his skin itching from fleas.

"To fight is an honor. Your challenger is obsessed with revenge. He wants to flog you, then kill you. He plans on killing the other commanders who humiliated him. He has devised a special revenge for Shanti. Zindar believes he could actually be king one day." Delartay shook his head. "Nunqua do not look favorably on traitors of any sort. He has served his purpose. Zindar's death is his own doing. War won't last forever. The resources of the Willovians will unite with the power of the Nunqua. Your existence here, this prisoner-of-war encampment, is temporary. I am not your enemy."

"Oh, yes, you are," Jun said.

"How very noble," General Delartay said. "And stupid."

*

Shanti emerged from the tunnel into a small space with dirt walls, which appeared much like the room she had just left. Aiden opened a door and led her into a tidy cellar where she could finally stand straight. She stretched her arms and stood on tiptoe, feeling like a snake that has just shed its skin. "How did you know where I was?"

"Come upstairs and see for yourself."

"Are you a Guardian?"

"I suppose I am now. Come on up. There's medicine and food upstairs. And a brush for your hair."

Shanti ascended the steps behind Aiden. They entered a

pleasant open room with carved wooden furnishings, a table and chairs, artistic knickknacks sitting on shelves, paintings on the walls, and a pot of tea infused with aromatic spices, simmering on a potbellied stove.

A woman, a stranger, approached and looked at the bite and scratches on her neck. "You certainly made her angry this time." Aiden's exact words.

"I'd like you to meet my mother, Kiana," Aiden said. He and Kiana had the same color hair and eyes, the same complexion, and the same easygoing manner. Aiden's father, the castle painter, was also present, with two young girls who looked to be 14 or 15 years old. Another Guardian, a brawny man, had come to check on Shanti, also. A woman with beautiful white hair and a pink shawl entered the room, supporting her broken arm. Shanti thought she looked like a broken angel.

"Madiza," she said. "Did you foresee this?"

"I saw the possibility of it. My dear Shanti, we need to talk. First, get some medicine on that bite and have something to eat and drink. You're safe here."

Aiden took Shanti's weapons and put them in a wooden trunk. His sisters helped their mother grind herbs with a mortar and pestle to apply to the bite wound. The vivacious girls talked—so different from their quiet mother and Aiden. They even brushed and braided Shanti's hair, chatting the whole time, asking a new question before she had time to answer the last. Quiet Kiana put a blanket around Shanti's shoulders then gave her a cup of hot tea before leaving her alone with Madiza."

"Good family." Shanti held the warm cup in both hands, sipping her tea.

"Yes." Madiza sat next to her and groaned when her elbow bumped the armrest of the chair. "Gy was hoping that Bayla would marry Aiden. The possibility exists. They both need to commit to that choice, though."

"Bayla doesn't always make good choices," Shanti said.

"She's young. Are you ready?"

"Ready for what? For you to hex me with a sleeping spell and look into my future? No, thank you. Speaking of which, how come the monks say they can predict the future with absolute certainty, yet you say the future can be altered?"

"The monks' visions are always true. My insight shows possible pathways. It's a natural gift to guide others. The monks obtain their information against the laws of nature and use it for themselves. That's why they are cursed."

"Better not to know," Shanti said.

"Afraid? You don't realize your potential. Come with me into the future. All you have to do is touch my hand and share my power." Madiza lifted her hand. On her wrist was the opal bracelet.

"That belonged to Queen Serova."

"Yes." Madiza touched the dark stones embedded with flecks of color. "I had to do a bit of magic to get it. Serova bequeathed it to Bayla, but the monks did not want the child to have it, so they buried it with Serova. Grave robbers searching for royal treasure are common. I could not let the stones fall into the wrong hands."

"The bracelet is powerful, then."

"It is helpful." Madiza again lifted her hand toward Shanti. "You came out of the tunnel, and you'll come out of this."

Shanti set down the cup of tea and pulled the blanket tight around her. She reached for Madiza's hand. The room disintegrated into a darkness so black, no Nunqua could penetrate it with their mortal vision. Shanti fell into another dimension, stretching as she descended. Her spirit contracted, then regained its regular shape as a familiar room materialized. Madiza stood beside Shanti, her broken arm still wrapped in a pink shawl.

"Interesting." Madiza took in the long room with portraits covering the walls. "Where are we?"

"The portrait room inside the castle," Shanti said.

"The portrait room. Perfect! Your power is surprising."

Power? Shanti observed the painting of King Magen. It had

changed. Magen didn't look strong and vigorous as in his youth; the painting portrayed a sickly monarch. A heavy chain weighted his shoulders, and he held up two fingers.

Shanti leaned closer to the portrait. "The painting is the same, yet different."

"Remember, you're not standing inside the castle. This is a vision. Everything is open to interpretation. The two fingers Magen is holding up, I believe, signify that he was never entirely in control of Willovia."

Shanti studied the portrait of Bayla's mother next. Serova's lips were black, matching the black of her dress. She gripped a leash around a wolf's neck and cradled a bundle wrapped in cloth."

"Serova was poisoned," Madiza said, "when she was pregnant with her second child. King Magen never knew that it was the monks who murdered his wife and unborn son. The monks feared Serova and the child in her womb, so they murdered her. If the king had ever found out, he would have butchered every monk and every friend and supporter of the monks, only to become a bitter man full of hate."

"Did the monks poison Magen, too, causing his sickness?"

"No, he wasn't poisoned."

Shanti looked at a torn portrait. Four scratches split the canvas surface. The portrait showed a sickly monarch whose eyes were rimmed in red. He held a book in one hand; the other hand was missing—cut off. "What happened?" Shanti said.

"Serova," Madiza answered.

The tiny hairs on Shanti's arms rose. A woman in a black dress, with pointed teeth and black lips, appeared next to her. Shanti jumped. Had the spirit of Serova always been with them?

"Her power is limited," Madiza said. "She cannot speak or hurt you."

Serova raised her arm. Attached to her sleeve were two bats exactly like the ones Shanti had killed.

"Enough of your games, Sera." Madiza turned to Shanti.

"Only when she became queen did she become Serova. Her name is Sera. Don't fear the dead; it's the living we must contend with." Sera changed her appearance into that of a normal, quite attractive woman. She lowered her arm, and the bats disappeared.

Another portrait had four slash marks down its center. "Your temper, Sera, is unrivaled," Madiza said. The portrait showed a bearded king wearing a shabby bearskin coat. On his shield was the small letter "g," the symbol of the Guardians of Willovia. A hooded hawk perched on his gloved arm, and the castle crumbled in the background.

"Trouble comes to every life, Shanti," Madiza said.

A strange sensation enveloped her as she moved toward three new portraits—pictures of the future. Baylova, in a red dress, graced the canvas. The fingernails of her left hand were black, and her right hand dripped blood. At her feet was an army of wolves and dogs. Vultures, crows, and bats darkened the top of the portrait. Hanging on a string around her neck was a lock of hair. Shanti touched her own hair—the same color as the lock in the portrait.

"It is possibilities that we see," Madiza said.

"Do the Nunqua conquer Baylova, or does Baylova conquer the Nunqua? Is that *my* hair?"

"It is . . . possible."

Next to Baylova's portrait was a painting of Commander Gy. He held a sword and a shield, yet he looked grim like the other monarchs. "Gy would make a good king," Shanti said.

"Look closer. Tell me what you see."

On Gy's chest, over his heart, were two holes, through which the background colors of the paint could be seen. Shanti moved her head from side to side. The holes gave the impression of moving with her. Smoke rose in the background: the castle on fire, near a red sea.

"The holes are for his children. If Gy becomes king, his children will be kidnapped, and he will lose them. He will have no heirs to inherit Willovia. Upon his death, civil war will consume the country."

"He knows this? Is that why he let Bayla be crowned even though she didn't pass the Guardians' tests?"

Serova's appearance reverted to a sharp-toothed, black-lipped female demon. She opened her mouth in an invisible hiss toward Shanti.

"Gy doesn't know, but his wife, Tova, does. I read her fortune. I suspect she has influenced his judgment."

One more portrait of the future hung on the wall before them. Long scratches tore the picture of a possible future queen. Ripped canvas obscured the face. Shanti smoothed the canvas to see herself. "Lies." She stepped away.

Serova, minus her demon mask, pushed Shanti toward the portrait.

"Not lies," Madiza said. "Possibilities. It takes true courage to look."

Shanti smoothed the torn portrait. She wore a blue dress with a red sash of mourning. In her hand was a globe, and two swords were strapped across her back. The painting showed her as she was at birth: a half-breed with faded spots. She looked grim and bone weary. Her left ear was deformed, sliced into upper and lower sections. Shanti felt her ear. It was whole. "Why is my ear like that?"

Madiza sighed. "Because the king is a powerful, often violent man. The globe means you will travel far. I think you travel to get away from him. You ran away from him once, pretending to be his spy."

"Caravey," Shanti said. "More lies."

"Is it so hard to believe? Have you truly forgotten? You had a relationship with him. Despite his cruelty, he still cares for you. General Caravey Delartay controls Lord Argu of the Nunqua." Madiza pointed to a thin string wrapped tight around Shanti's neck. "I once said that you are a string pulled so tight, it is bound to break. You are also the string that binds Willovia and the Nunqua together—a half-breed. Caravey knows your importance. It's why he protects you, why he hopes you'll return to his side. The people of both countries will respect you as queen, even love you. But you will have to sacrifice much."

"I will not marry Caravey."

"Then he must be defeated." Madiza sighed. "But how do you kill a healer? He cannot die by the sword or sickness. He cannot be poisoned. Only Baylova is powerful enough to kill Caravey. I cannot do it. And you won't."

Shanti gazed at the red sash she wore in the painting. She would not ask for whom she mourned. Serova's icy fingers touched the bite mark near her collarbone. The queen had long, dark eyelashes and brown eyes. She seemed young—in her mid-twenties, Shanti guessed. Serova raised one hand toward Shanti and the other toward Madiza. Her demon mask returned, and her hands morphed into claws. She raked the air with her fingers.

The opals on Madiza's bracelet transformed into black leeches. The leeches burrowed under her skin, leaving bloody pits on tattered flesh.

Serova advanced toward Shanti and slashed her face. Shanti's skin split, cut by knives of ice. She opened her eyes to throttle the neck of the black witch, break her nose and maybe a finger or two. But she was back inside Aiden's house. The blanket had fallen off her shoulders, and her tea was cold. Shanti felt her face with her hands: numb but unmarked. "The apple doesn't fall far from the tree," she said.

Madiza chuckled, then grimaced as she readjusted her broken arm and touched the opal bracelet. "Harmless tricks to protect Baylova. For you or Gy to rule, Baylova must be destroyed. The possibility exists that you destroy Baylova."

"You're the ivory ant. You told me that killing the queen would kill the colony."

"If Gy becomes king, civil war decimates Willovia upon his death. If Caravey rules, the Nunqua alter the landscape of the country by using up our resources without replenishing them. Within one generation's time, a famine devastates Willovia. Innocent people—children—will starve. Disease will be widespread. Willovia will be a wasteland. Caravey may be able to heal the sick, but he cannot conjure food out of nothing to feed the starving."

"But Baylova's portrait was not of a benevolent queen who rules justly," Shanti said. "You want me to spare her life so she can lead Willovia by instilling fear in its citizens. I don't understand."

"The portrait can change, Shanti."

"What kind of fortune-teller are you? You show me the future, then tell me it's not necessarily the future. Everything can change. This information is useless."

"I show you the pathways; you choose the path. If you do become queen, you must work to avoid the famine, and you mustn't run away. Please remember that."

"Why didn't you die when the owl was killed?" Shanti asked.

"For the same reason Baylova didn't die when you killed the bats. It's a simple matter of intent. Baylova wanted to hurt me. She used her power to break my arm, show me her strength, and stop me from interfering in her plans. The guard who killed the owl had no knowledge of my presence in the room. He had no power over me. Understand this, Shanti: to take a human life requires more effort than simply killing a possessed animal." Madiza rose from the chair, supporting her injured arm. "There's something important I must share with the Guardians. I suppose it can wait until tomorrow. Good night. Get some rest."

Madiza left the house, escorted by the burly Guardian, to stay at an inn for the night.

*

Shanti lay on a couch inside Aiden's family's house and stared up at the wooden beams in the ceiling. Horrible thoughts of the tunnel, Serova, and the bats swirled in her brain, and she couldn't sleep. She wished Madiza had hexed her with a sleeping spell before leaving. She also wished she didn't know the future, the awful possibilities.

Guardians gathered the next day in the home. The burly man told Shanti, "Your saddle and horse are in my stable."

"I was wondering if I could sell my horse or exchange it somewhere," she said. "It's a good horse when it's not possessed."

"That shouldn't be a problem," he said.

Guardians, including Aiden, his father, and three other men, congregated around the old woman with the broken arm. "I know who let the Nunqua warriors into the castle," Madiza said. "The monks have bought rare herbs and spices from the Nunqua for years to make their potions. They use the caves to conduct these secret transactions. These rogue warriors entered through a seldom-used area of the caves. Their superior eyesight gives them an advantage. They had no intentions of harming Baylova; they only wanted to create a reputation for themselves."

Shanti closed her eyes and leaned against a wall as Madiza droned on. She was tired of such dreadful topics: civil war, famine, kidnapping, death, poisoning, treachery. She left the Guardians and entered the kitchen.

Kiana and Aiden's sisters were making bread and soup for their guests. An opening in the brick chimney was situated above the fireplace where the bread was being baked. The warm kitchen smelled like dough. "May I help?" Shanti asked.

"Of course." Kiana gave her an apron.

Shanti rolled up her sleeves and kneaded dough while listening to the girls chat cheerfully about innocuous topics: studies and books and boys and dancing. It had been a long time since she last made bread. Her mother had taught her how to cook when she was a child. It was simple, comforting, and useful—a joyful task that cleansed her spirit, like helping deliver babies.

Shanti patted the soft ball of dough. Flour dusted her hands. Somewhere in life, she had taken a wrong turn, and now she traveled on a path that led only to devastation.

26
BURNING BOOKS

J UN LIMPED INTO the open-air arena. Tiered benches, some wooden and some carved out of solid rock in the side of a hill, surrounded a flat field with entryways in the north, south, west, and east. It was a filthy hole where most of the spectators, Nunqua men and women, watched in a drunken revelry. Armed warriors guarded the area and watched the show. Two men wrestled in the pit. Plumes of dust rose as their bodies smacked the ground and their feet kicked up dirt. Noisy onlookers placed bets and jeered. Jun would not fight like an animal to appease the Nunqua, and he would not kill a Willovian. He would rather be flogged.

Zindar stood on the other side of the pit and lifted metal balls that fit in the palms of his hands, preparing his muscles to fight. He wore the black uniform of the Nunqua and chatted with the warriors. He appeared clean, well fed, and properly groomed. A sudden fury burned inside Jun.

The wrestling match ended, and Zindar moved to the center of the arena, sword in hand.

General Delartay spoke to Jun. "He challenged you, Willovian. This has nothing to do with the war. Zindar wants revenge for the scars on his back." A short Nunqua, leather bands around his biceps, gave Jun an ordinary sword. Delartay continued. "Win, and you win food for your tent. Lose, and Zindar will kill you."

Jun stayed where he was. The short Nunqua shoved him into the pit. Jun could not bring himself to look at Zindar.

"I've heard rumors of how good you are with a sword, Commander Jun. Let's find out." Zindar swung puckishly at his opponent. Jun blocked the blow but did not fight in earnest. "What's wrong with your leg?" he chortled through his teeth as he continued fighting. "I heard you hurt your knee trying to escape a jealous husband after he found you and his wife together in bed."

Their swords clanked. Jun locked Zindar in a sudden arm hold. "Their defenses are weak at the east entrance," Jun said. "Horses are tied just outside the arena. We can fight the Nunqua and escape if we're quick enough."

Zindar's black boot kicked Jun's sore knee. He yelled in pain and listened to his opponent once again laugh through his teeth.

"You're a rapist and a traitor," Jun said. "And a dead man."

Jun limped as he exchanged blows with Zindar. He was hungry, tired, yet winning. The audience roared at the display of skill against strength. Jun cut Zindar's leg. The black uniform gaped open, blood flowing down and obscuring the color of skin. Zindar's heavy blade swung futilely again and again. Jun sliced open Zindar's side, the cut not deep enough to kill. He cut Zindar's back, then his chin, like a cat playing with a mouse. Zindar dropped his sword and raised his hands.

The audience waited for Jun to end the match, hissing at the delay in their entertainment.

Delartay, along with two other warriors, entered the pit. "Either cut his arm or cut his neck, Willovian."

Jun tossed the sword into the dirt.

"Then I shall do it for you." Delartay unsheathed his own sword, and the noise of the crowd quieted to an expectant murmur.

"I'm Willovian," Jun said, "not Nunqua. I will not mark his

arm. Zindar is Willovian. I want him brought into the same camp, the same flea-infested tent, where I'm forced to sleep. And I want him wearing the same black uniform he wears now."

"No!" Zindar reached for his sword on the ground, but a warrior stepped on the blade to stop him.

Warriors forced Zindar out of the arena, and spectators groaned in disappointment, denied the opportunity to witness a gory ending to the death match.

Delartay said softly to Jun, "I do not die so easily as this."

Jun shuffled back to the prisoner-of-war camp, escorted by warriors on horses, a short chain hobbling his feet. He surveyed the land and Nunqua defenses, trying to deduce a means of escape. They pushed him into the fenced-in camp. Soon after, Zindar was pushed into the same prisoner-of-war camp, weaponless and wearing the black uniform of a traitor.

Warriors found Zindar's corpse the next morning near the fence, beaten and killed by his own kind, the ruby ring still on his finger.

*

Shanti rode a brown and white paint into the Hedgelands. She entered the secluded camp in the woods and tethered her horse to a tree. Dried leaves had been blown inside the pavilion where the soldiers once ate. Wasp nests clung to the rafters. It was early spring—too cold for the insects to be active. A string hung from the rafters, the tuft of Mr. Pascha's hair gone, probably taken by birds to line their nests.

Shanti went to the stump in the middle of camp. She traced the grooves of the dragon carved by Aiden, its paint now faded. Things had changed so much in a year, it made her feel old. She took a small knife from her saddlebag and scratched the name "Pirro" into the stump as artistically as she could.

Shanti hiked on the narrow path winding through the woods to the picturesque spot by the stream. The cairn of rocks she had assembled in the fall was still there, although the topmost stone had fallen. She moved the rocks, then stabbed the earth with her knife to loosen the dirt. She dug into the cold ground with her hands, mud scrunching up under her fingernails, and pulled out the blanket—brown now from being buried in the soil for so long. She unwrapped Bayla's sword, which she had stolen at the obstacle course, hidden under her bed, and buried when she was alone at camp and the other soldiers were gone playing war games. The engraved dragon twisted around the blade, which was still shiny and sharp.

Shanti sheathed the sword and slung it over her shoulder. Two swords now crossed her back in the shape of an X. She knelt next to the cold stream to rinse the dirt from her hands, and a sudden queasiness twisted her gut. She couldn't bring herself to touch the water.

The strap from the weapon irritated the skin on her collarbone. She tugged the strap away from the bite wound to ease the painful itching, and spread mud on the wound, but it didn't help. The pocketknife could hack away the scab from the bite wound. Holding the dirt-encrusted blade to her neck, she prepared to scrape it across her skin.

The hole in the ground where the sword had been buried widened, and dirt around the edges fell into the depression. A pale hand emerged—a phantom escaping its hellish abode. Serova crawled out of the pit, her lips black and her dress tattered. She crept toward Shanti, smelling like meat left in the sun too long.

Shanti stabbed Serova with the pocketknife and encountered nothing but air. The hole was only a two-foot pit in the earth. She was alone in the woods, or had she descended into another dimension? Was she having a vision?

She pressed a cold, dirty hand to her scorching hot forehead and prayed for sanity. The journey would be long, and she was very sick. She must find Caravey.

"The monks?" Baylova questioned Commander Kyros. She placed her hands on the desk, her abdomen resting against the edge. The skin beneath the fingernails of her left hand was stained black from the poison, as it would always be. Sunlight poured through the windows and created elongated patterns on the floor. Six colorful flags decorated the walls of the room.

"The monks buy rare herbs and medicines from the Nunqua through the caves," Kyros said.

"It can't be. I had a vision of warriors at the camp in the Hedgelands when I returned to the castle for my father's last days. These warriors knew Shanti; I'm sure of it. She's the traitor who led the Nunqua into the castle—not the monks. Where did you get this information?"

He didn't want to tell her that the information came from a fortune-teller, communicated to him by Aiden. "My sources have been investigating the matter."

"Monks? Do you believe this information to be correct?" she asked.

"I do," he said.

Baylova paced back and forth in front of the desk. "But Shanti was a warrior—*is* a warrior. Where is she?"

"I don't know."

She stopped pacing. "You don't know, or you won't tell me. Where's the old monk?"

"Imprisoned at the south end of the royal guards' training grounds."

"Has he been interrogated?"

The question surprised Kyros. The monk was a fragile old man. "No."

"Take me to see him, Commander. Let's ask him what he knows. Bring ten guards at least. We leave now."

Kyros bowed to her command. He gathered ten of his best

guards. With the queen, they rode through the city streets to the prison.

The frail old monk, dressed in the blue robes of a learned man, sat nobly in a Willovian jail cell. Baylova remained outside the cage, flanked by Kyros and the royal guards.

"Is something wrong?" the monk asked.

She grasped the bars, scanning up and down their length. "Why did you do it?"

"Do what?"

"Help the Nunqua warriors into the castle."

"You're mistaken."

The queen spoke softly, her eyelids half-closed. "You know the castle even better than I do."

"Baylova, reinstate the order," the old monk pleaded. "We can work together to defeat the Nunqua. We can save the lives of many."

"It was you." Her eyes closed. "I can feel it."

The monk's attitude changed, and his lips curled into a snarl. "More will die." He rose from the hard chair, staying away from the bars and out of reach of Baylova and her guards. "Where's our brother you so favor? Does he remain at the castle, or has he gone?"

Bayla looked at Commander Kyros. Kyros signaled that the young monk, Tobian, was no longer a guest at the castle.

"My brothers are out there, waiting to return. You have to believe that we act with a sense of duty and responsibility. If you break the ancient pact, then you break Willovia. Accept your fate, or Willovia is doomed. It doesn't end with me."

"No, it ends with me. I will have no heirs to appease your bloodlust. The royal line of Willovia dies with me."

"You need us. Our powers of prophecy are essential to your rule. Reinstate the order!"

"Never."

"I know many things, Baylova," he said. "Commander Kyros, would you like to know the future? Would you like to know how you die? I can tell you. Baylova, I can tell you who is loyal to you and who isn't. Isn't that important for a monarch to know? What do you say? Reinstate the order, and I'll tell you everything." He chuckled from behind the bars, hands clasped in a virtuous posture in front of his chest.

Baylova bent her fingers in the shape of a claw. She lifted her hand over her head, then slashed downward in a startling gesture toward the prisoner.

His laughter increased at her childish behavior—until four deep scratches appeared on the thin skin of his face. Black ooze seeped out of the cuts. He felt the cuts and gaped at the dark fluid on his fingertips. "You're as evil as your mother."

"I will make sure you never say anything to anybody, ever again."

She sliced her clawed fingers sideways through the air. He opened his mouth, and black liquid spattered out. The monk choked on the thick fluid and spat out his tongue. She had cut it off. Disgust overwhelmed everyone in the jail as they watched the old man struggle.

"He will survive," the queen calmly informed the guards. "I want the monks found," she said to Commander Kyros. "All twenty of them. Put them in separate jail cells, in separate towns if need be. Find Tobian, and bring him to me. Burn the monastery. Make sure the guards salvage nothing from that building. To do so would bring grave misfortune down on Willovia. I'll go with you."

Kyros momentarily looked away from the sputtering monk to acknowledge the queen's command. He returned his gaze to the spectacle. The inky substance ran down the prisoner's chin and onto his robes.

The Queen and her guards left the prison. Commander Kyros stayed to watch the old monk try to speak. With an agility that belied his advanced age, the prisoner sprang at him, eyes bulging in hate. His arm reached through the bars to grasp at Kyros's clothing. Kyros backed away and left the imprisoned monk alone. The old man was now physically unable to enlighten anyone else with his twisted, foreboding secrets.

*

Tobian lurked in the shadows of buildings. He watched as flames consumed the monks' former residence. His eyes were rimmed in red, and it appeared as if some unknown illness ravaged his once strong body. Every day, he felt weaker without the miraculous potion that could save and enlighten him. He reached into his shirt and touched the last beaker, the only surviving sample of the mystical elixir. No, there was more, but it was walking around in the body of Baylova. Tobian longed for another taste of the future.

Baylova had imprisoned his mentor, set fire to his home, destroyed the vital history books of Willovia. She shouldn't have burned those books. The queen had too much power and was becoming a tyrant. He must destroy her. He hung his head, and reason fleetingly overtook the power of the spell. He must destroy the potion.

But Tobian could bring himself to destroy neither the queen nor the potion in his pocket. He ran as far as he could, away from the burning building and away from the capital city of Erbaut, but he could not escape his curse.

27
SNAPPING THE STRING

CARAVEY DELARTAY SAT on an uncomfortable chair as Lord Argu sauntered about the room and talked nonstop. Argu's fist smacked his hand, and he lectured the general concerning war. A dozen mismatched chairs were scattered about, and large maps were rolled up inside a canister on the floor. Caravey's feet rested on another chair, his legs crossed at the ankles. How he hated Argu's impromptu speeches. The pompous ruler knew nothing of military tactics or the ways of a warrior. The only reason he tolerated Argu, who considered himself the greatest warrior ever, was because of his money and connections.

One of Caravey's men opened the door and entered the room. "General Delartay . . ."

"How dare you barge in here!" Argu barked.

Caravey raised his palm. "It's all right. What is it?"

"A woman is here to see you."

"You interrupt me because of some *woman*?" Lord Argu put his hands on his hips. "Honestly, General, your warriors have no sense of things."

Caravey held back the urge to punch Argu in the head for

insulting one of his men. The warrior tossed a wristlet into Caravey's lap. The wristlet contained three poisoned darts. "My apologies, Lord Argu," Caravey said. "This is urgent, pertaining to the war. I have to go." He followed the warrior out, happy for any excuse to leave Lord Argu's company.

She stood between two black-clad warriors. Two swords were strapped to her back, and she wore Willovian attire yet looked like the half-breed she was.

"*Two* swords, Shanti?" He grinned. "You're not that good." He felt the sickness before he saw it in her weary features and glassy eyes. His smile disappeared. "What is it?"

"The queen . . . bit me. She's . . . no." She shook her head. "A bat."

"Take her inside," Caravey ordered. "Find a bed for her. How did she get here?"

"Horseback," a warrior said. "She was alone. She's been tracked since yesterday."

"See that her horse is taken care of," he said.

"What's wrong with her?"

Caravey regarded the wristlet in his hands. "She's dying." He went into a crudely constructed wooden building and commanded the warriors to leave him alone with Shanti. Sitting on the edge of the bed where she lay, he put the wristlet on a small table.

"Why did you cut my ear?" she said.

"You're hallucinating." He touched her ear. "There's nothing wrong with your ear." Caravey held both her hands. They were dirty, limp, and hot.

"You cut my ear in half. You tied a string around my neck. Can you help me take these swords off?" The weapons were still strapped to her body, wedged between her and the mattress. Caravey removed the swords and laid them beside her.

"Why do you have two swords?"

"She hates me. I stole her sword, and she hates me."

"Who?" Caravey pulled aside Shanti's shirt to view the bite wound.

"The bat is retribution. The queen. Can you help me? I can't . . . much longer."

Caravey lifted Shanti's quaking body to a sitting position. He put his hand gently on the back of her head and kissed her, tasting her lips and breathing in the sickness. His healing power flowed through her. She leaned against him, her cheek on his shoulder. He held her until the shaking of her muscles ceased.

"Why did you wait so long to come back?" he said.

She snored softly, her body exhausted. Caravey laid her back on the mattress and put a blanket over her. She hugged the two swords, in their separate sheaths, close to her chest.

"Shanti," he whispered, and his smile returned.

*

Baylova wore her brown uniform. The sharp talons of a hawk clutched her leather-gauntleted arm. She removed the hood covering the hawk's eyes. "Go. Find her."

The bird spread its wings and leaped from her arm, gliding high above the trees and into the cloudless blue sky. Baylova watched until it vanished from view.

Commander Kyros was with her. He, too, wore a brown uniform. "Baylova, we're ready."

"Have you captured any monks?" she asked.

"Six have been imprisoned. Tobian is still missing."

Baylova sighed. "I'm almost glad to be leaving. How many guards are there?"

"Four hundred and twenty two," he said. "We'll join another five hundred along the way."

"Tell the guards not to touch or kill any animals they see. The wolves are also for my protection."

"Your protection?" Kyros said. "What about food—rabbits and deer? The men will need to hunt for meat."

"So be it."

Baylova and Commander Kyros marched in front of silent soldiers standing straight. She mounted her stallion next to a soldier on horseback. Attached to his saddle was a blue flag adorned with a falcon. The flag flapped above their heads in the wind.

"Do you wish to speak to the men before we leave?" Kyros said.

The soldiers were lined up in an impressive display, motionless, ready to bow to her command. She searched for Aiden in the group but could not find him. "I have nothing to say."

"Baylova," he spoke through clenched teeth, "you must." His jaw tightened, yet she did nothing. Kyros mounted a black horse with a white streak on its muzzle. He galloped in front of the men and unsheathed his sword, holding it high above his head. His horse kicked the air with its front hooves. The men cheered, their battle cry rising up to the clear sky.

"We face the invaders and fight for Willovia!" Kyros's voice thundered above the noise. "For our families and our children. The Nunqua will not enslave us. We will not be second-class citizens to an inferior breed."

Men shouted, "Hell, no!" and "Filthy Nunqua beasts!"

Kyros continued, "I would rather die! There is no glory in war, in what we are about to see and do. But we must do what is right, and send the bastards back to hell, where they belong! You are the strength of Willovia. From this point on, I serve you. Willovia will be victorious only because of honorable men like you." Kyros returned his sword to its sheath and rode past Baylova, giving her a bitter, disrespectful glare.

*

Shanti woke to find a folded black uniform and boots on a table next to the bed. Never had she felt so grimy. She changed her appearance to full-fledged Nunqua, with scars on her arms. The sickness no longer weakened her body. She carried the swords, wristlet, and uniform outside. The warrior camp was flat with single-story wooden buildings—mere shells to break the wind. Young warriors gawked at Shanti as they passed. "Bathhouse," she barked in the language of the Nunqua.

They directed her to a wooden building with six doors on the front. Various-size kettles and pots of water steamed above a large stove. She strode into the bathhouse. A Nunqua woman poured water into an empty metal pot.

"It's about time," the woman said. "I haven't had a break all day." Shanti grabbed a towel and wrapped it around the heated handle of a pot. "What do you think you're doing?" the woman said. Then, seeing the black uniform and weapons in Shanti's hand and the humorless look on her face, she grudgingly returned to her task.

Shanti entered a private room inside the bathhouse. Oilcloth lined a square tub half-full of clean water. She dropped her things, emptied the steaming water into the tub, then returned outside to get a new pot.

"You only get one," the woman said.

Shanti ignored the comment and picked up another heated pot. A basket held rounded balls of soap. She took one and smelled it. "This all you have?"

The woman lifted a wet hand, red and irritated from the cleansers used in the bathhouse. "There's honey-milk and lavender-scented soaps in the storage area. Might even have some perfume for you, too. Perhaps a pretty bow for your hair."

"No one disturbs me," Shanti ordered.

She bathed, washing her hair three times, until the water was cold and the soap a mere speck. Putting on the black uniform—the tight underclothes, pants, comfortable boots, and midlength jacket—was like traveling back in time. She strapped the wristlet onto her scarred arm, swung the two swords onto her back, and left the bathhouse. A different woman worked there now, stoking the fire with scraps of wood. She saw Shanti and quickly averted her eyes.

The uniform gave her a grandiose feeling of superiority. Shanti wrung water out of her hair and combed it with her fingers. Warriors walked toward her, chests out, chins held high. They were masters of camp.

"I can't believe it," they said. "She's back."

"We thought you were going to sleep forever."

"I almost did." Five warriors surrounded Shanti. The short man with bands around his biceps put his arms around her legs and lifted her off the ground, draping her over his shoulder.

"Tracker," she said. "Don't you owe me money?"

He put her down. "Ah, you're still hallucinating, I see. How the hell did a bat bite you? Were you throwing rocks in a barn?"

"Actually . . ." She put her wet hair into a knot and secured it with a band. "The bat was possessed. I'll tell you about it as soon as I get some food. I'm *starving*."

"Same old Shanti," a burly warrior said.

"Gitonk." Shanti pulled a necklace of human hair from under his jacket. A lock of red adorned the morbid collection. "You bastard."

"It's war, nothing more."

"Bullshit," she said.

Tracker pulled her away from Gitonk. "Come on," he said. "I'll show you where you can eat."

"I need to find my horse and saddle first."

Tracker took her to the stables. Her horse grazed nearby, and her saddle perched astride a wooden wall inside a crude structure with a noticeable lean. Opening her saddlebag, she took out the feather, stained brown, and put it in her pocket. She searched for something else. "Somebody stole my money. I expected as much."

Tracker pulled Shanti's bag of coins from his pocket and threw it to her. "Just keeping it safe for you. Are we even?"

"Your debt is paid."

Next, Shanti opened a box from inside her saddlebag. She put on the necklace with one lock of hair and hid it under her jacket. "General Delartay expects me to wear it," she said. "Let's eat."

They went to a popular tavern a short distance away. Heaps of potatoes, eggs, and venison were mounded on Shanti's plate. She felt light-headed drinking her second mug of ale. Tracker, Gitonk, General Delartay, and other warriors listened to her. "I slipped on the stairs and fell down about . . ." She took a bite of meat, then a swig of ale. ". . . twelve steps, maybe twenty. The castle guests just stared at me. I swear, I was an absolute mess. They finally helped me to my feet. The queen couldn't very well come down in her night-gown—too busy pretending to be sick. So I ran out of the castle, got on my horse, and rode into the city. Then she sent wolves after me."

"Wolves?" Tracker said.

"And if that weren't bad enough, that witch turned my horse against me. Luckily, some people came out of their houses to help."

"She's powerful?" Caravey asked.

Shanti took a bite of eggs. "She's *scary*. I don't think she's reached her full potential."

"Why doesn't she turn your horse against you now, send a pack of wolves to tear us apart here in this tavern?"

She shrugged. "I'm not sure. Perhaps she needs to know my whereabouts before using her power against me. Maybe she needs to be closer or experience a strong emotional cue to initiate an attack. In all honesty, I think she's terrified. We're not defenseless children she can manipulate with fear. We are warriors!" Shanti lifted her glass in salute, and the men around her howled and beat their chests. Caravey remained quiet, nodding slightly to show his approval. "I went to the Hedgelands to get her sword," Shanti said, "and that's when I started hallucinating. Ghosts and demons chased me, tried to steal my soul, tear me apart. A small, sane part of my brain knew I was going mad. I'm surprised even I made it here."

Caravey took a drink of his ale. "Whose hair hangs at the pavil-ion in the Hedgelands?"

Shanti put down her mug and thought of Pirro's needless death. "Why did you go there? It wasn't right. The hair belonged to the cook."

"I doubt it." Gitonk said thickly. "You wouldn't insult the cook. You like food too much."

"Oh, he was a good cook, too. His chicken stew and sourdough bread were the best." Shanti gulped down the last of her ale and ordered another. "But he was an ass and needed to be dealt with." She clasped her hands together and cracked her knuckles. "Tied him to a tree."

A Nunqua woman in uniform, with a sword across her back, came to the table. "General Delartay, boys. Who's this?" She regarded Shanti as if looking at something foul scraped from the bottom of her boot. "I thought you weren't taking on new warriors, General."

"What do you want, Yasmine?" Caravey said.

Yasmine watched Shanti get bread from a dish, devour it, and guzzle some ale. "She eats like a pig."

"I haven't eaten in two days," Shanti said.

Caravey glanced at Yasmine only briefly. "I'm not taking new warriors into my group unless they have special skills I desire."

Shanti wiped her mouth with a cloth and scrutinized the woman warrior. Black braids hung past her shoulders. her uniform was tailored to accentuate her breasts. Her eyes were dark and her spots small. Body art, symbols of strength painted red, adorned her well-toned arms.

"What's her skill?" she sneered.

Shanti took another drink. "I forget."

"Surely not swords. Why do you have two? Do you think you can beat me?"

"I'm a little drunk right now, but . . ." Shanti stood, the mug of ale still in her hand. "what the hell."

"No," Yasmine said, scowling. "An official fight in the arena. If

I win, General Delartay allows me to join his warriors. The best of the best."

Shanti looked to the general for permission.

"You've been sick," he said. "Not to mention out of practice. But a challenge is a challenge. You will fight."

"All right." She sat back down, and Yasmine left. "Is she any good?" Shanti asked.

"She's more interested in *looking like* a warrior than being one," Delartay said. "What do you want if you win? And you'd better win."

"If it's acceptable to you, General, I'll wait until after the fight to make my request."

"Keeping secrets from me?"

His. tone hinted of a threat. It made the hidden scars and burns on her hands hurt in remembrance. She forced a laugh. "Like I said, I'm a little drunk. I don't want to waste my request on something foolish."

Caravey continued to drink, visibly displeased by the guarded answer.

"I need some time to think about it," she said. "That's all."

They stumbled back to camp, their spirits high. The sun sank under the horizon. They passed men, Willovian prisoners carrying firewood and guarded by warriors. A familiar voice said, "Filthy half-breed."

Hair covered his neck. His clothes were worn, and he limped with his back toward her. Iron chains shackled his feet, although he was still able to take small steps. Shanti passed the guards and approached the prisoners, pulling on his shoulder to view the bearded face. "Jun."

"It's the Willovian from the Hedgelands," Tracker said.

"Jun," Gitonk said. "Isn't that a girl's name?"

"Nice uniform." Jun viewed her with disgust. "Why don't you come into the Willovian camp for the night."

General Delartay moved behind Shanti and peered over her

shoulder. "You must have a death wish, Willovian. Killing Zindar is one matter. Shanti's one of my warriors. She belongs to me."

"Zindar?" she said.

"Oh, yes," Caravey put his arm around the front of her shoulders. "Zindar challenged Jun to a fight in the arena. Your friend is quite skilled with a sword. He won. But instead of cutting his opponent's arm, Jun here requested that Zindar stay at the prisoner-of-war camp, in the same tent where he sleeps. We found Zindar's corpse the next morning, beaten so badly we could recognize it only by the ring on his finger."

She felt as if someone had punched her in the gut. "You killed Zindar?"

"I killed a traitor."

"Beat him to death." Caravey ran his hand up and down Shanti's arm. "Do you want to know how we captured Commander Jun? We found him jumping from a second-story window—a woman's bedroom—trying to escape a jealous husband who had come home to find him in bed with his wife. That's how he hurt his knee, not in some glorious battle."

"A fight." Jun stared at Shanti. "Just her and me in the arena."

"Prisoners cannot challenge. Besides, someone else has already challenged Shanti. Gitonk, you'll fight Commander Jun, as I promised."

Caravey stepped away from Shanti. She took Baylova's sword off her back and showed Jun the dragon engraved on the handle.

"Traitor *and* thief," Jun said.

"You murdered Zindar and committed adultery. Don't accuse me of crimes without first considering your own actions." Shanti and the warriors left the prisoners.

She lay in bed that night with a knife under her pillow, two swords beside her, and poisoned darts within arm's reach. The wind blew, making the walls creak. A loose board banged on the roof. Shanti hoped Caravey wouldn't come to her bed to rekindle the flame that no longer burned for him. That fire burned for someone else.

Jun was locked in the prisoner-of-war camp. He appeared thin, scruffy, and full of hate. Was he acting, concealing his emotions to survive? What had happened with Zindar? How was Jun captured?

Shanti pulled a long thread away from the frayed edge of the sheet. She wrapped the thread around both hands. Was she a string pulled so taut it was bound to break, or was she the string meant to bind Willovia and the Nunqua together? She snapped the thread into two separate pieces—exactly how she felt.

28
UNCLE SEIKO

TRACKER AND GITONK sparred with Shanti, attacking her in a grassy field. Their swords swung smoothly, alternating blows blocked by Shanti in a dance of elongated arm movements and cautious steps. The exercise, the actions of her now healthy muscles, was invigorating.

"Technique over force," Caravey said. "Brain over body, head over heart. The sword is your will, and your will is strong."

She focused on the movements. Her surroundings faded. The only sound was the music of metal on metal. Her movements accelerated, her heart raced, and the sparring became easy. Gitonk and Tracker blocked her now, letting her take the offensive. Caravey talked; she didn't listen. Both Gy and Caravey had taught her to ignore distractions.

"Enough," he said. "Enough!"

She stopped, her chest heaving.

"Save it for the arena. Besides, someone's here to see you."

A Nunqua warrior with gray hair, a sturdy physique, and a wide nose waited at the edge of the field. His spots reminded Shanti of a puzzle. She returned the sword to the scabbard on her back.

Caravey, Tracker, and Gitonk stayed behind as she went to the warrior and lowered her head. He put out his hand. Shanti grabbed his wrist as he grabbed hers.

"General Seiko," she said.

"General?"

Shanti imagined that her father, if he were still alive, would have looked much like the warrior in front of her. "Uncle."

He pulled her into a quick embrace, then held her at arm's length. "You're not such a skinny kid anymore. Let's walk. I believe you wrote to inform me, in the utmost secrecy, that you weren't coming back from Willovia."

She walked on his left side, the proper position for someone subordinate in rank and family hierarchy. "I wasn't planning on it. Things have changed because of the war."

"And what of Caravey?" He glanced sideways at her. "Did you return for him? You can't play warrior forever. A woman's purpose is to *give* life, not take it."

"That's not the reason I returned."

"Caravey is a general, able—"

"You're worse than a woman, Uncle," she said.

"It would be good to see you more than once in three years."

"How goes the war?"

"I'll not torment you with details, half-breed. Your nature prohibits you from choosing sides in this war, no matter what uniform you wear. My brother should never have gotten involved with that Willovian woman." Angry wrinkles creased his forehead, then gradually smoothed. "He loved her, though. Would have married her if such a union were legal."

"I didn't see the light of day until I was six years old," Shanti said. "They kept me inside until I could control my appearance. I remember my mother and father. They didn't hide their feelings for each other from me—just from the rest of the world."

"I hear you're fighting in the arena already. You certainly have a way with people."

"That's not my fault. She challenged me. I think her name is Yasmine. Are you going to be there?"

"I'll stay, but as soon as the fight's over, I have to leave. Is that really the queen's sword?"

"Yes," she said.

"Always causing trouble, doing things the hard way. Just like your father, you are. We have word that Baylova's riding with the Willovian forces to the Outer Boundaries."

"The monks predicted she would."

"I better not see you on the battlefield, half-breed," he said.

She lowered her head in a show of respect. The battlefield was the last place she wanted to be.

*

Shanti lifted round weights to prepare her muscles to fight. Nunqua spectators packed the arena, making bets and getting drunk. Black-clad warriors watched from the stands or prowled around the edge of the pit. Jun waited at the west entrance for his turn to fight. His weight rested on one leg, and his hands were tied behind his back. He stared at Shanti, then directed his gaze toward the east entrance. He once again looked at Shanti, then fixed his attention on the east entrance.

She discreetly shook her head and bent forward. Too many warriors were present for her and Jun to attempt an escape from the arena.

"What's wrong?" Caravey said.

She dropped the weights and picked up a handful of dirt, rubbing it between her palms. "Nothing, General."

He put his hands on her shoulders. *"Anaya say midea."*

"Strength of will," she said.

"Bring me honor." Warmth and desire flashed in his eyes.

Shanti took the two swords off her back, handing the queen's sword, plus her wristlet, to General Seiko to hold during the fight. She entered the pit while gazing down at her feet, oblivious of the noise of the spectators. What if she lost the match with Yasmine? If she lost, no one would pay attention to her. She would be ignored, ostracized, and Caravey would not try to rekindle the old flame if she failed to bring him honor. Then she could concentrate on getting Jun out of the prisoner-of-war camp. She would let Yasmine win.

Shanti reached the middle of the pit and raised her head to look at her challenger.

Yasmine sauntered toward her, swinging her hips. Whistles, cheers, and vulgar comments erupted from men in the crowd. Yasmine wore a black shirt, tight black pants, and thigh-high boots. Red body art adorned her arms and neck, and her shiny hair was pulled back in a simple ponytail. Shanti switched the sword from her right hand to her left.

"I didn't get a chance to ask your name the other day," Yasmine said. "I like to know the names of the warriors I defeat in the arena. I would like to thank you in advance for—"

Shanti seized Yasmine's neck, digging her fingers into the soft flesh, and tripped her, knocking her to the ground. Never would she let this wench cut her arm!

Yasmine jumped up, swinging her sword and ready to fight. "You'll pay for that."

Shanti switched her sword to her right hand and changed her appearance from Nunqua to Willovian. The crowd quieted. Murmurs spread through the audience. Then loud shouts.

"Shanti?" Yasmine said. "It can't be. That's just a myth. Shanti hasn't fought in any arena, or even been seen, for years."

The crowd chanted, "Shanti, Shanti!" The two women sparred, Shanti blocking the sword from getting anywhere near her head or body. She kicked Yasmine in the gut and sent her sprawling into the dirt. Reverting to the skin of a Nunqua, she descended on Yasmine. She grabbed the smooth ponytail and pulled tight, her boot on Yasmine's upper back, and sword under the band of the ponytail. Nunqua warriors shouted in disbelief. Shanti was going to cut her opponent's hair—a serious gesture indeed. But Shanti thrust the tip of her sword into Yasmine's expensive boot instead, cutting the leather without cutting the leg.

Yasmine's face contorted in concentration as she attacked. Strands of hair stuck to her sweaty cheeks, and the top of her boot flapped as she moved.

Something watched, something unnatural. A hawk, possessed, perched on the topmost tier of the arena. Shanti glanced at Caravey, the only other person in the arena to notice the hawk and discern an abnormal spirit controlling the bird. Caravey's head tilted in bewilderment.

A blade bit into Shanti's shoulder, returning her attention to the fight.

"A warrior clothes herself in pain, not pride," she murmured as she swung her sword. Yasmine blocked the blow but was knocked off balance. "Pain is our teacher, sacrifice our duty. Brain over body. Head over heart." She pushed Yasmine down and cut the soft leather of her other boot. "Match is over. You lose." She stepped on the back of Yasmine's hand, twisting the sword out of her grip and slicing her forearm. The noise of the crowd pierced her.

Ending the fight was like regaining consciousness.

The hawk continued to watch. Shanti retrieved the Queen's sword from General Seiko and unsheathed it, holding it high in the air to show the bird as spectators slurred her name in a drunken stupor.

Caravey's fingers ran along the bleeding cut on her shoulder; the narrow wound sealed itself.

Shanti pointed to the bird. "Baylova."

*

Baylova smelled the bodies before her in the trampled field. The dead could not be moved, for fear of attack from the enemy. A bloated horse lay on its side, milky eyes unblinking and flies crawling over the carcass. Swords, arrows, and bits of clothing were strewn across the ground: a boot here, a water bag there, a bloody parchment, a letter from a loved one—the trinkets and trappings of lives wasted. She thought of Pirro and Aiden, then of Shanti, and closed her eyes. Through the eyes of the bird, she watched Shanti, wearing a black uniform and fighting a woman. Shanti held the sword engraved with a dragon. *Her* sword. Shanti had her sword!

Baylova opened her eyes. The dead spoke, mangled men pleading to be put in the ground. Blue lips of Willovian and Nunqua corpses called her name like croaking frogs on a hot night. Vision and reality entwined.

Shanti moved among the dead, licking the blade of Baylova's sword. "Rega. Princess. Unworthy queen."

Baylova's pupils rolled back into her head. Only the whites of her eyes could be seen. She walked away from her guards and into the open, stretching her arms wide.

"Baylova, get back!" Kyros shouted. "We're within range of their archers. You'll be shot."

"Baylova," Commander Gy said. His hair had grayed considerably since the start of the war.

The queen, Commander Kyros, and several hundred men had arrived in the Outer Boundaries only minutes before. The royal guards, mystified by her appearance, did not pull the entranced woman out of harm's way.

Her arms swung in fluid arcs, and a sudden wind swept the ground like a wave. High above, a buzzing black cloud darkened the sky. Wolves howled. Mice and rats skittered over the field, toward the enemy.

"Come get your sword, *Princess.*" Shanti ran toward her. Wasps flew through her. Mice jumped at Shanti's feet, unable to stop her swift sprint.

Stingers pierced the spotted flesh of real warriors. Red lips of Nunqua cried out—irritated, annoyed, their swords and arrows useless against the angry swarm sent against them. Behind battlements and breastworks, pestilent mice, harbingers of disease, skittered up black boots and pants to bite muscular men with their tiny teeth.

Commander Gy watched the events openmouthed. He grasped Kyros by the jacket and shook him. "We attack now. I know the men are tired, but now is the time to force the Nunqua from the Outer Boundaries. Now!"

Shanti jumped, holding the queen's sword high in the air. She landed and used the flat of the sword to sweep Baylova off her feet. Baylova fell onto her back. Her pupils returned to their proper place. Shanti crouched next to her, silent, calm.

The vision of Shanti evaporated like steam, while the wasps and mice remained to torment the warriors.

*

Shanti watched the fight with an uneasy feeling. Something was wrong.

The thin blade in Jun's hand bent when struck by Gitonk's large sword. The audience inside the open-air arena cheered. Gitonk was a brute, not a skilled swordsman. Jun worked day after day carrying firewood and performing other menial tasks. He was a prisoner, hungry and tired. The weapon given to him was substandard. Fighting in the arena was a sport—all competitors were supposed to be given a decent weapon and a proper chance to defend themselves.

"It's not a fair match, General," Shanti said. "You intend to kill him?"

"Why should that matter to you?"

Jun backed away from the sword, which ripped through his coat but did not cut skin.

"You're testing Jun?" Shanti inhaled. "No, of course not. You're testing me."

"Three years is a long time to be away. This Willovian was at the camp in the Hedgelands with you."

"I followed every one of your orders, became the princess's personal guard, told you about her power. I gave you the information you asked for, and it almost got me killed." Shanti took her weapon off her back.

"What is it you plan to do?" he said.

"I will not condone killing for the sake of killing, whether Nunqua or Willovian. I can't change what I am."

"Yes, you can change. And you have."

He knew. Caravey knew she had never intended to return. She came back only so he could save her from the sickness caused by the bite of a bat. "I never liked Gitonk anyway."

"Gitonk serves his purpose. He's an ignorant, reckless son of a bitch. But he never questions my authority."

Shanti moved to the edge of the pit, holding the sword inside its sheath, with the hilt facing out. She shouted to Jun above the noise of the crowd, "For Pirro!"

Jun ran and took the sword, dropping the bent, useless weapon.

"Shanti?" Gitonk said.

She lifted the necklace adorned with hair out of her jacket, then pointed to his neck. "For Pirro."

Jun fought with a new spirit and won, pushing Shanti's sword through Gitonk's thick middle. She averted her gaze from the gruesome spectacle. Warriors carried Gitonk out of the arena, still alive. Caravey would heal his obedient servant once again.

Six Nunqua warriors surrounded Jun. "Drop the sword," Caravey ordered. Jun threw the weapon down. "Impressive. You've won extra food for your tent, and a day's rest." Warriors tied Jun's hands together and chained his ankles before escorting him out of the arena. Caravey returned Shanti's sword to her, dripping blood.

"Death is an ugly business," he said. "Commander Jun is not so noble. He could have simply cut Gitonk's arm, but preferred to kill him instead, just like Zindar."

"Gitonk won't die. I'm certain you'll heal him, General."

"As I said, Gitonk serves his purpose, as do you. War won't last forever." Caravey moved close to her. "I was testing you, and you performed exactly as expected. You didn't just give Commander Jun a sword; you gave him hope. You're important, Shanti. So very, very important."

"I'm the string that binds Willovia and the Nunqua together. The Willovians will accept you only because of me."

"It's more than that."

Caravey's skin was unblemished, perfect. He had a strong chin, wide brow, and intelligent face, but the pupils of his eyes reminded Shanti of tunnels from which there was no escape.

*

Shanti lounged inside a tavern packed with Nunqua. Two swords were strapped to her back, and two women flanked her, combing and stroking her hair with perfumed oils on their hands. They made small braids in the long tresses. She could hear the Nunqua whisper, see them glance her way. Whether they said good things or bad about her, she didn't know.

Caravey came to the table and sat across from her, grinning at the women braiding her hair. "Enjoying your winnings?" Tracker and other warriors were with him. "There's the matter of your request," Caravey said. "What do you want for bringing honor in the arena to me and to my warriors?"

Shanti signaled the women to go away. They finished the braids and left, though the men pleaded with the pretty women to stay.

"What do you want, Shanti?" Caravey said. "Do you want me to free the Willovian?"

She reached into her pocket and pulled out a white feather spotted with brown. "Heal her."

Warriors standing nearby laughed at the request and called her crazy. Caravey ordered the men to leave. "Who is she?"

"A witch."

"What's her name?"

"Her name is unimportant."

"How did she get hurt?" he asked.

"Saving me from Baylova."

"Why does a witch take interest in you?"

"The same reason another witch hunts me."

"You really are infuriating," he said. "Can you just answer the questions?"

Shanti extended the feather toward Caravey. "Heal her."

Caravey took the white feather and placed it between his palms. He closed his eyes, and his breathing slowed. He returned the feather to Shanti. The brown spots on the feather were gone. He moved around the table to sit beside her, their thighs touching.

"Caravey," she whispered, not wanting anyone in the tavern to hear her call the general by his first name.

He ran his fingers down her forearm, tracing the parallel scars, then put his hand on her knee under the table. His hands were always so warm.

Two warriors came over to their table. General Seiko stood next to a Nunqua with red welts covering his spotted skin.

"Willovia has regained the Outer Boundaries," Seiko growled to Caravey, "while you drink and have a good time."

"How can that be? We outnumber their soldiers three to one."

"Wasps." Shanti looked at the warrior with the welts. "Baylova. She hexed me with wasps once."

"Wasps and mice and wolves and Willovian royal guards," Seiko said. "The men believe the battlefield is cursed. A quick death by the sword is one thing; a slow death by witchcraft is another."

Caravey turned to Shanti. "Can the witch I just healed defeat Baylova? Will she help us?"

"She's Willovian. She won't help. I've already asked."

"I cured her. She owes me."

"General Delartay," Seiko said. "We meet with Lord Argu now and discuss our options with the other generals."

Caravey left Shanti's side.

"Gather your belongings," Seiko said to her, "and leave at sunrise. You may stay with my family. I'm sure you remember the way. This isn't your fight, half-breed."

She nodded, and Seiko left.

With the generals gone, Shanti put her hand in her pocket and touched the feather. In a vision, Madiza appeared inside the tavern, her arm no longer supported by the pink sling. The Nunqua parted, and Madiza moved aside. Shanti saw Jun in the vision, saw Caravey's lie. Jun was not given extra food and rest as Caravey had promised in the arena. Instead, he had been tied to a pole at the boundary of the Nunqua camp, with a black eye and with a trickle of blood dripping down his chin. She released the feather, and the vision vanished. Shanti knew what she must do. "I'm sorry, Uncle."

29

A ROLL IN THE HAY

AIDEN WROTE A name and number on a fieldstone, with a piece of white chalk. He picked up a chisel and hammer, then began etching the inscription. Rubble from previously engraved fieldstones covered the table, and a rock held down pieces of parchment. Blisters bubbled under his skin. The hammer and awl rubbed the sores with each strike. The pain was therapy; the pain was good.

Baylova approached. He bowed, then continued his work.

The chink of metal on stone carried across the field. Soldiers dug graves nearby, and bodies wrapped in dark cloth lined the ground.

She examined the gravestones. "You're too talented to live your life by the sword."

Aiden wiped the pebbles from his work and blew dust from the unfinished inscription.

"I didn't . . . I'm sorry," she said. "Will you come back to the castle after this is over?"

He set down the tools, his voice hushed. "I'm not sure, Baylova."

"At least, can you come to the castle to see me?" A large

fieldstone engraved with "NUNQUA 38" caught her attention. "How did you know the age of this warrior?"

"It's not an age. Thirty-eight warriors are buried in a mass grave on the other side of this field. More mass graves are situated around the area."

Bayla looked at his rough and blistered hands. "I hate being queen."

"I know," he said. Aiden watched her walk away—a peculiar sight in the tragic landscape. Bayla was conniving, stubborn, sometimes cruel, but she was also sad and sweet. He wanted to paint her portrait to see if he could capture the essence of her. Aiden finished the grave marker and set it on a pile with others. Enough daylight remained to complete one more. He lifted a heavy fieldstone onto the table and looked at the parchment for the next name on the list. With white chalk, he wrote the word "UNKNOWN," then drew a Willovian falcon beneath it. Water seeped from his blisters as he chiseled, and the pain was good.

*

Her timing must be perfect. Tracker was busy trying to console the clothes off Yasmine, the generals and Lord Argu were off somewhere discussing the war, and most of the warriors were drunk. Shanti went to the edge of camp, where Jun was tied to a pole. She cut the rope. He collapsed onto knees and hands, his feet still shackled. Shanti fished from her pocket a master key she had taken from the guardhouse, then freed Jun from the chain binding his legs. She put his arm around her shoulders and tried to help him stand. His body was limp, the fighting spirit beaten out of him. "Horses are waiting," she said. "We must reach the horses." He remained on the ground, too weak to travel. "Now's our only chance. Jun, please."

A white fox passed them like a quiet phantom. Jun's head lifted curiously.

"We follow the fox," Shanti said.

Jun got up, one hand on his sore knee. He limped, chasing the bushy white tail of the animal. He groaned, and Shanti took his arm, trying to get him to move faster.

"Quiet," she said.

The fox dashed past a Nunqua warrior hidden behind bushes. He stooped at the waist and held the reins of two swaybacked horses without saddles. Shanti removed Baylova's sword from her back. Gitonk handed her the reins, and she handed him the sword—the trade agreed upon when Shanti had visited him, alone and shunned, in the infirmary.

Gitonk inspected the sword, stroked it, his eyes never leaving the treasure. "I'll give this to General Delartay—bring him honor. No longer will I be the least of his warriors."

Jun struggled onto the horse's back and followed the fox. Shanti trailed on the other horse, her legs sticking out at odd angles from the animal's fat barrel.

Baylova's sword remained with Gitonk.

*

"The war is at an end," Commander Gy informed Baylova and Kyros inside a tent. "We meet with Lord Argu and General Seiko to demand—"

"The war is *not* at an end," Baylova said.

"Only minor skirmishes remain at the far borders. The Outer Boundaries belong to us. We meet with the leaders of the Nunqua and declare peace."

"The war is not over until I say it is over! We march into Nunqua territory and find my sword."

"Your sword?" Gy said.

"I had a vision," Baylova said. "Shanti cavorts with the warriors. She wears a black uniform and carries the sword she stole from me in the Hedgelands."

Gy clenched then unclenched his jaw. "You would spill more blood to save a stupid sword."

"We sacrifice one life now to save two lives later. The Nunqua will continue to harass Willovia. They will continue their plans to take over our lands unless we show them our strength. We prove to the Nunqua we're not weak."

"*We*? Or *you*? I will not support this strategy of yours," Gy said.

"Then you'll be replaced. Commander Kyros, gather the troops to invade."

Kyros nodded.

"Baylova," Gy said, "not all your enemies have spots on their skin."

"No longer will I be voiceless in your presence, Commander Gy. That sword is more than a piece of metal. It represents something a highly regarded man such as yourself could never understand. You may leave."

Gy left, and Kyros followed. The blue Willovian flag with a gray falcon rose above the queen's tent.

"You'll send me messengers?" Gy asked Kyros.

"Of course."

Gy took the pipe out of his pocket. "Where's Shanti?"

"Just as Baylova said, with the Nunqua. She's helping Commander Jun escape the prisoner-of-war camp." He scratched his chin. At least, I think that's what she's doing."

"She's doing more than helping Jun." Gy rolled the pipe back and forth in his hands. "She's testing the queen, playing the part of a traitor to provoke Baylova to fight. Shanti's finishing what she started at the camp in the Hedgelands."

*

"I am a Guardian of Willovia. I swear it." Shanti held her palms toward a bald man with brown skin. The old man pointed a dagger at her chest. They were back inside Willovia, in the kitchen of an elderly couple's home. The old man's plump wife stood in the door frame, wearing a robe. Her black hair stuck out at odd angles, and she held a candle in one hand, a butcher knife in the other. Dried flowers and herbs, along with rabbit and skunk pelts, hung from nails on gray wooden walls. Stuffed owls and crows perched on the windowsill. The kitchen smelled like sawdust.

"You wear the uniform of the Nunqua. You're a traitor," the old man said.

"No," Shanti said. "I put the uniform on to help Commander Jun. Tell them, Jun."

"The Nunqua kept me and other Willovians as prisoners of war with almost nothing to eat. They tied me to a pole and beat me. Do you have any food? I have no money."

"You poor dear," the woman said.

"Jun," Shanti said.

The old man waved his dagger at her.

"I'm not going to hurt anyone," she said. "Jun!"

"Just a few bites to eat," Jun pleaded with the woman. "I'd pay you if I could."

The woman sidestepped Shanti, butcher knife at the ready.

Shanti held her hands at chest level. "Commander Kyros, the high commander in charge of castle security and the royal guards, asked me to help Jun escape the Nunqua. Commander Gy, the high commander who leads the Willovians at the Outer Boundaries, made me a Guardian of Willovia. I saw the symbol of the Guardians, the letter "g," carved into the entryway of your home."

"The wife and I just moved here. Never knew what that letter meant."

"I could really use your help, Jun."

The plump woman loaded Jun's arms with dried meats and flatbread. She took a brown jug off a high shelf and uncorked it. "Now, you be careful with that. That's Mama's special brew. Burn a hole right through your stomach if you don't eat something with it."

"Thank you for your generosity," he said.

"Glad to help a fellow Willovian—and a commander, too." She held the candle to his bearded face and saw the blackened eye clearly. "Nunqua bastards."

"Jun!" Shanti yelled. The old man held the dagger point to her belly.

"Never saw her before tonight." Jun winked at the plump woman with his good eye. "I don't know who she is."

Shanti glared at him.

"What's a Guardian's purpose?" the old man asked.

"To do what's best for Willovia," Shanti said.

"It's all right, Mama. Why are you wearing that uniform?" He lowered the dagger, and Shanti lowered her arms.

"Because I had to."

The man's eyes narrowed. "Guardian?"

"Yes, Guardian."

"Actually, the wife and I have lived in this house for thirty years. You two can stay in the barn tonight. You need to get out of that outfit, missy, before it gets you killed. Mama, you got any extra dresses?"

"Thanks a lot," Shanti said to Jun.

"Don't mention it," he replied through a mouthful of food.

*

"I tried to stop them, General," Gitonk said, "but I ain't fully healed yet. I grabbed Shanti, pulled the sword off her back. They stole two horses and got away."

Caravey turned the queen's sword over in his hands. "Technique over strength, brain over body. Do you understand what she's done?"

"She betrayed us."

"She let you have this sword for a reason," Caravey said. They stood near a dilapidated building, two warriors flanking the general. "I'm sorry, Gitonk." Caravey put his hand on Gitonk's shoulder and reversed his healing touch. The sword wound in Gitonk's gut opened, as did the belly slice from Jun at the Hedgelands. A wet, gurgling moan escaped his throat, and blood soaked through his shirt as the burly Nunqua warrior slid down the wall of the building.

"He shall be buried with honor," Caravey said to the two warriors with him. "Gitonk gave his life more than once for the Nunqua. The spirits tormented me to release his soul." Caravey cut off a lock of Gitonk's hair with Baylova's sword. He separated the strands, letting them fall to the ground and blow in the breeze, impossible to retrieve. "You're free, although your struggle continues."

"Get Tracker now," he ordered one of the warriors. "I need five men. We find Shanti and bring her back. Inform the rest of my warriors that they fight under the command of General Seiko until I return." He said to the other warrior, "Ensure that Gitonk is prepared for burial." Caravey picked up Baylova's sword, sheathed it, then strapped it across his back exactly as Shanti had intended.

The sword made him a target. *Though not for long*, he vowed.

*

Jun stayed with Shanti in the barn for three days. He washed, ate, rested, washed, and then washed again. Women from the town had come and cut his hair shorter than it had ever been. They burned his clothing, providing him with all new things to wear. Gifts, they said, in appreciation of his service to Willovia. They also gave him soap, food, a pair of boots, and hand-knitted socks and generally fussed over him the way a mother fusses over a sick child. These same women ignored Shanti as she tried to glean information about the war. Still, she did manage to procure a few items of used clothing for herself.

Jun gazed at his reflection in a cracked mirror hanging from a peg inside the barn. He shaved by lanternlight. He splashed his face with cold water from a bucket, rubbing skin that had been covered by a scratchy beard. The cut on his lip was small, and the bruise around his eye large. He picked up a piece of jerky to chew. Hot red pepper flavored the meat.

Shanti sat in a pile of straw, sewing a skirt. "Probably squirrel." She pulled up on the needle and broke the thread with her teeth.

"Tastes more like raccoon." He put down the half-eaten strip, then joined Shanti on the hay with the jug of alcohol. He took a swig, then offered it to her.

Shanti swallowed a few mouthfuls. "Not bad," she said, her voice raspy from the scorch of the alcohol.

"You're quite popular in the arena."

"I've lost as many fights as I've won." She handed him the jug. "Commander Kyros is at the battlefront with Baylova. From what I hear, Willovia has regained the Outer Boundaries."

"Then we go there," he said.

"*You* can go there. I intend to stay as far away from Baylova and Caravey as possible."

Jun got up and placed the jug of spirits on a roughhewn timber. He lowered the flame in the lantern to a flicker. Blankets were folded over a stall door. He picked them up, then spread them on the hay, reclining next to Shanti. She continued to sew, avoiding body contact even though they were so close. Jun nudged her with his knee. "Put it away."

She moved the skirt aside. "How did you get captured?"

"I was wondering when you were going to ask. I was stupid— let myself get trapped in a woman's bedroom. She worked for the Nunqua for money or . . . I don't know. She drugged my drink. Nothing happened."

"What about Zindar?"

"He's dead. I believe it was Zindar who told the Nunqua the location of our camp in the Hedgelands."

"A scratching noise came from the barn roof, and Shanti flinched.

"What's wrong?" Jun said. "Afraid of the dark? It's just a bat or a barn swallow. Could be an owl."

Shanti looked up into darkness. "Twenty bats, maybe more. We need to leave."

Jun unbuttoned her jacket. It was too dark to read her expression. A glimmer of silver reflected in her eyes, reminding him of what she was.

"I thought you were weak from your ordeal," she said.

"Not *that* weak. Besides, I hate seeing you in this uniform."

"This isn't the best place . . ."

He removed her jacket and tossed it by the skirt, then buried his fingers in her hair. "I thought I was going to die and never see you again," he said, "never have the chance to show you how I feel."

She lifted the back of his shirt and raked the flesh with her fingernails. He pulled her hair, though not enough to hurt. "Take the uniform off, Shanti."

"Make me."

Jun wrestled her out of the uniform—a power struggle she obviously wanted him to win. She yielded to the explorations of his hands, his mouth. Her response was fervent, sweet—the hidden side of Shanti, which he wanted for himself. He wished there were more light, so that he might see the pattern of her skin, kiss every faded spot. On a bed of hay and discarded clothes, Shanti enveloped him in softness, whispering words in a language he didn't understand. Fingernails raked his flesh once more.

Shanti belonged to him.

30
QUEST FOR A SWORD

JUN AWOKE, AND Shanti wasn't beside him. She moved about the barn, getting ready for the day. Her black boots stuck out from the dark skirt a village woman had given her. Above this, she wore a white shirt and a man's beige overcoat. The mismatched clothing was functional though not fashionable.

"Come with me to the Outer Boundaries," he said. "Commander Gy will be there; so will Commander Kyros. They can confirm your story."

"Baylova is at the Outer Boundaries. Do you remember how she hates me? I assure you, it's only gotten worse."

He wanted to pull her back onto the blanket and bury himself in her arms, her warmth. "Stay with me, Shanti."

"I . . . can't. Not right now. The Willovians think I'm a traitor, and I'm certain the Nunqua want my head for helping you escape. When the war's over, things can be different."

"You're so pigheaded sometimes. Where are you going?"

"I don't know." She strapped the sword to her back, and the dart wristlet to her arm. "Somewhere I don't have to wear these all the time. Somewhere I don't have to pretend to be something I'm not."

Jun buttoned his shirt. "Does such a place exist?"

Her movements slowed at the stinging remark. Why did he have to say something so dumb? It didn't matter to him that she was a half-breed. She should know that, especially after last night.

"I have money," she said. "Not much, but enough that we can trade the horses for better ones. I'll see if they're awake." She slid the barn door open enough to squeeze her body through.

The morning sky was gray, and fog settled in the distance. The smell of eggs and sausage came from the house. Jun folded the blankets and draped them over the stall door. It didn't make sense for her to be alone. Shanti would stay with him. They would go to the Outer Boundaries. That was final. After all, he was still a commander in the Willovian military and could vouch for her allegiance. She had saved his life; it was his turn to return the favor.

He put on his coat and looked in the mirror. The cut on his lip had healed, along with his black eye. His body felt strong. Too strong. Jun hopped up and down to test his knee. The persistent pain that had caused him to limp since being captured by the Nunqua was gone.

Shanti, that witch! She must have retained a measure of Caravey's ability to heal and unknowingly transferred it to him. Which meant she was a repository for Baylova's power, too. No wonder Delartay coveted her!

The old man entered the barn, dragging Shanti in by the arms. Her heels left two long tracks in the dirt. "We got trouble, boy." He dropped Shanti and pushed the sliding door shut. The shaft and feathers of an arrow protruded from her left side. Shanti panted. The color drained from her face, and spots emerged on her skin.

The old man backed away. "Wha . . . ?"

Jun knelt beside her and lifted the flap of her jacket. The bleeding was minimal. He broke the shaft in two, leaving the arrowhead buried between her ribs, to extract later. She would recover. A tear rolled down her face. Jun rolled her onto her uninjured side to ease her breathing. "Who's out there?" he asked the man.

His eyes widened. "She *is* a Nunqua."

"Who is out there?"

"Nunqua warriors. The wife left through the tunnels to get help from town."

Jun reached for Shanti's sword.

"No . . ." She struggled to speak. "Fire."

"Fire?"

Voices loomed outside the barn. Nunqua voices.

"Fire," she said. ". . . will hurt . . . their eyes. Blind them." Another tear rolled down her nose.

"Don't worry, Shanti. You'll get through this. Trust me." Jun took hold of the lantern. A small flame burned inside. He picked up the jug of alcohol. "I'm sorry," he said.

The man placed both hands on his bald head. "Not my brew! Oh, all right." He opened a trapdoor hidden under straw. Reaching down, he pulled up five jugs of the strong liquor and kissed the last jug. "For the good of Willovia." He pointed to the barn door. "You take that side; I'll take this one."

Jun put down the jug and gathered a handful of straw. He lit the end with fire from the lantern. The old man did the same.

Both doors slid open at once. An arrow flew by the man and stuck into the wall. Jun threw the jug in front of the opening. It broke, and he lit the spilled alcohol. Flames mushroomed outward to reach a pile of straw. Jun opened the stall gates to release the two horses, smacking them on the rump to get them out. The horses bolted toward the exit not blocked by flames. Warriors backed away from the charging beasts. The hooves of a horse just missed trampling Shanti.

The old man threw down the next jug, lighting the alcohol with the straw torch. "Over here!" he yelled to Jun.

Nunqua warriors crossed the fire. The old man tossed a third jug into the blaze, near the intruders, and they retreated from the dazzling flames, covering their eyes with their arms. Jun lifted Shanti, who was in too much pain to stand. Her breathing was labored. The arrow must have nicked her lung. He followed the old man to an unblocked exit at the side of the barn.

The spiked metal ball of a mace hit the old man in the chest. He soared backward into Jun. Two spotted hands grabbed Jun's coat, hauling him over the injured old man. Jun released Shanti and, pulling the sword from her back, grazed the warrior's side. The warrior blinked, his eyes darting back and forth. The mace whizzed through the air, missing its target. Jun lifted Shanti's weapon over his head and swung it, but a sword stopped him from killing the Nunqua armed with the mace.

General Caravey Delartay squinted as he fought with Jun. Fire shone on the blades.

"Get her!" Delartay shouted.

The warrior with the mace grabbed Shanti's arm and dragged her away.

Jun ran toward Delartay, ready to ram the weapon into his heart. Delartay repelled the attack and kicked Jun's knee, which, after a night spent with Shanti, was no longer sore. Jun picked him up and slammed him to the ground. The swords fell from their hands. Delartay punched, kicked, and tried to gouge out Jun's eyes. Jun, on top now, pushed his forearm against Delartay's throat. Delartay sputtered for air.

A monstrous blast knocked them over, shaking Jun to his core. He rose sluggishly. Had the fire reached a still or an entire barrel of alcohol hidden in the barn? Turning his head, he saw Delartay snatch Shanti's sword while shielding his eyes from the flames.

Jun was as good as dead. There would be no prisoner-of-war camp—none of Delartay's games this time. The bald man, his shirt spotted with blood, yanked Jun backward, close to the burning barn, toward the intense heat.

Willovian voices mingled with the crackle of the fire. Delartay stepped away from the burning barn and searched the flames.

"Can't see us," the bald man said. "Fire's too bright for Nunqua eyes."

A warrior on horseback brought Delartay his mount. Shanti slumped in the saddle with the unknown warrior.

Delartay got on his horse, and the warriors rode away into the fog.

"No!" Jun said.

"Papa?" a woman called out. She saw her husband, injured but standing. Clasping her hands together, she looked up to the sky.

A gang of armed Willovian men ran to their aid, but it was too late. Shanti was gone.

"A horse!" Jun grabbed the man's bloodied shirt, making him groan. "I need a fast horse."

"It's too late. Better this way, boy. She's back with her own breed."

*

The Nunqua stopped in the middle of the forest to regroup. The man holding Shanti dismounted and pulled her off his horse. He tied the reins of his horse to a tree branch, leaving Shanti thrashing on a layer of leaves. Warriors left her alone as they filled skins with water from the stream. Tree roots spread along the ground like giant snakes. Frogs and turtles jumped off rocks spotted with lichen and splashed into a nearby stream. The horse pushed her with its soft muzzle.

Kidnapped again.

Caravey knelt beside her. He opened her jacket and reached inside her torso. She shrieked, pushing the remaining air out of her one uninjured lung. Her eyes closed, and her body slacked. The warmth of his healing touch replaced the agony. The fibers of her muscles weaved together, and her lungs expanded with an inflow of fresh air. Caravey showed her the bloody arrowhead in his bloody hand. "Another scar to chronicle your disobedience. Do not test my patience. I'm not through with you."

Leaves tangled in her hair. She was too weak to stand. Caravey dripped water onto her lips and into her mouth from a bag. He lifted her sleeve and removed the wristlet. "Gitonk is dead." He waited for a response.

Shanti remained silent.

*

Commander Kyros and six other Willovian soldiers stood in an informal circle around a captured Nunqua warrior as Baylova interrogated him. They had entered enemy territory days ago with three thousand men. Sickly trees, bent by wind, dotted the grassy landscape.

Kyros watched the wolf snap at the warrior's legs.

"Where's my sword?" Baylova asked the prisoner. Another wolf, snarling, hackles standing on end, lurked about her feet.

"Shanti has it." The warrior's face contorted, and he tried to kick the beast away. Sweat dripped from his spotty skin. "She waits for you." The wolf tore at his boot.

"Where?" Baylova said.

"The arena. Death match. She wants to kill you with an audience watching." The wolf clamped down on his calf. "Get him off me!" Froth dripped from the wolf's mouth. "Shanti wants to show both the Nunqua and the Willovians that you're weak. Get him off!"

Baylova whistled, and the wolf released the warrior, licking its teeth and snout. She petted the snarling beast. "It's not a 'he.' It's a she-wolf."

He gripped his bleeding leg and sniveled. Baylova left the group, followed by the two gray beasts.

Kyros clapped when the queen was out of sight. "Bravo! What a brilliant performance."

The warrior stood to his full height, no longer sniveling.

"How many warriors await us at the arena? Four thousand? Ten thousand?"

"Personally," the Nunqua said, "I'd like to see Shanti fight your queen. It'd be a hell of a show."

"Your generals have planned quite a diversion," Kyros said. "The real battle occurs outside the arena while the royal witch is preoccupied. Whose idea is this? General Seiko's? Surely not Lord Argu's—he's a bit thick to come up with that sort of ruse."

"If you must kill me, do it now and spare me the conversation," the warrior said. "My duty's done."

"Take him away," Kyros ordered. "You'll live to perform again."

Soldiers tied the prisoner's wrists together and departed with him. Kyros held back one Willovian soldier. "Go to Commander Gy. He's at the Outer Boundaries. Tell him we're being led into a trap and need more men to fight."

"Commander, why not tell this to Baylova."

"Because she's a young woman, stubborn and foolish. I'll do all I can to slow our progress to the arena."

"Why not . . . ?" He closed his mouth, lips pressed tight together.

"Speak your mind," Kyros said.

"Why not turn around? The soldiers don't want to be here, inside Nunqua territory. Many will disobey Baylova's commands and follow you or Commander Gy. Why not leave?"

"This war will end and another begin if Baylova's orders are not heeded. *Civil* war. I'd rather kill a Nunqua warrior in battle than a Willovian brother. Arm yourself well, keep off the roads, and don't travel at night."

"Yes sir."

Kyros sighed and looked deep into the messenger's youthful face. "May the spirits protect you."

"And you."

*

Shanti sat on a bed inside a windowless room. Someone unlocked the door and entered. It was Tracker. He tossed a black uniform onto the bed. "You never planned on coming back. Only after you were bitten by the bat."

"He never burned *your* skin . . . cut you with a knife so he could heal you . . . pretended to be your savior."

"Do as he says," Tracker whispered. "The more you defy him, the more he'll hurt you. You can't fight a healer and win."

"Tell General Seiko I'm here," she said.

"He already knows."

Footsteps approached the room. "Only a coward follows blindly," Shanti said.

His sneer was like salt rubbed into open sores. She waited for him to spit on her, call her a backstabbing bitch, cut off a lock of her hair. But Tracker said nothing—the cold shoulder of a friendship gone sour.

Caravey entered the cramped space, shadowed by two warriors. "Shanti, my sweet, two-faced mongrel." He threw her sword and wristlet of darts onto the bed, by the uniform, and ordered Tracker to leave. "I saved your life twice: first from the sickness caused by the bat's bite, and then from the arrow lodged in your lung. You owe me. One last fight." He took Baylova's sword off his back and pulled the shiny blade out of its scabbard. "In the arena."

"No."

"Don't do it for me." Caravey pointed the sharp tip of the weapon at her throat, lifting her chin with the blade and forcing her to look at him. "Do it for the Nunqua. For yourself. Hell, do it for the Willovians. Baylova's no benevolent queen. You can defeat her. You *will* fight Baylova." He pulled the sword back from her throat.

"I will not."

Baylova's sword arced through the air. Shanti turned away from the blade. The sharp edge cut her ear, slicing it in two. The room spun, and the contents of her stomach lurched. The pain and nausea were not as great as the knowledge. Madiza's prediction had come true. Caravey had cut her ear!

The room dissolved. She was inside the portrait room of the

castle—a vision. Now? It seemed so real. Blood dripped from her mangled ear and pooled on the marble floor. The three portraits of Baylova, Gy, and herself hung on the wall. Pathways to the future. Nothing had changed. Nothing was set in stone. Madiza wasn't with her; neither was Serova. She was alone.

She had brought herself into the vision; she could bring herself out of it. Shanti willed herself back to the present.

Caravey's lips moved, but all she heard was the pounding of her blood. No fear paralyzed her. She put both hands on the wall for balance and jumped at Caravey, pulling his hair and wrestling him to the floor. She stole his power, and her ear was restored. He couldn't break free, and they thrashed about. Caravey's ear split and bled as she reversed his healing power.

The two warriors finally wrenched her away from Caravey.

He touched his mangled ear. "You witch!"

"I guess I am," she said. "I'll not fight for you. You don't control me anymore."

"I *own* you!" A vein on his forehead stood out. "Where would you be if I hadn't trained you? In a tavern, serving drinks? A servant in some rich man's manor? A second-rate seamstress? A pathetic loner always living in fear that people would find out your secret? I made you a warrior. I made you great. Your fame in the arena came about only because I taught you how to fight, to overcome pain, to succeed. I carved out your destiny, not you. *I* did. You owe me." Caravey pulled a small vial of out of his jacket and showed her a drug. "You will fight Baylova. And you will win."

*

The sight of the arena filled Kyros with dread. Armed Nunqua warriors watched the procession of Willovian invaders, letting them pass unopposed. Three thousand brown-clad soldiers rode or marched behind Baylova, Kyros, and the blue flag. Dust, blown by a harsh breeze, pelted their faces. Crows soared low over the landscape, and vultures circled above.

They reached the arena overflowing with Nunqua men, and Baylova dismounted. She patted the stallion's neck, then handed the reins to a soldier. He led her horse away. The two wolves approached and prowled about her feet. She looked to Kyros, terror evident on her face.

He remained on his horse. "I stay with the soldiers, Baylova. You do this alone."

She headed toward the arena built of wood and rock. The wolves followed. Crows flew in loose formations around her. Brawny Nunqua warriors in full battle array backed away from the diminutive witch. Baylova and the wolves disappeared into the structure. Spectators inside the arena cheered.

Kyros galloped to the rear of the assemblage of Willovian soldiers and out of earshot of the Nunqua. He bowed his head and firmed his resolve, hating what must do. "For the good of Willovia." He lifted his head and commanded the man on horseback beside him, "Tell the archers to prepare their arrows. On my signal, we burn the arena to the ground."

Over hills in the distance, thousands of Nunqua warriors came into view. Kyros spoke into the wind, "Gy, where are you?"

*

Shanti coughed as the drug was forced down her throat. A hand clamped over her mouth, and she swallowed the liquid. Hair fell over her face, and her wrists were chained to the wall. She wore the black uniform now. She kicked at the warriors.

"Save it for the arena, my sweet," Caravey said. His ear had healed, although it remained deformed. A wound inflicted by witchcraft. So a healer *could* be harmed. "Leave us alone," he said. The warriors left the room. "Baylova demands your allegiance. I know you won't bow to her. She tried to kill you, after all."

He spoke of honor, Nunqua might, and the death of Baylova. Caravey's speech became the purring of a leopard with padded feet and sharp teeth. The leopard rubbed its sleek head against her leg, wanting attention, but her arms were chained to the wall.

"So many cages," she said.

"Kill Baylova, and you'll be free," Caravey said, once again in human form. "What do you want when you win? What is your request?"

Separating illusion from reality had become difficult. She rattled the chains to escape her bondage.

"What's your deepest desire?"

She stared at him, her eyelids heavy, her mind confused from the vision. Or was it the drug? "Who are you?"

"You will is strong, but your mind is full of holes, my dear. You've blocked me out of your memory. Just as you blocked out the memory of the night we took you away from Willovia and you killed one of my warriors. When I gave you *this*." He touched the hair on the necklace around her neck. "Baylova is not worthy to be queen. You will be a magnificent queen. You will unite the Nunqua and Willovians. You and I can rule. No longer will you have to hide your true self. The name 'Shanti' will be legendary.

"You are the offspring of the celebrated warrior Shintar. You were hidden most of your life. I brought you out of Willovia after your mother died, and prepared you for greatness. A grand arena will be built in Erbaut after the war. We'll construct the best training grounds, host the finest fights. Thousands of spectators will cheer your name. The people of both countries will adore you, love you. And every night, you and I can feast, get drunk on the sweetest wine, sleep on sheets of silk. We'll be together again. Remember the good times. Think of the future."

Shanti licked her lower lip to taste the potion. Her surroundings became clear, as did her purpose. Blood pumped through her veins like ice water, awakening her senses and priming her to muscles to fight.

"Defeat Baylova," he said. "Today, you will bring us honor, my warrior queen."

31
THE ARENA

BAYLOVA'S BREATH CAME in ragged gasps. Nunqua filled the stands, shouting in a language she didn't understand. Wolves circled the pit.

Shanti entered the arena, unkempt hair in her face and dried blood splattered across her cheek and neck. A scar marred the skin above her collarbone, another scar her chin, and her hands looked burned. The cheering of the crowd intensified into a frenzy at the sight of Shanti, who held her sword with the dragon engraved on it, twirled it in her hand, flaunting the stolen scrap of metal.

"Lose something?" Shanti said.

Baylova lifted her hand, black fingernails held out like claws. A wolf charged, teeth snapping, poised to rip vulnerable flesh. Shanti slashed the creature's belly open with her sword, and pain ripped through Baylova's midsection. She lifted her other hand, and the second wolf charged.

Shanti, one sword strapped to her back, threw down the weapon and faced the animal barehanded. The crowd chanted Shanti's name. Shanti grasped the fur and forced the animal to the ground, pressing her body on top of the beast. The animal whimpered.

Debris inside the arena blew into a dusty whirlwind. Baylova dropped to her hands and knees. Energy drained from her like water squeezed from a sponge. Shanti was stealing her power through the wolf that she possessed.

A thump reverberated through the arena, and the ground shook. Light flashed near the topmost tier of wooden benches. Multiple fires flared in the arena. Nunqua spectators poured out of exits, armed and ready to do battle. A trap.

Bayovla's head dropped weakly to the dirt as Shanti absorbed more of her power. An eerie quiet enveloped her. She lifted her head. She was at the castle, inside the portrait room. A dream? A vision? *Now?* She studied the strange yet familiar place. The paintings of her ancestors were not how she remembered. Details had changed.

Shanti's footsteps echoed in the long hall. She stopped—a tall and terrifying apparition. "Serova," Shanti said. A woman in a black dress came into view.

"M . . . Mother?"

Serova touched Baylova's face with a cold hand.

"She cannot speak in this place," Shanti said. "You went to war with the soldiers, faced a traitor, faced death. You passed the final test. The Guardians of Willovia will accept you as queen. *Respect,*" Shanti hissed, "takes longer."

"I don't understand," Baylova said.

"I'll release the wolf when we return. You must enter the battle, use your power to defeat the Nunqua. You can end the war. Madiza has foreseen it. Show them your strength, and they will leave Willovia alone. "

Paint on the portraits bubbled, then blackened, spreading to the edges of gilded frames, to obscure past and future monarchs. Heat warmed her skin. Fire crackled. Burning portraits fell off walls to reveal smoldering seats inside the arena. Serova vanished. Shanti's spirit returned to her body, still pressed on top of the wolf.

A scowling Nunqua warrior appeared in the disintegrating

vision. He put a hand on Baylova's shoulder. The blade in his other hand slid upward through her. The warrior pulled the sword out. Baylova felt the warmth of her life's blood flow out of her. "Aiden," she said. The man took the sharp edge of the blade and cut her throat.

Over. It was finally over. Shanti's scream sang in her ears like a distant dream. The cumbersome body that encased her spirit crumpled to the ground.

*

"This is madness!" Commander Gy watched warriors thunder down hills on horses, toward men fighting each other. He rode toward the arena with reinforcements. It didn't matter how many Willovian soldiers he had brought—it was a fight they were certain to lose. The Nunqua would expend all their strength, every resource, to save their lands from invaders—lands the Willovians didn't even want.

Gy turned to a soldier with a horn fastened to his belt. "Sound the retreat." He looked for Commander Kyros and saw him near the burning arena. "Retreat!" Gy yelled as he rode toward the battle. The horn blew, a deep hum penetrating the chaos. Other horns followed.

The Willovian flag, carried by a man on horseback, flew high near the fire. "Take down the flag," Gy said. The soldier lowered the flag and rolled the material around the pole, tying it closed with leather strips. Gy searched for the Nunqua flag. He saw it on a hill not far away. The Nunqua Lord Argu, wearing black armor, sat astride his horse. Beside him was the gray-haired warrior, General Seiko.

The fighting subsided, replaced by an uneasy truce. Only a few casualties littered the ground. It could have been worse. Much worse. Gy weaved his mount through the horde. "Easy, men. It's time for diplomacy."

"Gy." Kyros bent over, one hand on his knee. The other hand held his sword, covered with gore. "Thank the spirits."

"Where's Baylova?" Gy said.

Kyros looked in the direction of the burning arena.

Jun ran to them on foot. "Where's Shanti?"

Once again, Kyros glanced at the fire.

An arrow flew past Kyros and hit Gy. His horse reared, and he was thrown off.

Fighting between Willovian soldiers and Nunqua warriors resumed.

*

Shanti picked the sword up off the ground and went to the body of Baylova, fighting back the surge of remorseful tears. "I can heal you. It's not too late."

"She's dead," Caravey said.

She knelt beside the corpse and put her hand over the wound on Baylova's neck, trying to seal the cut.

"You can't bring her back if she doesn't want to come back," Caravey said. "She tried to kill herself once. Death is what she wanted. Baylova was too weak to wear the crown. How many men died from her ill-conceived decrees? Now you are queen of Willovia, and I will be ki—" A finely crafted dart hit him in the shoulder. He tugged it out, threw it to the ground. "Stupid freak. You can't poison me. I'm—" Another dart struck him in the chest.

She knew that the poison wouldn't kill Caravey. If only she could touch him, steal his power, give him the sickness that once ravaged her body—the illness caused by the bite of a bat. Would it be enough? How did one kill a healer?

Caravey's mouth opened in an angry roar. He sprang at her, squinting in the brightness of the fire, sword in hand, ready to deliver another scar for her disobedience. Now was the time to break free of her bondage. She would die as he had taught her to live: fighting.

Shanti countered the blow with Baylova's sword. The force of his assault sent her staggering backward. She was no match for

Caravey with a sword. Her arm swung in a smooth loop. The uninjured wolf attacked and tore at his arm. Shanti stood and curled her fingers into a claw, slashing her hand through the air. Caravey's head, stung by the invisible force, whipped to the side. Although she never touched him, blood seeped from four gashes in his cheek. He had spilled her blood more than once; now, Shanti knew, she could spill his.

He scowled in anger—and a newfound fear that she could see in his face. Caravey was not indestructible. Shanti possessed the wolf. The animal jumped, clamping on to the exposed area of Caravey's throat with a determination stronger than death.

She felt the animal's rage, the thrill of the kill. Baylova's power was *her* power. She twisted her arm. The wolf twisted Caravey's neck with an unnatural force, snapping bone and nerves. His contorted body lay motionless on the ground.

Black smoke filled the arena. It hurt to blink, to breathe. Shanti coughed and went to Caravey's body. She wouldn't mourn. He had been dead to her for years. She cut off a braid of his hair with her sword. His hand contracted, and she backed away.

His fingers moved. The fingers of his other hand began to move. "Damn you," she said. A painful tightness constricted her chest at the thought of what she must do to ensure his death. Using the wolves to attack Caravey had given her a sense of detachment. This was different.

Flashes of a forgotten memory—the night she taken away from Willovia—now surfaced: the warrior's detestable grin, raspy voice, hands all over her, the flash of metal, other warriors staring in shock at the faded spots on her skin, which she could no longer control. A rag soaked with vapors had been forced over her mouth until her muscles refused to respond to mental commands. She was taken away from Willovia in a drug-induced stupor.

Shanti lifted the sword over her head in a two-handed grip and prayed to the spirits for strength, both mental and physical. This was the moment of truth. Everything else—the training, obstacle courses, endless hours of sword practice, competing in the arena for sport—was just a game. Was she a real warrior, a real soldier, or just an arrogant woman who prided herself on being something she wasn't? Shanti concentrated on Caravey's neck. Blood poured from the bite wound made by the wolf. She widened her stance. It must be a clean cut, a quick soldier's death.

Caravey's eyelids flickered. His arm bent slowly at the elbow.

She visualized an ax cleaving wood and swung the sword in a downward arc. Caravey's head rolled away from his body.

Shanti howled in revulsion. *What have I done!*

Smoke burned her eyes. She returned to Baylova's corpse, the brown uniform soaked with blood. The lunacy of war, of seeing people she knew die so violently, cut deeper than any blade could reach. She picked up the lifeless arm to heave the body over her shoulder and carry it out of the arena.

Baylova's blue lips moved. "Leave me."

Was she hallucinating, or had the corpse just spoken to her?

The lifeless eyes were half open. "Let my body burn."

"It wasn't supposed to end like this," Shanti said. "I didn't plan—"

"Don't let the monks find my body. Take my hair. End the war."

Shanti put the body down, cut off a lock of hair, and kissed the forehead.

She searched for a way out. Fire blocked the exits. A white blur passed her like a ghost. A white fox. It stopped by the benches of stone. *Madiza.*

Shanti coughed, followed the fox, crawled under seats to a hole in the rock. She entered a smoke-filled passageway that led to rooms and the outside. Two swords, hers and Baylova's, crossed in an X on her back. The wolf was at her side. Her tongue tasted like charcoal. She stooped at the waist and fell. The wolf pawed at her, yipping to get her to move.

Shanti crawled along the ground, chased by the licking flames. Cooler air entered her lungs. She escaped the burning arena. Rising smoke blocked out the sun. She moved away from the fire and stumbled upon the motionless body of a Nunqua on the ground. The cries of a wounded Willovian nearby filled her with dread. She had left the scene of one horror only to find another. The Nunqua had started the war, yet the Willovians had invaded Nunqua territory. Whose side was she on? Jun's question, as always, returned to her thoughts. Was she Willovian or Nunqua?

She was both, damn it.

Gathering what remained of her strength, Shanti walked into the midst of the battle, the wolf beside her. Tufts of smoke rose from her singed uniform. She lifted her bloody hands. In each was a long lock of hair. No men attacked her. They spoke her name in astonishment. She whistled for Baylova's horse, and the wolf left her side. The stallion, confined at the edge of the battlefield, bolted free of its tether and galloped toward her. Shanti mounted the horse and galloped through the multitude of men. "Argu!" she yelled.

Lord Argu and General Seiko rode toward her. She showed them the hair. "General Delartay is dead. Queen Baylova is dead."

Argu lifted his fist in the air. "Willovia is ours."

Shanti shouted for everyone to hear. "Willovia is *mine*. I faced Queen Baylova in the arena."

"You'll be rewarded with lands," Argu said. "A promotion. General Shanti—"

"I rule Willovia! Unless you wish to challenge me? Let's fight, Argu. Take Baylova's hair from my hand, and I'll let you have Willovia. Take Delartay's hair, and I'll let you lead the Nunqua." Shanti dismounted. "Afraid?"

Lord Argu dropped his fist and glanced at the unfriendly faces of those around him.

Shanti waited in the uncomfortable silence. Argu and his incompetence had been a pestilence to the people for too long. She put both locks of hair in her left hand and lifted her right hand to possess his horse. It kicked wildly. Argu held fast to the reins but lost more of his balance each time the horse bucked. Shanti went over and calmed the steed, then yanked Argu from the saddle. Taking the last dart from her wristlet, she plunged the poisoned tip deep into his neck.

"Arrogant witch!" He pulled the dart out. "You're nothing but General Delartay's whore."

She showed him the braid of Caravey's hair. "Not anymore."

"You'll never rule," Argu said, his hand covering the puncture wound on his neck.

"And you'll never know what it *means* to rule." Shanti backed away from Argu. "General Seiko, bring me Lord Argu's sword."

Seiko looked at Shanti as if he had never really seen her before. He ordered his men to take the blade encased in a black scabbard. Three warriors seized the weapon from Argu, who fought but eventually succumbed to the attack. The men gave the sword to General Seiko, who, in turn, dismounted and offered it to Shanti. She took it and spoke to Argu. "It's time for a new era—one that doesn't involve you."

She unsheathed the sword and lifted it for the benefit of those gathered around her. "Argu's lands are my lands; his castles are my castles." Shanti sliced the unmarked skin of Argu's forearm, then said to a group of warriors, "Take him to the edge of the battlefield, and tie him to a tree so everyone will know of his defeat. He'll be dead by morning." Nunqua men seized Lord Argu and took him away.

"If anyone wishes to challenge me," she said, "do it now."

No one spoke. Commander Kyros stood near, the abomination of combat reflected in his once proud face. She spread her arms, inviting a confrontation. He shook his head to show he had no intention of challenging her. "Where is Commander Gy?" she asked.

"Wounded," Kyros said flatly.

She returned Argu's sword to its scabbard, then mounted Baylova's horse, with two swords strapped across her back and another in her hand. She pushed the locks of hair into her jacket for safekeeping. "Commander Kyros, General Seiko, separate the troops. The fighting ends now. Post guards around the arena. Let the fire burn out. No one goes near the ashes. If anyone does, tie him to a tree next to Argu."

*

Commander Gy stomped to the tent with the Willovian flag flying high above it. Next to the blue flag embroidered with a falcon was the black flag of the Nunqua.

Gy's shoulder and chest were bandaged. The arrow had embedded in his muscle. It was removed, and medicine applied to the wound. It still hurt like hell. The pain only intensified his anger. *Damn that woman.* Shanti had used him. Baylova was dead—killed by Shanti—and that scheming, stubborn, murdering woman had declared herself queen of not just one country but two.

"Out of my way," Gy said to the soldiers guarding the queen's tent.

They barred him from entering. "No weapons inside, by Her Majesty's orders."

Then I'll kill her with my bare hands.

He gave the guards his sword, and they let the high commander pass.

He went inside, teeth clenched tight, and stopped when he saw the strange scene. Shanti was on the ground, her feet elevated on a chair. Commander Kyros was bent over her, as was General Seiko. Shanti babbled, her words jumbled in incomplete sentences. She was scarred, bloody, burnt. Faded spots covered her neck and forehead. On a table were three swords and two locks of hair, one braided.

Commander Jun was also inside the tent, standing away from Shanti with his arms crossed. "She's in shock."

A short warrior clad in black, with bands circling his biceps, and war paint on his face, stood at the other side of the tent. "She's not in shock. She's been drugged. The drug increases her aggression."

"Who are you?" Gy said.

"Tracker."

"What happened in the arena?"

Jun glared at Tracker as he answered Gy's question, "She won't say. Keeps mumbling about fates worse than death, retribution, *anaya say* something."

"*Anaya say midea*," General Seiko said. "Strength of will. Breathe, Shanti. It's over." Seiko moved toward Gy. "At least, *I* believe the war is over."

"I declared the war over once and got shot by a Nunqua arrow!"

"An honorable scar," Seiko said. "Wounded in battle with thousands of enemy warriors bearing down upon you. Fire raging, courageous men giving their last breath for love of country, and witch battling witch. My warriors respect such a mark."

"What about Shanti?" Gy said. "Where did all her scars come from? And I'm not talking about the ones on her arms."

"General Delartay," Tracker answered.

"I didn't know he mistreated her so," Seiko said, "or I would have killed him myself. She was always so careful, so full of secrets."

Shanti moaned, and Seiko glanced at her.

"Years ago, my brother was involved with a Willovian woman. She's my . . . I'm not sure of the word in your language. She's my relative? Kin?"

Jun's eyebrows rose. "She's your niece?"

"That's it. Yes."

"*You're* her uncle?" Gy said.

"Yes."

"You used your own niece as bait to lure Baylova to the arena?" Gy said.

"That was General Delartay's plan. I told her to stay away from the battle, invited her to stay in my home with my family, far away from the fighting. She's always been so defiant, just like her father."

Shanti moved her feet off the overturned chair and kicked it aside. She curled into a tight ball, with arms tucked close to her body. Kyros left her side to join the men talking. "Her pupils are returning to normal. The drug's wearing off."

"It's not the drug," Jun said. "It's the shock of what she's just been through."

"I failed," she said. "Baylova's failure is my failure. She's dead."

"Did you kill Baylova?" Gy asked.

"My sword did not strike the blow. Caravey . . . I think I'm going to be sick."

"Did you kill General Delartay?"

"I did my duty."

"Queen Shantova?" Gy said.

Her face had the faraway look of someone who had witnessed war for the first time. It was a good sign. Anyone who witnessed death, or caused it, and did not suffer was unworthy to rule. His anger faded, and he sneered at her, lying there on the floor in a fetal position. "You're pathetic, wallowing in self-pity like a pig wallows in its own shit."

"I know what you're doing, Gy," she said.

He sighed in relief. She would get through this. "Then be the leader I taught you to be. Be the queen."

"Shanti," she said. "Just Queen Shanti. Nunqua retain their lands, and Willovia leaves. The Outer Boundaries will be a memorial open to both countries."

"I believe that's a fair offer," Gy said.

"Agreed." General Seiko shook hands with Commander Gy.

A woman wearing a brown uniform entered. She carried a pouch on her back, with a strap over one shoulder. "Sirs, if you will please back up." The woman took a small container out of the pouch.

"Wait." Seiko raised his hand toward the woman.

"It's medicine," she said.

"Let me see it."

She handed Seiko the container. He sniffed, then abruptly turned his head from the fumes.

"Smelling salts," the woman said.

Seiko gave back the container.

"Out," she ordered. "With all due respect, I can't help her with everyone standing around. Out!"

"No one goes near the arena," Shanti said. "No one."

32
CATACOMBS

THE CITIZENS OF Willovia lined the streets for the funeral of Queen Baylova. Six horses pulled an open carriage. Red velvet covered the burnt remains inside the carved wooden casket, and an abundance of wisteria and gardenias draped the carriage. One royal guard led Baylova's stallion, saddled yet riderless, through the procession. Queen Shanti walked behind the carriage, wearing a blue dress and red sash. A simple gold band adorned her intricately braided hair, and faded spots covered her skin. Somber citizens whispered to each other as she passed. Whether they said good things or bad, she didn't know.

Commander Gy, Commander Kyros, and General Seiko walked behind Shanti. Royal guards and soldiers marched behind the high commanders to the beat of drums. Every Willovian in the procession wore a red armband. Two hundred Nunqua warriors in impressive black uniforms also marched in the solemn parade. No Nunqua wore red in mourning. Shanti noticed many Willovian citizens turn their backs to the Nunqua. She must be patient. Healing the wounds of war would take time.

The procession wound slowly through the cobblestone streets

of Erbaut and ended at the royal catacombs. A stone entryway narrowed to a tunnel cut out of rock, leading to the tombs of Willovia's kings and queens. Royal guards closed the lid of the casket, then carried the remains into a torchlit passageway. Commander Gy, Commander Kyros, and General Seiko followed. Shanti stared at the entrance to the tunnel. Petrified.

She had to see this through. It was her duty. Shanti entered the catacombs, and the ground immediately sloped downward. Sarcophagi of long-dead royals lined the subterranean maze. It was the burial place of kings and queens, heroes and legends. The air smelled like wet dirt, mold, and worms. Her skin itched. The bristly legs of an insect tickled her neck—a cockroach controlled by Baylova. Shanti swiped her neck and felt nothing there. She descended farther into the tunnels, past the tombs of Queen Serova, the stillborn prince, and King Magen.

Royal guards placed the casket on a stone table inside a vault. More flowers decorated the crypt. Workers layered bricks across the vault opening and mortared them into place. Almost over. A high-pitched squeak assaulted her ears. Bats—thousands of flying creatures she couldn't see or control with her newfound power—were somewhere in the catacombs. The brick wall was almost complete. A terrible idea entered her brain: this was a trap.

They must be sealing the entrance to the catacombs just as they were sealing the opening of the tomb. They planned to shut her inside forever, the half-blood witch and self-proclaimed queen of two countries.

Shanti stole away from the entourage of mourners to find her way out. Tunnel connected to tunnel. She wandered about, lost, terrified, covering her ears with her hands to shut out the squeaking of bats. She lifted her skirt and ran through the labyrinth with eyes dilated to see in the unlit passageways. The noise stopped. In front of her was an undecorated tomb. Above the sealed crypt was a plaque. On that sign was only one name, the letters covered in gold:

"SHANTI." A gentle tapping came from inside the vault. Then a strong pounding. Someone inside, trying to get out.

Buried alive. She would be entombed forever. Alone. No light, no food, no way out. And no hope of death to save her. A vision, a recurring dream. The reason she hated tunnels.

She ran, closing her eyes and feeling her way along the walls. When she opened her eyes, she saw a light that did not come from a torch. Shanti sprinted toward the light and up the slope until she was out of the catacombs. White clouds floated like balls of cotton in the sky. She filled her lungs with clean, sweet air. Royal guards and military leaders calmly stepped out of the catacombs. Kyros, Gy, and Seiko walked over to her.

Kyros bowed his head slightly, his face no longer reflecting the horrors of war but, in their place, a hint of amusement. "I would never have guessed you to be claustrophobic."

Shanti lifted her arm to blot the sweat off her brow with her sleeve. Then, thinking about the fine material of the dress, she lowered her arm. "We can't all be fearless of everything, Commander Kyros."

He gave her a handkerchief.

She wiped her forehead and offered to return the cloth.

"Keep it," he said.

"Commander Kyros, I need seven of your best royal guards to serve as my security and accompany me on a trip." She turned to Seiko. "I also need seven Nunqua warriors to serve in the same capacity. I'd like Tracker to be among them."

Seiko nodded.

"And Yasmine," Shanti said. "Have them meet me on the docks tomorrow morning. There's one more funeral to be taken care of."

Shanti went to Baylova's stallion and patted its gleaming coat while resting her head on the flank. She took off the saddle, blue blanket, and bridle, then awkwardly carried the gear over to the carriage, trying not to soil or wrinkle her expensive dress in the process. Soldiers took the gear from her and finished the job. Being royalty was going to take some getting used to. Shanti smacked the stallion on the rump. "Go."

The animal whinnied and galloped away. Free.

*

Heavy cloth sails billowed in the wind, moving the ship smoothly through the sea. Shanti stood alone at the bow, feeling the cool spray on her skin. Romantic notions of traveling to faraway places entered her brain. She longed to forget her responsibilities, leave Willovia, seek new adventures. She longed for anonymity. Those days were gone. Baylova's curse was now hers. In some warped way, it was right.

She walked about the deck with arms crossed behind her back. Willovian soldiers conversed on one side of the ship; Nunqua warriors congregated on the other side. The tension between the two groups was palpable. The captain had issued a stiff warning that anyone, whatever their breed or rank, caught fighting aboard his ship would be immediately thrown into the brig. How could she get the Willovians and Nunqua to work together? Her royal guards must set the example.

Shanti descended a narrow ladder to the cavernous hold below, to view the ship's only cargo: a simple pinewood casket.

She opened the creaky lid. Black cloth, the same color as the warriors' uniforms, shrouded the corpse. On top of the cloth rested Caravey's sword, cleaned of blood and gore and buffed to a mirror-like shine. Holes perforated the wood of the casket. The inside was lined with rocks. Heavy chains had been wrapped around the black covering to ensure that the body remained at the bottom of the sea. Shanti wiped away a tear, lamenting her mistake. Someone watched from the shadows—Jun.

She turned away to hide her emotions and heard his footsteps climb the ladder.

The casket was brought up to the deck and perched on the edge, ready to be slid overboard, into the deep. Nunqua warriors put their right hands on the casket and spoke short words honoring the fallen general. They closed their fists over their hearts in a final salute.

Shanti opened the lid to remove Caravey's sword. Ribbons of black and red were tied to the handle. "It will be melted down," she said, "for the scars he gave to me."

Warriors pushed the casket off the ship. It splashed into the sea, floated briefly, then sank as water filled it.

Shanti gave Caravey's sword to the captain, to secure in his quarters until they were back on land. She stood at the bow again, watching water sparkle in the rays of the sun. Jun joined her.

"I'll never understand you," he said. "You helped me escape the prisoner-of-war camp, slept with me, and yet I see you crying in private over his corpse. And then you order his sword melted."

A dolphin swam alongside the ship. Its glossy gray body emerged from the water, jumping in and out of the wake. More dolphins surfaced alongside the ship. "Do you really think I was crying over the corpse of Caravey?" she said.

"What do you mean?"

"Caravey's body isn't in that coffin."

He considered her words before speaking. "What did you do?"

"I kept my promise to Baylova."

Jun watched the dolphins. "You didn't. Not even you would be so treacherous as to . . . You switched the bodies?"

"There's a purpose to everything I do."

"If the citizens of Willovia ever found out . . . If the Nunqua ever found out . . ." Jun stared at her in disbelief.

"The people of both countries would tear the limbs from my body and feed them to the pigs."

A pelican flew low over the water.

"If Baylova were truly upset about my actions, those dolphins would be sharks. And they'd be angry. Everyone believes that because of the drug, I don't remember what happened in the arena, but I remember everything. I called her 'queen of Willovia,' told her she passed the Guardians' test. Then Caravey stepped behind her and cut her throat. She was unarmed. I stole her sword and led her to battle. I didn't think Caravey would stoop so low as to kill an unarmed woman. I was naive to believe that war was just a game. Her death is my fault. This is my punishment: being queen in her stead. I have something to ask you."

"What is it?"

"I'm making a trip to Tokana with my newly formed guards. I'd like you to go with us as commander of the guard."

Jun leaned on the wooden railing, his usual smug self. "Queen or not, you can't order me around."

"Yes, I can. I need someone good with a sword, able to lead these guards and form them into a cohesive unit. You can also teach me the code, at night—just you and I, alone. I'm not giving you an *order* to take the position; I'm giving you a choice."

"Why is Tracker part of your guard?" Jun said. "He was one of Delartay's warriors."

"Because he's the best at what he does. And we were friends once. If you accept the position of commanding my guards, you'll outrank him."

"I'll think about it."

They watched the dolphins cavorting in the wake until the animals tired of the game and disappeared under the water. Jun and Shanti headed toward the stern of the ship. Willovians and Nunqua were gathered together. Tracker sat in the center of the group and spoke in heavily accented Willovian. " When Queen Shanti was training, General Delartay made her ride the meanest, nastiest, foulest-smelling nag you ever wanted to see. Its hair was matted and gray except for the hindquarters, which had no hair and was a repulsive pink. It kept biting her and running away. What was the name of that horse again?"

"Boenase," Shanti said. "Bones."

"Bones, that's right. Anyway, we kept teasing Sha . . . Queen

Shanti about the darts she wore on the wristlet on her arm. Nobody believed they were poisonous."

"Teasing?" Shanti said. "I believe you mean 'tormenting.'"

"To prove us wrong, she shot that demon of a horse with a dart. The next day, Bones was lying in the field with its legs straight up in the air like four tree trunks."

"I put it out if its misery," Shanti said.

"The stench was horrible," Tracker continued. "And the flies. You should have seen the hole we had to dig to bury the carcass. We cut off its legs to make it fit in the hole. So what does General Delartay do when he hears Shanti killed one of the horses and wasted a whole day of training so the team could bury it? He gave her his horse. *Gave* it to her. She won every race from then on."

"He didn't give it to me. We bartered for it."

"What did you give him in return for his horse?" Jun asked.

"When's dinner?" Shanti said. "I'm starving." She saw Yasmine sitting alone and left the men to sit next to her. "You'll have to learn the Willovian language."

"Why did you choose me as your guard?"

"Because we both need a second chance. I want you to take the body art off, too—the symbols of strength you paint on your skin."

Yasmine said nothing.

"Have you ever been to the grand arena in Tokana?" Shanti said.

"Once, when I was a child."

"I remember the first time I went there with General Delartay's team. On the days before the competition, I wore a dress and wasn't allowed to practice with the men. Everyone thought I was Delartay's servant girl. The other teams would try to coax information out of me concerning the general's strategy. Believe me, the games start much sooner than on the first day of the contest. When the other competitors saw me riding into the crowded arena with the team, wearing a black uniform with a sword on my back and a lock of hair around my neck, they were stunned. On the third day of the contest, when they found out I was the daughter of the great warrior Shintar, they went wild. And on the last day of the competition, when I changed my appearance in front of everyone, well, let's just say, even you knew who I was before I had the chance to tell you my name. We had such fun!"

"It takes at least ten warriors to enter the competition at the grand arena. Most teams bring more to replace the warriors who get hurt. You have fourteen personal guards. Are you planning on making us compete?"

"Perhaps," Shanti said. "Convince people of your strength by your actions and not the symbols on your skin, learn the Willovian language, and we'll work on your fighting skills."

"There's a rumor that you and General Delartay were . . . close. Why melt his sword?"

"Caravey and I were close before I realized that not all his actions were honorable." Shanti smelled fish being fried in the ship's galley—maybe shrimp or crab—and her stomach growled in response.

"Thank you," Yasmine said, "for the second chance."

"Welcome to the team."

*

Shanti walked through the halls of the castle to the portrait room and found Aiden there. Splotches of paint spattered his shirt and hands. He moved the lower left corner of a frame on the wall, then backed away to gauge its straightness. The portrait was of Baylova. A graceful gold crown adorned her head. Long hair tumbled down her right shoulder, and her skin had the appearance of porcelain. The fingernails of her left hand were black. "It's perfect," Shanti said. Sealed in a case directly below the portrait was Baylova's sword.

"What do the symbols you made me put in the portrait mean?"

"The wolf and wasps represent her power, the Willovian hawk symbolizes her going to war with the soldiers, the blue robe she's stepping on shows her defeat of the monks, and the two red rose-buds in her hand, never to open, are for you."

"*Me?*"

"The last word she spoke was your name. Did Jun tell you what happened in the arena?"

"Yes." Aiden readjusted the portrait's frame. "I hear you're going to Tokana with your personal guards."

"I'm planning on it."

"I was wondering if you needed one more guard."

"It would be a waste of your skills as a—"

"I'd like to go," he said.

Shanti permitted the interruption. "Agreed." She gazed at the richly detailed portrait: Baylova's light features against the dark background, the proud yet sad expression on her face, the supple folds of the black dress with delicate lace, the realistic wolf sitting at her side. "You truly are talented, Aiden."

*

The Nuncovian Council met in the caves beneath the castle by the sea. The council consisted of Commander Kyros, Madiza, General Seiko, and General Thaktos—a gaunt, often overlooked Nunqua warrior considered by all to be a logistical mastermind. Commander Gy had been asked to serve on the council but decided instead to retire to his farm and family. Queen Shanti ruled over the proceedings.

"Can we expect a coup attempt from Lord Argu's relatives?"

"A coup would require an army," Seiko said. "I doubt any warriors would follow the command of those once loyal to Argu, especially since the generals have pledged their allegiance to you. They are no threat to your reign."

"General Thaktos," Shanti said, "the northern castle in Prigone is yours to use. General Seiko, you may live in the royal residence in Tokana. I urge you both to promote trade between our two countries. Keep the borders open and safe for all who wish to travel.

Commander Kyros, I want you to see that sufficient stores of grain are stockpiled. Nightly feasts here in Willovia will be scaled back to take place only during a full moon and on festival days or special occasions."

"Done," Kyros said.

Jun entered the cave and stood in front of the council.

"Commander Jun," Shanti said, "have you considered the offer to command my personal guard?"

"I accept."

Madiza rubbed a dark opal on the bracelet around her wrist. "They will attack tonight."

"*Who* will attack?" Jun said.

"The monks." Madiza smiled at Jun, as if at an open book that was easy to read. "Do not underestimate them, Commander. They may seem sickly and old, but they are desperate men intent on corrupting the crown."

"With all due respect to the council, the queen's guards have yet to work together. The royal guards under the leadership of Commander Kyros are better prepared to defend an attack against the castle."

"The attack will not be at the castle," Shanti said. "Capture the monks and put them in prison for conspiracy to subvert the monarchy. Tracker can translate your orders to the warriors."

Jun nodded, and the meeting adjourned.

*

A yellow moon crept out from its hiding spot behind a cloud. At the edge of the city, six men, in clothing that hung loose from their skeletal bodies, used a long iron rod to break apart the chains securing the entrance of the royal catacombs. They stole into the depths of the earth with torches, pickaxes, and burlap bags. Stoic stone faces carved into statues stared at them as they passed. The monks finally came to the tomb of Baylova.

They worked without needing to speak. Each chink of a pickax on the sealed wall of the vault brought them closer to the object of their obsession. It wouldn't be long before the remains were theirs. True, it wasn't Baylova's life's blood, taken moments after her heart stopped beating. The burnt corpse and bones would make a weak potion compared to still-warm blood, but it would help the monks see into the future, if only faintly. There was a new queen and a chance to create a new pact to secure their destiny alongside royalty. They would peer into Shanti's future, discern how to gain her confidences. Then they would go back to the old ways. Shanti's flesh and blood would be bartered for the good of both Willovia and the Nunqua.

The order of the monks would be a cherished organization once more, held in the highest esteem, able to come and go into the castle and caves as they pleased. They would live in an opulent residence with the best of everything and with servants to cater to their needs.

Pebbles and mortar crumbled downward with each feeble stroke. A hole in the wall opened up. Desire drove them faster as they bashed away chunks of wall until the hole was large enough to go through.

The sickly-sweet scent of decaying flowers wafted out of the vault. Two of the monks entered the tomb with torches. They opened the lid of the casket, caressed the red velvet covering the corpse, and salivated.

One monk carried an empty sack over his shoulder. They pulled back the covering to reveal the prize they had risked their lives to retrieve. Fire had blackened the corpse. Long, frizzy hair stuck out from the scalp. Muscle had melted away to reveal milky bone, and white teeth jutted from loose lips that slumped down the jaw and cheeks. The head was detached from the body. Leopard spots patterned the skin on the arm.

"Something's wrong." One of the monks reached out and touched the corpse. Instead of bloodlust, he felt only revulsion. He scrutinized the body: the limbs were long and thick, the shoulders too wide and hips too narrow for a woman, especially a petite woman such as Baylova.

The monk's shrill howl ricocheted inside the vault, "No-o-o-o-o!"

*

Shanti stepped onto her balcony. She wore a white nightgown, and her feet were bare. In her hand was the long lock of Baylova's hair that she had taken when they were in the arena. She separated the strands and let them blow in the breeze. The hair swirled in a current of air, drifting down to the earth and sea below. Impossible to retrieve. "Your spirit is free," she said.

She returned to her chamber, a comfortable room with a bed, desk, wardrobe, hinged privacy panel, and chaise. Books from the library were piled in an untidy heap on a table beside the chaise. Also on the table was a candle burning inside a glass urn.

Shanti went to her wardrobe and returned with two more locks of hair. She went outside again, unbraided and released the strands of Caravey's hair, and spoke the simple words of the ritual: "Your spirit is free." She also scattered the Nunqua warrior's hair from her necklace, to blow in the wind. "Your spirit is free."

The words meant nothing. She accepted her status as a witch, but she didn't have the ability to control another person's spirit. No one did. Releasing the hair was symbolic. And cathartic. She was no longer a string pulled so tight it was bound to break.

Shanti lounged on the chaise, with a blanket pulled up to her waist. She perused a handwritten book of geography, containing drawings and incomplete maps. Her thoughts wandered to Jun. She wished he would use the ledge to come into her room tonight, but he was busy following orders. Her eyelids grew heavy. She blew out the candle, hugged her pillow tight, and fell asleep on the chaise. The bed made especially for her, overflowing with blankets and pillows, remained empty.

*

The monks bellowed in anger. Their wails of frustration mixed with the sound of . . . what was it? Laughter? They raised their torches. Someone had followed them into the catacombs. The laugh belonged to Baylova. Alive! Her phony death and deceptive funeral must have been a trick.

She stood before them in a black dress with lace trim. In the dark surroundings, her pale skin looked like wax.

"Queen Baylova . . . ," breathed a monk holding a pickax

Red-rimmed eyes stared greedily at the body that held the warm, flowing blood they craved. The monks licked their lips and surrounded her.

Her skin darkened until it was black and burnt. Flesh dripped down to reveal bone. She smelled of the salty sea. Heat rose inside the tunnel until it felt as if they were being cooked inside a cast-iron pot over a roaring fire. The monk with the pickax, raised it over his head and swung downward, right through Baylova. The pickax encountered nothing but air.

They ran from the laughing ghost, leaving behind tools and the evidence of their crime. A snarling spirit wolf chased them out of the tunnels, and they shouted in terror.

Seven Nunqua warriors, their eyes shining silver in the dark, and nine Willovian soldiers captured the monks as they emerged from the catacombs.

Commander Jun ordered Tracker and half of Shanti's guards to escort the monks to prison. The other half, including Yasmine and Aiden, entered the catacombs with torches. They descended to the site of the desecrated grave with a bucket of mortar, tools, and a handcart filled with bricks. Jun and Aiden crawled through the hole to inspect the open casket. The burnt remains of a man had been uncovered. The unburned patch of skin on one arm was spotted.

"Delartay?" Aiden asked.

Jun nodded.

"And Baylova?"

"At the bottom of the sea. It must be kept secret. If word of this ever got out, the people would turn against Shanti."

"I'm not so sure," Aiden said. "Tonight only proves she had a reason for switching the . . . whoa!" Aiden pointed to the gap between the head of the corpse and the rest of the body. "Shanti did *that* in the arena? I knew she killed him, but I didn't realize . . ."

"She avenged Baylova's death, freed herself from Delartay's twisted grip, and ended the war."

Jun returned the red cloth over the gruesome remains, then closed the lid. They crawled out of the vault, and Shanti's guards resealed the tomb.

*

Shanti studied a map on a wobbly table inside a tack room of the royal stables.

Jun traced his finger along a line of the map that ran from the Willovian castle in Erbaut to the Nunqua capital. "We'll take this road."

He wasn't wearing a uniform—just regular clothes comfortable for riding. All around, Shanti's guards saddled their horses in preparation for the journey. They weren't wearing uniforms, either, just inconspicuous attire with swords and various other weapons to safeguard the queen.

No sword weighted Shanti's back, and she no longer wore her wristlet with darts. Bearing weapons might provoke hostility, and Shanti wanted to be a symbol of cooperation and trust. She wore a man's wide-brimmed hat of tanned leather to keep the sun and rain off. She pointed to a blank area of the map. "We'll travel through here."

"That land is uncharted," Jun said. "It's easier to take the main thoroughfare, and it will give you an opportunity to meet with the people."

"Willovia considers this area within its borders and, therefore, part of our kingdom," Shanti replied. "There's plenty of time to explore this region before we arrive at Tokana for the tournament. We'll return along the main roads when we have more supplies, guards, and equipment."

"What tournament?" Jun said.

"*The* tournament, in the grand arena. Uncle Seiko is taking care of the arrangements: a place for the guards to stay and train, my residence at the royal palace, wardrobe, attendants, a feast in my honor."

Jun tapped his finger on the map. "Exploring these lands with only fifteen guards is dangerous. As queen, you cannot take such a risk."

"As commander of my guards, you have the responsibility of uniting this group into a dedicated fighting force that will strike fear into the hearts of those who wish to harm me. What better way than to rely on each other as we travel through these lands?"

"There's a reason this area is uncharted."

"Come on, Jun. Don't you want to know what's out there? *Who's* out there? I do." Shanti folded the map and put it in a bag containing two leather-bound journals. More maps, a few small books, and writing utensils were also in the bag. She left the tack room to find Aiden, adjusting the straps of his saddle. She gave him the bag. "Cartographer and chronicler." She entered a spacious stall to find her horse already saddled and ready to go. Sometimes, it was good to be queen.

Jun followed her into the stall. "You're still keeping secrets from me." He moved close. "Just remember, I don't take orders from you."

"Yes, you do." Shanti felt the usual flush creep up her face. Memories of the night they spent together resurfaced. One night with Jun was not enough.

He took a scrap of orange cloth out of his pocket.

"What's that?" she asked. "Is that my armband from the Hedgelands?"

Jun put it back in his pocket and left the stall.

He had kept the armband he won from her on the night they played capture the flag. Did he have it with him all this time, even when detained at the prisoner-of-war camp? Maybe she meant more to him than he had let on. Maybe she didn't have to sleep alone every night. Maybe Jun had thought about being king. Her heart filled with hope. He would have to give up his freedom, though, his anonymity. Not an easy thing to do. And he would be a king in name only; the authority to rule would always be hers. The Nunqua wouldn't accept a Willovian king, just as the Willovians would never accept a Nunqua king. An *heir*, on the other hand . . .

She led her horse out of the stable. Her guards had assembled in an informal group at the edge of a field. Kyros and Gy stood by a wooden fence to see them off. Shanti went to them and hugged Gy. "I'd like you to come to the tournament. Bring Tova and the kids. You're welcome to stay at the castle as my official guests; then you can see that the Nunqua are not as brutish as many believe. You and your family will be treated with honor."

"We'll be there," Gy said. "Good luck, and be careful."

Shanti turned to Kyros. "Not planning on gathering an army in my absence to topple me from power, are you?"

Kyros answered in his usual lofty attitude. "Hardly."

His contrived indifference was a good sign. Kyros had, after all, risked his life by defying Baylova's orders and helping her escape the castle. All men wore masks. "Keep Madiza safe," she said, "and stockpile food—"

"You act as if you don't trust me."

Should she shake his hand? Give him a hug? Bow in gratitude for his service to Willovia? Or wait for him to bow first? Her horse pushed her impatiently with its nose.

"Everything will be satisfactory here." Kyros lowered his head a finger's breadth. It was enough—the last thing she wanted was overenthusiastic flattery.

"Thank you, Commander Kyros." She got on her horse and joined her guards, already on horseback. "Tracker, northeast. Take

Aiden and scout ahead for the best route." The two men rode away. Shanti addressed her remaining guards. "Last chance to change your minds, girls . . . and Yasmine. Anyone here want to quit?" She repeated the question in the Nunqua language. No one responded. "Let's go." Shanti didn't ride in front of her guards or behind them, but among them.

A pack of feral dogs emerged from the underbrush. The animals acted tame, even playful, and the horses were not alarmed. "Are you doing that?" Jun asked.

A dragonfly with iridescent wings landed on her arm. "It's Baylova. In some small way, her spirit is with us."

Shanti wondered whether she would have done anything differently had she known beforehand that stealing Baylova's sword and provoking her to enter the battle would result in Baylova's death. She wasn't sure. The dogs and dragonfly soothed her guilt.

Experiencing war gave her a better appreciation of peace. She accepted her responsibilities as queen, wielded her power when necessary, listened to her advisers, and vowed never to let the crown crush her as it had crushed Baylova.

Shanti, Jun, and her royal guards, both Nunqua and Willovian, traveled away from civilized society, toward uncharted lands.

End